Letters to Abby

Mandy Hayes

Kissmann Books

This is a work of fiction. Names, characters, events, and incidents are either the products of the author's imagination or used in a fictitious manner. Any similarity to actual persons, living or dead, events, or locales is purely coincidental.

No part of this book may be reproduced in any form or by any electronic or mechanical means, including information storage and retrieval systems, without the written permission from the author or publisher.

Copyright © 2021 by Mandy Hayes

All rights reserved.

Editing by Editing Fox

ISBN-13 (print): 978-1-7779305-0-9
ISBN-13 (ebook): 978-1-7779305-1-6

For anyone struggling;
You are not alone

Dave
September 8, 2026
Present Day

"We need to go!"

Dave checked the time on his phone again as he gulped down the last of his coffee. It was too bitter and he shook his head, making a mental note to pick up creamer on his way home from work. The empty cup clinked into the sink, and he picked up his phone on the way to the front door.

The steady sound of rain beat down on the roof and it complemented the bittersweet feeling Dave had in his heart. He stared at his reflection in the mirror beside the front door, a man aged from the one he remembered. Streaks of silver more than peppered his dark hair, and when he grew his beard out now, it was only grey. Lines etched across his forehead, and there was a familiar tiredness under his eyes that had been there for the last fourteen years. But it was not the aging of his face that had him feeling bittersweet. It was that he could recognize himself despite that he had aged, yet when he turned towards the sound of the stomping steps hurrying down the stairs, he could scarcely believe how much *she* had changed.

Abby came running down the stairs in her favourite pair of cropped jeans, the pinnacle piece of her summer wardrobe, and one of the new tops she had picked out for the school year. It was a mix of bright oranges and pinks, louder than the blue one Dave told her he liked when they were in the store, but she reminded him he knew nothing about what was "in" or "cool" (or that nobody even used the word "cool" anymore). They bought both shirts in the end, but Dave doubted he'd ever see the blue one.

It was hard to believe that this was the last first day of school. Abby graduated next summer and by next fall, she'd be off to university. Or traveling, she was undecided. When he closed his eyes, Dave could still see his little girl running down those same stairs, pigtails bouncing with mismatched socks and a doll in her hand, as though it were yesterday. He could still hear her little voice, the way she pronounced "tomatoes" as "tee-os," and the way she would throw her head back when she laughed. He smiled to himself, and when he opened his eyes, it faltered, the memory gone, his little girl replaced with the grown woman before him. Time was a cruel master.

Abby grabbed a lip balm out from her backpack and nudged Dave out of the way as she applied it in the mirror. His breath hitched, as for one brief moment Abby looked so much like Ronnie that it knocked the wind out of him. These moments were scarce, thankfully. Abby was the smitten image of her mother, save for the blonde hair instead of brunette. But their personalities were as different as night and day, and that helped Dave see past the resemblance. He recovered before Abby noticed, and when she turned and smiled at him, he smiled back.

"Ok! Here I go. Have a great day at work," she said. She planted a quick kiss on his cheek and then spun on her heel towards the door. Dave clucked his tongue and wagged his finger at her.

"We need to do the sign first," he said. Abby groaned as she reached down and slipped on her shoes.

"Really, Dad? Don't you think I'm a bit too old for this now," she sighed.

Dave chuckled and picked up the "Abby's First Day of Grade 12" chalk sign from the floor. The permanent letters were faded and chipped, the colours dulled by age, much like how Dave felt about his appearance. The spot where he wrote "Grade 12" in chalk was worn and discoloured from years of different grades, levels, and activities. Ronnie had bought it years ago and never got to see Abby use it.

"Come on," he said with a smirk. "It's the last one. Last time."

Abby let out a dramatic sigh and rolled her eyes to the ceiling. "Okay."

Dave handed her the sign as he moved to get his coat out of the closet and then slipped on his own shoes. He grabbed two umbrellas, one for each of them, and as Abby unlocked the door and put her hand on the knob, the doorbell rang. The sudden sound made Abby jump, and Dave chuckled. He zipped up his raincoat as Abby peered through the peephole and frowned.

"It's some kid," she said.

Dave wasn't sure what it was, but all at once, butterflies filled his stomach. Goosebumps ran over his arms and a chill up his spine. Time suddenly slowed down and the sound of Abby turning the knob was as loud as a gunshot. Without having even seen the kid yet, Dave had a premonition of sorts. He knew, just *knew*, who was on the other side of that door. And now, no matter how many times he had dreamed of this moment, of all the different ways this scenario could go, Dave found he did not know what to do or say. He never thought this day would come.

Abby swung the door open, and a young teenaged boy stood on the porch. Rain poured nonstop behind him, pelting down on the mailbox at the end of the drive. The manhole next to it flooded, blocked with leaves again, which was normal for this time of year. A floorboard underneath the boy's sneaker squeaked as he shifted when Dave stepped up beside Abby.

In an instant, Dave felt winded. A mop of brown curls fell into the boy's blue eyes, eyes so familiar to Dave not because they were like Abby's, but because he remembered them so well. Fourteen years changed a lot, if not everything about a person, but his bright blue eyes were the same. As Dave stared at him, he recognized some of his other features too. The shape of his nose and lips were only recognizable because Dave would say goodnight to his picture every night. In the picture, though, he was only five months old. That was the last time Dave had seen him. And now, like Abby, he was all grown up.

"Can we help you?" Abby asked impatiently, breaking the held breath Dave didn't realize he was holding. Normally, he would have reprimanded her for her rudeness, an unusual trait for her, but she was still bitter from the summer.

The boy glanced at Abby and then settled his gaze on Dave. His hands shook, but his stare didn't waver. "Hi. You probably don't recognize me… but my name is Eli. I'm your son."

BEFORE

Dave
April 18, 2009

Dave had been home all of five minutes when Ronnie came waddling down the stairs as fast as she could. Tears streamed down her face as she buried her head into his chest, and said something hurried, the words muffled in his shirt.

"Say that again?" Dave asked.

"I think my water just broke," she said between sobs as she lifted her head and looked up at him.

Dave felt his face drain. The baby wasn't due for another two weeks. He had never gotten around to reading the book Ronnie had bought him on labour, babies, parenting, all of it. In that moment it hit him that he was very unprepared for what was about to happen. They were about to bring a new little person into this world, or more accurately, Ronnie was about to, and Dave didn't have the slightest idea how to handle it.

But he knew he had to figure it out soon and to take it one step at a time. By the panicked look on Ronnie's face, the tears streaming down her cheeks and the imprint of the pillow on her cheek from where she had been sleeping, Dave knew that the first step he had to take was to be calm. Because if he mirrored her panic or let on just how terrified he was about what was about to happen, how much their lives were about to change, Ronnie would panic more and then shit would hit the fan.

After a deep breath, Dave pulled apart from Ronnie, placed his hands on the sides of her arms and looked at her square in the face. "Tell me what you need."

The next few minutes were a whirlwind. As the baby wasn't due for another two weeks, nothing was packed. At least he had installed the car seat. Ronnie dictated from the bathroom, where she sat on the toilet as her water continued to leak, what he needed to grab for the baby, for her, and for himself. Because of his calm demeanour, Ronnie calmed a bit as well. She took her time, as much as she could, as Dave raced around the house collecting diapers and onesies, throwing everything hastily into their small blue suitcase. On the inside, Dave was anything but calm. Although she seemed fine now, he knew that the pain would start soon. And a million questions ran through his mind. What if something happened to the baby? What if there were complications, and the baby didn't make it? Or if something happened to Ronnie? What if their car wouldn't start, or if there was traffic, or the hospital was full, or… or…? He couldn't remember a time when his thoughts raced so fast.

"We should call the hospital first, to let them know we're on our way," Ronnie called from the bathroom as Dave carried the suitcase downstairs. "The number's on the fridge."

A nurse picked up on the first ring, thankfully.

"Hi, yes, my wife's water has broken," Dave said in a flourish.

"Ok," the nurse said. "What is your wife's name?"

"Veronica Sanders." A keyboard on the other end clicked as the nurse typed in the information, and Dave wondered why a nurse would type so slow in a situation like this. He was not prepared to deliver the baby at home.

"Veronica… Sanders. Ah yes, with Doctor Hauer. How far along is she?" the nurse asked.

"Uh…"

The nurse sighed. "When's the due date?"

"Not until May 3rd," Dave said.

More keys clicked on the other end. Dave listened for Ronnie upstairs, but she was quiet. That had to be a good sign, right?

"Any contractions?" the nurse asked.

"Uh... no. I don't think so. She seems fine, but she says her water has broken," Dave said.

The typing stopped, and the phone rustled as the nurse adjusted it on her end. "Alright, well, you'd better come on in. We'll test to make sure it's broken water and admit her as needed. Just come in through emergency, register there, and they'll send you up to the fifth floor."

As Dave hung up the phone, Ronnie came waddling back down the stairs with her bedroom pillow under one arm and her favourite sweater draped over the other. She clutched the banister as she moved, her knuckles white with her grip, and she took slow, deep breaths.

Dave rushed to her side and grabbed the pillow from her as she came down the last few steps. "Are you OK?"

Ronnie nodded as she exhaled a deep breath, and smiled, happy tears in her eyes as she looked down at her protruding belly. She ran her hand over it. "We'd better get going."

Once he helped Ronnie into the car, Dave threw the suitcase and pillow into the back, locked up the house, and they were off. Thankfully, traffic was on their side, but with each passing stoplight, Ronnie seemed to get more and more uncomfortable. The hospital was only twenty minutes away. The roads were dark, streetlamps flashing as they drove by. Dave didn't want to drive too fast, worried that the motion or bumps might cause Ronnie additional discomfort.

Dave relaxed a bit as the hospital appeared in the distance. He loosened his hands on the steering wheel, unaware of just how hard he had been gripping it. Ronnie continued to breathe deeply in and out beside him, but her breaths became closer together, and now and then she'd intake a sharp breath with a wince on her face.

The parking lot at the hospital was packed. Dave managed to grab a spot, worried he'd have to park across the street, but it still seemed miles from the emergency entrance. He ripped off his seatbelt and ran around the car to help Ronnie out. The contractions were kicking in now.

"Head inside, I'll catch up to you," he said. Ronnie nodded and walked towards the emergency entrance, while Dave raced past her to pay for parking. Pay parking at emergency was ridiculous, in his opinion, but he didn't want to get a ticket and knew that Ronnie would scold him for not paying. As he dug out his wallet at the slow meter, he glanced up to see Ronnie still steady on her way to the entrance. Maybe he would start a petition to get designated "my wife is having a baby, I'll come back and pay for my stall when I can" spots.

Inside the hospital, Ronnie was just approaching the registration desk as Dave ran in with their bag and her pillow. The nurse took down Ronnie's information and then pointed them in the elevator's direction where they could go up to the maternity ward, and she'd send the paperwork up to the printer there. At the elevator, Dave jammed the button so many times that he worried he broke it. Ronnie shifted back and forth on her feet with her hands on her back. She was uncomfortable, and the stairs would not be an option.

"Are you doing OK?" Dave asked her. She nodded her head curtly but said nothing. The elevator arrived and they shuffled in. Dave was thankful nobody else joined them and they went up to the fifth floor uninterrupted.

The ward gleamed in front of them as the doors opened and the elevator chimed, "Fifth floor, Maternity." Dave led Ronnie down the hall and to the reception desk.

"Hi, I called ahead about a half hour ago. My wife's water has broken. Veronica Sanders," Dave panted.

The nurse looked up at them and then wheeled down the desk a bit further. She grabbed a piece of paper from the printer, rifled through a pile of files next to it, and pulled out one of them. Another nurse walked behind the desk and the two exchanged a few brief words. Ronnie let out a moan and her breathing quickened. The second nurse took the file from the first, pressed a button behind the desk, and a pair of double doors next to the reception area swung open.

"Come on in, we've got a room set up for you," she said. "My name is Chelsea."

Ronnie walked through the doors and Dave trailed behind her. Chelsea asked her a bunch of questions, while Dave glanced around the ward. He didn't like hospitals much; the way they smelled of antiseptic and decay, the scuffed floors, and the terrible lighting.

Chelsea led them to the last room down the hall on the left. The room was bright and clean, the shades on the windows drawn. There was the bed in the middle and a section off to the right to weigh and check the baby. A small TV hung up next to it, and there was a small couch, more of a bench, really, for Dave to sleep on, as well as a few chairs and a small fridge. The room also had its own private bathroom. Here in this hospital, Ronnie would deliver the baby in the same room they would be staying in. It was quite the setup, and he thought for a moment, of rescinding his earlier thought of how horrible hospitals were.

As Ronnie undressed and Dave helped her into a gown, he was thankful that the maternity ward at their hospital was all private rooms. Another positive check for this hospital in their corner of Canada. Ronnie's discomfort was turning into pain, and Dave wasn't sure how he could help. He and Chelsea helped Ronnie onto the bed where she lay on her back and cringed her way through the contractions.

"I'm just going to see how far along you are," Chelsea said. Dave pulled out a water bottle from their bag and offered it to Ronnie. She took a few sips and nodded her head once she was done, and he kept it close as he took her hand. As another contraction came on, she squeezed his hand as hard as she could, and Chelsea smiled. "Eight centimetres. Shouldn't be long."

After a few contractions came and went, Chelsea suggested that maybe Ronnie should try another position to help ease the pain. Dave helped as Ronnie tried to switch to a squatting position, but she shook her head halfway through and said it was too intense. Dave helped her return on to her back, and Chelsea then asked if Ronnie wanted to try the laughing gas. They didn't have a concrete birth plan in place. No music, chants, or calming sayings. They had attended no birthing classes, and now Dave wondered if they should have. The timing of the classes just never worked out, and Ronnie had questioned if the cost was worth it when they could just look up tips and advice online. All she had told him was that she wanted to do it as naturally as possible, which is what their hospital encouraged, but if she ended up wanting the epidural, to make sure she got it.

Ronnie nodded at the suggestion, and the nurse moved to the other side of the bed. There, she opened a panel in the wall, pulled out a hose and mask, and handed it to Ronnie.

"Breathe in during the start of the contraction," she instructed. Ronnie took the mask and placed it over her face as another contraction came. She squeezed Dave's hand and took a deep breath. The gas seemed to help ease the pain, but then Ronnie made an odd face.

"She's going to throw up," Dave said in an instant, the instinct coming over him. He grabbed a bowl the nurse had set aside and placed it beside Ronnie's head just as she moved the mask away from her face and retched. Her mouth barely moved an inch, and Dave brought the water bottle's straw to her lips, and she took a deep sip. The nurse stealthily took the vomit bowl away, and Ronnie squeezed his hand in thanks as she moved away from the straw. Dave pushed a stray strand of her dark hair out of her face and kissed her hand.

Time went by both quickly and slowly. Ronnie didn't get sick again from the laughing gas, and before Dave knew it, the nurse said that she was ten centimetres and could push. Ronnie could not use the laughing gas while she was pushing, and Chelsea packed it back up into its hidden panel.

Dave was thankful that it was time for the pushing. Seeing Ronnie in pain was hard. He couldn't imagine what the contractions felt like, but he wished he could take the pain away. He thought once it was time to push that it would be over, but he was wrong.

Time now slowed. Another nurse joined Chelsea. They monitored the baby, who was doing well, but taking her sweet time coming out. With each push, she kept going back up, and Chelsea explained it was because she was at a slight angle.

"Usually, the pushing is only about thirty minutes," the other nurse said in sympathy. Dave didn't want to look at the clock ticking above the bed, but he did. Poor Ronnie had been pushing for an hour and a half. She let out a horrible shriek, envy of a banshee, with every push. The sound had caught Dave, Chelsea, and even Ronnie off guard. Chelsea suggested trying not to scream each time, but Ronnie explained she couldn't help it. Dave could see that she felt embarrassed, but the nurse worried about her losing her voice. Dave knew Ronnie would worry about disturbing the other mothers and babies on the ward.

"OK, I think this is it," Chelsea said as Ronnie pushed again. She turned to the other nurse and instructed her to go get the doctor on call. It was a busy night in the ward. Dave would later learn that they were admitted into the last available room, and that there were two other women giving birth in the maternity's triage room, and another poor woman was on a stretcher in the hall somewhere, with not enough time to send her to another hospital.

"It's baby time," the doctor announced as she returned with the nurse. They set all the equipment up at the end of the bed, and Ronnie pushed again. "Long, deep pushes, OK Veronica? You're doing great."

Ronnie pushed. Dave reminded her to breathe as she kept holding her breath when she pushed. She grunted and groaned, and the nurses and doctors kept encouraging her to push. They mentioned something called the "ring of fire," which sounded terrible, and Dave could only imagine that it felt worse. And then, before his eyes, the top of a head began to come out from his wife. It was both the craziest and most inspiring thing he had ever seen. It was incredible, the miracle unfolding before him. How Ronnie was doing this, pushing this little person out of her body, was beyond him. She could barely open the peanut butter jar some days, and yet here was, a small human exiting her body.

"One more, Veronica!" the doctor said. For a brief moment, Dave stared as his wife had a baby's head poking out from between her legs, and then with another big push, the rest of the body came sliding out. "She's here!"

Their tiny daughter let out a cry and the doctor placed her on Ronnie's chest. Ronnie looked down and smiled at the baby as Chelsea put a hat on her head and a towel over her body.

"She's here," Ronnie whispered, and as she looked up at Dave, he leaned over and gave her a quick kiss. The baby snuggled up to Ronnie, and as the two stared at each other, Dave glanced back at the other end of the bed. The placenta pushed out and there was blood everywhere. Dave had never seen so much blood in all his life, and the organ was bigger than he expected it to be. Ronnie looked relieved once the placenta was out and smiled again at Dave. He tried to smile back, but all he could notice was how pale his wife was. Ronnie did not take to sun easily, but he had never seen her this white before. She was like a ghost.

Ronnie focused on the baby, and Chelsea invited Dave over to cut the cord. His hands shook a bit as he readied the scissors over the piece of flesh and he tried to take in the moment, but all he could see was the blood on the cord, the blood on Ronnie's hospital gown, the blood on the baby. It was like being inside a happy horror film.

"Take a picture," Ronnie murmured just before he cut. The nurse grabbed Dave's phone and snapped a pic as he quickly cut the cord.

As he handed the scissors back to the nurse, he glanced at the doctor. Concentration wore on her face as she surmised the damage to Ronnie's private area.

"I need more sponges," the doctor said. That's when Dave noticed a bowl filled with used, bloody sponges off to the doctor's right. "I can't tell where the bleeding is coming from and where to stitch to make it stop."

Chelsea handed the doctor more sponges. She then exchanged a look with the other nurse and moved over to talk to her. Dave tried to focus on Ronnie's serene face as she stared at their little daughter who was still snuggling up with her peacefully. He thought he overheard Chelsea tell the other nurse to get an IV ready for Ronnie. She had lost a lot of blood.

"Ah! Got it," the doctor said just then. "Eleven sponges later, and I've found the problem. You might want the laughing gas again as I stitch you up; it'll make it a bit more comfortable."

Ronnie agreed, and the second nurse, whose name Dave never learned, set up the laughing gas. As she did so, Chelsea came back over to take the baby from Ronnie.

"I'm going to weigh and measure her while you get fixed up."

"Dave, make sure you take pictures!" Ronnie said between huffs of gas.

Relieved that his wife was going to be OK and didn't need the IV, Dave walked across the room to the little baby station. Chelsea put her on the scale and Dave snapped a pic when the numbers came to a halt. Six pounds, ten ounces. Chelsea then put a diaper on the baby, which she did not like. She fussed a bit and wriggled, and she did not like it when Chelsea stretched her leg out and measured her, nineteen and a half inches long. Once done, the nurse wrapped her up in a blanket and turned to Dave.

"Would you like to hold her now?" she asked.

Before he gave a solid answer, Chelsea moved in and carefully set the baby in his arms. It was like cradling a weighted football with a tiny pink cap, wrapped up in a yellow blanket. The baby yawned, her tiny mouth making a perfect O, and she blinked her dark newborn eyes up at Dave. She looked just like Ronnie. He was holding a miniature version of his wife in his arms, and he could not be prouder.

"What's her name?" the second nurse asked. A clipboard of paperwork was now in her hands, and she had her pen poised and ready for his answer. The doctor finished the last stitch on Ronnie, and Chelsea whisked away the mess.

Ronnie set down the laughing gas and beamed brightly. Her voice sounded relaxed and slurred, loopy from the gas she had been inhaling, but there was no mistaking her happiness as she said, "Abigail Donna Sanders."

Once the nurses and doctor left, Ronnie looked over at Dave and smiled. He leaned in and gave her another kiss, and then handed their daughter back to her. "Is there anything you need?" he asked.

"A snack might be nice," she sighed. The high from the laughing gas wore off, and she sounded exhausted now. "There's a Tim Horton's in the lobby."

"Say no more."

Dave gave her another quick kiss on the forehead and headed towards the door. Behind him, he heard Ronnie let out a blissful sigh, and he looked over his shoulder to take in the scene. The way the light came in from the windows, the rising sun peeking through the blinds made it look as though he were in a dream. This was the first relaxed look of his new family, and he watched as Ronnie looked down at their new baby. His little Abby.

April 19, 2009
Dear Abby,

    She's here. I can't believe that she is here! Two weeks early. We were not ready for that, let me tell you. She's only eight hours old and I can't stop staring at her. She's perfect in every single way. Even the nurses gawked at how beautiful she is and said they always tell everyone that their baby is cute... but that Abby actually is, ha ha! She doesn't look like a wrinkly old man or a hairless monkey or something. She came out this perfect little cherub angel.
    I'm enjoying a few moments to myself before everyone comes to visit. Or at least, trying to enjoy myself. Dave is asleep on the couch the hospital provides for the fathers, and he's snoring up a storm, as usual. I'm surprised the nurse hasn't come in to tell him to be quiet, as I'm sure it's echoing down the halls of the maternity ward. The funny part is that little Abby is snoring away in her bassinet beside me. Thick as thieves these two will be, I can just tell. A few moments ago, I had her asleep with me in the bed. She didn't want to leave my side, nor I hers.
    My water broke at 10:45 last night, unexpectedly, as I was only 38 weeks along. Dave scrambled to pack the bags and drove like a wild man to the hospital. We got the last room available. Busy night to be giving birth, apparently! I tried to get comfortable in a few different positions but being on my back was the only thing that

helped. Everything else made the pain more intense. Laughing gas helped take the edge off and let me focus on something other than the contractions.

Dave was a wizard at one point, as I threw up without warning, and he somehow had this pan under my face to catch it. I had to push for an hour and a half, and finally she was out at around 4:00 this morning. I don't even remember her crying, they just placed her on my chest, and she looked up at me, this sweet, chill little baby. I tore quite a bit, and it took the doctor a while to get the bleeding to stop. They didn't know where it was coming from, and the nurse was about to bring an IV in when the doctor figured it out and began to stitch me up. It was all worth it and I'd do it again in a heartbeat though, for this sweet little girl.

We named her Abby, of course, after you. Abigail Donna Sanders. We'll see if Dave's mom snarks about not being included in the middle name, but I just couldn't go through with two. Two middle names are too many.

Her hospital bracelet says she is zero days old. So surreal and odd to see. She isn't even a day old yet! She's 0! Her age is only in hours at this point. She has the entire world ahead of her, a blank slate, ready to be anything and anyone she wants to be. I can't wait for the memories we'll make together, the traditions, the messes, the bond that we'll share.

Not to brag, but she looks just like me. So often do I see pictures of newborns who look identical to their fathers, but not in our case! There is a caveman theory that the baby looks like the father, so the father doesn't abandon the family… I hope that's not nature trying to tell me I'm the flight risk here. What mother would abandon her child? What mother could abandon a baby as sweet as this one? I couldn't even go to the bathroom without wheeling her bassinet in there. I've been dreaming of having a little girl ever since I started thinking about having kids.

Life is about to change, but only good things could come from something like this, right? Isn't that what happens when dreams come true? I've pinched myself a few times already to be sure that I'm not dreaming. It's real. She's here now. And we're both so in love with her.

May 10, 2009
Dear Abby,

    Everyone always warns expectant mothers about labour, the pain, etc., and then the sleepless nights with the newborn... but nobody ever warns you about breastfeeding and how PAINFUL it is! You'd expect that the baby would know what it's doing or since, you know, this is what breasts were made for, that it would be easy-peasy, lemon-squeezy. But I can't take it! I cringe every time Abby cries and she's hungry. I dread it because I know of the pain about to come. And then I worry I'm going to squeeze and crush her little head from trying to cope with the pain, which is such an irrational fear, but it's there. What if I break her little skull?
    Dave says I'm being silly, at least about the skull crushing fears. He's so supportive. He holds my hand, which I can then squeeze the life out of while I cry, and we start to nurse. Once she starts going, it's not too bad, but my nipples are so cracked and sore. Abby doesn't seem to mind, but I do. I think I might just switch to pumping exclusively, so she's still getting breastmilk, but it won't be as hard on my nipples. Everyone says once you get to the six week mark that the pain goes away and your body gets used to it, but I don't think I can last another three weeks.

August 7, 2009
Dear Abby,

    Have you ever loved something so much that it just makes you want to shout it out to the world? I can't get over how much I love our little Abby. She is just the cutest thing in the world, and I could stare at her all day. She rolled over from back to front for the first time at Mom and Dad's house the other day, and Dad was lucky enough to capture it on video. I keep re-watching the moment over and over again, and I am so proud of her! I almost missed it too because I was on my way to the bathroom when it happened, but Dave quickly yelled for me. She's sleeping beside me right now and I can't stop looking down at her and smiling. This has to be the purest form of joy I've ever experienced.

Dave
August 26, 2009

 The house was dark as Dave pulled into the driveway. Another shift gone late, this time because of a malfunctioning freezer at the store. It had been a hectic day to begin with, and the freezer was the icing on an already rotten cake. He fumbled in the darkness, trying to fit his key into the slot, muttering to himself that he had to fix the damn porch light soon. It burnt out at the beginning of the summer, and he had been muttering the same thing to himself each night ever since.
 The alarm keypad downstairs beeped softly in the night once the door swung open and Dave stepped inside. One cat meowed from the top of the stairs, and Dave paused for a moment. He heard something else coming from the kitchen upstairs. It was Ronnie's breast pump.
 The sound had become a familiar one over the past few months, as she decided to exclusively pump for Abby. Breastfeeding didn't end up working between the two of them. The doctor mentioned something about a lip-tie or tongue-tie, and after three and a half weeks of trying and crying at every feed, Ronnie switched to pumping. This way, Dave could help feed Abby too, and he liked the bonding experience. He hated seeing Ronnie's face cringe each time she'd have to breastfeed or sometimes she would squeeze his

hand so hard because she worried she'd squeeze Abby's head from the pain.

It was hard for him to see her in agony. Her recovery hadn't been going so well to begin with, and at least by switching over to pumping she found relief somewhere. Dave wished he could just take the pain away instead, as Ronnie had wanted to breastfeed Abby to at least a year old. But sometimes life just didn't work out the way one expected.

Dave could hear the pump upstairs, but all the lights were off.

"Ronnie?" he called into the darkness. Maybe he was just hearing things. The pump had become a bit of a white noise during the day, as she pumped every few hours.

When she didn't answer, Dave flipped the hall light on and trudged up the stairs. Down the hall, Ronnie sat at the kitchen table. The pump was on the table to her left, the baby monitor on her right. Her face was blank, zoned out as she stared at a spot on the table.

"Hey honey," Dave whispered. There was something off about the whole scene. She looked tired, but a sad tired. Not the type of tired that a good night's rest would relieve. "Why are you sitting here in the dark?"

"Mmm?" Ronnie murmured. She looked up from the table and over at Dave. For a moment, it was as though she didn't see him, like she was looking through him. Dave's brows furrowed in concern. He pulled out the chair next to her and placed his hand over hers as he sat down.

"Everything OK?" he asked.

Ronnie sighed. "Yeah… just depressed."

Dave's heart sank a little. Ronnie had depression. Now and then she would get into these "down moods" as she would describe them. She wouldn't want to do anything and would just lie on the couch, be mopey, and then snap out of it after a few days. Each time it happened, he would ask what he could do to help, give her space if that's what she wanted, or try to make her laugh and smile. It was hard for him when she was like this, but Dave loved her for who she was and that included the parts that weren't as glamorous as the rest.

"Anything I can do to help?" he asked. This is when she would normally ask him to do a random task around the house, usually something he had been putting off or something he didn't realize was bugging her.

But Ronnie just shook her head and gazed off at nothing over his shoulder. "No… not really."

Dave nodded. The clock in the kitchen ticked behind them on the wall. Whiskers, their cat, meowed as she came down the stairs and brushed against Dave's leg. Ronnie pulled her hand out from under Dave's and turned off the pump. She placed the full bottles of milk on the table and tears welled up in her eyes as she snapped her nursing camisole back into place.

"What is it?" Dave asked softly. Sometimes she just needed a bit of further prodding to get to the root of what was bothering her.

Tears fell from her eyes. She let out a shaky breath, and Dave stood to pull her into a hug.

"I think I need help," she mumbled into his chest. He pulled her close and placed his chin on the top of her head. Her hair smelt like the new shampoo she was trying out, like a summer's breeze wafting through a field of daisies. "I just… I think I have postpartum depression. I just feel down all the time. Some days I worry that you'll come home, and Abby will be crying, screaming her head off, and I'll just be—I'll be—I don't know… just gone."

Dave squeezed her a little tighter. The trail end of her sentence was not something he wanted to think about. He couldn't imagine his life without her and needed her here.

"OK," he said slowly. "Why don't you make an appointment with your doctor and talk to her about it?"

Ronnie nodded. She pulled back a bit and looked up at him. "Would you judge me if I had to go on medication?"

Dave shook his head. He didn't understand why she had this insecurity around him sometimes. There was nothing she could do that would make him think less of her. The stigma around depression and women being more emotional than men made her self-conscious. It was unfair to her. There was no reason that she should have to feel insecure around him, but Dave reminded her of that again and again.

"Of course not." The tears cleared out of her eyes and Ronnie took a calm breath. She smiled up at him and then gave him a quick kiss on the cheek.

"Thanks honey," she whispered.

Dave reached over and grabbed the two bottles of milk off the table.

"You go get some sleep. I'll put these away and clean the pump parts for you," he said. He grabbed two bottle lids out of the drawer and placed milk into the fridge. Ronnie stretched her arms over her head. Stretch marks on her stomach peeked through as her shirt rode up a bit. They had all appeared after Abby was born, as Ronnie's body shrunk back down. Dave didn't mind them, but Ronnie hated the way they looked.

The stairs creaked under her soft footsteps as Ronnie went upstairs and disappeared into the darkness. Dave let out a deep breath, one he didn't know he had been holding, and stared up at the darkened staircase. All he wanted was for her to be happy.

October 15, 2009
Dear Abby,

Sometimes I feel like if someone were to open up my head and take my brain out, it would be grey and black. It would be obviously sick looking, oozing some sort of toxic substance, and when placed next to a normal pink and happy brain, people would cringe and gag. Like those smoking commercials where they show the healthy lung and the smoker's lung. That's what my brain would look like, except not because of smoking, but due to a dark mental illness that I had no control over getting. A genetic sickness that I am so worried I will pass on to Abby and any future children we have. Seeing her as a happy baby now, I can't imagine her turning out like me. I can't predict the future and that scares me. I would just die if she had the same dark, terrible thoughts that I do, that consume me some days to the point where I don't know what to do to get out of it, where some days I don't even know how I'm still moving forward. I can only hope that she takes after Mom, who, as you know, is the sunniest person there is.

April 19, 2010
Dear Abby,

 I can't believe she is a year old already. Where has the time gone? How is this possible? What started out as one of the hardest years of my life certainly has transformed into the best. Once those first three months went by... every moment since has been nothing but happiness. I just love her so much and can't wait to see her continue to grow. She isn't walking quite yet, but she's so close. She is such a sweet little girl, my sweet baby. It makes me want another one, but I want more time with just her first. We'll start trying when she's at least two, if not older.
 I'm not looking forward to going back to work. I don't know how I can be away from her. It's only part-time, and Dave and I have worked out our schedules so that while I'm at work he's at home, so we're fortunate that way. No need to look into daycares, which seems like such madness. It makes me feel better knowing she'll be with him. They have such a sweet relationship together. She is such a daddy's girl, and she has Dave wrapped around her little finger. There is nothing he wouldn't do for her.
 We're having a big party for her tomorrow with all the family. I've been planning it for weeks. It's going to be floral themed, and I made her a floral crown, and we'll have bouquets of flowers everywhere. The weather is supposed to be nice too, so Dave is

planning on having hotdogs and hamburgers on the barbeque. It's going to be wonderful.

Dave
May 1, 2010

"Dave!"

Ronnie's shriek from upstairs stirred Dave from his half-sleep state. He bolted upright on the couch and rubbed his eyes, unsure if it had come from a dream or if she had really shouted for him. It had been a long day at work, and he had just meant to close his eyes for a minute. That minute had turned into twenty-five-or-so by the look of the clock on the wall, and Dave shook his head slightly. Last he saw of Ronnie, she had gone upstairs to change Abby's diaper. He wondered what they were still doing up there.

"Dave! Come quick!" Ronnie shrieked again. This time he knew it was real, and he jumped off the couch and sprinted for the stairs.

Ronnie was sitting at the top of the stairs with a huge grin on her face. Strands of her dark hair fell out of her messy bun and into her eyes, and she shook her head to one side to get them out of her way.

"Watch, watch, watch," Ronnie whispered once she saw him over her shoulder.

A foot or so away, Abby stood at her plastic music table. That thing annoyed the hell out of Dave. If they forgot to turn it off and walked too heavy footed near it, it went off on it its own, playing its little music and flashing its lights. Dave was sure it was possessed, as sometimes it seemed to just go off on its own regardless of if anyone was near it, but Abby loved it. It was her favourite toy, and any time Dave joked about breaking it, Ronnie would scold him.

Abby looked over at Ronnie, who had her hands outstretched. She smiled at her mother, two little dimples appearing on her fat, chubby, baby cheeks. Ronnie had her dressed in a pink headband and matching pants, and a white shirt with a kitten on it.

"Come on, Abby. Come to Mama," Ronnie said with a big smile on her face.

All week Ronnie had been trying to get Abby to walk. Twice she had come close, but Abby couldn't do it on her own yet. She would walk a few steps while holding one of their hands, but that was it. She'd either demand to be picked up or she'd fall down onto her poufy diaper bum and crawl instead.

Dave watched as Abby, still smiling, let go of the music table and took a step forward. Her chubby arms wavered at her sides for balance as she took another step forward towards Ronnie. The steps were slow at first, unsure and unsteady, but then she gained confidence and picked up speed. Ronnie wiggled her fingers, eager to catch Abby in her arms as she stumbled towards her, all on her own. Dave watched in amazement, pride swelling within him as Abby walked unassisted into Ronnie's arms. Once within reach, Ronnie wrapped her hands around Abby's waist and pulled her into a big hug. She swung her side to side, and the two of them laughed and smiled. Ronnie showered Abby with kisses all over her face.

"Abby! Way to go, kiddo!" Dave cheered and Ronnie let Abby go. Abby looked up at him and Ronnie scooted out of the way. She stood a little unsteady on her feet, but then took the three steps she needed towards him, her chubby arms outstretched.

"Dada!"

Dave scooped her up and threw her into the air. Abby shrieked and giggled, and as Dave caught her, he planted his own set of kisses on her cheeks. She squirmed and giggled, and then leaned in and gave him a sloppy kiss on his cheek.

"Her first steps," Ronnie sighed happily. She smiled up at Dave and he smiled down at her.

With Abby secure in his arms, he sat down on the top step and leaned up to give Ronnie a kiss. She met him halfway, and a familiar warmth spread within him, the comforting feeling he always had when he kissed his wife. As they parted ways and he opened his eyes, he smiled again at his beautiful wife, lost within her ocean blue eyes for a minute. Everything was perfect within his little family, and Dave hoped that this feeling of pride and happiness would never end.

June 8, 2011
Dear Abby,

 Abby is so sweet, but I feel so bad. Morning sickness has kicked in full force now, and as I was starting to make dinner, I threw up. I ran over to the sink and vomited, and at first, Abby thought it was funny. She was colouring at the kitchen table and began to laugh and giggle, likely because Dave pretends to gag whenever he needs to change her diaper.
 Then a second wave hit, and I threw up again, and she said, "Mommy?" in a concerned voice, but still laughed a bit.
 The third wave she began to cry and told me to stop. I felt so terrible, and told her I was fine, but that I couldn't stop. She didn't stop crying until I could physically go over and give her a hug once I had finally stopped throwing up.
 Hopefully this sickness dies down soon, and then we can enjoy the summer together. She's at such a fun age right now, and I don't want to miss any of it.

August 27, 2011
Dear Abby,

    Today on the news there was a report on a missing woman who is suspected to have postpartum depression. Police are pleading with the public to keep their eyes open, as her family believes she is at risk of harming herself. Surveillance at a local corner store caught her on camera buying some diapers and other little necessities. I hope they find her. My heart goes out to her worried husband and their infant daughter. At least the baby isn't with her. I can only hope that this has a happy outcome. I understand how this woman must be feeling, and if her family is worried about her and labelling her as "missing," then what she is feeling and going through must be very serious.

September 2, 2011
Dear Abby,

 I am heartbroken and can't stop crying. They found the body of the missing woman today, the one who had PPD. She threw herself in the river sometime shortly after the video of her at the corner store had been taken. I can't imagine the change in feeling from buying diapers to suicide in what may have only been a few minutes or hours. I can't stop thinking about her poor husband and their infant daughter, who will never get to know her mother now, because this horrible darkness overtook her. I am thankful that her baby was not with her. I've read too many stories of mothers who perish with their babies. It breaks my heart, and I am going to give Abby an extra tight hug tonight.
 I think back on those days, those dark nights, when I would feel consumed by my depression and just imagine Dave coming home and me not being there, not knowing where I'd be or in what condition... just that I would be gone. Imaging it and going through with it are two very different things, but all it takes is a bad day, a bad moment to take that leap. I can't imagine what that trigger would be for me, and I'm happy that I'm in a place now where I don't think it'll ever be a possibility. I hope this woman finds peace in whatever sort of afterlife she believes in, and that one day, her family finds peace too.

Dave
February 2, 2012

"I think my water just broke."

Dave opened his eyes and rolled over. The room was dark, but he could see Ronnie's large outline beside him and her face staring at him in the muted glow of the moon through the curtains. He reached behind him to grab his phone off the nightstand, and when the screen lit up, it said his alarm was going to go off in five minutes. There would be no going into the store today.

"Dave?" Ronnie whispered again. "Did you hear what I said?"

"Yes," he yawned. He put the phone down and leaned over to give her a kiss. She smiled in the darkness, and he smiled back. Their baby boy was on the way.

This time their bags were packed and had been for a few weeks. They had learned from Abby's early arrival and would not make that same mistake again. Ronnie worried the baby would be early again, but here they were, three days overdue. The doctor had opted out of inducing, at least for now, which made Ronnie feel relieved. Now there would be no need.

"I'll call the hospital," Ronnie said as she sat up slowly. She winced as she turned to move out of the bed, and Dave quickly jumped up to help her. The last few days had been rough on her, especially her hips. Dave came home the other night to find her crying in their room because she could not get into bed without his help. He didn't remember her ever being this uncomfortable or in pain while pregnant with Abby, and he didn't like it. Apparently, subsequent pregnancies could be harder and harder on the body. And Ronnie still wanted a third. Dave wasn't sure if he'd be able to see her in pain for a third time, and they hadn't even finished getting through the second.

"I'll call your parents," Dave said. "And I'll get Abby ready."

The plan was to meet with Ronnie's parents at the hospital. They would take Abby home with them, and Dave would stay at the hospital overnight. Flashbacks of the panicked feeling he had with Abby played through his head, and he let out a sigh of relief. No panic this time. Not yet at least.

As Dave got off the phone with Ronnie's mother, Abby came skipping out of her room. The kid woke up with instant energy, always from zero to one hundred once she was up.

"Morning, kiddo," he said. "Guess what?"

"What?" Abby asked.

"Baby Eli is coming today!"

Abby's face exploded with excitement. She threw her hands up in the air and started shouting, "Yay, yay, yay!" as she ran up and down the hall. It took Dave a few moments to get her to the potty and get dressed. Once she was ready to go, Dave quickly changed, grabbed everyone's bags, and off they went.

Ronnie's mother, Donna, was already at the hospital as they pulled in. Ronnie's contractions started during the car ride, but they weren't full blown yet. She took her time getting out of the car and Dave took care of the rest.

"How exciting!" Donna clapped as she approached their car. Abby jumped out of her seat and into Donna's arms.

"Gramma! Baby Eli is coming!" she said.

"You go head inside." Dave waved off Ronnie, and she took deep breaths and leaned against the car. "I'll catch up to you. Just take it slow. I just need to pay for the parking."

Ronnie nodded. She waved goodbye to her mother and gave Abby a quick kiss.

"Good luck!" Donna called. Dave unpacked the bags and handed Donna the overnight bag for Abby.

"Be good for your grandma," Dave said as he slammed the trunk closed.

"She's always good." Donna winked at Abby and Abby giggled. Dave smiled at the two of them and then headed towards the parking meter. Ronnie was still slow, waddling her way towards the hospital. He paid quickly and went to catch up with his wife.

It was a calm feeling he had this time as he caught up with Ronnie. They casually walked in through the hospital's front doors, not the emergency department like last time. They registered at the desk and then made their way towards the elevator. Ronnie would take in a deep breath now and then but seemed to be doing well overall. Of course, things would escalate later, but for now, Dave breathed in the calm.

Once up in the maternity ward, the nurses brought them into the triage where they assessed Ronnie to confirm that her water had broken. It wasn't as much of a gush as it had been with Abby, Ronnie explained to Dave when they were still at home, so she wasn't one hundred percent sure. But the contractions started earlier this time than they had with Abby.

As Ronnie was in the bathroom giving her sample, a nurse brought in another expectant mother to be assessed. Dave looked up from his phone and the woman gave him a dirty look. The nurse then pulled the curtain across that separated the two beds and assessed the other patient. Dave overheard that she wasn't as far along as Ronnie was in her pregnancy. That meant little. When Ronnie was pregnant with Abby, they had gone in for an assessment at one point because she had become concerned that the baby wasn't moving as much. It all ended well, and Dave hoped the same for this other woman.

Ronnie came back out of the restroom and smiled as she climbed up onto the bed. She patted her round belly and closed her eyes as another contraction came.

"Doing alright?" Dave asked. Ronnie nodded through the contraction and Dave timed it on an app he had installed on his phone. Their nurse came back and confirmed that Ronnie's water had broken. She then questioned Ronnie on a few things and jotted down her answers on a sheet on her clipboard. Dave, however, didn't pay attention. The woman on the other side of the curtain was talking and it distracted him.

"Will I get my own room?" the woman was asking. The blue curtain shifted and bulged as the nurse moved around.

"Well, we're still assessing you in here. There's only one room left, and the other couple were here first, I think," the nurse answered.

"But I asked about it first. What if there's something wrong with my baby?" she snapped.

"We don't know that yet," the nurse replied. "It's first come, first served. The other woman's water has broken. Her baby is coming now. You still have thirteen weeks to go, and from the way your baby is kicking now, things are looking fine..."

Dave stopped listening when Ronnie climbed off the bed and the nurse led them out of the room. He picked up their bags, and as he walked by the woman on the other bed, she gave Ronnie a nasty look. Ronnie didn't notice. Dave just smiled at the lady and gave her a thumbs up. It just made her angrier, which made him chuckle.

By some stroke of fate, they were in the same room as when Ronnie delivered Abby. This time, Ronnie had more of a plan of what she wanted. At first, she bounced on the ball that the nurses provided. After that became less desirable, she moved to the shower, where Dave waved the shower head over her back, where the contractions were the most uncomfortable. She only lasted twenty minutes in the shower before she moved to the bed, and that's where she stayed for the next few hours. They mostly sat in silence, save for when Ronnie had a contraction. She would either breathe deeply or let out a low moan. During her pregnancy she had decided she wanted to bring stress balls in to squeeze during the contractions, and they seemed to help her. Dave was proud of his wife. He couldn't imagine voluntarily going through the same horrendous pain twice.

Things moved at a steady pace. The nurse moved around the room setting things up as Ronnie's contractions came and went at even intervals. Dave sat at her side, ready with her water bottle or his hand for her to squeeze. She preferred the stress ball, which was becoming mangled under her nails.

All at once, Ronnie gave out a loud cry. "I think I need to push!"

The nurse came running over as Ronnie began to push. A waterfall erupted out of her, and Dave sat close by her side. He didn't remember this much liquid coming out last time. A second nurse came into the room with the doctor and the doctor resident, and they prepped themselves at the end of the bed. The nurse got the baby's station ready to their right. Ronnie took deep breaths, squeezed her ball, and gripped Dave's hand with her other.

"OK, let's concentrate on our pushes," the doctor said. The resident doctor put on his gloves and put his hands between Ronnie's legs. Ronnie let out a low moan and a long push. Dave could tell that she knew what she was doing this time. Her pushes were concentrated, and she synced her breathing better. Already he could see the baby's head coming out.

"Stop!" the doctor blurted at once. Ronnie paused what she was doing and took quick breaths. Dave couldn't imagine trying to hold a half-exposed baby in place.

"Cut the cord," the doctor said in a hurried voice. The resident doctor did as he was told and cut the cord. "Push!"

Ronnie pushed and the rest of the baby came out. They placed him on Ronnie's chest and Dave's heart stopped. There was no cry. The baby boy was bigger than Abby had been, but he was blue and limp. Ronnie hadn't seen him yet, her eyes still closed from exhaustion, and the doctor grabbed the baby and whisked him away. Both doctors and nurses all huddled around the baby at the station across the room. Ronnie opened her eyes and looked over at Dave. The colour in her cheeks drained and there was a look of pain on her face.

"Is he…?"

"He's fine," Dave reassured in a calm voice. But he didn't know. He had never seen anything so scary in his life. Their baby was blue. He didn't cry. The cord had wrapped itself around his neck, and Dave didn't know what he would do if he didn't hear the baby cry soon. There was no way that this was happening to them, that Ronnie had to go through weeks of terrible morning sickness, painful, aching hips, hours of labour, only to have their sweet baby boy not survive. It wasn't fair. He wouldn't know how to shield her from it, as it would be a reality they would both have to face. He wasn't sure if they'd be able to survive it.

A shrill cry ripped through the air and Dave let out an enormous sigh of relief. A nurse turned and smiled at them, and the resident doctor returned to help birth the placenta. After a few more moments, the nurse gasped and laughed as the baby peed on her. Once cleaned up, she came over and placed the baby on Ronnie's chest. The colour was back in his face, and he looked up at Ronnie with great big eyes, so alert for a newborn. Relief flooded through Dave, and he chuckled as he looked down at his son. A little troublemaker already.

February 2, 2012
Dear Abby,

 Eli was born today. My water broke at home this morning, and then it was showtime. It was gruelling. When you have your first child, you're nervous because you don't know what to expect, but that naivety sort of protects you in a way as well. You go in blind because you don't know what's about to come. But with your second, you're nervous because you know <u>exactly</u> what to expect. I don't remember it being this intense with Abby, but it must have been! I laboured for longer with Eli but pushed him out a lot faster. There was a moment though, when the contractions were on top of each other, that I was sure I was going to die. There is no way that I am ever doing this again.
 He's a big baby, much bigger than Abby was. I could really feel him coming out, which was both a blessing and a curse. A blessing because I knew it would be over soon, a curse well, because you know… he was bigger. It was also terrifying because he came out with the cord wrapped around his neck, and he was unresponsive for what felt like forever. It was only maybe a minute at most though.
 None of that matters now of course. I love him so much already. He looks so much like Abby did as a baby, it's unreal. He's like a little masculine version of her. She's visited him already and was so enamoured by him. Right away she wanted to hold him and was so

delicate when I handed him over. She couldn't stop talking about how cute he is, and when Mom went to take her back home, I overheard Abby tell her how excited she is to play with Eli once we're home. I wonder how bored she'll be when she realizes that he can't quite "play" with her just yet. She's going to be an amazing big sister though, I can just tell.

Everything about today has made me think about when I was here last with Abby. We were coincidentally in the same hospital room! I remember it like it was yesterday with her snoring in the bassinet beside me, then with me in the bed. It's so hard to remember her ever being this small—smaller even.

Eli is very alert already. He's quite calm and keeps looking around the room with these great big eyes. Breastfeeding seems to be going quite well already, so I am optimistic about it this time. New baby, new blank slate. My recovery seems to be a lot better already too!

I just have a very positive, peaceful feeling about everything to come.

April 20, 2012
Dear Abby,

    Practice makes perfect, am I right? I feel like I'm dreaming some days. We've transitioned from one to two kids so well. I feel like I've mastered this already, which of course makes me question it. It shouldn't be this easy, right? Don't get me wrong, Eli is a hard baby. He's not the hardest baby out there. It's not like he has colic or anything. But he's so much harder than Abby was. I never realized what a calm baby she was until now. And yet somehow, I just feel amazing right now. We've got a routine down, and every day, everything just falls easily into place.
    Abby turned three yesterday, which is just insane. Where did the time go? She's blossomed into such an endearing and kind-hearted little girl. The bond between her and Eli is so sweet. Even though he can't do anything yet, she tries to include him in everything. He's the first thing she thinks of in the morning and the last thing before bed. They're going to be the best of friends growing up. I can't wait to see them actually interact with each other as he gets older. She sings him this little lullaby she made up for him if he's crying and I'm unable to tend to him right away. "It's OK, little Eli…" Those are the only lyrics, but she's consistent in her melody every time. I love it. I love everything about our life right now.

April 27, 2012
Dear Abby,

    Having kids is like getting a puppy, or like when people get their children bunnies for Easter gifts, and then a month later they're at the SPCA. Or at least, that's how I feel. I just love babies. I want babies. I want all of the babies until they're about two... and then that's it. I'm done. Where's the farm where I can drop them off and let them roam free? Oh, there isn't one. Babies/children, like puppies and pets, are a lifelong commitment. That's in the fine print of parenting somewhere, in the invisible manual that nobody hands out.
    Despite him being absolutely miserable half of the time, I'll gladly take Eli screaming and just wanting to be held all the time, over Abby's constant non-stop chatting, and wanting to be played with, and "Look at me! Look at me!" repeatedly. I love her to pieces, and more often than not, she makes me smile. I love seeing her grow and discover new things, and she makes me genuinely laugh out loud at the things she says at times. But I need a break. All of that "I feel so good, blah blah blah" that I wrote last week has suddenly taken a turn, and I don't like where it's heading.

Dave
May 4, 2012

"Hello, hello," Dave called as he came in through the garage door. Another long workday was behind him, and he was happy to be home. It wasn't quite dinner time yet and Dave's stomach rumbled. If he recalled correctly, Ronnie wanted to make tacos tonight. He had picked up a few of the fixings on his way home from work and marched up the stairs with the grocery bag in his hand. He also had a chocolate bar for Ronnie, and a cookie for Abby.

Up the stairs he heard music coming from the TV. As he rounded the corner, he saw bright colours flash on the screen, and Abby stood a few feet from it. She stared at the people on the screen, a children's singing group that she had become obsessed with, and followed along with the dance they were doing. It was all she ever wanted to watch or do. Dave stood quietly in the stairwell for a moment, smiling to himself as he watched her try to copy the dance, her version not quite as synchronized as the adults on screen. Her pigtails bobbed up and down as she moved with the rhythm and brought her arms above her head.

Dave walked into the room and glanced towards the empty kitchen. Ronnie and Eli weren't there. Abby was alone in front of the TV.

"Hey kiddo," Dave said. He placed the grocery bag on the counter and Abby looked over at him and smiled. "Where's Mommy?"

"Shower," Abby responded as she geared up for the next dance segment. As she said it, Dave then noticed the sound of the shower upstairs over the music from the TV. He also noticed the shrill, nonstop cry of a baby mixed in with the sound of the running water.

Dave hastily put away the food fixings and went upstairs. Setting sunlight shone through the bright open windows, and he looked forward to their vacation in a few weeks. Donna and Gerald had given them the keys to their condo in Maui, and Dave had taken two weeks off work. It was a much-needed vacation for him, just as it was for Ronnie. Though she was on maternity leave, he knew that she needed a change of scenery, and that maternity leave was no cake walk.

Eli was a hard baby. Harder than Abby had been at least, and therefore more difficult than what they had experienced before. He was clingy and did not like to be put down. It was hard to hold him all the time with a three-year-old to also look after. Ronnie tried a few different carriers and wraps, but Eli did not like those either. And so, the housework had gone undone, dust coated countertops, and laundry made mountains in baskets and corners. Dave entered their bedroom, the bed unmade, and a few dirty diapers sat on top of their dresser, plus a small pile of cat vomit in one corner. All signs of a hard day, Dave thought to himself.

As he got closer to their ensuite, the sounds of Eli crying over the shower became clearer. Dave pushed the door open and paused. Ronnie hummed quietly a lullaby that went unheard in Eli's ears as he squealed. She had placed him snuggly inside a laundry basket, on top of one of their comforters and what looked like one of her shirts. Babies could smell their mothers and it was an attempt to calm him so that she could put him down. The attempt was in vain, for his face was scrunched up and red as he wailed from within the basket.

Ronnie didn't notice Dave at first. She stood facing the shower head, the hot water trailing down her body, her soft voice echoing on the surrounding tile. A section of the glass was rubbed clean, a viewing point for her to see the baby. Her shoulders slumped as though in defeat, and it was hard to tell from the running water whether she was crying or not. Dave watched the water run down her fair skin, the scars, and marks from bringing their precious children into the world visible on her naked body. It sagged and stretched, no longer the smooth facade it had been when they met six years ago. She was beautiful.

Not wanting to disturb her, Dave crept in quietly and scooped up his crying son. Almost instantly, Eli's cries settled, and Ronnie looked up. A wary and thankful smile spread across her face, and Dave blew her a kiss.

"Thank you," she whispered. It wasn't something she needed to thank him for. He was his father; they were in this together as even partners. He'd told her this before, but Ronnie said thank you whenever the occasion called for it. Dave had long given up the battle, and just accepted it now.

"Any time," he said. He bounced Eli in his arms and looked down at him as they left Ronnie to have a peaceful shower alone.

Dave placed Eli down on the bed and waved his fingers in front of him. His son stared up at him with great big, dark blue eyes, still undecided on what their permanent colour would be. Eli then let out a giggle and Dave waved his fingers in front of him again. The baby kicked his feet excitedly and turned his bald head from side to side as he followed where Dave waved his fingers.

"Stop giving your mom a hard time," Dave said playfully. Part of him meant it, a small bit. Not that Eli did it on purpose. He was just a baby, after all, but Dave worried about Ronnie. Lately, she just seemed defeated all the time. He hoped that their vacation would bring some life back into her, and that maybe, just maybe, she wouldn't have to go through postpartum depression again. But if she did, Dave would be there for her, to help her through it. He'd always be there for her.

May 25, 2012
Dear Abby,

 What is it about Hawaii that is just so relaxing? Is it the sound of the ocean waves? The warm sand? I feel like part of it must be the constant sun. I think I have SAD. There would be no SAD symptoms if we just lived here though. Too bad it's so expensive. Maybe if the exchange rate was better... ah, daydreaming.
 Remember when we used to come here as kids and pretend we were mermaids in the pool? Abby and I played that today. I used it as a game to help teach her some basics about swimming. At first, she wouldn't even enter the pool, but now, on our last day here in paradise, I had her swimming a bit without her life vest on! I was so impressed by her and how far she progressed. I wish we didn't have to leave. Everything about these past two weeks has been wonderful. Maybe it's because we're in Hawaii. Or maybe it's because Dave was here all day to help with the kids. I definitely do better when he is around. He's my rock. I don't know where I'd be without him.

June 4, 2012
Dear Abby,

I lost my shit today. I don't know what is wrong with me, but everything feels ten times harder than it should be. I feel like I can barely keep my head above water.

It all started at dinner time. Dave was at work of course. Eli was having a tough day, just being his usual grumpy self. I finally had him settled down and all I'd been looking forward to all day was making turkey wraps with tzatziki.

Abby was pretty well behaved, albeit chatting non-stop as usual. The girl just doesn't know when to stop. I held it together enough to get dinner on the table while Eli was having a calm moment. I gave Abby her plate and sat down to eat mine, when she suddenly looked up from her plate and said, "Mommy, I need to pee-pee!" just as I was about to take a bite. Perfect timing, of course.

So, I set my food down and we rushed upstairs, Abby does her business, etc. I try to remind her to go when Mommy first asks if she needs to go, which I had done before making dinner. I feel like all potty training is an uphill battle.

We go back downstairs, Eli is fussing a bit, but nothing too bad, and then I see Whiskers on the table, her face in my plate and eating the turkey out of my wrap. And I just <u>lost</u> it. I screamed at her and chased her all over the house. Dinner ruined, I threw it in the bin and just broke down crying behind the counter while I snapped at Abby to be quiet and go eat her food when she asked me what was wrong. At some point, I heard her little voice go, "Bad Whiskers, eating Mommy's dinner" and now, above the still lingering feeling of anxiety and rage, I just feel so guilty for the way I acted in front of her.

But I lose my patience so much easier now than before. Everything sets me off and I don't know why or how to fix it. I felt like I was doing so well and had transitioned to two kids so easily, despite Eli being so much more difficult than Abby. Breastfeeding is still going well, thankfully, but I'm just finding myself struggling with the two of them. If Eli starts crying and Abby starts yapping her head off, I can't take the noise of both of them. And of course, since Eli doesn't understand and isn't doing it on purpose, I end up snapping at Abby for her to be quiet until I get Eli to settle down. But it's so unfair on her too because it's not her fault. She's just learning and developing her skills and growing into this beautiful little person with such a positive, sunny, and friendly attitude... she doesn't deserve this.

I don't know what to do, and aside from making sure I cover my damn plate next time, I don't know how to stop these feelings from taking over. Is postpartum rage a thing? I know anxiety is, but this is just... I was seeing red when I saw the cat eating my food. This can't be normal. And it definitely can't be healthy. I don't know how I'm going to survive if I have this on top of my depression and this developing anxiety.

__Dave__
June 28, 2012

Ronnie sighed a cheerful sound. It was late in the evening. The early summer sun started to set, and Abby was tucked into bed. She had passed out right away, worn out from a long day of playing at the park and walking along the beach. It had been a great day as a family, and Dave felt worn out too. He sat on the other end of the couch from Ronnie, his eyes glued on the TV screen as he played his Xbox. Ronnie snuggled with a light blanket, seated next to the window, the warm summer breeze wafting in. Eli was asleep on her chest, his soother bopping up and down every few minutes as he dreamed of nursing.

"I want another one," she murmured quietly. Dave glanced at her but said nothing. His stomach flipped a bit, but he focused on his game. Ronnie wanted another baby. Eli was only four months old and already she was thinking of the next one. Dave didn't have a problem with having a third child. He had known from the beginning that Ronnie wanted to have three kids. Part of him hoped that since they had one of each, she would be fine with two. But he knew that wouldn't fly. It wasn't the idea of a third child that had him bristling at the thought, it was Ronnie herself.

At first, Dave thought they got through this new baby unscathed. For the first few months, Ronnie was happy. Her spirits were up, despite the deprived sleep, and she had transitioned from one child to two in a breeze. Her recovery had been a lot smoother this time, and she was a pro with this baby.

But slowly, especially these last few weeks, Dave could see the postpartum depression setting in. It was a bit different from last time, and when Ronnie admitted it was happening, she explained it as such. She wasn't so much depressed or sad like with Abby; she just felt overwhelmed, at everything. And Dave could understand that. Eli, as adorable as he was, was more difficult than Abby had been. He was clingy and didn't sleep fully through the night. Breastfeeding was going better for Ronnie this time, but Eli couldn't be set down without the constant sound of crying in the background. And it wasn't a normal baby cry; it was this terrible hoarse sound that made Ronnie anxious the second it would start. She worried about his vocal cords, and while Dave tried to assure her that Eli would be fine, she couldn't handle it.

Abby was in a bit of a difficult phase, the "threenager" phase, and went from angel to devil at any given moment. When she acted up while Eli was crying, Ronnie broke down. More than twice now, Dave had come home from work to find Ronnie sitting in another room with her back to the wall, taking deep breaths as she tried to calm herself down. More than once, she had put Eli down in his crib and had to walk away to compose herself. She was short with Abby all the time when all Abby wanted to do was play.

Dave helped as much as he could. The minute he was home, he would spend his time with Abby to give Ronnie a break. Abby was a very high energy child and depression sucked Ronnie's energy away. Or when he was home in the mornings or had his day off, he would hold Eli so that Ronnie could eat breakfast in peace.

Despite the difficult phases the kids were currently in, Dave could see himself with another. But he worried about Ronnie and the state of her mental health. Twice now she was diagnosed with postpartum depression. It was worse this time around. Ronnie received medication a few days ago for it. He worried about how bad it might be a third time and what it might do to Ronnie. He could see himself with three kids but could not handle three without her. They were a team.

"Honey? Did you hear me?" Ronnie asked in a loud whisper. She did not want to wake Eli. Dave didn't blame her. He had cried for ten minutes straight in his hoarse scream. It was not colic, thankfully, but it was still hard to hear. Like nails on a chalkboard through a megaphone.

"Yes, I know hon," Dave said. He glanced over at Ronnie again and she smiled at him. She closed her eyes and settled back into the couch and rubbed Eli on his little back and bum.

As he looked back at his game, he mentally sighed. He didn't know how to bring up his concerns without Ronnie being hurt. She would think that he didn't want another baby or that he was trying to put it off or delay it. He worried she would think that he was trying to use her mental state as an excuse *not* to have another baby when he would never use her mental health against her. But it wasn't responsible for them to have another baby while she was still recovering, both physically and mentally, from the last. He knew that. Dave hoped Ronnie was taking her mental health into account as well.

He glanced over at her again and calmed. She looked peaceful and happy, her eyes still closed, as she snuggled with Eli on the couch. The depression aside, she did great with babies. Abby was the one she was having more difficulty with. Toddlers were hell. But this phase would pass, and her postpartum depression would pass too. They would probably try for another baby once Eli was a year or a little over. They still had plenty of time to adjust and then reassess their plans for a third child. Dave could then bring up his concerns about a third bout of postpartum depression with Ronnie closer to then. It would be best to wait until she got over this round before worrying about the next.

July 4, 2012
Dear Abby,

People always say when you get married, that a spouse is like a ball and chain. "The ol' ball and chain" they say. They could not be more wrong. A ball and chain is like a sentence, something unintentional that you cannot escape of your own volition. Marriage is happy. You willingly tether yourself to that person, and you are equals. The tether stretches; it is light as air, and you can spend time apart, and always come back to each other. If needed, I can take the tether off. It's not heavy.

Children are the balls and chains. They drag you down despite their small size. You carry their weight everywhere you go, even if you try to forget about it, it's there. They're there. There is no escaping them, you can't just take the chains off. You can force them off, but it's painful. And as much as you wish the chains would come off, that you could go back to the chainless life you once had, taking them off hurts. A lot.

Dave
July 28, 2012

    The night air was cool, a relief from the hot summer's day it had been, and the townhouse was dark as Dave approached it. Ronnie didn't wait up for him. With aching feet, Dave dragged himself up the porch, and the creak of the stairs echoed the feeling of his tired bones. It had been a long and exhausting day and was almost midnight now. A discrepancy between the cash in one of the tills and the final printout report kept him later than usual, which had caused him to miss his bus and have to wait a half hour for the next one. It would be a relief when his car was back from the shop in two days, and he wouldn't have to rely on public transit again. Ronnie had offered to pick him up from work, but Dave didn't want her to have to wake up the kids as they'd be asleep by the time his shift was over.
    The alarm beeped softly as Dave opened and closed the door, and he sighed, comforted to be home. The next two days he had off, and he was ready to relax. As he reached out for the light switch, he tripped over something that squeaked, and Dave cringed at the loud sound as he flipped the lights on. He looked down at one of Abby's toy ducks and kicked it out of the way as he listened to hear if the fumbling had caused Eli to wake. The last couple of nights he had been fussy and knew that the frequent wakings were taking a toll on Ronnie. Though she seemed to do better now that

she was taking medication, Dave wanted her to get a good night's sleep. It was hard for him to help her with the late night wakings. There wasn't much he could do when all Eli wanted to do was nurse.

Whiskers meowed softly at Dave as she slipped out of the shadows. He reached down and patted her head as he walked down the hall and into the kitchen. There, he turned on more lights and the disarray of the living room made him smile. The remnants of a fort stretched across the dining room chairs and back of the couch painted a picture of a fun afternoon. A pile of dolls poked out from the bottom of the half-fallen blanket roof, and the couch's pillows were strewn all over the floor.

Dave helped himself to a tall glass of cold water, and Whiskers wove herself around his legs, purring loudly. The glass clinked on the counter next to a spot of dried spaghetti sauce. Dried noodles littered the floor where Abby had sat, and the last of the dishes that were not yet packed in boxes filled the sink. It was hard to believe that next week they would be in their new house. The feeling of not having to share walls or pay strata was a joy, and Dave was proud that they moved up to the next level. A bigger house had been on Ronnie's wish list for a while, and now that he had been in his new position at work for a good period of time, Dave knew it would be no problem for them. It was a dream come true. The sale had gone through yesterday.

Moving boxes piled up against one wall of the living room and Dave flung his tie over one as he kicked off his shoes and unbuttoned his shirt. He sank down onto the couch, the cushions sighing with him as his feet throbbed. Whiskers jumped up next to him and meowed again. Dave turned on the TV and turned the volume to low, not wanting to wake the kids. The cat settled beside him as he got comfortable, and as a commercial about organic fruit juice came on, Dave closed his eyes and drifted off to sleep.

When he woke up, his feet no longer throbbed, but his back did. The old grey couch wasn't as comfortable as it had once been, and it was one of the first things they planned to upgrade in the new house. Whiskers had moved over to her cat tree at some point.

Dave turned off the TV and yawned as he reached to check the time on his phone. It was just past 3:30 in the morning.

As he slowly made his way towards the stairs, Dave turned the lights off. The walls looked empty without their pictures hung up, all of them now safely wrapped up in boxes. He made some mental notes of patches and touch ups that would need to be done to some walls before the new owners moved in. He'd have to get started on those tomorrow.

Up the stairs, the banister squeaked and shifted as he pulled himself up. He nearly tripped over Ginger sleeping on the landing at the top, and she hissed angrily at him when he stepped on her tail.

"Stupid cat," Dave muttered as the angry fat feline slunk down the stairs. The nightlight in the hall was off. Dave pushed it back into the socket and it flashed back on. Abby must have knocked it out as she did her nightly running up and down the halls. How she had so much energy throughout the day, Dave didn't know. It was a superpower only toddlers seemed to possess.

Abby's room was the first one off the stairs. Her door was ajar, and Dave poked his head in. Stars shone on her ceiling, her nightlight twinkling softly to fight away the dark. He smiled at the pile of books at the end her bed, a few of them fallen on the floor, and she snored softly from her pillow. At least she slept through the night.

Dave padded down the rest of the hallway to the master bedroom to check in on Ronnie. The light was off, which meant that she and Eli would be asleep. He looked forward to sleeping in his own bed with his wife at the new house. Ronnie was ready to be done co-sleeping too, he knew, because Eli was a lot wigglier than Abby had been. But it made no sense to put him in his own room if they were moving into their new house so soon. It would be better to do the transition into his crib all at once, in the new house.

The door creaked softly as Dave opened it as quietly as he could. He held up the light on his phone to find his phone charger. It was over on the dresser where he had left it. As he moved towards it, the empty bed caught his eye. He did a double take and flicked the light on in the room as though the light of his phone was deceiving him. But it wasn't. The bed was empty. Dave scratched his head, not sure what he was seeing, and then padded back down the hall. Maybe they were sleeping in the spare room for some reason, on the futon where Dave had been sleeping. The master bedroom got hot during the summer, and maybe the heat was bothering Eli's sensitive skin. The spare room was much cooler as the setting sun didn't hit it like it did the master.

But the spare room was empty. The door was wide open, the blanket left in the same crumple Dave had left it in that morning, and the pillow was half fallen off the futon. The window was open, and a car drove by outside, the headlights flashing through the room briefly as a worrying chill ran up Dave's spine. For some illogical reason, he ran back to the master bedroom as though they would appear there, sleeping on the bed. But the room was still empty, stark, and too bright with the light still flicked on.

Dave thundered down the stairs, all the way to the bottom floor of the townhouse. The den was filled with boxes ready to be moved into the truck when they picked it up on Tuesday. A memory of Ronnie sleeping on the futon when it was down here flashed through his mind. She had slept down here with Abby as a baby for one night during the summer when she was still small, when the heat was too intense, and the screens weren't on their windows yet.

The door to the garage squealed as Dave ripped it open and he slammed his hand against the light switch. Ronnie's car was there and empty. A part of Dave sighed with relief. More than once, he had worried about Ronnie committing suicide by carbon monoxide poisoning by running the engine. They had always been fleeting thoughts. This was the first time he thought it could have come true, but he stared, puzzled, at the empty car.

Slowly, he closed the door and stood there staring at it, the house silent around him. As he made his way back upstairs, back up to the master bedroom, he looked down at his phone. Ronnie had texted him around 10:30 to say goodnight. He stared at the screen and then quickly typed, *Where are you?*

As he passed Abby's room again, he walked in and checked on her. He didn't like to think that Ronnie may have done something to her, but with her and Eli not home… Abby was fine, still snoring away, and she muttered in her sleep something about spiders as Dave stroked her chubby little cheek. Back in the hall, he turned on the light. He turned on the light in the spare room and the bathroom. When he went back into the empty master, he turned on the light in the ensuite, hoping with each flipped switch that somehow Ronnie and Eli would appear. The text he sent still went unanswered.

Dave sank onto the bed and stared around him, wondering what to do next. As he scanned the room, he noticed something missing. The pile of onesies and sleepers that had been on the nightstand, the clothes that Ronnie had kept out while packing everything for the house, were gone. So was the extra soother that she kept next to the change pad on the dresser, the main diaper ointment she had been using, and half of the freshly opened diaper sleeve. Then he noticed Ronnie's laptop, last seen on the chair in the corner, missing. When he ripped open the closet door, her favourite sweater wasn't there, her makeup bag from the ensuite was gone, and the dresser drawers seemed emptier. He raced out into the hall, and his heart sank when he opened the closet door. The small blue suitcase was missing.

Panic, confusion, and hurt rushed over Dave all at once. He raced down the stairs, his phone glued to his ear as he dialled Ronnie's number. It rang and rang and went to her voicemail. Dave didn't know what to say, so he just hung up. Ronnie hated checking her voicemail, anyway. He dialled her again as he headed for the front door, now noticing her purse was missing from its usual spot on the console table beside the fridge. His chest began to hurt, and he prayed for Ronnie to pick up the phone, to explain that there had been some sort of emergency for Eli, so urgent that she left Abby asleep in the house knowing that Dave would be home soon. Something that would have caused her to bring a suitcase, and her laptop, and favourite sweater, but forget the car…

As he moved towards the front door, he stopped dead in his tracks as something bright shone from the dining room table.

Ronnie's phone lit up as he tried calling her again. She had left her phone behind. Dave's hand shook as he reached out to touch it. He touched the screen and it lit up again, a photo of Abby and Eli smiling back at him. It was one of the professional ones they had gotten when Eli was a newborn. They hadn't been able to afford professional newborn shots with Abby, and Ronnie was overly excited that they could do them with Eli.

Dave unlocked her phone as he walked towards the front door. Ginger now slept on the couch, with Whiskers curled beside her. She lifted her head and yawned as Dave walked by. He went through Ronnie's texts, something he had never done before, looking for some sort of sign of where she had gone. But she had texted only him today, and other than a joke from her mother, nobody else in the past few days. There were no clues as to what was happening right now. No explanations.

A cool summer breeze greeted him as he opened the front door. Dave stared out into the night, the dark sky, and the quiet street, with his phone in one hand and Ronnie's in the other. He sat down on the front step and stared, a numb feeling overcoming him, as he realized they were gone.

July 28, 2012
Dear Abby,

    I'm writing this on the airplane right now. We've just taken off and I can see the lights below us as the plane continues to rise. Eli is fast asleep on my lap, and we're on our way to the condo. I feel like I am floating outside of my body and not in control of my actions. I am a robot, and an outside force has taken over, and all I can do is sit back and watch as this impostor makes decisions on my behalf.
    All I can think about is how I just packed up our bags and we left. And I left Abby behind. My sweet baby girl. I feel so numb. Her cheeks were warm when I kissed them goodbye. I can't even write about her without my eyes going blurry and tears staining the page. I was worried she was going to wake at the sounds of my sobs, but she's a deep sleeper. She's always been such a good sleeper. And I just left her there. By herself. What if she wakes up before Dave is home, and sees that we're gone, and she's all alone? Or if the house catches fire or somebody breaks in? I timed it right so that Dave would be home within thirty minutes of us leaving. But what if that wasn't close enough?
    I don't know what the future holds. I don't even know what I'm doing right now. All I know is that I can't handle it. I can't handle anything. Every time I'm left alone with the two of them, I feel trapped. Like I'm drowning. Their sweet faces keep me from falling

beneath the surface, and still, sometimes I can't catch my breath. It's not Abby's fault. It's not Eli's fault. It's not Dave's fault. The fault lies within me. I have a darkness that I can't escape, a feeling that I've lived with my whole life, that's grown stronger and inescapable since having Eli. I just need some space. Some time. I don't know what I'm doing. I just know that I need to go away for a bit, and that Eli needs to come with me. He needs me. He's too little to leave behind.

And maybe it's good that he needs to come too. I don't know what I'd do if I were on my own. I don't know if Dave would have understood if I had told him that I needed a vacation on my own, away from everybody. He would have worried, but he would have let me go. I should have talked to him instead of wrestling with this decision on my own for weeks. I don't know what I'm doing. I don't even know how I got the fake ID documents together, and yet here I am, here we are, on the plane, unnoticed. It worked. But I'm not so sure it was a good thing that it did.

I am tipped over the edge and now can't seem to figure out how to get back up. I don't know if this will be permanent or temporary. I don't know how to turn back now that this is in motion. I'll call Dave when we get to the condo. Just the thought of hearing his voice is calming me already. I should have just talked to him. The medication isn't enough, I need more help. I just don't know what exactly. Maybe I'll call him in a few days. I just need to get myself under control. I just need a break. Not from Dave, not from Abby, but from myself. I just need a fresh setting, to find some way to dig myself out of this hole that keeps swallowing me up.

Dave
July 30, 2012

"I just don't understand," Donna sobbed. A snotty tissue in hand, she shifted on Dave's couch in the living room. "She was over just that morning to drop off something. She seemed fine, completely fine. I don't understand..."

Dave massaged his temples and rubbed his hand down his face. Everything was still a blur. He had waited until the next morning to see if Ronnie would come back. She did not. He then had the hard task of making phone calls to the police, to family, both his and hers. He had the difficult task of trying to keep a calm and cheery demeanour for Abby. It was too soon to explain to her that Ronnie may never come home; that she would never see her baby brother again. Neither of them would.

Their townhouse suddenly felt violated. It was appropriate that most of their items were packed up and ready to be moved into a new house. The walls that held so many memories, the spot where Abby took her first steps, and the kitchen that had many late-night dance parties for two, all seemed tainted now. All Dave wanted to do was be anywhere other than here. It was too painful.

The police asked a lot of questions. They searched through the house, which Dave had already done. Ronnie's car was still here, as were her and Eli's passports. But her wallet, favourite articles of clothing, toiletries, and most of Eli's essentials were missing. The police reprimanded him for not contacting them sooner. As Ronnie's mental health was a risk, that meant Eli could be in danger. They agreed on issuing an Amber Alert for Eli's return, just to be safe. Dave hated the thought of it. The idea that his wife would hurt their son, he knew wasn't possible. People don't pack their essentials when they plan to commit suicide. As they left behind their travel documents, it was logical to assume they were somewhere in the country.

Dave's chest had ached at his next discovery. Their joint account was empty. Whatever Ronnie's plan was it was permanent. Or at least she thought it would be. He hoped she would come back; that she would get whatever time away she needed, away from the stress of both kids, of moving into a new house, and from whatever else may have been bothering her, and once she was calm again, she would come home. He had wrestled with whether to tell the police about the money, but in the end, he did and let them know that he didn't consider it stolen. If Ronnie came back or if they found her, he wouldn't charge her with theft. Dave's job was stable enough that he could provide for himself and Abby and pay for the new house on his own. It would be tight, but it would be manageable.

"Hey look! Mommy's picture is on the TV," Abby said. Excitement filled her voice as she pointed to the TV, and she beamed over at Dave. The morning news was on, and beside the anchor were the pictures of Ronnie and Eli that Dave provided to the police. A lump formed in his throat, and he reached over and changed the channel quickly. "Hey! When's Mommy coming home?"

Donna erupted into a new set of sobs and Dave had to turn away from them to keep from crying. He couldn't tell Abby the truth yet. He didn't know how to.

"I'm not sure yet, kiddo," he answered at last. The blank walls around them stared at him, and he had to get out. "Say, why don't we walk over to the park and play there one last time before we move to the new house?"

"Yay!" Abby squealed. She jumped down from the couch and ran over to her shoes near the front door. As she fumbled to put them on, the wrong feet no less, she looked up at Dave. "Will Mommy and baby be at the park?"

Dave bit his lip and took a deep breath. It was going to be a long day.

August 4, 2012
Dear Abby,

    I hate to admit it, but I am doing well. I have a range of conflicting feelings throughout the days, but overall, I feel calm and relaxed. Eli and I spend the mornings on the beach, in the sun. He didn't like the feel of the water at first when I dipped his toes in, but we've slowly gone in further and further each day, and now he'll happily sit on my hip with the water up to his knees, and kick and splash. The sand is a whole other thing though. He hates it, and I don't blame him. It just gets everywhere and it's irritating.

    I nap when he naps back at the condo, and it feels refreshing to have no other commitments during the day. I just go with his flow, as he's still quite fussy and clingy. But it's easier to handle when it's just the two of us. And that's when the conflicting emotions come in to play. I miss Abby so much. Yesterday at the beach there was a girl around the same age as her, and I just couldn't stop watching her play. She built sandcastles with her father and came up with an elaborate story on what was happening in the castles. Abby would have done the same, were she here. It makes my heart ache.

    At night when Eli is asleep, I cry thinking of Abby (and Dave). None of this is or was her fault, and I feel like the worst mother in the world for feeling relief when she's not here. It's easier to take a break when it's just Eli and I. Three is such a hard age... and yet,

Eli will be three one day too. I don't know where we'll be then, if we'll be back at home with Dave and Abby, or if we'll still be on our own. If it's just the two of us, how will I handle it then if I can't handle it now? I like to think it's just the post-partum hormones, that everything will settle down in a few months and then maybe things will be back to normal. But I haven't called Dave yet. We've been here a week, and I haven't contacted him. And I don't know what to do.

There is this feeling of shame that is building up and starting to consume me. I know the longer I wait to reach out and connect with him, the harder it will be to do so. Do I just turn up at home again in another week? Seeing him usually makes me feel better. It would be better to talk about it all in person, apologize then, and get back into the swing of things. But I just can't do it yet. What if it's already too late?

I'm surprised they haven't thought to come check here yet. I guess leaving the passports behind has thrown them off. How else would we be able to enter the United States without them? It won't be long though until they figure it out. We'll need to move on soon or go back home...

There's an anxiety that is growing too, both about going back and not going back. I can't have it both ways, but I can't decide which way to go because I still don't know what I'm doing. I don't know how I got here, where I am going, what my end game is, what I plan from here...

Dave
Present Day

The clock ticked on the wall. The sound filled the void of silence that had fallen over the house. Dave did not go to work, and Abby did not go to school. Instead, they both sat at the dining room table, Dave at the end and Abby to his right. On his other side was Eli. His son.

Eli looked like Ronnie, just as Abby did, only in different ways. Abby was like a miniature version of her, with subtle differences. She had blonde hair, with Dave's dimples and lips. Eli had her same curly brown hair, same eyes, and same expressions. He held his mug of hot chocolate the same way Ronnie always had, and there were other subtle things, like the way he moved or the way he spoke, that were all Ronnie. There were small pieces of Dave too, though, his nose, his build, and the shape of his face.

Dave never thought he would see his two children together ever again. Abby stared at Eli, her expression blank. Dave wished he knew what she was thinking, wished he had a better way to ease her into this. While she had remained angry and hurt at Ronnie for much of her life, she had rarely spoken about Eli. Dave didn't know what she felt at this moment, and that scared him. She had been so little when Eli had left but so attached to her baby brother. Did she even remember him now? Aside from the few pictures they had of him, was there anything from her memories that remained?

Eli, on the other hand, kept avoiding eye contact. Especially with Abby. She could be intimidating, Dave knew, but he supposed in this case that Eli had returned for him and didn't know how to feel around Abby. Maybe he didn't know about her, and it came as a shock. Dave liked to think that Ronnie would have told him about his sister. She may have left them, but she wouldn't have forgotten about them. He knew that she would have told Eli about his family. Maybe not often, but she would have at some point. She had to, for here he was. He had known where to find them.

"Are you sure you're not hungry? Nothing I can make you?" Dave asked to break the silence. The ticking of the clock was driving him mad. There were so many questions for Eli, but Dave knew he had to ease into them. Eli shook his head. His curls fell into his eyes as he looked down into his hot chocolate. Abby tapped her fingers on the side of her mug impatiently. Dave gave her a look, and she sighed and stopped.

Eli took a deep breath. He didn't look up from his mug as he said, "I guess you're wondering why I'm here."

"Yes," Dave said. *And where you've been all these years. What your favourite colour is. How you're doing in school. What your life has been like. How your mother is doing.* "But we can ease into that if you're tired from traveling. I'm assuming you took the red eye?"

Eli nodded. "There will be time for rest later," he mumbled. There was a glint in his eye.

Dave's stomach flipped. He gripped his own mug. It should have been too hot to touch for so long, but he couldn't feel it. Something was wrong. He didn't want to go there, to think of what Eli's next words would be, but he should have known. There was only a handful of reasons that his son would return to him at a young age instead of an adult looking for his own volition.

Eli's lip quivered. He cupped his mug and continued to stare into it as he took another deep breath before his next words. "Mom passed away."

Time stopped as everything came crashing down around them. The clock ticked louder, and it hurt Dave's ears. He closed his eyes as a white noise overtook the ticking and he took a few moments to breathe. She was gone. Not just from his life, but from the earth. He would never see her again. It was for certain this time. Any lost hopes and fantasies he had over the years of bumping into her on the streets, of her returning his unanswered messages on Facebook or e-mails, of getting a random postcard or letter in the mail, or even a like on an Instagram post, they were all gone now. They would never be realities. Eli said the words he dreaded. There was no taking them back. They hung there between them above the tabletop. He would never get his answers from Ronnie, and he could never give her his forgiveness.

When he opened his eyes, Dave looked over at Abby. Her knuckles were white from gripping her cup, a neutral expression on her face. Her eyes looked glossy but shed no tears. Eli let out a sniffle and when Dave turned to him, he saw him quickly wipe a tear away. There was no shame in crying, Dave wanted to say, especially over the loss of a loved one. He wanted to reach out and take Eli's hand but couldn't. They were still nothing more than strangers related by blood.

"What—" Dave cleared his throat as his voice cracked. "What happened?"

Eli glanced up at him. Dave could see the hurt and tired in his eyes. For whatever reason, he was burdened with this task, to come and find the father he did not know, the sister he could not remember, and deliver to them the news that the wife and mother that abandoned them had died.

"There's no easy way to say it," Eli said. Dave inhaled sharply. In that moment he knew. He gave a curt nod and Eli said the dreaded word, worse than the ones he'd already spoken. "Suicide."

Dave struggled to keep it together. There were many nights when he worried about coming home to find Ronnie had taken her own life. The post-partum nights were the worst. He recalled when he came home, the lights off in the house, to find her pumping in the dark. He had hoped that was the lowest she would ever get. What he had really hoped was that amid all the hurt she had caused himself and Abby, that Ronnie had found peace and happiness. It was the main reason he could forgive her for what she'd done. And now, though he still forgave her deep in his heart, he was mad. Not at her, but at the universe. For the darkness that had plagued her in the life she had with them, followed her into the new life she had built for her and their son. And it had taken her away from all of them now.

"When?" Dave asked once he had the strength.

"Few days ago," Eli mumbled. "Sunday."

Two days ago. Two days ago, Dave had been shopping with Abby for the last of her school supplies and for a few new pieces of clothing for her last year of school. If he had known that sometime on that same day Ronnie was going to end her life, there would be nothing he wouldn't give to have been able to stop her.

Dave stared at his son. He could only imagine what he felt at this moment. The pressure he must have felt to come out and tell them, two people he didn't even know, to share with them this painful experience. Dave knew nothing about his son's life. Did he have a stepdad back at home? Was there nobody else who could have dealt with this task? Did Eli set it upon himself to come find them or was it one of Ronnie's last requests?

"There's a funeral planned for next Friday," Eli said at last. He looked up and met Dave's eyes. There was so much emotion there. Pain, confusion, and something else. Something Dave couldn't quite put his finger on. "You need to be there."

"Why?" Abby said. Both Dave and Eli turned to her in shock. Angry tears spilled from her eyes and her face twisted in pain. "What does it matter if we're there? She abandoned us."

"Abby," Dave hissed.

Eli winced at the accusation but looked offended at the same time. He opened his mouth as though to retort, but then closed it and looked back at Dave. "There's some legal stuff. And she'd want you there. *Both* of you." He shot Abby an angry look before turning back to Dave. There was that odd look in his eye again, and Eli kept glancing down at his cup and then back up again. There was something else, something that he hadn't told them yet and struggled with. "And Dave—Dad—you are our legal guardian."

"What?" Abby asked at the same time as Dave said, "*Our?*"

Eli inhaled deeply. He looked up from his mug and stared straight at Dave. "Our. Me and my younger sister, Lisa. Your other daughter."

AFTER

August 10, 2012
Dear Abby,

I am in absolute shock. I can't believe what I'm about to put down here. I'm pregnant. I'd been feeling off the last few days and started throwing up yesterday. It was all too familiar, and I was in disbelief, but finally went to the pharmacy after over-the-counter meds weren't helping. And it came back positive. Positive.

I don't even know what to think right now. We hadn't even really been trying. Of course, I'd mention to Dave about having a third. I've always wanted three, and though the age gap between Abby and Eli was good in some respects, I kind of wished they'd be closer together. And now... well, careful what you wish for, I guess. Eli is only six months old! They'll be like, thirteen... fourteen months apart!

Do I call Dave? I mean, how can I not? But how can I after everything that's gone down? It's been almost two weeks since we came here. I see me and Eli's faces still in missing posts on the internet, the pleas and cries... I try to avoid social media and the news because of this.

But I can't stay here any longer. Not only because having a baby in the States would be ridiculously expensive, but because I feel like we've been here for too long already. I'm surprised that Dave, or Mom and Dad, haven't come bursting through the condo's front door. I think I've found somewhere new for us to go, but now this *recent development has me wondering what's the best thing to do. Dave deserves to know. But how can I face him after disappearing for two weeks? After having my face plastered all over the news, being (likely) charged as a kidnapper and a thief? Where do I really go from here?*

Dave
August 12, 2012

Whiskers meowed and rubbed up against Dave's leg. He reached down and patted her head as he sank onto his new couch. It had just arrived earlier that day and was the perfect fit for the new living room. Moving and unpacking was an arduous task to tackle on his own. The physical labour of moving furniture and boxes had been a great distraction at first. The aches and pains of his muscles and bones took focus away from the aches and pains of his heart.

Abby was excited about the new house. She ran all over the enormous space, from one room into the next. She slid down the stairs on her bum and would run back up to the top to do it again. When Dave brought in the boxes from the truck, she would tell him where they should go.

"This is baby's room," she'd said when he came up the stairs with a box. That was the first hit of the heartache returning, pushing itself to centre stage and into the spotlight. Dave hadn't thought about how painful the unpacking would be. At the townhouse, he had hastily thrown the last of their belongings into boxes and labelled them all "Misc." Dave wanted to get out of that townhouse, their first home together, as fast as possible. He wanted to leave behind the tainted memories that now haunted there and move on to a new place. A place where he would either move on and raise Abby by himself, or a place where a miracle would unfurl, and Ronnie and Eli would rejoin them.

But when Abby showed him the third bedroom that would have been Eli's, the dawn of the task before him became clear. He'd have to unpack and open up those memories again and relive them as he decided what to do. So, for now, all the things that were labelled "Eliot's Bedroom" sat in the room, in the dark, with the door closed.

Once all the furniture and the physical labour was over, Dave unpacked boxes from the most neutral to least neutral. He started with the kitchen, and his and Abby's everyday necessities. Then he set up Abby's room and playroom. While those boxes contained things for Abby and wouldn't stir up too many painful memories, it was bittersweet unpacking and setting up the rooms. Ronnie had been so excited for the playroom. Abby's toys took over the townhouse while they were there, and the prospect of having a room to contain the toys and create an imagination haven for Abby was one of the key features that sold Ronnie on this house. Every day she would bring up a new idea for the playroom or talk about the way she wanted to configure it, and what new toys they would finally have room for. Ronnie particularly wanted to get Abby a train table, since she played with the one on display each time they went to the toy store.

Ronnie also had ideas for Abby's new bedroom. Paint samples were tucked away in an envelope somewhere, each one labelled with what room Ronnie wanted to add a splash of colour to. Dave didn't want to paint, and now he definitely wouldn't. When he unpacked Abby's room, he paused whenever he went to set something up. Where would Ronnie have put the dollhouse? Would she have put Abby's cube shelf horizontal or vertical? Which books would she have put on the shelf and which ones would she have showcased on Abby's headboard, and where would she have hung the floating shelves?

Whiskers meowed again and jumped up on the couch next to Dave. He ran his hand over her black fur, and she purred loudly as she settled next to him. Most of the boxes were unpacked now, but he avoided the ones that were obviously Ronnie's. Earlier in the day though, as he unpacked the last of the office, he came across their wedding mementos, the engraved wine glasses, cake topper, and their wedding album. He should have known they were there as they kept them displayed in their glass cabinet in the office, but for whatever reason, he forgot about them. And they knocked the wind out of him when they appeared beneath the paper wrapping in the box.

Now, he sat on the couch with the wedding album in his hands and he stared at the cover. A black-and-white photo of him and Ronnie silhouetted against the sun stared back at him. It was one of her favourite pictures from their wedding. They also had a copy of it framed somewhere in one of the unpacked boxes in the master suite. He ran his hand over the album and took a deep breath, ready to spiral down into a dark hole as he went through memories of happy times and tried to figure out how he got from there to here.

Just as he placed his finger under the cover to open the book, his phone rang. Dave sprang up from the couch and jogged over to the counter to grab his phone before the loud ringer woke up Abby. The screen flashed his in-law's number.

"Hello?"

"Dave." It was Donna. Her voice was quick and serious. "The condo keys are gone."

Dave's stomach flipped. Donna and Gerald's condo in Maui. Brief memories of their vacation a few months earlier flashed in his mind. Abby loved swimming in the pool and Eli had been good the entire plane ride.

If Ronnie had gone back to Maui, maybe she was just taking some time to herself. And she had needed to take Eli with her because of the breastfeeding and because he was still so young. Ronnie just needed a break. Though her post-partum depression stemmed from hormone imbalances since having Eli, it seemed to be Abby who set it off more. Three-year-olds were difficult. Maybe after a few weeks or a month in Maui, she would come back. He'd forgive her, because somewhere deep in his heart he had already forgiven her. Depression was a disease, and you couldn't blame someone for having a disease. They would pick up where they left off. Dave would make sure that Ronnie got the help she needed, better than whoever she had spoken to before, and he'd take time off work to help more with the kids or see if they could afford a part-time nanny or something.

"But their passports are here," Dave said, the small glimmer of hope fading. He had briefly thought that maybe she had run away to the condo, but never said the idea aloud because it seemed impossible. They couldn't be in Maui if their passports were here. They needed passports for international flights.

"Gerald already called the building," Donna continued. There was an excited undertone to her serious voice. "The security guard said that he'd seen them. They're there, Dave. They're at the condo. Gerry's going on the next flight."

Dave closed his eyes and brought his free hand up to his face. They were alive. Before he could stop it, a relieved sob came out of him and he tried to stop the tears from coming, but a few dropped and rolled down his cheeks. A realistic part of him had tried to prepare himself for the possibility that Ronnie's depression had pushed her over the edge and that she and Eli were gone from this world. He had seen stories before of new mothers committing tragic acts because of post-partum depression. It was an unfair side-effect that too many women went through, yet they rarely talked about it. Maybe if it had been more normalized, Dave would have known how to handle the situation better.

"I should go," Dave said as he composed himself quickly.

"No," Donna cut him off. "Listen Dave, I understand. We know you want to see her. We don't blame you for this." Dave wasn't so sure he believed that. He certainly blamed himself.

"But Gerry and I feel it would be better if he went. Catch her by surprise and then help her come home. He's already on his way to the airport," Donna continued. "We just worry that if you go, it might cause some tension. We don't want her to spiral and things to get worse. You need to be here for Abby."

Dave sighed. There wasn't much he could do if his father-in-law was already on the way to the airport, and it was *their* condo. There was some logic at sending Gerry instead of himself. While he was sure that he would have been able to persuade Ronnie to come home, Gerry wouldn't bombard her with questions. Dave wouldn't have either, or at least he didn't think he would, but he *would* be an emotional mess when seeing her. She needed someone calm to approach her. And Gerry was the calmest out of the three of them.

"Alright," Dave agreed. "But please tell Gerry to get her to call me. I just want to talk to her." To hear her voice, even if it was just to hear her cry over the phone. Maybe hear Eli giggle in the background. Shrieking would be fine too. Just something from both of them.

"Yes," Donna said. She paused a moment before she spoke again in a soft, hushed voice. "But you know nothing is for certain. While the security guard said he had seen her, it was a few days ago. They rotate daily and don't see every single person go in and out the door. At most, we can be certain that they *were* there. I got ahead of myself by saying they were *still* there. I hope they are."

Dave hoped so too. If they weren't, he was certain he would never see his wife or son again.

August 20, 2012
Dear Abby,

 Well, after a little over a week living in the motel, I've found a place for Eli and I. It's a quaint little house in a small town on the coast in Newfoundland. I absolutely love it. It's something out of a fairy-tale, with white shutters, ivy climbing up one wall, and a rounded-top door. There are three bedrooms, though one is ridiculously small. It'll work for a nursery. I'm thinking down the road of converting the attic into a bedroom, and then maybe Eli can sleep up there when he's older. But I'm getting ahead of myself. Thinking things like that makes my stomach sink and my heart break. It's admitting that this is permanent, this new separated life I've carved out.
 For now, it's one step at a time. And that next step was finding a home for us. This motel is horrible, but I didn't want to pick somewhere that was going to eat up our money. I need to find a job, but that will be hard to do while I'm pregnant. Nobody will want to hire someone who will be going on maternity leave in seven months. But I can't even begin to apply for jobs until my morning sickness dies down. It's not as bad as it was with Abby, but worse than it was with Eli.
 One step at a time though.

Dave
August 27, 2012

    Ronnie had been at the condo, but by the time Gerry got there, she and Eli had moved on. Those were the thoughts that went round and round Dave's mind as he started to navigate life without his wife and son. There was no telling where in the world they were now and Dave knew, with a deep, heart-wrenching feeling, that he would never see them again. It was a heavy feeling that sunk deep down into the pit of his very core. Ronnie had somehow gotten them fake IDs. There was no telling what else she could do or how far they could go. There was only so much that the police could do here. Even with social media and how small it had turned the world, the planet was very large, and they were just two people. One of whom was still tiny.
    It broke Dave's heart when he thought of all the things he was going to miss with Eli. So many firsts that he had gone through with Abby were lost on his son, and all the father-son bonding was out the window. He would never know the person Eli would become. Whether he would be as fiercely outgoing as his sister or if he would be quieter and more observant. Would he be athletic or intellectual, musical or mechanical? There were too many missed things to count. Whatever he ended up being, Dave just hoped he'd be happy. Somewhere in the back of his mind, he already hoped and figured that perhaps Eli would seek him out in the future, once

he was a grown man and curious about this father. He would see Eli again, one day. But Ronnie, he didn't know.

What he knew was that he had to put all the current hardships behind him and deal with them in private. Abby still did not quite understand what was happening. She didn't know the finality of what occurred, and he had to keep on as though it was all normal. To explain it to her as simply as he could, hope that she would accept it in that special way that kids comprehend serious things, and he could go on being both a father *and* mother to her. And give her the best life he possibly could, on his own.

One new positive that had come around in the past few weeks was that there was a boy who lived up the street of their new neighbourhood, and he was about the same age as Abby. Greyson, he thought he recalled. Abby had played outside a few times with him already, and Dave had briefly met his mom and dad. They also had a baby girl who looked to be around the same age as Eli. It tugged at his heartstrings that this family lived up the road. They would have been the perfect friends for the four of them. The wife, Stacey, recognized Dave from one of his TV interviews about Ronnie's disappearance, and had offered her sympathies. Dave was thankful that she only did it the one time and then treated him and Abby like normal human beings the next few times they ran into each other.

Now, Dave sat on the steps of his new porch as Abby and Greyson played on the sidewalk. They drew elaborate pictures in Abby's new set of chalk as the sun set behind them. Summer was nearing its end. A new season would help Dave carry on.

Dave watched as Abby drew a rainbow and chatted excitedly to her new friend. All she knew was that Mommy and Eli had gone away. Dave hoped that the less he explained, the less she would ask. The first few weeks she had accepted that, but just the night before she asked when they would come back. As he sat there watching them play, trying to figure out what his answer would be when she asked again, his phone *pinged* from within his pocket. He took it out and opened the new e-mail that came through.

> **Hello! Reminder to all parents that the first day of our ballet 3-year class starts on Saturday, September 15, at 9:30am. Students should come to class wearing...**

Dave sighed. The sinking feeling in his gut felt heavier. Ronnie had signed Abby up for dance class and he had completely forgotten about it. The registration had been under her e-mail, which meant she must have logged in to change the account to fall under his. It was like a nail in a coffin. Ronnie was still looking out for Abby, but in a way that confirmed she wasn't coming back. Dave just wanted to know why. Why did she leave? Why did she give up on their relationship, their life together, when he *never* would have given up on her? It wouldn't have mattered how bad her depression had gotten. He would have been there for her. For better or for worse, like they had promised to one another.

Dave also felt suddenly panicked. There were so many little things Ronnie had done for them that he hadn't noticed until now. Like schedule keeping. He had jokingly laughed at her various calendars and agendas, always paranoid that she would forget something. But now he understood. As Abby got older, there were more things he had to remember. Not only his work schedule, but her activity schedule and daycare schedule. Preschool two days a week, and now dance class. Greyson's mom had also mentioned something about a music class and Abby had gotten excited about that. He had a whole new respect for single parents now.

As the sun continued to set, Abby and Greyson abandoned their chalk and raced up and down the sidewalk. Abby laughed and flung her head back, her blonde hair dangling down her back and her dimples showing on each cheek. He knew that as time went on, Ronnie's disappearance would get easier for him to deal with. But for Abby, it would be the opposite. The older she got, the more she would understand and the more questions she would have. While he would go from painful to content, she would go from happy to hurt. There would come a day when she would realize that her mother didn't just leave, she abandoned her. And it was Dave's job to keep her happy. It would be a shame for those smiling dimples to fade.

Dave
September 4, 2012

"Say cheese!"

Abby squeezed the "First Day of Preschool" sign in her hands. Dave held up his phone and smiled.

"Cheese!" she said. She squinted her eyes and threw her head back as she did so. Dave clicked the picture. It was perfect because it was Abby. It embodied her silliness and high energy. He laughed and changed it to his phone's wallpaper, his new favourite photo.

"Ok! Let's go, kiddo," he said. He shuffled her into the car and helped buckle her in. Abby smiled as he did so. She was wearing her new sparkly sneakers, the bright orange ones she had picked out the week before, and her favourite ladybug shorts. Her new kitty-cat backpack sat on the seat beside her. Dave closed the car door and took a moment to himself before he climbed into the driver's seat. The past few weeks had been hard. Once it was clear that Ronnie and Eli weren't coming back, Dave went all out on focusing on Abby. He talked about how fun preschool was going to be, went out and bought her a bunch of new clothes, a new backpack, water bottle, and lunch bag. If he distracted Abby from Ronnie's absence, he distracted himself as well.

On the way to preschool, Dave drove quietly. Abby sang along to the kids' songs from the CD he had put into the player. She chatted about the birds she saw in the sky, the mailbox that was in the shape of a house, and about the different things she would do at preschool that day.

"I'm going to make new friends," she chatted as they stopped at a traffic light. "And I'll paint some pictures and learn about letters and play at the playground."

"Yeah? That all sounds really fun," Dave said. The light turned green, and he continued to drive. The GPS on his phone told him where to go. Ronnie had picked out the preschool. It was one that was near their old townhouse. They didn't know they would move when she had enrolled Abby, and Ronnie decided it was still best to keep her there.

As they pulled into the parking lot, Abby got more excited.

"Look! I see kids out there," she said.

"Mmmmm," Dave murmured as he pulled into a parking spot. He wasn't sure why, but he worried about Abby and her first day. He worried that Ronnie's disappearance would affect Abby's independence. She'd always been independent and outgoing. This would be the first time Dave would leave her with someone she didn't know for an extended amount of time.

As they climbed out of the car and Dave helped Abby with the straps of her backpack, he could already see some of the other kids having meltdowns about leaving their parents. But of course, the other thing he worried about the most was Abby seeing the other kids with their mothers. Nearly every one of them had their mother there. Some of them had both parents. There was only one other kid there with just his father.

Dave and Abby joined the other kids and parents as they waited for the teacher to open the door. Abby chatted to the boy behind them. His mom smiled at Dave, and Dave nodded back. He didn't want to make small talk with the other parents and have to explain where Ronnie was. Maybe they wouldn't ask, as single dads were more common nowadays. But some people were nosy. Maybe some of them would recognize him from the news. It wasn't something he wanted to talk about yet, especially with strangers.

The teacher opened the door and invited the children inside. "Say goodbye to your mommies and daddies!"

Some children cried and clung to their parents harder. Dave winced at the word 'mommies' and glanced down at Abby, waiting for the realization to hit her and for her demeanour to change. He didn't think he'd be able to handle her crying. It would make him break down and cry too.

But instead, Abby barely looked at Dave. She had a smile on her face and threw her hand up in a wave that could have been directed at anybody as she said, "Bye Daddy!" and walked into the classroom. She didn't look back. And she certainly didn't notice that she was the only one without a mommy.

October 27, 2012
Dear Abby,

 I miss Dave. I miss him so much that it hurts. I miss the way he makes me laugh without even trying, or how he always just knows what's wrong before I tell him. I miss his homemade waffles and his warm embrace. I miss the smell of him, even his disgusting gym shoes he refuses to clean. I even miss his snoring. Eli snores softly sometimes in the bed next to me, and he reminds me of a mini-Dave, even though he looks much more like me and Abby. I miss Abby too, of course. She's going to be a big sister again. I wonder how she'd feel about that. Would she be excited for another baby? She loved Eli so much. I should have left him with them. But he needs me. And I need him. If I hadn't brought him with me... I don't know where I'd be now. Dead? Alive? Maybe I'd be back at home, and we'd all be together.
 I am just starting to feel flutters from the baby and usually I would rejoice, but it is just making me sad. He doesn't even know about his third child. I don't even know how I would go about telling him now. Just show up with a pregnant belly? Call him? Send him an anonymous e-mail? There is no way to make this any less complicated. I don't know how to fix what I've done.

Dave
November 6, 2012

    The lights of a passing car shone through the window as Dave sat down on the floor next to Abby's bed. She lay in bed looking at the pictures of her favourite storybook as Dave read from the pages. They had survived two months of activities together and Dave felt things were going well. Abby loved her preschool and ballet classes, and he had managed to enroll her into that music class with the neighbour boy from up the street. He supposed that if Ronnie was destined to have disappeared from their lives, that she had picked an appropriate time. These new activities kept Abby distracted from the fact that her mother and baby brother were gone. Or at least, Dave had thought so until that night.

    As he turned another page, now halfway through the story, he paused and looked at Abby. She was staring at the pages with a slight pout on her face.

    "What's wrong, Abby?" Dave asked. He closed the story with his finger keeping place in the book and brushed a strand of blonde hair out of her eyes.

    Abby sighed. She shifted under her blankets and then shrugged.

    "Come on, what is it kiddo?" he pressed.

    Abby sighed again. "I just miss the way Mommy reads the story," she said in a small voice.

Dave's chest ached. He didn't know how to respond. This was the first time since the incident that Abby mentioned Ronnie in a non-passive way. It was dawning on her, and Dave wasn't ready for it. He had bought a book on how to help young children grieve but didn't find it helpful.

"Mommy does the voices in a gooder way," she continued. "And sings the song at the end."

Tears filled Abby's eyes. She looked away from Dave and down at the book. She grabbed it out of his hands and the paper from the page cut his finger as it slipped by. Abby threw the book across the room, and it hit the floor with a thud.

"Abby…" Dave said, his words lost.

"I want Mommy!" she cried. Full sobs escaped from her small body and tears welled up in Dave's eyes too. He didn't want to cry in front of her, but he couldn't stop it. "I miss Mommy and baby!"

The stars from her night-light twinkled on the ceiling above them. Dave wrapped his arms around Abby, and she cried into his chest. He stroked the top of her head as he tried and failed to withhold his tears.

"I know, kiddo," Dave whispered after some time. Abby had stopped crying and was quiet, asleep in his arms. He continued to stroke her hair and held her tight, as though she might also slip away and leave him alone in the dark. "I miss them too."

Dave
January 31, 2013

There had to be a conspiracy, Dave thought, about all waiting rooms having obnoxiously loud ticking clocks. As if the stress of waiting for a doctor or dentist, or in this case therapist, to emerge with your child wasn't bad enough, there had to be an unwritten rule somewhere about adding in the sound of time ticking away as you waited. That constant reminder that time was slipping away had to be present in all stressful situations, for Dave couldn't recall a waiting room that was calm and silent.

The disposable coffee cup in his hand was a crumpled mess as he gripped it hard. It wasn't until droplets of cold coffee dripped onto his pants that he realized just how badly he had mangled the white piece of plastic, and he hastily stood up to throw it away in the trash. A woman sitting across the room with her son glanced at him as he walked by with a snarky look, as though crushing his coffee was a stain on her day. Or perhaps she was wondering what was wrong with his kid that he was here too at the pediatric therapist's office.

None of your business, Dave thought as he walked back past the woman to his seat. After all, who was she to judge him? Her kid was here too.

It became clear pretty quick a few months ago that Dave needed to get Abby in to see a therapist. Even if all they ever did was play together, she needed an outlet other than just him for her feelings. Or, better yet , she needed another adult, a third party away from the situation, to help guide her through this time. They both did.

Dave sighed as he sat back down in the chair and exhaled slow and loudly as he looked up at the clock. Next week it would be his turn speaking to someone. He had mixed feelings about going to therapy. Just the word *therapy* brought up an uncomfortable feeling inside him. He wanted to wrinkle his nose at the word and the notion. Other people needed therapy, not him. Not an average person. But he was no longer just an average person. He was an average person with a traumatic experience. And wasn't that just the type of person that therapists helped? The only other time Dave had ever thought about a therapist was when Ronnie developed post-partum depression. And now he needed one *because* of Ronnie. There was irony there, somewhere.

The blue door across from him opened and Dave stood at once. It was like waiting for the doctor to come through the surgeon's doors. Here he was, hoping the therapist would say "She's cured!" and it would all be behind them.

Of course, that didn't happen. The therapist smiled at him as Abby skipped out with a lollipop. He knew he couldn't ask the doctor details of what went on between them because of this therapist's confidentiality rules. If there was anything serious, the therapist would let him know. But otherwise, this was Abby's private time to vent about anything, including him. It killed him not knowing what went on, but if she came out happy, then that was all he needed.

April 4, 2013
Dear Abby,

    It's a girl! She's here. The baby is here, and I am overcome with emotions. Happiness, relief, elation... sadness, nostalgia, guilt. It's a jumble of everything, and all I can do is hold her and cry. I didn't know going into this birth what she would be, and though Dave and I always wanted another girl, part of me was really hoping she'd be a boy. Then I wouldn't feel so guilty for keeping this from him. But she's perfect in every way. She actually looks more like Dave than Abby and Eli ever did, which just makes me feel worse again.
    Maybe I should call him. It feels so wrong to have gone through this without him. Everything is different this time. Different hospital, not in the same room that I gave birth to both Abby and Eli in—it's like a new chapter in a book that I never meant to pick up in the first place. I am glad that I went with a midwife this time. Without Dave, I needed some sort of extra support, more than just the nurses that would have been in and out. I also had a doula-in-training and am so happy I found her during my pregnancy. Her name is Tracy, and she was there just for me.
    The scariest part was leaving Eli with Mrs. Hannigan. But she brought him over once I told her that the baby was here, and all seemed well. She said Eli was behaving, and she is fully aware of his allergies, so no worries there. I lucked out on having such a

wonderful neighbour. She treats me like a surrogate daughter, and just dotes on Eli all the time. These things help make me feel happy and settled in this new life that I abruptly chose for myself. My old life feels like a dream, something fuzzy and far away.

I've named her Lisa. That was the name Dave always had picked out if we had another girl, so it only seems right that she has this part of him. One day they'll meet, I know they will. One day soon, I hope. As fuzzy as that old life seems to be in my head, distanced by these last few months, it's a dream that keeps calling out for me. I want to turn around and grab it, take it back, but I don't know how. The shadows that plague me tell me it's too hard, impossible to go back now, but my heart keeps the dream alive. Maybe one day, when the depression and anxiety tangled around the chaos I've created gives an inch, my courage will push through, and I'll go back to fix what I've done.

April 26, 2013
Dear Abby,

    Thank God Eli is a deep sleeper. Lisa is difficult. She won't let me put her down. I can't get anything done without the sound of her crying. Today, while Eli napped, I had her in the laundry basket on the floor of the bathroom so I could shower. She was crying the entire time. The sound of the shower was not strong enough to drown her out. I felt as though I was drowning in the sound of her cries, and I wished the hot water would take me with it down the drain. What I really wished was for Dave to open the door and scoop her out to soothe her. He would have if he were here, if he knew that he had another daughter and that we're just on the other side of the country. I don't know how single mothers do everything on their own. It's so much harder without him. But the only thing harder than this would be to go back. How do you put the pieces back together again when you keep stepping on them and making them smaller?
    I think she has finally fallen asleep, which means I need to sleep too. Eli will be up in a few hours. Sometimes I'm not sure I have the strength to face another day. But each day it gets a little better. Or at least, that's what I keep telling myself will happen.

Dave
May 9, 2013

Dave paced the halls as the clock ticked on the wall. A car drove by the front of the house, and he peered through the peephole to see if it was Donna, but it wasn't. Whiskers meowed at his feet, and he almost tripped over her as he paced again.

"Stupid cat," he muttered. Whiskers meowed louder and followed him, back and forth, back and forth.

Donna would be home with Abby at any moment. All day at work, Dave's thoughts were preoccupied with his daughter and mother-in-law. Abby's preschool had a tea lunch today for Mother's Day. Ever since the month's newsletter for the school had come out and Dave had seen the event marked down, he dreaded it. It wasn't because Abby would be upset that Ronnie wasn't there for Mother's Day. She was too young to remember doing anything special with her on the previous Mother's Days, and Dave could easily spin it into Grandmother's Day going forward. He worried about Abby being surrounded by her classmates and *their* mothers. He worried about the other kids asking questions or hurting Abby's feelings, or her feeling left out in some way.

Donna had taken the day off work in a heartbeat, which Dave was thankful for. He knew Donna would make sure that Abby felt special. The whole situation was hard for all of them, but everyone focused on making Abby happy. And yet, any time something like this came up, Dave still worried about her.

"OK! Go away, you dumb cat!" Dave shooed after he almost tripped over the black cat a second time. He nudged Whiskers away, and she meowed grumpily as she slunk off and sat in the corner. The doorbell rang and Dave jumped over to open it.

"Daddy!"

Abby ran and gave him a big hug as Donna came up the walk behind her. Abby's pink dress was bright in the early evening sunlight. It was an obscene color, but she liked it and wanted to wear it to the special tea. Dave looked over at Donna for some sign as to how the day went. She flashed him a thumbs up and he let out a sigh of relief.

"Abby! How was your day?" he asked as they walked into the house. Donna came in behind them and shut the door.

"It was fun!" Abby said. "We had special cookies and I drawed a picture with Gramma!"

In the kitchen, Abby dumped her backpack on the floor and sat on her chair up at the counter. Dave pulled out a box of juice from the fridge and prepared her an after-school snack of cheese and crackers. Donna pulled up a chair beside Abby and smiled as she continued to regale Dave about their day. All was going well, and Dave set the snack in front of Abby. She grabbed a handful of crackers and continued with her chattering.

"... and the other kids' mommies were there, but since Mommy is gone, I haded to bring Gramma," Abby said. Dave froze and he shot Donna a concerned look. She frowned and the two of them didn't know how to respond. Then Abby continued without skipping a beat. "But it was OK because James brought his Gramma too, and Lily brought her aunt."

Dave felt relieved. They had survived their first Mother's Day tea without Ronnie. Each one would be easier than this, and if her absence did not upset Abby this time, then they had nothing to worry about going forward. With this event, at least.

July 16, 2013
Dear Abby,

    I'm not doing so well. I locked myself in the bathroom for fifteen minutes, curled in a ball with my hands over my ears to drown out the noise. All Lisa does is cry if I put her down. I'm just trying to make dinner for Eli, and she won't stop screaming. Eli is screaming too over a toy not working the way he wants it to. I need some quiet.

Dave
August 1, 2013

    Abby laughed at something, tears streaming down her face, as her older cousin, Elena, continued making a silly face at the kids' end of the dining table. Dave smiled at her. Her laughter was the one positive to agreeing to dinner at his mother's house. Abby rarely got to see her three cousins, the daughters of his older brother, because they lived up north, along with his mother and stepdad. Part of him had considered moving back up here last year, after everything that happened with Ronnie, but then he remembered how much he couldn't stand his older brother, specifically his wife, and knew that as painful as it was to stay where he had built his life with Ronnie, it was the better choice. He loved his family, of course, but a weekend with them was enough. It wasn't long after dinner that they reminded him of that.
    It was his mother and Bruce's fifth wedding anniversary. They had been together since Dave was about seven, three years after his father died, but never tied the knot until Bruce's cancer scare a few years back. Everything worked out happily ever after, for which Dave was grateful because Bruce was a great guy. He had brief memories of his mother being lost once his dad had died, and all of that changed when Bruce came into their life. They had tried to have children together, but it never worked out. And so, Bruce had taken Dave under his wing, and the two of them formed a

relationship that Dave imagined he would have had with his real father. In fact, Dave was closer with Bruce than he was with his mom. His mother strained that relationship though.

Jeremy, Dave's older brother, could do no wrong. He was older by six years, married his high school sweetheart whom their mother *adored*, and had given her three sweet little granddaughters. Miranda, Brigitte, and Elena were sweet little angels when around their grandmother, but Dave had seen them for the little devils they were. He saw how Courteney, his sister-in-law, screamed at them, the fits and tantrums that they'd thrown. Abby, so far, had never acted how his nieces did. He worried each time they'd get together that Abby would pick up some nasty habit, but so far, she had come away unscathed. He knew it'd be a problem the older the girls got. If they were anything like their father, his nieces would be quick to pass on bad habits to their little cousin. It was a wonder Dave survived his childhood.

"Well, she seems happy enough," his mother suddenly said as she chewed through her steak. There were no fresh vegetables on the table, just meat, potatoes, and some sort of coleslaw doused in sour cream Courteney had brought. It wasn't until he was looking for it that Dave realized how much he wanted a salad. Ronnie was always the one to bring a fresh salad to dinner. Somehow, she had snuck good eating habits into his diet, and Dave scratched his head as he wondered when the last time he ate a good salad was. His mother's cooking was good, but the lack of fresh vegetables was suddenly obvious to him.

Pam, his mother, nodded down towards Abby and the girls. Abby stuck her tongue out, mimicking Elena, and the two of them fell into a fit of giggles. They were only a year apart, Elena the youngest of the three. Miranda was eight, and Brigitte was six. Courteney shot the girls a reprimanding look, but once she turned back to her food, the girls fooled around again.

"Can't have been an easy year," his mother continued. Dave took a deep breath and gripped his fork harder as he helped himself to more potatoes. He told his mother many times on the phone that once they were up there, he didn't want to talk about Ronnie. He didn't want to talk about what happened last year because it was still raw in his mind. Abby still asked about Ronnie every night. He mentioned that *if* she could not keep the subject mum, as he knew she wouldn't, that he didn't want to discuss it within earshot of Abby. And yet, here he was.

Good ol' Bruce shot his wife a look, but Pam either ignored or missed it. Jeremy shifted uncomfortably, which surprised Dave because half the time his brother wasn't paying attention to what was going on unless it involved himself. Even now, as Courteney shot the girls another look to behave, he did nothing to help keep his rambunctious daughters under control.

"I'm not surprised though, really," his mother continued. "I always knew there was something off about her. You can just tell by someone's character that something is off, but you can never pinpoint it until it happens."

"Pam," Bruce hissed. Pam finally looked up from her plate. Jeremy shifted again and Dave stared at his food, trying to deep breathe his way through his mother's hurtful words. He knew that Ronnie and his mom had a cordial relationship at most, and that they weren't as close as she and Courteney were, but he'd never realized that his mother felt this way before.

"What, it's been a year," Pam continued, unable to take the hint. "Time to move on, really. I just feel bad for Abby the most. To be abandoned like that, at such a young age, unable to understand."

"What's abambom mean?" Abby asked suddenly. The girls were no longer making faces at one another. The giggling stopped and they were hanging on to their grandmother's words. Dave's head snapped up quickly and he looked over at Abby. She looked confused, but not hurt. Not yet at least.

"Mom, can we talk about it later please?" Dave asked sternly. This was exactly what he had wanted to avoid.

"If you can't talk about it now, you'll never be able to," she continued. "Of course, the worst part was that she took away our only grandson. Our sweet Eli."

Dave huffed. He could feel steam coming out of his ears as his temper rose. Anger and hurt bubbled inside him. It was one thing to bring up Ronnie and the hurt she had caused, but Eli was a whole other matter. Dave never allowed himself to think of Eli, of his chubby cheeks and bald little head. How he'd blow raspberries repeatedly, his little tongue poking out between his lips. The way he'd stare at Dave's hat like it was a second head on his shoulders. He had at least gotten to spend some time with Ronnie, live a bit of life with her before she had become overtaken by a dark emotion Dave didn't understand, but he had only gotten a sliver of time with Eli. His sweet son that he didn't know if he'd ever see again.

His mother prayed for a grandson. For whatever reason, despite that she had two sons of her own, his mother had never craved a daughter. Her close relationship with Courteney was a surprise because of this, and apparently just the right amount of a mother-daughter relationship she needed. She loved her granddaughters, Dave was sure, but she had been over the moon with joy when they had Eli. Eli was the new sun in the sky, and Ronnie had taken that away from her.

"Daddy, what does abambom mean?" Abby asked again, this time with impatience in her little voice. Dave looked over at her, unsure how to respond.

"It means you're left behind on purpose," Miranda piped up. Courteney tried to shush her, but it was too late. Hurt filled Abby's eyes as she tried to process what this meant.

"Mommy… forgot me on poipose?" Abby asked. Damned kids and their undeniable ability to hear the things you don't want them to hear every time. The one time a swear slips out, and it's the only new word they'll say. The one time you sneak a cookie, and they catch you, and the one time your damned mother mentions aloud that your wife abandoned them, they hear you.

"No, of course not sweetie," Dave said at the same time that his mother said, "Yes, honey, she did."

Dave fumed. He slammed his utensils down on the outdated brown floral china and pushed back his chair.

"Mom! This is exactly what I wanted to avoid," Dave said as Abby cried. "I told you I didn't want to talk about Ronnie! Can't you just leave it alone?"

"Leave it alone? How could I!?" she said back, aghast. "She ruined your lives, David. She kidnapped your son, stole your money, and left her daughter and husband behind. How can I not bring it up? You're my son and she hurt you. If she ever resurfaces, you should press charges for what she's done!"

Dave moved around to the other side of the table and picked Abby up into his arms. He stroked her soft blonde hair as she cried into his shoulder and spilled a million questions in her small voice about her mother. Dave didn't understand any of what she said. The setting sun shone through the window and made the entire room an ugly orange hue. The striped wallpaper in the room, horrendously outdated, just angered him more.

"Just stop, Mom," Dave said. Jeremy sat stupidly in silence, pretending that nothing was happening.

"Courteney would never abandon her girls," his mother continued. It was incredulous how she couldn't let it go, couldn't keep her damn mouth shut. "That's a proper mother, there. You're better off, really, you and Abby. Good riddance, I say."

Everything turned from orange to red. Bruce dropped his fork in shock and tried to stutter apologies on Pam's behalf. Courteney sat a little straighter at the praise, while Abby continued to cry confused questions into Dave's ear.

"How can you say that?" Dave roared. Abby jumped at his loud voice and cried harder. He continued to stroke her hair but couldn't control his anger anymore. "I love Ronnie. What happened isn't fair to anyone, including her, but it happened. There's no changing that. And if she does ever come back, it'll be to open and forgiving arms. Depression is a mental illness, Mom, not some made up bullshit like you think it is. She's not a bad person. She just made a rash choice."

Pam rolled her eyes. "Oh David, you—"

"Shut up!" Dave yelled. "I'm done. We're leaving. If this is the garbage that you're going to spout about my family, the truth of what you think of my wife, then I don't want to talk to you. This isn't how family treats family. When you're ready to grow up, call me. Because until then, Abby and I don't need you and your negativity in our lives."

That shut her up. His mother opened and closed her mouth, unable to retort for once. And Dave didn't stick around long enough for her to do so. He held Abby close, roughly packed their suitcases, and left the house within ten minutes.

Bruce ran out to meet them at the car as Dave was pulling out of the driveway. His face was flush, and he pushed his glasses up his sweaty nose. "Please, Dave. Stay for the weekend. Your mother was really looking forward to it."

Dave shook his head. "Sorry, Bruce. I can't. Happy anniversary."

Bruce opened his mouth again, but Dave, still rife with anger, pulled back out of the drive, and left before his stepdad could speak again. It looked like Dave wouldn't have to worry about his nieces being a bad influence on Abby after all, for he was sure they wouldn't be seeing each other again for a long time.

November 1, 2013
Dear Abby,

    Tonight was one of the scariest nights of my life. Eli had an allergic reaction, bigger than the one he had when I first discovered his allergies. He got into the Hallowe'en candy before I had a chance to remove anything that wasn't safe. I don't even know how he managed to open the wrapper. He cried immediately and spat it out, but the damage was done. He scratched at his throat and hives erupted everywhere. I was a mess using the EpiPen but managed to do it. Lisa screamed in the background of it all, of course, since I had to put her down.

    Mrs. Hannigan rushed over when she saw the ambulance stop in front of the house. She stayed with Lisa while I went to the hospital with Eli. He's fine now, everything back to normal. I'm shaking thinking about it still. I need to be *so* careful with what I give him. Being an allergy mom is hard. I wish Dave were here to navigate this with me. I'm not made to handle this. If the thought of calling him didn't make the pit of my stomach drop and push me over the edge, I'd do it. He would know how to comfort me. He would know how to fix everything.

March 1, 2014
Dear Abby,

 Well, it finally happened. The day that I've been dreading since finding out I was first pregnant with Abby. Eli threw the entire roll of toilet paper into the toilet and flushed. I was nursing Lisa in the other room and heard the toilet flush, and knew it was trouble right away because he was supposed to be napping. I ran over, Lisa still on my boob, just in time to see the water overflow like Niagara Falls in my bathroom. Eli looked up with his wide-eyed "Wow" expression, and just said, "Uh-oh!" which was both adorable and frustrating.
 Not sure whether to cry or laugh at this point. I just rushed him out of there, threw a bunch of towels down on the floor, closed the door, and walked away. Eli's now back in his crib, which obviously can no longer contain him, but at least he is actually napping now. I'll have to survey the damage and see if I can fix it myself or need to get a plumber. Or maybe I'll just switch to using an outhouse.

Dave
April 19, 2014

"Daddy, Daddy! I can see Cinderella!" Abby whispered excitedly as she tugged on Dave's arm. Her bright blue eyes were wide in wonder as she stared past the line ahead and into the velvet alcove where Cinderella was waiting.

Dave smiled. Abby continued to whisper in excitement as she held her autograph book tight in her small hands. They had just come from the boutique where Abby had her hair done professionally, tied up in a tight sparkly bun and finished with a small shiny crown, and she had picked out a shiny blue Cinderella dress. Cinderella was her current favourite princess, though she cycled her favourite through the group every few weeks. But right now, as they waited in line to greet her, as well as two other princesses that were waiting further in the meet and greet area, Dave was glad that fate had been on his side and Cinderella was one of the princesses on duty on Abby's birthday.

It was their third day in the happiest place on Earth, and Abby's fifth birthday. The warm California weather was perfect and a welcome change to the dreary spring rain they had nonstop at home. Every day was magical since they arrived, and Dave was glad for it. This trip was something that he and Ronnie had been planning since Abby was born. The idea was to take each child, one-on-one, for their fifth birthdays. It was meant to be a time of quality parents-and-child interaction, no siblings allowed.

Dave had wrestled with the idea of going by himself. He knew it would be an amazing experience for Abby, something to take her mind off Ronnie and Eli, because the situation still seemed quite fresh to her. At least once a week she still brought up Ronnie or Eli, wondering what they were doing, when they would be back, why their trip was taking so long? And while Dave knew it was natural for her to ask these questions and that his therapist said it would be a while before it died down for her, it was still hard for him to give her adequate answers. As she got older, her questions became more complicated. For the first time just a few months ago, instead of the usual straight forward, "When is Mommy coming back?" Abby had asked, "Did Mommy leave because she didn't like me?" That was the first in a while that Dave had broken into tears after she had gone to bed.

Abby swished from side to side as they moved up the line. Her dress was like the actress's ahead, and she buzzed with excitement. Dave could feel her vibrating beside him, and he placed his hand on her shoulder. She was both excited and nervous. It was her first princess interaction. She had been quite excited to meet the other famous toons in their respective houses the day earlier, but this was on a whole new level.

As they approached the princess, Dave smiled. Abby was too shy to walk up at first, but then Cinderella complimented her dress and hair, and Abby came out of her shell and started chatting nonstop. The actress laughed and smiled, signed her book with an elaborate signature, and was picture-perfect as Dave took a few photos of them together. Abby waved, and they moved into the next line to see the next two princesses.

When they finished with the princesses, Abby announced loudly that she wanted chicken nuggets, and they set off to find a place to eat. Abby skipped beside Dave as he held her hand, and she went on and on about the princesses. She pointed in awe every time they passed the castle, and crew members around the park would stop and say, "Happy Birthday!" to her when they noticed her birthday pin.

Once their chicken nuggets were secured, they found a seat at one of the outdoor tables and chowed down. Dave had opted for a grilled cheese instead of the chicken nuggets, and as he dunked his sandwich into the hot tomato soup accompaniment, his stomach growled loudly. Meeting princesses must have been hard work, because when Dave looked back up after taking two bites of his lunch, he saw that Abby's plate was almost empty already.

"Whoa, kiddo, you ate that fast," Dave said.

Abby dunked her last nugget into the cup of ketchup and shoved it into her mouth. "I'm five now, Daddy, my tummy is a lot bigger than it used to be," she said as she moved onto her mountain of fries.

"Alright, well slow down," he said. "You don't want to be sick on the rides."

"Let's do the carousel again!" Abby said. They had ridden it at least six times yesterday alone. It went without saying that it was her favourite ride. That was fine with him, as it was her birthday and this trip was for her, but a small part of him felt annoyed. It was also in the busiest section of the park.

The sound of the crowds was easy to tune out as Dave listened to Abby's merry chatter. He knew that for the rest of the day all he would hear about would be the princesses, and he was fine with that. Whatever made her happy on her birthday, made him happy. And that was all he would ever strive for, for the rest of their lives. To make her happy, and make her forget the feelings of abandonment, hurt, and confusion that had befallen on them.

Abby
September 2, 2014

    Abby took timid steps through the door and into the brightly coloured classroom. There was a coat rack and hook for her backpack on the back wall to her left. She also noticed a door that led to a private bathroom back there. Good. She worried about having to use the big kids' bathroom all by herself, but it looked like the kindergartners got their own. There were four round tables in the middle of the room, each with five chairs around them and bright coloured construction paper set up in front of each one. To her right was a circle time area, set up in a much similar fashion to the one at her preschool. She relaxed a little more when she saw it. Further to her right was a play area abundant with toys, including the dollhouse she had been admiring in a store the other day. She eyed it greedily and made note of the fastest route to get to it, determined to play with it first.
    "Go on, kiddo, looks like all of the other kids are sitting down in a circle over there," Daddy said. He put a hand on her shoulder and steered her toward the circle time area. A gaggle of kids were sitting down in a circle together, and a friendly looking woman walked over to sit in front of them.
    Abby pulled away from her father and moved towards the circle. It was the first day of kindergarten, and unlike when she went to preschool where everything felt safe and familiar, she had been

quite nervous about going to the new, big school. She plopped down next to a girl with long hair the colour of chocolate. The girl looked nice enough, so Abby introduced herself.

"Hi, I'm Abby," she said. The girl barely looked at her and continued to stare straight ahead. Abby cleared her throat and tried again. The girl turned and looked at her, somewhat disinterestedly at first, but then gave her a big smile.

"I'm Scarlet," she said. "That's my mommy over there." Scarlet pointed at a pretty lady talking to another lady off to the side. All the parents stood together, crammed into the space. Abby noticed that there were a lot of mommies there, but only a few daddies.

"That's my daddy," Abby said. She pointed at him, and he smiled and waved at her. Abby smiled back.

Scarlet, however, frowned slightly. "Where's your mommy?"

The question caught Abby off guard. But she answered anyway. "I don't have one."

Something about the words hurt. Abby felt yucky inside, and the ickiness made her feel like she was about to throw up. The lie fell off her lips and she didn't know why. She *did* have a mommy; a mommy that she had loved very much, but she didn't know where she was now. She never came back, so in a way that meant that she didn't have one any more… right? Lying was bad, but Abby didn't know how to tell the truth in this circumstance. Because she didn't know where her mommy was. And saying she didn't have one felt easier than trying to explain that she didn't know where her mommy was. Mommies just didn't go missing. They weren't like toys that get stuck under the couch. But her mommy *did* go missing and had been missing for a long, long time.

"Oh," was all that Scarlet said.

The teacher then sat down in front of the class and welcomed everybody. Her name was Ms. Marigold or Margarine or something. Abby wasn't sure because she couldn't concentrate now. Her eyes wandered past the colourful papered sections of the walls, the ABCs, and past the dollhouse back to where the parents were standing. The ickiness in her had turned into a panic as she scanned past all the mommies until she found her daddy standing in the back. He smiled at her again and Abby calmed. He was still there. He hadn't left her too.

Slowly throughout the orientation of her first day, she relaxed more and more. She laughed with Scarlet, and the two of them played with the dollhouse. At one point, each student went and picked out a spot at one of the tables. That would be their spot for the year. They used the colourful paper to make leaves that they hung around the classroom, as the teacher, whose name Abby still forgot, explained how they'd be talking about fall for the first few weeks, and how the leaves change colours and fall off the trees. And her daddy stayed the whole time, smiling, praising her leaf, and watching her play. He was there, always watching her. And she knew, deep down, that he'd never leave her. He would never go missing.

Dave
November 6, 2014

As Abby came down the stairs for breakfast, Dave tried to act nonchalant. Bacon sizzled on the skillet and Abby's omelet was just about done. He glanced at her as she sat down at her chair at the counter, and she rubbed her eyes sleepily.

"Morning, kiddo," Dave said in a casual voice. Inside, he buzzed with excitement. With steady hands, he moved the omelet from the pan onto Abby's plate, next to the orange he had already cut up for her.

"Morning," she mumbled. She picked up her fork and poked at her omelet a bit before finally taking a bite. Dave turned back around and turned off the stove. He lifted the bacon from the skillet onto his plate, where his own omelet was waiting. As he took his first bite of breakfast, he leaned against the counter and looked over at Abby with a twinkle in his eye.

"Hey Abby." He paused for a moment and then continued. "How would you like to have a braid for school today?"

Abby gasped. Her fork clattered against her plate as she dropped it and she looked up from her food with wide blue eyes, excitement drawing on her as she smiled from ear to ear. "Really?"

Dave nodded. Two weeks ago, Abby came home from school down in the dumps. She had been quiet walking out of the school to the car, when usually she was a chatter box.

"What's wrong?" Dave asked once they had gotten in the car.

Abby sighed and sniffled. In the rear-view mirror, Dave saw a tear run down her cheek and it tore him up inside. It did every time he saw her cry.

"Scarlet had a really nice braid in her hair today," Abby started off. She then took a deep breath and her voice trembled as she continued. "I told her that I really liked it, and then she said that I couldn't have any braids because I didn't have a mommy and only mommies can do braids."

Dave closed his eyes and exhaled slowly. A range of emotions ran through him. He wondered if there was any way he could kick a five-year-old girl's ass, but he knew he couldn't. He felt mad at Ronnie for leaving when her daughter needed her. This was just the first of the mother-daughter things that Abby would miss out on, things that Dave either wouldn't understand to do or wouldn't understand were important. And deep down, he was mad at himself, mad that he hadn't been able to stop Ronnie from leaving. Every day he wondered if there was something he could have done to prevent it. People told him that over time it would get better. But two years later, he still ran over everything from the last day he saw her over and over in his head.

They drove home together quietly that day, after Dave told Abby that Scarlet was wrong, that everybody can do braids if they learn. Abby wouldn't listen to him, positive that her peer's knowledge on the matter was fact. And so, for the last two weeks, in every spare moment Dave had, he practiced braids. YouTube tutorials and Abby's dolls' hair took up his nights, but now, he felt ready.

"Yes, really!" Dave said. "I've been practicing. Let's eat breakfast and then we'll get ready for school, and we'll do a braid in your hair."

Abby nodded with a big smile on her face and gobbled down her omelet. Dave smiled to himself and ate his breakfast with a satisfied feeling in the pit of his stomach. Once her plate was empty, Abby ran upstairs to pick out her clothes.

Dave cleared the dishes once he finished, and packed Abby's lunchbox in her backpack. A few minutes later she came running back down the stairs in her favourite unicorn t-shirt and a pair of sparkling blue leggings. She climbed back up onto her barstool and placed her brush and a hair-tie onto the counter.

"OK, Daddy, I want it like Elsa's braid," she said. Frozen was her current favourite movie, and everything she did recently, she did pretending to be Elsa.

"I'll do my best," Dave said. He picked up her hairbrush and brushed her blonde hair. It had grown longer than he realized, and he wondered if he'd be able to talk her into getting a trim. "Sit still."

Abby sat as still as possible. Dave saw her concentrating on her stillness, her fingers twitching at her side. He parted her hair and then slowly wove the strands together. It was much harder to braid on an actual person than he thought. Abby's hair was fine and slippery, and random strands kept getting stuck together here and poking out over there. Doubt crept in as he continued down the braid. It looked nothing like the one he had been practicing on the video and his trial runs on the dolls turned out much better. Perhaps he had spoken too soon, and now he had gotten Abby's hopes up and he would have to bring them back down.

"Are you done yet?" she asked with excitement.

"Yeah," Dave said flatly. The confidence he had felt earlier disappeared. He tried to keep his voice positive, but it faltered. "Almost."

The braid was uneven and leaned to the left. Dave sighed as he tied the elastic around the ends at the bottom, and he patted Abby's shoulder. "All done."

She let out a little squeal and jumped down from the stool to run to the mirror in the powder room. When she re-emerged a few moments later, her face was straight. Dave felt a lump in his throat and his thoughts rushed as to what to say. She was disappointed and he didn't blame her.

"Kiddo, I'm so—"

"Daddy," she cut him off as she walked over to him with long strides and stopped right in front of him. She looked up at him and all Dave could see was how her hair stuck up on the top. It did not brush down smooth like he wanted. A smile lit up her face and she wrapped her arms around him. "It's perfect! Thank you!"

A warm feeling of relief overcame Dave. He hugged her back and then told her to grab her coat and put on her shoes. As she skipped back down the hall to get ready, her crooked braid swishing behind her, Dave smiled to himself. Daddies could do braids too.

November 24, 2014
Dear Abby,

Today was a hard day. Dave posted Abby's school photo on Facebook. She was smiling in a bubble-gum pink shirt, long hair brushed behind her shoulders. Seeing her dimples flashed me back to the first time she smiled as a baby, and all I've done this evening is cry. Eli heard me sobbing at one point and crawled out of his bed to see if I was OK. He's such an intuitive little two-year-old. I showed him the picture of his big sister and told him that I just missed her, a lot. "A lot" doesn't even begin to describe it. Eli's asleep beside me now in my bed. He wanted to stay with me to make sure I was OK. How did I get to be so lucky to be his mom?

Dave rarely goes on social media, so I know he posted this for me. Just in the off chance that I still checked my page, which I do. I already plan to print off a copy of the picture and frame it on my wall. I can't believe she's in kindergarten already. She's all grown up and I've missed it.

Abby
December 5, 2014

    The mall was packed. Colourful lights twinkled in trees and bright snowflakes hung from the ceilings. Green garlands with red bows wove round banisters and matching wreaths were on every window. The holiday spirit was in full force, and as Abby stood next to her daddy in line to see Santa, she felt determined. Six kids stood ahead of her now and she could see Santa sitting on his green velvet chair. He laughed at something the current girl on his lap said, they took a picture, and then his elf assistant escorted the girl off to the side.
    From a distance, he looked just like Abby remembered. Every year since she had been born, she had gone to see Santa at this very mall. Every year before on this special occasion had been wasted, wasted by a little girl who only asked for toys or sometimes for treats. She knew she had been younger then and didn't understand the power, the *magic* that Santa had. She wouldn't waste her time with him this year.
    This year, she understood the gravity of what meeting Santa meant, knew that it was by good fortune that she happened to always see him during his visit to this mall. Abby imagined that Santa visited hundreds of malls to meet with other children, but there was no way he could visit them all. She was one of the lucky ones. And she wouldn't take her good luck for granted this time.

"Are you excited to see Santa?" Daddy asked as they stepped up in the line. He shook her hand in anticipation and smiled when she looked up at him.

"Yup." Abby smiled back and then her focus returned to Santa. Eyes on the prize. She repeated in her head over and over how she would ask him. Last night she watched a movie that involved a genie, and the princess didn't ask her question properly, and the genie got her wish wrong. Abby wasn't sure if Santa was like a genie or if his magic worked like wishes, but she didn't want to take that chance. She only got one shot, and this was it.

This wasn't something you could ask Santa for in a letter. She asked for toys in her letter because her daddy helped her write it. Abby glanced back up at him. Daddy was looking around the mall, not really paying attention to anything. He did that sometimes. This was something that he couldn't know about. This was going to be a Christmas surprise for him too. It wasn't just a present for Abby. It was going to be a present for their family.

When there were just two kids left in front of her, Abby felt nervous. When she was the next one in line, her hands began to sweat. She wiped them on her gold sparkly dress and took a deep breath.

"Don't be nervous, sweetie," her dad said. When she was younger, Abby was afraid of Santa. But she was a baby then, not a big girl like she was now. Santa could help her, and he *would* help her because she had been good all year. She made sure of it. This wasn't just something she had planned on a whim. Abby planned this for months.

"I'm not," she said in a firm voice. The elf led the boy in front of her off to the side, and Santa turned to her with a smile. He beckoned her forward and her daddy patted her back.

"Remember to smile!"

With timid steps, Abby stepped forward. Halfway down the red carpet, she found her courage and walked on with firm steps, her head held high. She climbed up on Santa's lap and looked up right into his eyes. They were kind, twinkling behind bushy white eyebrows. His beard tickled her cheek as he leaned in to talk to her.

"Hello there," Santa beamed. "You've been extra good this year, haven't you?"

A buzz of excitement ran through Abby. He knew. He had seen her hard work, and she felt a bit of relief flow through her. "Yes, yes I have."

"And what would you like for Christmas this year?" he asked with a smile.

Abby took a deep breath. She looked him square in the face and spoke with clear words. "I want you to bring my mommy and my baby brother home."

Santa's smile wavered for a moment. Abby quickly pushed on. She didn't phrase it as clearly as she should have. "Their names are Veronica Sanders and Eliot Sanders, but you know that already. They've been missing for two years now."

Santa's smile vanished. He looked up with an uncertain look in his eyes, and over toward Abby's daddy. She quickly looked over too. Daddy shot her a questioning look and Abby flashed him a smile. He couldn't know.

"Don't tell my daddy," Abby said. Santa looked back down at her, his expression neutral this time. "It's a Christmas surprise for him too."

Santa sighed deeply. He shifted in his chair and Abby stared up at him expectantly. It took him a moment to respond. "I only make toys in my workshop, sweetheart. I wish there was more that I could do."

Abby's heart sank. Her confidence wavered and she wilted. "But you have magic."

"My magic only lets me travel very fast, so that I can deliver the toys to all of the good children in a single night. And so that my reindeer can fly," Santa said in a sad voice. He looked up again over at Abby's daddy. Abby looked over too and her daddy looked concerned now. Tears filled her eyes. Her Christmas surprise was not going as planned. And she had been so good all year too.

Then something Santa said clicked in her head. She looked back up at him, her hope renewed. "OK, well if you can't bring them home to us, can you at least give them a message? Because you'll be bringing a toy to my baby brother, right? Except he won't be a baby anymore. He'll be two."

A pained look that Abby didn't understand crossed Santa's face. But he gave a small smile and nodded as she continued. "Can you just tell him that we miss him and mommy, and want them to come home?"

"Sure, sweetheart." Abby smiled, and when she smiled, Santa smiled again. They both turned and looked at the photographer. The flash was bright and left Abby blinded for a moment. Santa then wished her a Merry Christmas and gave her a candy-cane as the elf came over to escort her back to her daddy.

"Remember," Abby said as she turned away from Santa, "Eliot Sanders."

"I'll remember," Santa said in a sad voice. Abby skipped back to her daddy.

"Everything go OK, kiddo?" he asked when she reached him. Abby opened her candy cane, the wrapper crinkling as she did so, and popped it into her mouth. The cool tingling sensation of peppermint filled her mouth and went down her throat.

"Yup!" she responded. As her daddy went to go pay for the picture, Abby looked back over at Santa. It wouldn't be the Christmas morning she had imagined with Mommy and Eli waiting under the tree, her daddy happy again and their family whole. But if Santa got the message to Eli, her Christmas wish could still come true. It would just be delayed a bit as they found their way back home.

December 29, 2014
Dear Abby,

 Do you remember when we were little, and we used to wish on stars? We'd find the brightest one in the sky and whisper to each other what our wishes were? I never told you this, but as we grew older, I wondered if maybe the reason our wishes never came true was because we told each other what they were. Isn't part of the magic behind wishes that you can't tell someone what you've wished for?
 Regardless that they never came true, wishing on stars with you is one of my favourite memories. It makes me feel warm and fuzzy inside when I think back on it. And now, as I look up into the night sky, I see one star twinkling much brighter than the others. I like to think that it's you looking down on me.
 And I like to think that Abby can see it too. I often wonder, as I'm looking up at the stars or the moon, if she's looking up and seeing the same ones at that same moment. I know it's not possible because of the time difference, but it comforts me to know that we're blanketed by the same night sky, that the same winter's snowflakes or summer's warm breeze touches us both. Sometimes I'll whisper into the wind a message for her, and hope that it finds its way into her ear with the passing of a ladybug or the twirl of leaves.

Starlight, star bright, first star I see tonight, I wish I may, I wish I might, have the wish, I wish tonight... I wish that Abby will forgive me. That one day she'll understand. I know I can't wish to turn back time and fix what I've done, but I <u>can</u> wish for a peaceful future, and one where we may be together again.

April 4, 2015
Dear Abby,

 Eli has really gotten into baking lately. I think part of it is because of how careful I need to be with his food, that he always sees me checking ingredients and such, that he does it too even though he can't read. Explaining allergies to him was interesting, to say the least, since Lisa and I don't have them.
 Anyway, as a result he wants to help me with everything in the kitchen. And when I mentioned that Lisa was turning two soon, he was very adamant that he wanted to help me bake a cake for her. And so, we did. Thankfully, Lisa napped through the whole thing, for it was quite the ordeal. The kitchen still hasn't recovered, there's flour and sprinkles literally everywhere, but he was so happy with the result and so proud when he told her that he made it. Lisa didn't quite understand of course, but they both enjoyed the cake and are playing with the wooden block set I got her for her birthday in the other room. All I can hear are giggles. The sound of it warms my heart.

Dave
June 14, 2015

"OK," Dave exhaled with a deep breath. Abby took a deep breath too and eyed him uncertainly from the top of the driveway. She held her teddy bear tight in her arms and scratched her chin under her helmet's strap. Dave smiled at her and patted the seat of the pink bike beside him. It was her birthday present this year from Donna and Gerald. Abby's eyes had gleamed when she saw it, and she had gone out riding every nice day since. Now they both decided, though it was only a few months later, that it was time for her training wheels to come off.

"Come on over, kiddo," Dave said. "It's really no different with the training wheels off. You already know what to do. Just pedal like normal and go!"

"OK," Abby said with doubt in her voice. She walked with slow steps down the concrete drive and to the sidewalk where Dave stood with the bike. The smell of fresh cut grass, the beginning of summer, filled the air, and the flowers he and Abby had planted in spring were blooming brightly in the garden. "But what if I fall?"

"Then you pick yourself up, get back on the bike, and try again. I'll be here the whole time," Dave said as cheerfully as he could.

Abby shook her head. She didn't like the sound of that. Her confidence and trust were still wary from Ronnie's disappearance, but it improved each day. The best thing Dave could do for her, according to his therapist, was to be as present in her life as possible. He put away his phone when he spent time with her, he listened intently to her stories and imagination, despite how often it repeated itself, and most importantly, he constantly reassured her that he was there. It was important that he spoke it aloud so that she could hear it. It was something she never heard from Ronnie but assumed would be true. Ronnie had broken that assumption, Dr. Freemont had told him, and so Abby had to *hear* it now in order to believe it and have that inherent trust back.

"I don't know…" Abby said. "Can't I just leave the wheels on?"

"You could," Dave wheeled the bike closer to her as she'd stopped walking. "But it's more fun without the wheels. All of your friends will ride without them soon. I ride without them. When you get bigger, you'll need a bigger bike, and they don't make training wheels for bigger kid bikes."

Abby frowned. She fingered the bright tassels that hung from the handlebar and hugged her teddy closer to her chest. The bear also had a helmet on, bright purple like Abby's. "You won't let go until I tell you too, right?"

"Promise," Dave said. Abby stared at him straight in the eyes, as though searching for some untruth. Dave didn't blink and stared back, and after a moment, Abby nodded with confidence. She placed her teddy into the basket at the front of the bike, climbed onto the seat, and then Dave guided her towards the sidewalk.

"OK." He gripped the back of the bike seat and helped Abby stay balanced. "Just start to pedal like you normally do. Try to feel the balance of the bike."

"OK…" Abby said. Her feet pushed down the pedals slowly, and they began to move. They wobbled a bit at first, but then Abby picked up speed and she felt steady. Dave gripped for as long as he could, encouraging her as he jogged along beside. Soon they were going almost too fast for Dave to keep a grip on the seat, and he let go. She was steady and straight, riding along all on her own. Dave watched as she went on down the street and heard her say something happily.

"Way to go, Abby!" Dave called. It was a mistake.

Abby turned to look behind her, shock on her face as she realized he had let go. The bike wobbled, and her confidence wavered. A look of betrayal crossed her face, and she screamed as she lost control of the bike and teetered over into the bushes three houses down. Dave's heart sank into the pit of his stomach as he ran over to her. A few small twigs stuck out of her purple helmet, and her left elbow was scratched. Dirt smeared her legs and tears streamed down her face as she sobbed.

"You promised!" Abby screamed at him. Dave picked the bike up off her, a large scratch now down the body, the pink paint chipped. There was no hiding the hurt in her eyes. He had broken her trust, and she'd never forgive him. "You said you'd hold on!"

"You were doing so well though, kiddo," Dave said. "I thought you could do it on your own! Why don't we try again? I *promise* not to let go this time until you tell me."

"NO!" Abby shouted. She furiously picked up her bear, thrown out of the basket and now sticking out of the bushes, and clutched it close. "I never want to ride that bike again!"

Before Dave could try to convince her otherwise, Abby turned her back on him and ran towards their house. Dave looked down at the scratched bike and closed his eyes. The look of hurt in his daughter's eyes burned into his mind, and he promised himself that he would never be the reason behind that look again.

Abby
September 21, 2015

All week long, Abby was nervous about the presentation she would give today. Her teacher, Mr. Dawson, decided that to get to know everybody in the class, they'd do an *All About Me* day. Abby would have to go up in front of the class and talk about her family in a presentation. Her daddy had to explain to her what a presentation was, and once she understood, she decided it was something she did not want to do.

As hard as she tried to refuse the project, Daddy told her that everybody had to do things they didn't want to do sometimes. Even he had to do presentations at his work that he thought were boring or that he just really didn't want to do. But the difference was that her daddy's presentations were about boring numbers and coloured charts that she didn't understand. He would have all the answers to the questions people asked. But when Abby did *her* presentation on her family, and the kids in her class all saw that she was missing a mommy, they would ask her about it. And Abby wouldn't know how to answer.

Somehow, she made it through kindergarten unscathed by not having a mommy. Nobody asked her about it, they didn't draw any pictures of their families, and nobody batted an eye when it was her daddy who always picked her up from school. But Grade One was different. Already it proved to be a lot more grown-up and serious than kindergarten, and Abby had asked her daddy if there was a way to just skip Grade One. It horrified her when he told her it only gets harder the higher the grades go.

So, after much convincing and tears, and a few tantrums if Abby was being honest, she made her poster with help from both her daddy and grandma. Once she started colouring on it, she felt better, and her grandma bought her sparkly stickers to make it a bit more special. Even so, Abby just knew that her classmates were going to ask why her family picture didn't include a mommy, and Abby wasn't sure how she was going to answer it.

She sat nervously in the circle at school while Mr. Dawson set up the presentation space. Everyone else had their posters beside them, and Abby was a bit envious to see that Scarlet had put hers on bright pink paper. That would have been a fun idea. She would need to remember that for the next presentation. From what she could see though, Scarlet didn't have sparkly stickers like Abby did.

Since Abby's last name started with an S, she didn't have to go first. This relieved her because it gave her time to figure out what she would say when her peers would start asking her about the absence of her mommy. Abby herself still didn't fully understand what had happened, where her mommy had gone and why, and why she had left her behind but took Eli.

Abby often wondered what Eli was like now. When she'd ask her daddy about him, he said that he'd be a bit more grown up now, that he'd no longer be a baby. It was hard for Abby to imagine Eli being anything but a baby. That was all she had known about him. She wondered if he still cried a lot and if his eyes were still blue.

Her mind wandered in and out as she went back and forth between paying attention to what her classmates were saying, to wondering what Eli was like now, to trying to figure out how to answer the prospective questions about having no mommy. But as Abby paid more attention to her classmates and their posters, she relaxed, and the answers she had been prepping in her head slipped away.

Brian only lived with his mom and not his dad. Tina's parents were divorced, whatever that meant, and she had a stepmom in addition to her regular mom. And Sally just had two moms, no mention of a dad. As each child finished their presentation, each one with a more different looking family than the last, nobody asked questions about missing parents or siblings. Nobody questioned why Brian's dad didn't live with them, or why Tina's dad had a new wife, or why Sally had two moms and no dad at all. It was all just accepted.

So, when it was Abby's turn to present, she stood up tall and confident, and placed her poster on the stand Mr. Dawson had provided. The stickers sparkled under the classroom's light, and Abby looked down at her classmates sitting in front of her.

"This is my poster," she said. It now dawned on her that she was so worried about what to say if her classmates asked about her missing mommy, that she didn't prepare what else she would say during her presentation. "Uh… this is me and my daddy, and our cat Whiskers. Whiskers is getting pretty old, but she still likes to play with jingle balls and my hair elastics. We used to have an orange cat too, Ginger, but she passed away. So that's why she's flying in the sky, with wings. She's an angel now."

Mr. Dawson nodded along. When Abby looked away from her poster and at everybody else again, she saw that Mr. Dawson seemed to be the only one really paying attention. She directed her attention at him.

"We live in a house with blue walls, and we see my grandma and grandpa a lot. This is a picture of them I drew here," Abby continued. The words just seemed to come out naturally to her now, and she felt silly for being so scared earlier. As she had seen from her peers, everybody had different families. And on a whim, Abby decided that even though they weren't there, everybody in her family deserved to be mentioned. "I have a mommy and a baby brother too, but they live somewhere else."

Nobody said anything. Nobody asked where her mommy or the baby lived or if they ever saw them. Abby finished her presentation with a sense of relief and calm.

As the rest of the presentations continued, Abby learned that she was not the only one whose siblings didn't live with them, and that some siblings didn't even have the same mom or dad. In the end, it was an eye-opener, this *All About Me* day. She learned that there was no one way that a family should look, and even though she had a sneaking suspicion she was the only one who *didn't* know where her mommy or brother was, it helped to know that not everybody lived happily ever after with their mommies and daddies. And that made her feel normal.

Dave
October 16, 2015

"Thanks again, Donna," Dave said. It was Friday evening and his workday had gone awry. Someone tried to steal from one of the tills and the paperwork and police reports had taken more time than Dave expected. Thankfully, Donna was able to pick up Abby from school and take her for the afternoon until Dave could come get her. He was looking forward to a relaxing weekend with his little girl after this hectic week. They had plans to go see a movie and then check out the new indoor playpark that Abby was dying to see. One of her friends at school went the weekend before, and Abby begged Dave nightly to play.

"Any time, any time." Donna waved her hand and closed the front door behind him. Dave took off his shoes and followed her into the house.

Donna and Gerry had renovated their house soon after Ronnie disappeared. She had been their only child left and Donna wanted a change of scenery. They loved their house too much to sell, as they had a magnificent view of the bay and marina but needed to purge their painful memories. Like Dave and Abby had their new house, Donna and Gerry needed a new house too, in a sense. Not that they were trying to erase Ronnie, nobody could do that. But they needed a way to move on. Something cathartic to get over the hurt of her deliberate disappearance. And so, renovation it was.

Though Dave had been to the house several times since they renovated, it still took his breath away each time. Fancy new light hardwood floors throughout the main floor, paired with blue toned walls and bright white shutters. It made the main space bright and airy, much like the bay it overlooked. Clean white cabinets over marble counter tops in a newly opened kitchen just off the dining room and open concept living room made entertaining a breeze. They spared no expense in re-doing their home and it showed. Twice Gerry had invited Dave over to watch a movie in his new theatre room downstairs, and they had transformed Ronnie's old room into a room for Abby.

"Are we still on for dinner next weekend for your birthday?" Donna asked as they walked into the kitchen. She poured a glass of water and set it down in front of Dave. He was the only child they had left now and had adopted him into their family. He and Abby were all they had.

"Yes," Dave answered. Personally, he didn't enjoy celebrating his birthday. The novelty had worn off at a young age. But it was something that Ronnie and her family had always done, and now Abby was into it too. And Dave supposed it was nice to have a day that was about celebrating him and not pitying him. Time to time he still got sympathetic looks from coworkers or people off the streets who knew his story. Three years later and people still whispered about how his wife left him and stole his son. He didn't know how long those whispers would take to die down, but he hoped they would soon. It was bad enough to live with it for the rest of his life, but he didn't need people whispering about it behind his back for the rest of his life too.

"Perfect. Six o'clock," Donna confirmed. She then turned toward the stairs and yelled, "Abby! Your dad is here!"

Dave took a sip of the water as he waited for Abby to come up the stairs. When a few minutes went by and she didn't emerge, he frowned. Donna sighed as she prepared dinner for her and Gerry. "She's been down in her room for most of the afternoon. I set her up with some of Ronnie's old dolls, and she's been entertaining herself. Abby!"

"It's OK," Dave said. He set down the empty glass and licked his lips. "I'll go down and get her."

Automatic lights flicked on the side of the stairs as Dave descended, and when he reached the bottom, he could see the light on from underneath Abby's closed door. He knocked on it and asked, "Abby, can I come in?"

"Yes!" came her cheerful voice from the other side. Dave opened the door and was not prepared for what he saw.

Abby stood in the middle of her room wearing Ronnie's wedding dress. Her small frame was swallowed by the layers of sparkling tulle and her small hands held up the cream silk bodice to her chest. She had on one of her princess dress-up crowns and had tied her blonde hair into a messy bun.

"Daddy, look! I found this princess dress in Mommy's closet," she said. Despite that Donna, Dave, and Gerald all referred to the room as Abby's, somewhere Abby had learned that it used to be Ronnie's room. And now she always referred to it as "Mommy's room."

Dave stared dumbstruck at his daughter. Flashbacks of Ronnie walking down the aisle in the same dress came hurdling back at him and it took him a moment to focus on the reality in front of him. He had forgotten that Donna had kept Ronnie's dress in the closet. Abby rarely used the closet as they also had a large dresser in the room that had more than enough space necessary for the small set of extra clothes they kept at her grandparents' house. Abby was afraid of her own closet at home. Dave would never have suspected that she would go into the closet here.

He knew inevitably, one day, Abby would try on her mother's wedding dress. But to see her now, so small and sweet, swishing from side to side, the layers of skirts pooling around her… it was bittersweet. He could only imagine what Ronnie would think if she saw this, how cute she would exclaim Abby looked, how she would probably do her hair up in a real princess bun and would give her a bouquet and done a mini photoshoot or something.

"I'm a princess!" Abby exclaimed. She smiled and beamed at Dave, oblivious to his hurt and shock. He knew he should take a picture of this and take it in as a sweet moment of childhood, but he found it difficult. Perhaps he could focus on that Abby didn't know that it was Ronnie's wedding dress and play up the princess angle.

And that's what he did once the shock wore off. He put a smile on his face and told her how pretty she looked. He pulled out his phone and took a picture or two. But relief flooded through him once he got her to climb out of the dress, carefully pack it up, and put it back into the dark closet next to where he kept all his happy memories.

October 25, 2015
Dear Abby,

 Today is Dave's birthday. I bought a cupcake for myself and once the kids were in bed, I put a small candle on it and blew it out for him. I miss him so much. There isn't a day that goes by where I don't think of him. Some days I still pull out my phone to text him, to tell him about my day or some funny antic about the kids, to just rant or just to tell him I love him. I always want to share everything with him, and now I've made that impossible. It's so hard. I just feel swallowed in this big black hole, except this time, it's not a hole caused by depression, it's one that I've dug myself. Most days I am trying to figure out how to climb back out of the hole, but it keeps getting bigger and bigger with each day that passes. And on some days, when the days are dark, I am just hoping that I'll be buried here, and that all the pain will end.

Dave
May 18, 2016

    Most days, Dave did not like downtown Vancouver. It was too loud with the nonstop sound of traffic and cars honking at one another. It was crowded, too. People lined the sidewalks waiting for buses or moved in groups, university students on a study break, or work colleagues going out for lunch, and took up the narrow sidewalks from end to end. And it wasn't just the surplus of people that made the city crowded, but it was the buildings too. A mix of old row homes or historic hotels thrown in with the new, towering skyscrapers made of reflective glass, with solar gardens on the roofs.
    The normal rules didn't seem to apply here either. Pedestrians walked out in front of cars, regardless of the potential outcome. Vehicles ran reds, trying to sneak another inch forward in the blockade of traffic. It was perfectly acceptable, to some, to not hold a door open for the person entering behind them, and the transit seats were first come first serve, so it was best not to be elderly, injured, or pregnant. Or at least, these were the observations and feelings Dave had when he ventured into the city.
    Today, however, was different. He was downtown for a work convention and was on a break between meeting with potential new vendors for the store. This year's convention was quite spectacular, with a lot of new innovations and ideas on health

foods and healthy living. The trend was heading towards more plant-based eating, a practice he recently had been considering for himself. He wasn't sure yet if he could truly give up a good medium-rare steak.

The sky was bright and cheery, and it put Dave in a good mood. The hustle-and-bustle of people around him brought him an odd sense of comfort, and it made him realize he had needed a change in routine. He tried so hard to upkeep a sense of normalcy the past few years, for Abby's sake, that he had forgotten about spontaneity and change. Usually, he dreaded the annual convention, groaned, and moaned throughout the day of it and was happy to head home. But today he welcomed the chaos of the downtown core with open arms. He smiled at people as he walked down the street, eying the different food trucks that lined the sidewalks, trying to decide which one he would try. There was an aroma in the air that he couldn't quite place, but it made his mouth water and determination set in to find it.

At last, he found the source of the mouth-watering temptation. A hotdog truck on the corner of a busy intersection loomed before him, and he followed the scent trail right to the back of the line. The place was popular with at least seven people ahead of him, and one of the cart's servers was handing out paper menus to those in line so that they had their orders ready when they got to the counter.

"Thank you," Dave muttered as he took the menu. Already, three people lined up behind him. He was not the only one enticed by the smells that wafted down the street. He opened the menu and perused the different combinations at hand. There was a classic hotdog with mustard, ketchup, and relish, but from there they become more complex. There were different types of dogs, classic, beef, turkey, chicken, vegetarian, and an array of different toppings, the combinations endless. There were different spices and herbs, seasoning combinations he would never have thought to try together.

The line moved up, and Dave would spy on each happy customer's purchase. It was almost too hard for him to decide, and he felt anxious as the line in front of him diminished. At last, he decided on a spicy barbecue flavored hotdog, with cheese and gravy, the thoughts of his future plant-based lifestyle thrown aside by the temptation of a good hotdog, when he glanced up and something across the street caught his eye. His breath caught in his chest and his mouth fell open. It was Ronnie.

"What can I get y'ah?"

Dave didn't hear the server at the front of the truck. He didn't even realize he was at the front of the line, and that the server repeated herself almost immediately, for the line behind him was quite long. The menu dropped from his hand; the barbecue-dog forgotten as he abandoned his spot in line involuntarily and moved further down the sidewalk.

Ronnie was across the street, mixed into the crowd of people. She wore her favourite black zip-up hoodie with a pair of blue leggings, and white sneakers. It was the baseball cap on her head that caught Dave's attention. It was a bright fuchsia colour, and on the front, it read *Aloha*. Dave had bought it for her on their honeymoon after she had misplaced her original hat and had sunburned her face badly on their first day there. It became her favourite cap ever since, worn nearly every day in the summers after. There was no mistaking it.

The people around him blurred as he focused in on her and pushed his way down the sidewalk. She stopped at the light across the street and waited for the pedestrian sign to cross. Dave's pulse quickened as he moved to cross the street over to her, determined to run across even though the signal had changed and the *do not cross* hand flashed at him. His foot left the curb, but he quickly jumped back up as a bus cut him off and came roaring around the corner, a loud honk and profanity coming from the driver's window. Once the bus cleared the way, Dave's light was red, and Ronnie was starting to across the street the other way.

Dave jumped into the crowd crossing parallel to her. Maybe he could catch up to her on the other side. Or better yet, maybe after crossing ahead of her, she'd then turn left and cross over onto his side. But she turned right and moved further away from him. His eyes stayed locked on the fuchsia hat and blue leggings, as they wove in and out of the crowd, and he'd dart glances over at the walking signal, waiting for it to let him cross over onto her side. Just as the signal changed and Dave hurried to cross the intersection, to his horror Ronnie suddenly turned left and out of sight, down into the SkyTrain system. If Dave didn't catch up to her before she got onto a train, she'd be lost forever. Again.

Dave elbowed people hard as he moved through the crossing crowd. An old woman scowled at him, and he quickly muttered his apologies as he broke free from the crowd and sprinted toward the SkyTrain's entrance. A train squealed into the station just as he raced down the stairs, and for a panicked second, he thought his moment disappeared and that she boarded the train. But in the distance, he saw that bright hat bobbing in the throng of people and turn down another corridor towards the southern train. Dave ran after her.

A million thoughts raced through his mind as he ran. What would he say to her? Would they embrace? Would she turn him away? All the questions that had first come to his mind when she left four years ago resurfaced, the biggest being *why*. But he couldn't ask her that right away. They'd have to take it slow. Would she even be happy to see him? Dave knew one thing for sure, he'd be happy to see her. Overjoyed, really. He never thought he would see her again, and yet here she was, so close to him. Maybe she had been in the city the whole time, returned with Eli once they'd left Hawaii.

And Eli... where was he now? Daycare, probably, or maybe even preschool. He'd be walking and talking, his own little person. Maybe if things didn't work out with Ronnie, the thought of which already broke Dave's heart, he'd at least be able to see Eli again. They could arrange some sort of custody agreement. He knew he'd be a stranger at first to his own son, but Eli would only be four. They still had time to build a relationship.

All these things flashed in his head as he rounded the corner toward the southbound train's platform. Dave had never felt so determined about something in his entire life. He could *not* let her go again. Once they met, he'd hold her so close and so tight, and would never let go. He couldn't bear the thought of losing her again and would do everything in his power to prevent that from happening.

Once he rounded the corner, Dave caught sight of her again and jogged towards her. He could smell the scent of vanilla wafting from her, the same as the shampoo she used to love, and the aroma calmed him as he reached out to grab her elbow.

The woman turned around and everything came to a crashing halt. Dave stood there, breathless from rushing after her, and felt the wind knock out of him. He almost doubled over in pain from heartache as an icy stillness began to envelope him. It wasn't Ronnie, not even close. While the hat was identical, that was where the similarities ended. The woman looked nothing like Ronnie now that Dave saw her up close. This stranger had a wide face, big brown eyes, and freckles splayed across her nose. She was much younger than Ronnie would be, and Dave now noticed a strand of red hair poking out under the cap. He felt a fool for not noticing it before, for it was obvious now, as were the other differences that were suddenly screaming at him, wide hips and square shoulders, a round face, and small forehead.

"Can I help you?" the woman asked after a long awkward minute of Dave just staring at her.

"I-I'm sorry," he stammered. He let her elbow go, and she drew it back in close to her, as though he were a psychopath and was about to grab her again. Dave didn't blame her. "I thought you were someone else."

The woman raised her eyebrow, much too thin to be Ronnie's, and turned away to head to the opposite end of the platform, far away from him, to wait for her train. Dave watched her go, his dream of reuniting with his wife going with her. All the small hopes that had built up within him over the past ten minutes came crumbling down, and a deep sense of grief filled him, one he hadn't felt in a long while.

It wasn't until long after the woman's train had screeched in and out of the station, as Dave still stood there on the platform, that his stomach growled, and he remembered about his abandoned lunch and the hotdog truck above. The idea of the hotdog now was not as enticing as it had been before, and instead made Dave feel sick to his stomach. The downtown core was no longer an escape from normalcy, but an embarrassment and point of heartache. He hated downtown, now more than ever.

Abby
June 4, 2016

The smell of waffles wafted up the stairs and into Abby's bedroom. She took a deep breath and sighed as she smelled the deliciousness that was waiting for her downstairs in the kitchen. The sun shone brightly through her bedroom window, where she stared down at the street. Their neighbour was already out and mowing the lawn, and she could see Greyson a few doors down, playing basketball in his driveway. Summer was on the way, and everybody seemed to be getting a head start. Abby, however, felt like she was already behind. And it was her own fault.

"Abby! Breakfast is ready!" Daddy called from downstairs.

Abby climbed down from her window seat, and quickly got changed. She put on her comfiest pair of shorts, a pale pink pair that her grandma had bought her recently, and her favourite t-shirt. The unicorns on it were fading because she wore it so often, but today called for a favourite t-shirt. Nerves set in, and she hadn't even asked her daddy yet if he'd help.

Daddy was at the stove, nodding along to the beat that came through the radio. A pile of waffles was on Abby's plate already, syrup and butter on the table. The sight of them made her mouth water. As she entered the kitchen, her dad turned and smiled at her.

"Milk or juice?" he asked.

"Milk please," she said after some thought. She'd need some protein, she decided, and she could celebrate with juice later.

Once her daddy set the glass of milk in front of her, Abby took two bites of her waffles as he sat down at the table across from her. Abby took two more bites, a big gulp of milk, and then a deep breath as she turned to him.

"Daddy?" she asked. He grunted in response as his own mouth was now full of waffle. "Can… can you teach me how to ride my bike today?"

Abby held her breath as she waited for his response. The clock ticked on the wall, and he looked up from his plate at her question. Abby had thought about this for a few weeks now. She went out riding with Scarlet and Greyson a few times when the weather was nice, and both of them had their training wheels off. And then the other day at school, somebody else in the other Grade One class still had training wheels on their bike and had ridden it to school. At recess, some older boys stood by the bikes and laughed at it.

Thankfully, the owner of the bike hadn't been nearby and didn't get to hear their rude comments. But Abby had been nearby. She heard the mean things the boys said and knew that if it had been her bike and she had heard what they said, her feelings would have been hurt. A lot. And even though it wasn't her bike, she suddenly felt embarrassed and bad that she still had her training wheels on. She'd flash back to when her daddy tried to teach her to ride last summer, and she kicked herself for not trying harder. Yes, it had been scary when he let her go and she crashed into the bush, but he had been trying to help. She understood that now. And despite that the thought of crashing to the ground again terrified her, she would not learn unless she tried.

"Of course!" Daddy said with a big smile.

"I'm sorry about last year," Abby blurted out.

Her daddy scoffed. "Kiddo, no need to be sorry. You just weren't ready then, and I let go too soon. But we'll work on it today, together."

This made Abby smile. The two of them finished their breakfast quickly and headed out to the garage. It was a beautiful late spring day, summer just around the corner. Birds chirped, flowers bloomed, and there was something positive buzzing in the air. As her daddy took her bike off the wall and unscrewed the training wheels from the back, Abby nodded to herself in confidence as she clipped on her purple helmet. Today was the day. She may fall off her bike, but she'd get back on it again and keep trying.

Training wheels off, her daddy opened the garage door, and Abby was out on the driveway before it had squealed all the way to the top. Her daddy wheeled the bike outside and down to the sidewalk. He patted the seat and Abby took a deep breath as she made her way over and climbed on top.

"OK," he said in a clear voice. "Whenever you're ready. I *promise* not to let go until you tell me to."

"OK." Abby knew he meant it this time.

The handlebars bit into her palms as she squeezed them tight, and slowly, she pedaled the bike. The beads on the spokes clicked and clacked as they fell up and down the faster she went. Her daddy gripped the seat behind her, and the two of them concentrated on the task at hand. The front wheel wobbled at first as Abby concentrated on her balance, but soon she felt the center of her gravity. The bike became steadier and the ride smoother as she gained more confidence.

Abby inhaled deeply and then glanced over her shoulder at her daddy. "Let go," she said in a firm voice. Her stomach flipped at the idea, but she knew it was time.

"Are you sure?" Daddy asked.

"Yes!" Abby said. She could feel it in her bones.

Daddy let go of the back of the bike, and Abby was on her own. The bike wobbled again, and Abby swallowed her panic. She kept the handlebars straight in front of her, and even though she wanted to stop pedaling as her anxiousness screamed at full force, she pushed through it. If she stopped pedaling, she knew she'd lose her balance and fall over. Her feet pushed down on the pedals, and she kept moving forward. And before she knew it, Abby was riding her bike all on her own down the street. Something suddenly clicked inside her, and she knew just what to do.

"Woohoo! Go, Abby, go!" Daddy shouted from behind. Abby glanced back at him for a second and smiled. He was quite far behind her now.

"Weeeeeeeee!" Abby squealed with glee. It was exhilarating, the wind in her face, the houses and gardens of the neighbourhood whizzing by her. She sped past Greyson, still shooting hoops, and looped around back to her house where her daddy was waiting.

It was as she was speeding towards her dad that she realized she didn't know how to stop. Her daddy seemed to realize this too, for as she approached him at top speed, he reached out and caught onto the bike. Abby stopped pedaling and the two of them slowed to a stop. Once she came to a full stop, she jumped off the bike and into her daddy's arms. She hugged him as tight as she could, happy beyond belief.

"I did it!" she cheered.

"I'm so proud of you," he said. And she was proud of herself too.

August 29, 2016
Dear Abby,

What is it about bubbles that are so magical? Lisa and Eli have been playing outside in the yard nonstop for an hour and a half now. I can't think of any one time where they've been this entertained for consistently this long. Mrs. Hannigan bought them this little bubble-making machine on a whim, and we set it up today. I had to drag them inside for lunch at one point, and once they were done, they ran right back outside. It's a mixture of dancing in the bubbles and trying to catch and pop them. I think tomorrow I might turn the sprinkler on too at the same time. It's too bad we didn't have this at the beginning of the summer!

September 5, 2017
Dear Abby,

 Today was Eli's first day of kindergarten. I can't believe it! He was so nervous and shy. The whole orientation he was glued to my hip, except the last ten minutes when he made friends with another little boy named Robbie. It makes me worry about him when he goes back tomorrow and I'm not there.
 I always worry about Eli when we're apart. I still think of him as this little baby who needs me, likely because he is part of this dark secret that I have, my past life that nobody here knows about. I keep waiting to be found out.
 Sometimes I feel like Mrs. Hannigan knows the truth. Sometimes I notice these quick sad glances towards me, and it just makes me wonder if she knows. Maybe she is old fashioned and just pities a single mother with two kids. She knows that I have an estranged husband, but that's it. I was surprised she didn't press me with more inquiring questions when we first met, because she can be quite nosy, but for whatever reason, with Dave, she's never asked more. Part of me wishes she would. There are some days when I want to tell someone my secret, to let it out. Instead, I just keep on swallowing it and let it rot me from the inside out.

Abby
October 18, 2017

Abby skipped along the sidewalk with Scarlet, butterflies fluttering in her stomach. Their school day was behind them, and the two were on their way to Scarlet's house. She lived just down the street from the school, and her older brother walked home with them. Abby felt a bit exhilarated walking around without a grown-up present.

The leaves on the trees were bright and bold, a collage of reds, oranges, and yellows. Some trees were bare already, naked in the crisp fall breeze that drifted by. Tendrils of Abby's blonde hair poked out of her knit cap and blew into her face, her cheeks pink from the chill.

Today, finally, Abby got to meet Scarlet's new little sister. Mrs. Watkins had the baby a few weeks ago, and Scarlet's dad had explained that they just needed things to settle a bit before Abby could come over to meet the new baby. She wasn't sure what he meant by that but waited patiently until Scarlet could invite Abby over again.

When they entered Scarlet's house, the smell of freshly baked cookies greeted them. Mrs. Watkins always had something freshly baked for when company came over. Sometimes it was bread, one time it was pie, but usually, it was cookies. Abby's mouth watered just thinking of them as they walked through the front door. Scarlet's mom made the best cookies.

"Hello Scarlet, hi Abby," her mother said. Mrs. Watkins's smile was warm, but she looked tired, Abby thought. But it was a happy tired.

The girls sat at the counter and helped themselves to some warm cookies as they told Mrs. Watkins about their day. Scarlet's older brother grabbed a few cookies and then went up into his room.

"When you're done with your snacks, come and see the baby," Mrs. Watkins said. "She'll be up from her nap by then."

Abby smiled and ate faster. Scarlet was in no rush.

Once they finished, Scarlet led Abby up to the baby's room. Abby loved Scarlet's house. Warm and cozy, it had a homey feel to it that she never experienced at any other friend's house. It always smelled fresh and was something, Abby thought, that was only achievable when there was a mom in the house. Not a homey feeling, she realized—that was how *her* house felt. It was a *mom* feeling. Abby loved her own house, of course, but there was something special about Scarlet's that she'd never been able to put her finger on, until just now.

When they came to the top of the stairs, Scarlet turned left towards a room at the end that had been a spare room for as long as Abby had known her. One time, there was a desk and a chair in there, another time they had used it as a playroom. Now, as Scarlet stopped and carefully turned the doorknob, a dainty purple sign with the name *Emmy* was on the front.

Scarlet slowly opened the door. It smelled like baby powder as they stepped inside, and Abby smiled at the cute decor. A duckling lamp with a purple shade sat atop a bookshelf, with lavender chiffon curtains over the windows, and a soft hand-knitted yellow blanket strewn across a rocking chair. A duckling mobile hung above the white polished crib, and from inside the bed Abby could hear soft little noises.

"Well, this is her," Scarlet shrugged.

Abby looked over the rails and her heart stopped. Baby Emmy looked just like any other baby out there; small, pink, with a squished face and dark eyes. There wasn't really anything special about her, but as Abby looked down at her, flashbacks of baby Eli raced past her eyes. His bald head, blue eyes, and the way he would laugh when she'd stick her tongue out at him. Abby didn't think about her baby brother often. Their time together had been so short, and if she were honest with herself, she didn't really remember much about him. But now, as she looked down at baby Emmy, she felt a quiet, sad nostalgia creep inside her.

Emmy's little face scrunched up and turned red. She cried, a shrill sharp sound that pierced through the room. Mrs. Watkins yelled from down the hall that she'd be there in a minute. Scarlet sighed and rested her cheek on the crib, looking down at her baby sister.

"This is pretty much all she does," she said in a bored tone. "Cry, cry, cry, cry…" She then sighed and looked over at Abby. "Come on, let's go play in my room."

Abby nodded and Scarlet left the room. Abby turned to follow but hesitated and looked back at the crib. Emmy's fists were in tight little balls, and her tiny feet kicked inside her pink sleeper. She reached into the crib and took one of the baby's small hands into her own.

"It's OK, little Emmy," she whispered. Emmy stopped crying for a moment and looked up at her. She wrapped her tiny hand around one of Abby's fingers, and Abby marveled at how her finger was bigger than the baby's entire hand. The baby cooed and gave Abby a small smile, which she returned. And she stayed a few moments longer, remembering her baby brother, and wishing she'd have been able to spend more time with him. Even if mostly all he did was cry.

November 6, 2017
Dear Abby,

I'm so heartbroken. Eli is being bullied in school. I knew he was having some troubles recently, but his teacher pulled me aside today and said there are two boys who keep picking on him. Apparently, they call him names and make fun of his curly hair, and the teacher separates them immediately. There is a strict no bullying policy at the school, and I am glad to hear that they are on top of it already, and that the other boys' parents are being spoken to... but it just breaks my heart. On top of it all, she says that Eli takes it in stride. He just lets it roll off his shoulders and will laugh with the other boys, but she notices that he'll retreat into his shell afterwards and will then play on his own. I don't know what happened with the friendship he had started with Robbie on the first day. I think Robbie moved recently.

I don't know what to do. I had no idea. He always seems so happy and cheerful when he comes home. I never thought that my kid would be the one to be bullied. What makes it harder is that since this is such a small town, there are no other school options. I've thought about homeschooling him and Lisa before, but I don't think I have the patience for that. My mental health is too fragile. Plus, I really do enjoy my job.

This was something I never thought of when sending him to school. Naturally, now it makes me wonder about Abby. Has she *been bullied? Is she a bully? I would hate for it to be reversed. I wonder how Dave would handle this.*

Dave
December 2, 2017

 The hazy smoke made Dave feel sick. Or maybe it was the cheap beer. Whatever the cause, he decided he needed a break and stood up from the table. His companions around him did not take notice, too preoccupied with the dancing ladies and booze around them. One lady tried to get his attention on the way out, her bright pink lingerie causing him to linger longer than he'd like to admit, but then the haze of smoke and perfumes hit him again, and he declined her offer and slipped out of the club.
 Cold winter air hit him hard in the chest and it was a breath of fresh air. The beat from the music drowned out as the doors closed behind him and Dave sighed in relief. The streets were quiet, most people asleep at this hour, save for those who were partaking in the same type of risqué activities. Neon lights from the strip club flashed behind him, and Dave moved away from the doors and sat down on the curb of the sidewalk. Stench from the smoke and sultry perfumes left his nostrils, and the winter cold filled them instead. He closed his eyes for a moment, letting the chill fill his body, and he wondered if it might snow soon. Abby would be happy if it did, she had wanted to make a snowman for a few days now. Dave promised her if it didn't snow soon, they'd go up the mountain to find some and build one there.

"But I want him to guard the house," he recalled her saying. He chuckled to himself and could picture the snowman in front of their house. Abby had plans that involved a wooden sword and shield, a metal bucket for a helmet, and rubber boots.

The sound of the club's doors opening interrupted his thoughts, and Dave turned around to see a silhouette in the light approach him. As the doors closed again, Dave relaxed as Paul came out and handed him a beer. He took a swig from his own as he sat down beside Dave, and exhaled loudly, also relieved.

"Needed a break too, eh?" Dave chuckled.

Paul sighed again and took another drink. It was his bachelor party, organized by his older brother, Dwayne, and Dave knew it was not in his taste. Paul had been Dave's best friend since they were fifteen. He had been the best man at his wedding to Ronnie and had been there for him when things fell apart. The only reason Dave wasn't his best man in return was because his mother had pressured Paul for his older brother to be best man, and the strip club bachelor party had been Dwayne's idea. It was one he refused to relent on, and so, begrudgingly, Paul went along with it, and therefore so did Dave. Neither of them were the type to really enjoy the seductive dances from naked strangers, and both knew that it was because Dwayne's marriage was falling apart that he was so eager to go to the club.

"All I wanted to do was play some poker," Paul muttered under his breath. Dave chuckled again and took a slow sip from his drink. "How are you doing?"

Dave rolled the bottle between his hands and looked down at the concrete under his feet. It was a question that Paul asked him a lot of late, at least once whenever they hung out in person, which wasn't that often since Dave was usually busy with Abby and Paul busy wedding planning. This year marked the five-year anniversary of Ronnie's disappearance. Five years had gone by, and when Dave thought about that fact, it usually knocked the wind out of him. It had both flown by and made him think, *it's only been five years?* Life without Ronnie felt like an eternity of misery, and some days he still wasn't sure how he went on. It felt like just yesterday that he came home to that nearly empty house, his son and wife gone without a trace. He could see the empty bedroom, the confusion at finding the car in the garage, the hurt as he realized what was happening and that he and Abby were left behind…

"Doin' just fine," he said at last and took a long drink at that. Paul nodded and didn't press the issue. What more could be said about it, anyway? The case of finding them was cold, they had vanished without a trace. Some dark part of Dave muttered that they could be dead. The more optimistic side, which prevailed mostly when he thought about his missing family, said that somewhere Eli was a happy five-year-old now, living with Ronnie. In his mind, Eli had Abby's blonde hair and bright blue eyes. As an infant, he had resembled Ronnie, but maybe as he grew, he'd resemble Dave a bit more. It would be nice to know that one of his children looked like him, as Abby was all Ronnie, save for her blonde hair.

"Nervous about next weekend?" Dave asked to change the subject. He glanced over at Paul. His friend's face turned bashful for a moment, a small smile on his lips as he thought of his impending wedding.

"Nah," Paul said with a full smile. "You know me. I'm crazy about Trish. She's freaking out a bit, but that's more to be expected of the bride."

Dave smiled at his friend's happiness. Paul had gone through a rough breakup shortly before Ronnie's disappearance. He and his ex-girlfriend had been together since grad school. Carline had been his high school sweetheart, and Dave worried about him for a long time. Carline had been Paul's world, and she shattered it, much like Ronnie later shattered Dave's. It was actually Ronnie's disappearance that helped Paul snap out of his own misery to help Dave through his. And from there, he met Trish and the rest, as they say, was history. His friend had newfound happiness, and Dave liked to think that maybe, someday, he'd have the same… if not happiness, then some form of closure.

"She'll be fine day of," Dave said. "Once the dress is on, the rest of the details don't matter anymore. Or at least, that's what Ronnie told me."

Paul clapped Dave on the back and nodded. "The one thing that's bothering her," Paul said, not going to acknowledge the mention of Ronnie, to which Dave was grateful, "is the lack of snow. This winter-wonderland-Christmas themed wedding has been all she's been thinking about since she was a little girl, and ugh, if I could control the weather… there's nothing I wouldn't do for her, you know?"

Paul sighed and looked off into the distance, his head in the clouds. Dave nodded in silence as he looked down at his drink. He knew exactly how Paul felt, for he had felt the same way about Ronnie. There was nothing he wouldn't give or do to have her and Eli back.

"Ah, well," Paul said with another clap on Dave's shoulder. He stood up, brushed off his pants and shivered in the cold. "As much as I don't like it in there, it is a lot warmer. Coming back in?"

"Yeah, in a minute."

The music sounded again briefly as Paul went back inside the club. Dave downed the rest of his beer and sighed as he stood. Just as he turned around to head back toward the door, he paused as something caught his eye. A single, bright white snowflake fell from the sky. He smiled to himself as he looked up and a cloud of snowfall began to come down. It looked like Trish would have her winter wonderland wedding, and that Dave would soon have a snowman guarding his house.

Dave
January 18, 2018

Abby was quiet on the way home from school. Dave drummed his fingers on the umbrella handle as they walked home in silence. The sounds of the rain pattering on their umbrellas and their boots squelching in the puddles filled the lapse in conversation. Usually, she was quite chatty on the way home, regaling him tales of what happened on the playground that day, or what they had learned in class.

"So, kiddo, how was school?" Dave finally asked. He looked down at her, her face expressionless underneath her purple umbrella.

Abby shrugged without looking up at him. "Was OK."

"Nothing interesting happened today?" he asked after she failed to go into any details. She shrugged again and didn't answer.

Dave didn't want to press her. Once they got home and she had a snack in front of her, she was sure to open up. Maybe she just needed a safe space to express herself. The kitchen table was usually that place. Instead of fruit, Dave decided when they got home, they'd have a plate of cookies. He didn't like to see his little girl upset.

Their front door squeaked as they walked in. Abby kicked off her boots, wet footprints left at the front door, and slammed her closed umbrella down into the stand. The stand shook and Dave steadied it before it fell over.

"Careful, Abby," he said in a calm tone. It wouldn't help to reprimand her if he wanted her to open up about what was wrong. A mumbled "sorry" came out from Abby as she stalked off into the living room.

Dave stopped and caught his own eye in his reflection in the mirror. It was a circular silver mirror, with rings weaving in and out around the reflective surface. Ronnie had picked it out when they first moved in together. She'd gotten it from a dollar store. Brands and labels had never meant much to her, and this simple, yet trendy mirror had fit its original space in their townhouse perfectly. He had a sudden thought of panic as he stared into it. Was it—could it be that Abby was hitting puberty early? Was this a sudden influx of hormones, and a preview to how her teenage years would be?

The colour drained from his face as he tried to pull up as much as he knew about female puberty in his head. It was too soon, he decided with a firm nod to his reflection. Despite he had done no research on the subject yet, though maybe he should start sooner than he'd originally thought, he knew it was too soon. Abby was only turning nine this year. He had three, four, five years still to go. Or so he thought. Better start research now just in case. It was not a conversation he was ready to have with her.

Abby was lying face down on the couch when Dave walked into the living room, his mini-internal freak-out over. She let out a deep sigh.

"Abby, what's wrong?" he asked.

"Nothing!" she whined. She abruptly stood up from the couch and walked into the kitchen. After a moment of slamming cupboards open and closed, she let out a frustrated huff.

"Come on, what is it? What happened today?" Dave asked her again in a soft voice. Opening one last cupboard, Abby reached in to grab a fruit cup. She ripped it open and the sticky juice inside went flying everywhere. Tears welled in her eyes, and Dave swooped in with a paper towel to clean up the mess.

"Nothing happened!" Abby said. "I just… I have all these *feelings* and I don't know what to do with them!"

Dave took a deep breath. Now and then, Abby would have these episodes of being quite grumpy or upset for no reason. When she was younger, they'd come out in tantrums because she couldn't express herself properly. As she got older, she could explain herself more coherently, but sometimes, like today it seemed, it was still hard for her to work through what she was feeling and why. Dave usually gave her some space and she'd snap back to her normal self quickly. But today, this seemed a little different.

Silence, save for the ticking of the clock on the wall, filled the kitchen as Dave worked out how to respond. He wanted to help her, but he didn't know how. It was something he struggled with. All he ever wanted to do was take all her problems away and keep her happy. But the biggest problem was that her mother left, and that wasn't something he could fix for either of them. He closed his eyes for a moment and listened to the clock tick away. Ronnie popped into his mind. He pictured her smile, could smell the fragrance of her lavender night cream, and could see her writing in her journal. A lightbulb went off in his head.

"Have you ever thought about writing in a diary?" he asked.

Abby looked up from her fruit cup, spoon in her mouth. She sighed and shrugged. "Carol has suggested it a few times, but I don't know…"

Dave nodded. Carol was Abby's therapist and had been for the last five years. Abby still saw her once every few months, and she was the saving grace in getting her through this entire ordeal. Carol was a safe space for his daughter to express how she was feeling, not just towards her mother, but towards him too. Now though, it seemed like the therapist alone wasn't enough.

"Yes, you should try it," he said with enthusiasm. "Your mother used to write in her journal every night."

This piqued Abby's interest. She put the empty fruit cup on the counter and dropped the spoon into the sink. It clattered against the other dishes piled up and Dave made a mental note to empty the dishwasher later. "She did?"

"Yes," Dave said in a soft voice as he thought back again. He could hear her pen scrawling across the page. Some days he wanted to be nosy and see what she was writing about, especially when it seemed like a long passage or on days when they'd bickered. But he never did. It was a place for Ronnie to let her thoughts out, no matter how ridiculous, mean, or sad. Everybody had the right to vent, and some liked to do that in private. "It was a great way for her to unwind after a long day."

Abby frowned, and Dave went on, hellbent on helping his daughter out in this small way. "It's not just for tough days, but for good days too. Days you want to remember, funny things that happened, a place to vent about your frustrations or stress. Heck, you could even just doodle in it."

"I guess I could try it." Abby shrugged.

Dave clapped his hands suddenly. "Yes! Let's go out and get one now. I need to get a few groceries, anyway."

The two of them bundled back up and drove out to the mall. The rain was coming down heavier on their way back a few hours later. Abby took her time picking out a sparkly blue and green covered journal with a stainless-steel lock on it. It sat on her lap now and Dave glanced back to see her admiring it in the back seat. They'd even found a matching pen and had stopped for ice cream in the food court between errands.

"Who do I write to though?" Abby asked.

The light in front of them turned red and Dave drummed his fingers on the steering wheel. "Well, you don't have to write to anybody. It's just for your own thoughts. 'Dear Diary' I think is what most people write, but you could write to yourself, I guess. Or you could write to your mother."

The light turned green, and Dave glanced back at Abby at that last suggestion. It just popped into his head at the last minute, and as he thought more about it, the more he thought it was a great idea. Maybe it would help her not only get through all of these "feelings" that she had, but also cope with the loss of Ronnie.

"Carol has suggested that before too," Abby said in a quiet voice. "I don't know though. I think it's weird to write to someone who is gone."

Dave turned into their garage. He put the car into park and turned off the engine as he turned around to look at his daughter. "That's what your mother used to do."

"Really?" Abby asked. Her eyes were bright as she looked up at him, and Dave nodded.

"Yes. She used to write to her sister, who passed away when they were teenagers," Dave said.

"What happened to her?" Abby asked in a sad voice.

"She got hit by a drunk driver walking home one night from a friend's house," he answered. "She was seventeen and your mom was fifteen. That's when she started writing in journals. It helped her feel connected to her sister. You're named after her, you know."

Abby looked down at the journal in her lap. It sparkled under the car's interior light. "I guess I could try it. That's really sad what happened to Mom's sister."

Dave watched her for a moment. Blonde hair fell into her face as she continued to look down at the pretty diary. The shape of her face was so much like her mother's, it was like seeing what Ronnie must have looked like as a child. It made him ache. He hoped she would take him up on the advice. It would make him happy knowing that she felt connected to her mother.

Abby
June 1, 2018

    Hands stretched over her head, Abby took in a deep breath and exhaled slowly. The sun was bright, and the air was warm, the first sign that summer was coming. The spring had been unusually warm, but Abby didn't mind. She liked the warm weather and looked forward to summer. Her dad had started an annual tradition of camping for the first two weeks of summer last year, and she had looked forward to it ever since. But first, she had to get through the last few weeks of school. More importantly, today she had to get through her first big track and field meet.

    Parents and other spectators filled the stands as Abby continued to do her stretches on the track. It would be her race soon, the 500m dash, and she surveyed the competing girls as they stretched next to her. There was Jenny, who was also from her school but from a different class, and then three other girls whose names she didn't know, all from different schools. Then there was Joanna Newcamp. She was from the prestigious elementary school across town, prestigious because all the parents who dropped their kids off had fancy, shiny cars, and came from big houses. Rumor was that Joanna was the primary competition to beat. She was taller than Abby, with beautiful long blonde hair swept up in a perfect ponytail. Abby self-consciously tucked the wispy strands that strayed from her own ponytail behind her ears and moved on to stretching her quads.

Through the crowd of grown-ups mingling, she spotted her dad sitting on the bleachers. He was near the front, third row, and waved at her the minute she spotted him. Unlike the other parents who looked down at their phones, her dad watched her stretch, and gave her a thumbs up as she balanced on one leg and pulled the other behind her. A sense of relief and calm flooded through her, and she smiled back at him as she finished her stretches.

One coach signaled for the girls to move to the starting line. As Abby moved to her lane, she rolled her shoulders, took a deep breath, and then turned towards Joanna. She was beautiful and intimidating, but Abby stood tall and faced her square on. Joanna made a weird *what are you doing* face at Abby, but Abby ignored it. Then Joanna's expression changed to surprise and caution, as Abby stuck her hand out and said, "Good luck, Joanna."

"You too." Joanna said. She hesitated as she shook Abby's hand but did so, nonetheless. Her dad told her that the two most important things in sports were to have fun, and good sportsmanship. And even though she wanted to beat Joanna and come in first more than anything, Abby knew she also had to be a good sport.

She then turned away from her competitor, centered herself in her lane, and narrowed her eyes at her target down the track. The white line seemed so far away. It stretched out further than Abby remembered when she practiced her runs at school, and the more she tried to focus on it, the further away it got. That was impossible though. The line couldn't move. Abby could move closer to it, but it couldn't move further away from her.

As she contemplated this idea, the coach in front of them counted down from three and the whistle blew. The other girls *whooshed* past Abby as fast as they could while she continued to stare at the line that seemed further and further away. She then caught a single voice out from the parents shrieking in the stands and heard her dad call her name. Without looking back, Abby snapped out of her trance and took off.

The wind blew through her hair, the loose whisps of blonde tickling the sides of her face, as her sneakers slapped the pavement. She breathed in through her nose and out through her mouth like her coach had taught her, and before she knew it, Abby was pushing past through the crowd of girls. Joanna was just ahead of her now, her neat blond ponytail swishing at her back like a pendulum swinging on a clock. Abby's legs ached, her lungs burned, and she knew her pacing was off. But she was so close, and the line wasn't moving any further away. It was within her reach now, the shrieks of spectators behind her growing louder and louder the closer she and Joanna got. Soon she could hear Joanna's feet hitting the pavement, and Abby was pulling up beside her. They were shoulder to shoulder now and the finish line was right there.

The line was suddenly beneath her feet and Joanna's toes clipped Abby's heels. She won. *She had won!* Abby cheered and threw her arms up in the air as the other girls crossed over the finish line. Joanna panted hard beside her and when she stood up after catching her breath, she seemed to tower over Abby. Abby lowered her arms and felt alarmed for a minute. While she tried to be a good sport about losing, others didn't always have the same attitude. And Joanna looked pretty annoyed at her. She had her hands on her hips and a mean look on her face. Abby shrunk away slightly, not sure what to expect next. But just as she had surprised Joanna, Joanna surprised her. She stuck her hand out and Abby shook it.

"Good run," she panted. "I'll have to train harder for next year."

Abby smiled. "Maybe we should train together," she said. It never hurt to have more friends.

Joanna smiled too. "I'd like that. I've been looking for a good running buddy. Maybe our moms can exchange phone numbers."

Abby didn't even skip a beat, as often she would whenever someone assumed she had a mom. She looked over her shoulder and pointed at her dad, who was coming down to greet her, a huge smile on his face. "My dad's just over there. Let's go set something up."

As they walked over to their respective parents, Abby felt proud. Not only of winning the race and dodging what could have been an uncomfortable mother situation, but proud because she had just made herself a new friend.

June 24, 2018
Dear Abby,

 In a strange turn of events, Eli and Tommy are now best friends. They're inseparable. Ever since Jackson moved away, Tommy is now nice to Eli. I guess Jackson was the real troublesome one, because the bullying has stopped now. Eli is so happy to have a best friend, and Tommy is actually quite sweet. His mom... I think her name is Rhonda, she's nice too. Also a single mom. It's just her and Tommy. Jackson's mom was nothing but a snooty bitch when the principal tried to get us together, so I'm not surprised that he was the problem. I hope he learns compassion from somewhere because it certainly won't be from his mother.
 It's been a wild school year. Hard to believe that it's over now, and soon Eli will start Grade One, and it'll be Lisa starting kindergarten! Across the country, Abby will start fourth grade in the fall. All of my babies are grown up now. I feel like I didn't soak up their tininess as babies enough. I close my eyes and can still feel the weight of baby Abby in my arms, hear Eli's giggle, and smell Lisa's special shampoo. If I blink again, they'll be in high school.

Dave
March 22, 2019

    Dave took a deep breath as he sat in his parked car. He gripped and relaxed his fingers around the steering wheel as he stared at the restaurant's door ahead. This was a day he had been dreading for a long time. It felt wrong in many ways, and he felt sick to his stomach; nausea mixed in with butterflies. But he knew it was time, and that was why he finally agreed to be set up on a date.
    Tiffany from his work was adamant for a while now that she had the perfect friend to set him up with. Tiffany was one of the few people who Dave talked a little to about what had happened with Ronnie. So, she knew his history, knew that he was still technically married and hurt by what had happened, that he still loved his wife dearly, but it was nearly seven years now and who knew where Ronnie was. There would be no harm in going out on a date with someone.
    It wasn't like this was the first time Dave had been in the company of other women. It would be his first date since Ronnie left, but he'd had a few one-night stands. They weren't fond memories. He never liked to think about them afterwards, and he didn't like to use the excuse of "men have needs" because, really, he could take care of those needs himself. But sometimes, another warm body lying next to him made him feel better, briefly. He missed the companionship of having another intimate person in his

life, but he loved his wife still, missed her every day, and hadn't been ready to move into a new relationship. And so those odd one-night stands stayed as such and he never called back or got to know the woman afterwards. It made him feel dirty.

This was going to be different though, he reminded himself as he finally stepped out of his car. He texted the woman, Kathy, a few times as they set up their date and place, but they hadn't met in person yet. There was just something about the *finality* of dating that made Dave feel uneasy. It was like admitting that Ronnie was never coming back. And that was something he wasn't ready to grapple with yet because he kept that hope alive in his heart, not just for himself, but for Abby too.

Griffons was a hip new restaurant that was a mix of classy steaks and hipster fusion dishes. Dave heard nothing but good things about it since it opened a few months ago. The facade outside was classy, like one of the historic buildings found further downtown, with bright marquee lights and red velvet awnings. Inside was similar, fancier than Dave had expected, with red velvet seats, and sparkling chandeliers, but the art on the wall was all new and abstract, some backed with neon lighting. He wasn't sure if it worked together, in his opinion, but it must have because the place was quite busy.

"Reservation under Sanders," Dave said once it was his turn at the hostess's desk. She clicked away on her computer without even looking at him. Every one of her obscenely long nails was a different colour, and she smelled too strongly of peppermint. Once she found the reservation though, she looked up and smiled at him.

"Perfect, your date is already here," she said. This made Dave feel more tense and nervous. He hoped to arrive first. The hostess snapped her finger, and another host appeared at her aside. "Alfredo, table number 119 please. Enjoy your evening, Mr. Sanders."

Dave followed Alfredo through the bustling restaurant. Every table was full, either with couples, friends, or even a few families with small children. A variety of aromas wafted through the air and Dave's stomach growled loudly. He was sure it was loud because it *felt* loud, but the chatter of the patrons covered it up. The last thing he wanted was to have his stomach doing impressions of a dying whale when he met Kathy. First impressions were important.

Alfredo rounded the corner and the butterflies in Dave's stomach flew too quickly. He spotted the table at once, the only one that had a single occupant seated by themselves. Her back was to them, and she already had a glass of white wine in front of her. It looked half empty too, which made Dave feel a bit more at ease. She was nervous too.

"Here we are," Alfredo said as he pulled out Dave's chair.

"Hi," Kathy said a bit too quickly as Dave sat down.

"Hello." Dave's voice cracked like he hadn't spoken in years, and he cleared his throat so he sounded human again.

"Can I get you something to drink?" Alfredo asked. Dave ordered a beer and Alfredo hurried off. Now it was just the two of them and Dave felt his heart pounding in his ears and his hands sweating in his lap.

"Hope I didn't keep you waiting too long," Dave said, despite that he knew he was early. He didn't know how else to break the ice though, and this seemed to be just the ticket. Kathy's grip on her glass of wine relaxed, and she smiled at him.

She had straight white teeth and prominent smile lines. Dave liked to think that this meant she was a cheerful person, and it relaxed him a bit. Once Alfredo returned with his beer, and the two of them ordered their meals, they went through the usual first date small talk.

They started off by talking about Tiffany, their mutual contact, which lead into Dave talking about his work, and then Kathy talking about hers. Dave learned she was a stay-at-home mother for eight years before her marriage fell apart, and that she was just tiptoeing back into the workforce.

"Tiffany actually set me up with a great gig through her sister-in-law," Kathy said as their food arrived. "She's my person, Tiff, she's always been there for me."

"Yes, she's a great person," Dave agreed as he eyed his burger. He didn't know how to pick up the monstrous thing without making a mess of himself, and now regretted ordering it. Nothing like being a slob on a first date to leave an impression. After a few minutes of delegating, he figured out the optimum hold and just went for it. It was delicious.

"So, you have two kids?" Dave asked at some point when his mouth wasn't full of food. Tiffany had given him a bit of a background run on Kathy, so he already knew the answer. Her husband had cheated on her, extensively, though Dave didn't know the details of that, and he didn't really need to know. He had no respect for cheaters, which was another reason going on a date while still married to Ronnie made him feel so uncomfortable.

"Yes, two girls," Kathy said. There was pride in her voice, a feeling that Dave knew all too well. There was nothing he was prouder of than his daughter. "Alicia will be eight in the fall, and Melody is five. And you?"

Dave nodded. The last bite of his burger was still in his mouth, and he took his time finishing it before answering. There was no avoiding the mention of his family, and he knew that at some point during the date it would come up. He figured Tiffany had given Kathy the run down on him, as she had on her, and so Kathy already knew the answer.

"Yes, I have a daughter," Dave said. "Abby. She'll be ten soon."

An elephant appeared before them, and Dave wasn't sure how to broach it. He took a quick sip of his beer as he tried to figure out how to continue next, or whether to just ignore it, when Kathy spoke up between bites of her chicken salad.

"And a son too, I think Tiff mentioned?" she said. Kathy didn't look at him as she mentioned it, but Dave was grateful she spoke up. The elephant suddenly seemed to shrink all on its own, and Dave relaxed again. The way she said it indicated that she already knew his story, maybe she even remembered it from when it was everywhere on the news. And it also showed that they didn't need to talk about it, that this was all they had to say about it for now.

"Yes," he answered.

And that was it. Kathy smoothly changed to the next topic, raising daughters, another point that they had in common, and Dave found that talking to her was easy. She was so different from Ronnie, the way she spoke and gestured with her hands. Her voice was high and sweet, a bit nasally but not obnoxious. Kathy was quite pretty too, Dave thought, with soft blonde hair and dark brown eyes.

He sat back and watched Kathy as she regaled a story about a broken-down car, her two girls, and a salvaged ski trip, and he smiled. Tiffany had been right. Kathy was a suitable match for him. She was smart and kind, and they had a lot in common in terms of life experience. Dave knew from Tiffany that she was the same age as him, older actually by a few months. He couldn't imagine trying to date someone younger.

And although, at this point, he wasn't sure where the end of their date would take them, whether there would be a second one, or whether he had just made a new friend instead of a potential partner, Dave was glad that he agreed to be set up. At the very least, Tiffany had given him an enjoyable night out with a pretty woman, which was something he hadn't had in a long time.

May 23, 2019
Dear Abby,

 Today while Eli was at Tommy's house, Lisa and I had a girls' day. It was wonderful. I took her to the salon in town, and we got our nails and hair done. I got a trim, but the stylist added some purple streaks into Lisa's hair, and she's been smiling about it ever since. It was the first thing she showed off when Eli got home, and now he wants blue in his. Lisa is such a little girly girl, I love it. She only wants to wear dresses, is constantly trying to sneak into my makeup, and is always carrying some sort of little purse. It's cute now, but it makes me worry for when she's a teenager. Her teacher said she was in tears the other day because she spilled paint on her dress. Little diva in the making. She and Eli are such opposites, yet the best of friends. Kind of like how we were. I miss you so much. I think if you were still here, I wouldn't be in the mess that I'm in. You were what tethered me to the ground when my demons started to rear their ugly heads, and they've been out of control ever since.

August 7, 2019
Dear Abby,

 Rhonda is trying to set me up again. This time with a friend of her brother's. She insists that this guy would be great for me, but I just can't. I love Dave. There is nobody else out there for me other than Dave. Just because we're apart, doesn't mean that I don't love him, that I don't wish I were with him right now. I wish I could get that through to her without telling her everything. All she knows is that I'm separated. I wear my ring still. That should be a hint enough. I'll never be with anyone else. But I also don't know how to go back. It's been seven years. Some days it still doesn't feel real, like it's all a dream, and I'll wake up back at home. I just can't seem to wake up.

Dave
October 15, 2019

The soft ticking of the clock on the wall was soothing as Dave tried to process his set of thoughts. Dr. Freemont, Rebecca as she insisted he call her, sat patiently in her chair, notepad in hand. The teal leather chair was a familiar sight, and yet it always caught Dave off guard. It was bright against the otherwise modern grey walls, shiny silver details on the desk legs, the couch he sat on, and the abstract colourless art on the walls. The chair was out of place, and yet it spoke the most of the therapist's personality.

Dr. Freemont was his therapist of seven years. He started seeing her a few months after Abby had seen her therapist. She had come highly recommended by a neighbour of Donna's, and after much debate and pressure, Dave agreed to start therapy to work through what had happened. He didn't hesitate to take Abby to see a therapist once it became apparent that Ronnie wasn't coming back, at least not any time soon, but seeing one himself was a different story. It took him a lot of time to accept help and accept that it was OK to get help. It still made him uncomfortable to attend each session, but he felt better every time. It worked.

"How long have you been seeing Kathy?" Dr. Fr— Rebecca asked.

Dave took a deep breath. "Six months or so now."

"And you haven't introduced her to Abby at all?" Rebecca asked. Her pen scribbled softly on the notepad, but she kept her eyes up and peered at Dave through her steel frames. Rebecca's dark hair was streaked with silver, and her wardrobe matched the sleek and grey decor of the office, except for her shoes. Her shoes matched the teal chair.

"No," Dave said. He sank into the grey couch a little further, his shoulders slumped like a child in trouble. He let out a long exhale. "I haven't. I don't know how."

"Are you more nervous about Kathy meeting Abby or Abby meeting Kathy?" Rebecca asked. Dave wasn't sure he knew what the difference was, but that didn't stop him from knowing the answer immediately.

"Abby meeting Kathy," Dave replied without hesitation.

"And why do you think that is?" Again, Rebecca peered at Dave through her steel frames. That's the one thing that irked him about therapy, or at least how Rebecca did it. She seldom said statements. It was always questions, and Dave coming up with the answers within himself. He didn't like to dig deep within himself and face his emotions. Just once it would be nice for someone to hand him the answers, but he knew that wouldn't be helpful. The point *was* to look within himself, face it head on, and come out the other side better for it.

Dave sighed. Rebecca knew why, just as he did. Anybody could guess the answer. "Because I don't want her to think that I'm replacing Ronnie," Dave replied at last. Something felt tight in his chest, and he didn't like it. Breathing became difficult, but he took in the air slowly and let it out even slower.

"And is that what you feel you're doing?"

"Of course not!" Dave said. He sat straighter then and fiddled with his hands, twisting his wedding ring around his finger. "Nobody can ever replace her, and that's the problem. Abby is so angry with her but misses her all the time. She hasn't given up hope. I don't know. We don't talk about Ronnie much anymore, and I worry that introducing Kathy to her will bring up a lot of things that she's worked past already."

Rebecca nodded and scribbled on her pad in silence. Dave watched as the pen moved across the page, and the ticking from the clock on the wall continued behind him. It was one of those big, open-faced clocks where the numbers were just lines on the wall. It wasn't his style.

"And you're worried that introducing Kathy to Abby will mean admitting that Ronnie isn't coming back?" Rebecca asked once the silence had passed.

Dave said nothing. He looked down at his hands, at the callouses on his palms, and the dull shine from his ring. It hadn't been cleaned in a while. He couldn't remember the last time he took it off, actually.

"Because that's something that you still struggle to admit to yourself, isn't it, David?" Rebecca asked softly after Dave stayed silent. He slowly nodded his head and didn't look up at the therapist. He heard the pen softly scratching at the pad, and a low white noise from within overtook the sound of the ticking clock.

"How long were you and Ronnie together?" Rebecca asked.

Dave looked up, a bit confused. Rebecca already knew the answer. They had talked about this many times. His first few sessions had been about working through his relationship with Ronnie, what Ronnie was like, how her leaving wasn't his fault. Most of his other sessions were about Abby, how he was doing as a single father, how he felt she was doing, parenting advice, and such.

"Seven years," Dave said.

Rebecca nodded and brought her pen to her lips. "And she's been gone for seven years now too. You're entering a time where you've been apart longer than you were together. Commonly, it takes half the time a couple have been together to move on. You've given yourself the full amount of time. Granted, your parting was unwanted and abrupt, but it's time, David. There is nothing wrong with moving on. You've given Ronnie plenty of time to come back, and she hasn't. It's time to let go, and it seems you have started to do that. And I'm proud of you for it." Rebecca sat back in her chair and paused for a moment, looking Dave in the eye, before clearing her throat and continuing.

"Abby has already lived longer without her mother than with her. There's no doubt that introducing a new female figure in her life might bring about some struggles, emotionally, but you can't put your life on pause forever. It will always be difficult for her. There will never be a perfect time. You can introduce it slowly. Let her know that you've made a new female friend. And then go on from there," she suggested.

Dave sat back and listened. He let out a sigh of relief as the doctor talked. This was one of those sessions that going in he knew he just wanted her to tell him what to do. Because truth be told, he did not know how to introduce Kathy to Abby. The thought of it terrified him. He and Kathy spoke about it a few times, and she was patient and understanding. Both of her daughters had met Dave a few times already, they had even gone to the movies together once. He felt guilty that Abby hadn't been there, but he wasn't ready, and he knew Abby wasn't ready. Kathy wasn't pushing the matter, thankfully, because she understood to the best that she could, but he knew she wanted to meet her. It would be the next step in their relationship. The idea of them moving forward in a more serious direction also terrified Dave, but in a way that also excited him.

Dr. Freemont was right though. He had been separated from Ronnie the same amount of time that they had been together. He had to let her go and realize that she wasn't coming back. She had left them, for reasons that he'd never know or understand, but he forgave her. But *she* left them. *She* was the one who had given them up. And if she ever came back and Dave had moved on happily with Kathy, she had nobody to blame but herself. He couldn't wait forever.

"Yes, that's a good idea," Dave said once he realized he hadn't spoken in a while. He'd do it, eventually. He'd have to. But it still wasn't a band aid he was quite ready to rip off. Talking about ripping it off helped though.

Abby
November 16, 2019

    The Pink Ocean Spa was the crème de la crème of spas, or at least that's how Joanna's mother described it. Abby had walked by the spa before, the few times her dad had taken her out to the big, expansive mall out in the middle of nowhere, and always wondered what it would be like to go inside. It looked like such an expensive and grown-up place, and she hoped that one day she'd be like one of the fancy ladies who went inside to get their nails done. And that day had come.
    As she stepped over the threshold and transitioned from bland mall tile to shiny marble, Abby felt a transformation come over her. Shoppers eyed her as she stepped inside with Joanna and her mother, and it made her feel important as they watched the glass doors close behind them. The doors blocked out the sound of the busy mall, and the soothing sounds of flutes and waves greeted them. Abby was one of those fancy ladies now, and a warm happiness spread through her.
    A water fountain tinkled softly off to their immediate left, and as they passed it, Abby saw red and gold koi fish swimming inside. A sparkling chandelier hung above the reception desk, where two glamorous ladies in white coats smiled at them as they approached. Expensive body products lined the walls behind them, and scented candles sat in neat pyramids on the corners of the desk.

"Newcamp, party of three," Joanna's mother said as they got to the front desk. Joanna looked over at Abby and grinned, as the receptionist clicked behind the desk and then summoned another glamorous looking woman to take them in.

The calming aromas became stronger the further they walked into the spa. Joanna's mother chatted with the woman in the white coat, who led them into a grand waiting room. Soft plush couches were scattered about, where waiting men and women sat either chatting softly or reading magazines. Some of them were in light coral robes, while others were still in their regular clothes. A buffet was up against one wall and there were platters of cheeses, crackers, and fruits, as well as carafes of teas, coffees, and different flavored waters.

Joanna's mother led them over to one couch, and Abby sat down next to Joanna. The woman in the white coat offered them some of the flavored water, and Abby picked the one that had orange slices and blueberries floating in it, the same as Joanna. It tasted like the summer that had just passed and brought back warm memories of playing on the street, swimming at the beach, and running through the woods.

"Have you ever been here before, Abby?" Joanna's mother asked as she settled into the plush sofa with a glass of wine.

Abby shook her head as Joanna said, "No, mom, I told you. She's never even had a manicure or pedicure before."

"Oh! Well, glad we can change that then," her mother responded.

Abby felt her cheeks go pink, and she looked down into her water and the fruit floating around. What Joanna said wasn't *entirely* true. Her grandma had done mani and pedi parties before, just for the two of them at her house. Those experiences didn't count, Abby knew, though they had still been fun. But that was when she was a little kid, and this was the real deal now. Her grandma had talked about bringing her to a salon to get a real manicure a few times, but Joanna's invitation beat her to it.

Another woman in a white coat came and called for their party. She led them down a different maze of halls and into a room where the smell of nail polish was prevalent, albeit slightly masked by an array of oil diffusers that misted into the room. Three empty, large, black leather chairs sat in a row near the back of the room, and that's where the woman led them. Joanna's mother took the one on the end, while Abby took the one on the other and Joanna sat between them. Two more women in white coats were already waiting by the chairs, and the one at Abby's chair introduced herself as Cheryl. She had bright orange glasses, dark red dyed hair, and a friendly smile.

"Is this your first time?" Cheryl asked Abby as she filled up the tub at her feet with water. Abby nodded and Cheryl smiled. "Let me know if the water is too hot for you, OK? You let me know if you need anything."

"You're going to love it," Joanna's mother purred. She leaned across Joanna and winked at Abby. "When I took Joanna for the first time, it was magical."

Joanna rolled her eyes once her mother looked away and Abby forced a grin. As she sat there with Joanna and her mother, who idly chatted to Joanna about some family event that had nothing to do with Abby, she wondered if she should have waited to go with her grandma for her first time. It seemed like one of those small milestones that was usually a mother-daughter experience, one that her mother had robbed her of because she left, but one that could easily be made up by going with her grandma.

As the esthetician worked on massaging her feet, Abby looked around the pedicure room and felt a bit out of place. There were a few groups of older women chatting together, a few singletons, but there were also quite a few obvious mother-daughter duos. There was one mother with two teenaged daughters laughing uproariously about something, another older woman with her adult daughter, and then a mother-daughter duo around Abby and Joanna's age. Abby questioned whether she had robbed a first time experience from her grandma, the same way her mother had robbed it from her. There was nothing she could do about it now, except sit there and feel guilty.

When she returned home later, nails done in shiny and bright sparkly colours, Abby was surprised to find her grandma there.

"Your dad had to step out last minute for a work emergency," her grandma said as she shut the door behind Abby. "Did you have fun with your friend? Did you say thank you?"

Abby groaned on the inside. Her grandma was the "thank you" police.

"Yes, Grandma. I said thank you," Abby mumbled. She looked down at her feet and sighed.

"What's wrong, sweetie?" her grandma asked. "Did you not have fun?"

"No, I did," Abby said. She had a lot of fun once Joanna paid attention to her again and ignored her mother. The two of them giggled as they went through the vast array of colours to choose from, and Cheryl had done a little extra work on Abby's nails since it was her first time. She drew a heart on one of her thumbs, and a sun on one of her big toes. "But I just... I feel bad."

Her grandma lifted her chin and looked down at her. Abby had long forgotten what her mother really looked like. She would sometimes appear in her dreams, and nightmares, and Abby secretly looked through old photos of her when she was alone. But she knew she had the same eyes as her grandma, the same eyes that she had herself, and seeing those eyes look down at her full of concern and love, made Abby tear up.

"Why do you feel bad, sweetheart?" her grandma asked in a soft voice. Grandma's voice was always soothing and made her relax, just like her father's voice did. It made her feel secure, safe, and loved.

"Because I should have gone for my first time with you, Grandma," Abby blurted. "I'm sorry I went with Joanna instead."

Tears spilled from her eyes as her words came tumbling out, and before she knew it, her grandma pulled her into a warm embrace. She chuckled softly and stroked Abby's hair, and as she pulled back, she wiped the tears from her face.

"Oh Abby, you are such a sweet girl. You have nothing to be sorry about!" her grandma reassured through her smile. "I'm glad that you went and had fun with your friend. And you know what? It doesn't matter that I wasn't there for your very first time, because it will still be so, so special when we go together for *our* first time. Nothing can take away from that."

Abby didn't think of it like that. Her grandma, as usual, was right. It *would* still be special the first time they went together, because it wasn't something they had done together before. It would differ from when she and Joanna went, because it would be with family, likely at a different spa, with different colours to choose from and different flavored waters. And it would be magical, like Joanna's mother had described going with Joanna the first time had been.

"Now," her grandma said. She held Abby out at arm's length and grinned at her. "Let me see what colours you chose."

December 24, 2019
Dear Abby,

    Lisa and Eli are fast asleep on the floor of the living room. They set a trap for Santa and were trying so hard to wait up to see him. They spent the entire day coming up with a plan and drew various diagrams and made this sort of trap-thing out of our new fridge's box. Their imagination makes me smile. I snuck over to Mrs. Hannigan's to borrow one of her deceased husband's old black work boots and am going to put them into the trap, configure it in a way that it looks like their trap almost worked. There is nothing more magical than being Santa for your children. I wish I could send a bit of this magic to Abby. I wonder if she still believes at this age. I remember you let me believe until I was nearly thirteen. Sometimes I still do believe.

Abby
January 18, 2020

The house smelled like chicken. It was warm and comforting, and Abby's stomach rumbled, and her mouth watered just thinking about it. It was her favourite recipe, the one that her dad saved for special occasions or when she felt sad. Today, however, she felt apprehensive.

Soft music tinkled through the speakers, the sound interrupted by the doorbell's ring. Abby stayed where she was on the couch, staring at the page of her book she'd been trying to read for the last ten minutes. The words just sat there on the page, her brain unable to absorb them and the story stood still. The music in the background faded into white noise as she listened to her dad open the front door, and his comforting soft voice greet an unfamiliar, high-pitched laugh. She felt her shoulders tense. The door clicked behind them as their voices melded together in greetings and giggles, and soon they appeared around the corner and into the living room.

"Abby," her dad called. Abby didn't want to look at them, but it was too late. She glanced up briefly and then couldn't pretend she didn't hear or see them. She couldn't pretend she didn't see her dad's smile, how his eyes sort of lit up, and just how plain happy he looked. It was there, right in front of her, and now she couldn't ignore it like she had been since she figured out he had a girlfriend.

"This is Kathy. Kathy, this is my daughter, Abby."

Kathy smiled at Abby. "Nice to meet you, Abby."

Abby nodded as she surveyed Kathy. Her sandy blonde hair was pulled back with a clip, and she wore a cream-coloured cardigan over a white top. When she smiled at Abby, expecting some sort of reaction from her, lines bracketed each side of her mouth and showed her straight white teeth. It was a friendly smile, and she looked nice enough, but something flipped inside Abby's stomach, and it didn't make her feel well.

"Hi," Abby mumbled after a minute. The delay was obvious, and Kathy smiled nervously at her dad.

"Come in, I'll get you a drink," Dad said. He headed over to the kitchen. Kathy hesitated for a minute before sitting on the couch with Abby. Their couch was a big L-shape, and Abby was thankful for it. Kathy sat on one end, while she stayed where she was on the other.

After another moment of awkward silence, Kathy pointed to Abby's book. "What are you reading?"

Abby closed the book and flashed the cover to her quickly before hugging it close to her chest. She didn't want to talk to Kathy. The pit in her stomach turned, and she felt queasy. She tried to relax because she knew this was important to her dad, and when he came back from the kitchen with drinks for him and Kathy, Abby noticed again how happy he was. This was a special moment for him, and she wanted to keep it that way. But it was difficult.

All Abby thought about throughout the evening, as she gave brief answers to the questions Kathy asked and weak-returned smiles to her father when he smiled at her, was her mother. Sometimes her mother would visit her in her dreams, and would tell her to keep up hope, that she was coming back with Eli. Her brother was still a baby in her dreams, even though Abby knew that by now he'd be a grown-up kid like she was. And even though those dreams came when she was in her deepest sleep and when she'd wake up, she'd barely remember them, that feeling of hope would still be there. She'd wake up feeling renewed and full of purpose.

Now though, as she looked across the table at Kathy, that feeling of hope rotted within her. Abby looked back down at her chicken. It was her favourite meal, but it tasted sour in her mouth. Her dad said something, and Kathy laughed. It sounded like a duck quacking and bothered Abby's ears. When the laughter stopped and Abby looked up, she realized they were both looking at her.

"Remember, kiddo?" her dad said. When Abby didn't answer right away, her dad's smile faltered, and his look changed to concern. Abby quickly forced out a small laugh and nodded before looking back down at her chicken.

The rest of the evening was a blur. Abby faked not feeling well to get out of playing a board game with them. She knew by the look on their faces that they knew she was faking it, but Abby couldn't go through with it any longer. The feeling in her stomach, the uneasiness and heartache, continued to grow and grow, and she just wanted Kathy to leave. She couldn't tell her dad that though, so faking a stomach-ache was the next best thing.

Once up in her room and out of earshot of them, Abby burst into tears. It surprised her and made her cry more. She crawled onto her bed and under her blanket. The last thing she wanted was to cry too loud and to ruin the rest of her father's evening.

Under the safety of her blanket, she let her tears flow freely and loudly, and she pulled out a photo from underneath her pillow. It was worn and crinkled, a photo of her mother and herself when she was a baby. Her mother's smile was bright and shone in her eyes, and Abby's chubby cheeks were dimpled and red. She looked like Eli, or at least how she remembered him. Abby had found the photo in a frame once while looking through boxes for a long-lost toy, and she hid it under her pillow to keep her mother close. She looked at it often, particularly when she was sad. Now when she looked at it, it made her cry harder. Why did she have to leave?

At some point, long after her tears had ended, her dad knocked softly on the door.

"Abby?" he asked as he opened the door an inch.

"Come in," she mumbled from under the comforter.

The bed shifted as her dad sat. Abby took a deep breath and came out from under the blanket. There would be no avoiding him.

She hoped to fall asleep before she'd have to talk to him, but her mind wouldn't stop racing.

Her dad looked at her with that look of concern in his eyes. It was mixed with something hopeful and something hurting as well. The second she looked at him, her eyes watered, and tears streamed down her cheeks.

"I take it you didn't like Kathy then, huh," her dad said. There was a twinge of disappointment in his soft voice, and he looked away from her for a moment.

"I'm sorry, Daddy," Abby cried. Her voice quivered, but she tried to keep it steady. She tried so hard to keep it together for him, but she couldn't. She just couldn't. "It's not that I don't like her. She seems really nice. But… but…"

Her dad sighed. He pulled her close to him and she buried her face into his shoulder.

"I miss Mom," Abby sobbed. "Do you not love her anymore? Is that why you're with Kathy now?"

It was a question that she wanted to ask him when he first told her about Kathy, but she didn't know how to. Now there was no holding back. She had to know if her dad had moved on. She had to know if this meant that he had given up on Mom coming home or maybe he knew she wasn't coming home. Maybe there was something he was hiding from her, and he knew what had happened to her and Eli.

"No. I will always love Mom," her dad said without hesitation. "I just don't know if she's ever coming back."

"What if she does though?" Abby asked. She wiped the tears as they ran down her cheeks.

Her dad sat quietly for a few moments. "Then… that would be great," he said at last.

Abby smiled at that thought and snuggled in close to him. He hugged her close and rubbed her shoulder. The feeling was soothing and soon she felt herself drifting off. Just before she fell asleep entirely, she had to ask him one more thing.

"Promise me you won't go out with anyone else," she mumbled dreamily. "Promise me you won't give up on Mommy."

Her eyes were heavy, and she could not keep them open any longer. Just as the last few moments of consciousness drifted away, she heard her dad whisper back, "I promise."

March 18, 2020
Dear Abby,

 There is nothing worse than seeing your child in pain. I can't handle it. Poor Lisa dislocated her knee. It was horrible because at first, we had no idea what was going on. She and Eli were playing in the living room, and the next thing I know Eli is running to find me to tell me that Lisa is in pain, and she can't move her leg. She'd been sitting cross-legged and lifted her foot up to look at something on the bottom of it, and her knee popped out.
 I had to carry her to the car, and we went to the hospital. Of course, hospitals make Eli nervous since he's been there so many times because of his allergies. He started having a mini-panic attack, while also trying to be strong for his sister. Then I almost had my own anxiety attack trying to hold it together for the both of them as the nurse popped Lisa's knee back into place. This is why parenting is a two-person job. Vomit, diarrhea, I can handle. Pain, I can't.

Dave
July 28, 2020

    The sound of the campfire's crackle was calming. The dark night sky above them was clear, stars twinkling high in the midnight blue abyss. The moon was behind them, its reflection shimmering on the lake, and Dave took in a deep breath of the fresh air. It was late, and he procrastinated about going to sleep.

    Abby slept in her canvas chair on the other side of the fire. Wrapped up in her favourite fleece blanket, she looked quite peaceful. They spent this last day of camping on the lake. Dave bought them each one of those big animal floaties and it was the hit of their trip. Every day Abby raced down to the water to jump onto her giant unicorn. Dave bought himself one of those inflatable mattresses in the shape of a pizza slice. Abby thought it was hilarious.

    In the morning, they'd be packing up their tent and sleeping bags, and heading back home. Their trip was amazing. Dave really focused on his time with Abby. He made sure there was a smile on her face every day. He let her pick which paths in the forest to explore, what they ate for dinner, and what games they played on the grassy patch next to their tent site. Anything to keep his mind occupied. Dave dreaded going back home. Their annual camping trip this year was a distraction of the heartache he left at home.

It was months after the dinner debacle with Kathy, when Abby asked him to break up with her. At first, Dave was just bummed out by the situation. Abby was his first priority and if she was that upset about him moving on, then he wouldn't. Not until she was older, no longer a child, and could accept the fact that Ronnie was not coming home. Had things gone well, Dave hoped to bring Kathy and her daughters on this trip. Abby would have friends to play with. They'd laugh, play tag, and all jump on the giant unicorn together. Kathy and Dave would cuddle with one another in front of the fire. It would be the start of them all moving forward together.

Dave sighed as he looked away from Abby and into the flames in front of him. Oranges and yellows blurred together as grey smoke rose into the air. He wasn't mad at Abby. As hard as it was on him that his *wife*, the person who he vowed to love and live with for the rest of his days, had left him, he knew deep down that it was harder on Abby. It was difficult to explain to a child why someone might leave, even if that situation was not violent or abusive. Mental health was hard to describe even to adults and sometimes, unless you felt the same suffering, it was hard to relate to. There was no way that he could have continued with a relationship, no matter how happy it made him, if it upset his daughter so much.

At some point in her life, Abby would accept that Ronnie was gone, and they would all be able to move on. And he hoped her therapist would help her see that, sooner rather than later. For now, though, he promised her that he wouldn't give up on Ronnie returning, because deep down he wanted to believe it could be true.

A light summer breeze wafted by as Dave closed his eyes and took another deep breath. When he opened up his eyes, he imagined another way that this camping trip, how all the camping trips, could have been. Next to Abby, in a matching canvas chair would be Eli. He too, would be curled up with his favourite blanket, fast asleep. Dave imagined him blonde like Abby. Eli would have picked a dragon or shark inflatable for the lake, and he and Abby would have had balancing contests to see who could stay standing on theirs the longest as they tried to push one another off.

Cuddled next to Dave in front of the fire would be Ronnie. Her hair would smell like lake and lavender, and she'd be in her favourite pair of floral yoga pants. Dave would have his arms wrapped around her, and the four of them would be at peace. The kids would whine about having to leave the next morning, and Ronnie would cheer them up with promises of riding bikes and running through the sprinklers. She would make homemade popsicles and Dave would cook meat on the barbecue for dinner in their home together.

The fantasies of summers-that-would-have-been were interrupted as he heard Abby stir across the fire. The ghosts of Eli and Ronnie disappeared as he opened his eyes, and a sinking feeling filled his soul. But then Abby smiled sleepily at him from across the fire and as she yawned, Dave smiled back as the feeling slowly went away. At least he wasn't left completely alone when Ronnie disappeared. If she could have left him only one gift, she'd left the best one.

August 30, 2020
Dear Abby,

Why must summer end? The late nights, the laughs, the memories. The kids are excited for school to start, and while I am definitely looking forward to them being at school all day, there is also this part of me that just dreads being away from them. They keep me tethered and grounded, and lately I feel like I've needed more of that. Maybe I'm just not looking forward to the cold and dark of winter. Sometimes I think we should have just stayed in Maui.

November 25, 2020
Dear Abby,

On the days when I can't see clearly, I think about how I should have left Eli with Dave. Setting aside that I didn't know about Lisa at that time, if I had done that, then if I had to leave again it would be easy. Today is one of those days. What would happen to the kids if I were to leave now, if I were to join you on the other side? Winter is so dark and long. It's so hard to get through, and if it weren't for the kids and their smiles... I think I'd have left by now.

I was close to joining you once. So miserable and depressed, lower than I'd ever felt before at the time. It was scary. And then I met Dave, and everything changed for the better. For a little while, at least.

Dave
May 5, 2021

Dave stared at the fridge and sighed. Dinners lately were difficult. Abby was suddenly selective in what she wanted to eat, and he worried it was because the other girls at school were dieting. It was insane that the thin mentality started at such a young age. He thought he had at least until she started high school in two years before he'd have to worry about body-issues. But the other night, halfway through their spaghetti dinner, Abby's favourite, she pushed the plate away and said she no longer ate carbs. He wasn't sure what had changed in the three weeks between now and her birthday, where if he'd let her, she would have had half her cake in one sitting.

So now he stared at the fridge, wondering what kind of healthy meal he could get into her without worrying what it might do to her self-esteem. Dave tried to make them healthy meals often. It was something he struggled with for much of his young adult life, and it only turned around for good once he met Ronnie. She had been a pro at meal planning and budgeting, and when she left, it took him a few years to get back on track. He still held some grief weight around his middle, but most was gone.

The fridge still stared back at Dave ten minutes later, offering no inspiration. Abby came trudging down the stairs and into the kitchen.

"Well, I'm stumped," Dave sighed as he closed the appliance's door. He turned around and faced Abby. "What do you want for dinner?"

He resisted the urge to add "kiddo" at the end of his question. The long-term endearment he used on her since she was a toddler was no longer allowed. Abby informed him after her birthday that at the tender old age of twelve, she was no longer a kid and didn't want to be referred to as such. It broke his heart when she told him that, but Dave obliged. Kids grew up, he knew that. Every parent did. What they didn't know was when it would hit them, that pinnacle moment of change from when they stopped being a kid and evolved into an adult.

Abby shrugged and didn't make eye contact. She wore one of his old sweatshirts and it hung down to her knees, her legs skinny sticks in her black leggings. "I dunno, spaghetti."

Dave's eyebrow rose, and he crossed his arms. "The other night you said you didn't want spaghetti anymore."

"Oh yeah," she mumbled. "Well, I've changed my mind."

Dave frowned. Something was bothering her and lately, it took more and more effort to pull information out. He felt like he was losing his daughter already, and he didn't know what to do about it. Ronnie would have known what to do, how to handle it. She used to tell Dave how he was the better parent, how he had a knack of figuring things out and helping the kids in calm ways. He wished she was here now to tell him that, if not to resolve the situation itself. But she wasn't. And he couldn't allow himself to lose Abby too.

"There's nothing here that I want." Abby's voice was stilted, and she talked too fast. "We need to go to the store."

"OK," Dave said slowly, "we can go to the store. What did you want to get?"

"Nothing!" Abby snapped. Her cheeks turned red, and she avoided his eye further. "I mean, I'm just not sure yet. We just need to go to the store, OK?"

Dave watched her for a moment as he tried to figure out what was bothering her. She tucked a loose strand of hair behind her ear and tugged down on the sleeve of the sweatshirt. He noticed now that her eyes looked puffy, as though she had been crying upstairs. The clock ticked on the wall behind him, filling the silence, as he took two steps forward and gently placed his hand on her shoulder.

"Abby," he said. "What's wrong?"

"I just need to go to the store," she said. "Like, right now."

"What is it?" Dave pressed. "What do you need to get so badly that you won't just ask me outright?"

A sob escaped her. She sniffled loudly and when she finally looked at him, her bright blue eyes were full of tears. "I need to get some pads, OK? There. I said it."

Dave felt his own cheeks go red as he caught on. It made sense now, the big baggy sweater, the black leggings, avoiding his eye, and he felt foolish for not having figured it out. He thought he had more time before Abby hit womanhood, but when he Googled it later after they'd returned from the store, he learnt that twelve was the average age. He was unprepared for this moment and didn't have time to prepare or know any more on the situation than what he already knew.

"Abby," he said in a soft voice. He smiled, despite how uncomfortably he felt about the situation, uncomfortable because of his unpreparedness, not because of his daughter's biology. "It's completely natural. This is what your body is designed to do, what a woman's body does. It just means you're transitioning out of being a child."

"I know that," Abby snapped.

Dave was taken aback. "Then what's wrong?"

"I'm mad at Mom!" she yelled.

The clock ticked louder on the wall and surrounded the elephant in the room that was Ronnie's absence. It wasn't something that they talked about or acknowledged often anymore. Whenever Abby brought her up, Dave would answer her questions or regale her with stories. He always tried to keep Ronnie in a positive light, despite the negativity her absence brought. Otherwise, they just tiptoed around the elephant.

"She should be the one telling me about this, not you," Abby continued through her tears. "All of the other girls in class had their talks with their moms. I learned everything for the first time through the health video Mr. Berner showed in class, and everyone else already knew everything. It was so embarrassing! And Casey's mom took her out for a mother-daughter date when she got her first period and—"

Silence filled the end of her sentence and she looked away from Dave again. He took a deep breath and as he pulled her into a hug, she sobbed. He held her tight and let her cry. The last time she had an outburst like this against Ronnie, it was a tiny detail about the situation that was really bothering her. True, she was mad at her mother; Dave was mad at Ronnie too. The hurt of what she had done to them was small, and dull, but still there. And it always would be. They had adapted and moved on, become a dynamic duo, but now and then a bump would come up, like menstruation, and it would send them back to where they felt confused, hurt, and angry.

"I don't know which kind to get." Abby's words muffled as she spoke into his shoulder. But there it was. The main underlying cause to her outburst. The little thing that was really a big thing to her. She was mad at her mom because she didn't know what kind of pads to buy, and she didn't think Dave knew what to do. He didn't blame her. He did not know about the different products.

"Me neither, kiddo," Dave said. He mentally winced at his "kiddo" slip, but Abby didn't react, so he pressed on. He pulled back so he could look down at her face and wipe away her tears. "But you know what? We'll figure it out together. Like we always do."

Abby
June 18, 2021

"Ugh, slow dance," Scarlet said as the songs changed over. She and Abby stopped dancing and moved towards the wall on the right-side of the gym. Twinkling lights hung all around, along with a variety of blue, white, and silver streamers. The theme of the dance was "Under the Night Sky," and the teachers and school staff had done a wonderful job transforming the gym. Abby glanced around at the beautiful decorations and wondered if her dad would let her put a string of lights up in her room. There was something magical about them that she wanted to capture and take home. She had fairy-lights as a child, but she was too old for those now.

This was Abby's first dance. It was for the Grade 6 & 7 students, as a farewell for the year. All month long, Abby and Scarlet talked about the dance and how amazing it was going to be. Scarlet's older sister always showed off her fancy dresses when she went the last two years, and the two younger girls were envious. Scarlet's older sister always reminded Abby of Cinderella in her fancy dresses, and so that's the look Abby had gone for when she searched for a dress. It took three shopping trips later between her dad and grandma to find the perfect outfit, but they found *the* dress just last weekend.

A pale blue, made of flowing chiffon, it matched the hue of some streamers hanging from the gym's ceiling. It tickled the bottom of her knees and swished as she swayed back and forth as the slow dance began. Her silver shoes sparkled under the light of the disco ball. It took some convincing, but her dad let her buy shoes that had a bit of a heel. Scarlet's sister called them kitten heels, which Abby thought made little sense because they had nothing to do with cats. But they made her feel fancy and grown up. Only two other girls had any sort of heels on, and finally Abby felt like she was the one ahead of the game. The motherless girl for once was on the up-and-up with growing up into a woman.

Most of Abby's classmates gravitated away from the dance floor and onto opposite sides of the walls as the slow song started up. None of the twelve-year-olds dared to ask each other to dance. When the fast songs played, they'd all get together in their respective friend circles and dance like crazy. But as soon as those slow songs came on, they'd suddenly turn into strangers and pull apart, boys on one side, girls on the other. Some of the older kids from the Grade 7 classes would dance together. They were mostly from the popular crowd, and so far, it was always the same three couples who got together to dance slowly.

Suddenly, Scarlet jabbed Abby with her elbow. Abby snapped her attention away from the popular kids slow dancing in the middle of the gym and gave Scarlet a dirty look. She had pointy elbows and Abby's side hurt.

"Ow," Abby hissed. "What is it?"

Before Scarlet could answer, Abby looked up to see her friend Greyson standing in front of her. He stared down at his shoes mostly but kept glancing up at Abby.

"Abby, do you want to dance with me?" he asked.

The light from the disco ball swirled around her as she stared at Greyson. Her heart suddenly pounded, and she felt her cheeks flush. It was ridiculous to feel this way, she thought, because Greyson was her friend. He was one of her good friends, and all he was doing was asking her to dance. As friends. But it was a slow dance and somehow that made it different. Slow dances were for couples.

"Sure," she said once she thought her heart stopped pounding. Only, it didn't stop pounding. It hammered more as she followed him out into the middle of the gym floor. Greyson stopped and turned to face her. He looked nervous as he reached his hands out and placed them on her waist. His hands were sweaty through the chiffon fabric, and Abby felt her own palms sweat as she placed her hands on his shoulders.

They stood far apart and swayed awkwardly to the music. Abby was happy that he couldn't see how red her cheeks were in the gym's low lighting. She glanced back at Scarlet who was having a fit of silent giggles as she watched the two of them.

"You look really pretty," Greyson said.

"Thank you," Abby blushed. She loved the dress she was wearing, and her grandmother had come over to help curl her hair. Once her dad had dropped her off at the school, she and Scarlet snuck on some eyeshadow in the bathroom. When her eyes met Greyson's, they both looked away quickly and avoided eye contact for the rest of the song. A few more couples braved the dance floor before the song ended. Butterflies flitted in Abby's stomach the entire time.

Once the song was over, Greyson let go of Abby, and hurried back towards his group of friends. Abby turned back towards Scarlet who grinned from ear to ear and demanded that she tell her everything.

"There's not much to say," Abby shrugged. Her cheeks still felt flushed, and she couldn't stop smiling as Scarlet continued to prod her on what it was like to dance with a boy.

"Besides," Abby said as they made their way back onto the dance floor as the next fast song started. "It was only Greyson."

Dave
August 23, 2021

It was a boring Monday evening. The sunset was long gone, and the weather slowly changed from dry to wet. Light rain pattered against the windows as Dave finished loading the dishwasher. They had barbecue for dinner and ate outside on the patio in the warm summer air. The season ended, and Dave tried to soak up the last bit of it with Abby as much as he could. She was going into her last year at elementary school, and next year would be a teenager. His baby was growing up so fast in front of his eyes, and he felt like he couldn't keep up.

His phone suddenly buzzed on the counter next to him. The screen lit up with a text message and then went black again. A second later, another one came in, and then another one after that. Dave wiped his hands on his pants, and picked up his phone, squiggling the unlock code on the screen. A bright picture of Abby laughing at the beach was his background, and he smiled. It was one of his favourite new pictures, taken during their camping trip this past July, and it was one of their best trips yet. There wasn't a day that they hadn't laughed together, and neither of them had wanted the trip to end.

The messages were from Kathy. Dave felt like a snake whenever he messaged or spoke to her. Despite promising Abby over a year ago that they would break up, and that he wouldn't give up on

Ronnie, which deep down he never would, he continued to see Kathy in secret. It was much more casual than what it had been before. It hurt Kathy at first when Dave told her he didn't think they should see each other any longer. Hurt, but understanding to an extent. And yet, somehow, at least once a month they still got together.

It started last summer, right before the school year began. Sometimes it was for a romantic date, other times it was just for a quickie. Maybe, if it kept up, in a few years he'd get a feel for where Abby was at, and then reintroduce Kathy. His feelings for her had stalled as they maintained this friends-with-benefits relationship, but if they were to *really* pick things up again, he knew they'd go the distance. But for now, they kept it casual. Dave hated betraying Abby, but Ronnie disappeared nine years ago. At some point, as she grew up, Abby would accept that she was never coming back.

You need to come over. Now, read the first message. It was blunt and unlike Kathy.

I don't want to explain over the phone or text, said the second.

The girls are at dance and won't be home until 8; try to come before then, read the third. Kathy's daughters never had a problem with Dave, but for the sake of consistency, they also thought the two of them were broken up.

Dave glanced at the clock. It was a quarter after seven. Kathy lived about ten minutes away. Depending on what this emergency was, he could be in and out before eight. He knew this wasn't a booty-call. There was an urgency behind the messages.

"Abby!" Dave called up the stairs.

"What?" she called back. She appeared at the landing, already in her pajama pants, iPad in hand.

"I need to pop into the store for a bit," Dave said. His stomach flipped, and he felt greasy as he said it. There was nothing more that he hated than lying to Abby. "There's an emergency, and the assistant manager isn't able to handle it. I'll be back around eight."

"OK," Abby said. Her attention was already back to her screen, and Dave could hear the music from the candy matching game she played.

"Don't answer the door for anyone," Dave instructed, "and—"

"I know, Dad," Abby said, annoyed. Now that she was twelve, Dave let her stay home alone for small amounts at a time. It always made him feel nervous, but he knew it made Abby feel grown up and independent. It was an important rite of passage, and he knew she was responsible. Still, he couldn't help but parent her every time he left her alone.

On the drive to Kathy's house, Dave tried to think of what she would want to say to him in person that she wouldn't want to over text. He had a few scenarios in mind, but nothing prepared him for the real reason.

"I'm pregnant," she said as he followed her into the living room once he arrived at her house.

Dave felt the colour drain from his face. A range of shock, fear, queasiness, and guilt ran through him. He sank onto her couch, mouth slightly agape, as he tried to think of what to say.

"Or at least, I think I am." Kathy's hand shook as she ran it through her light hair, and she sat down in the chair across from him. "I had a negative test a few days ago when I realized I'm a bit late. Tested yesterday morning, and it was positive. It could have been a false positive because I started spotting a bit this morning, and…"

She trailed off and put her head into her hands. A small sob escaped her mouth, and Dave went to comfort her. He crouched down before her and put his arm around her shoulders.

"So, what does this mean then?" Dave asked. It was a dumb question, but he didn't know what else to say. He didn't know how to act or feel at this moment, only that he needed to comfort her. One step at a time, he thought.

"I'm sorry," Kathy sighed. She lifted her head and pulled away from him as she wiped the tears from her face. "I just couldn't keep this a secret. I have a doctor's appointment tomorrow to get some bloodwork done, just to be sure. But I have another home test I can take now. I'm sure it was a false positive, maybe a chemical pregnancy…"

Kathy trailed off again. Dave nodded, and she stood up to go to the bathroom. The clock ticked loudly on the wall. It was an antique clock that had once belonged to her grandmother. It was big and brass. Dave thought it was ugly, but Kathy loved it. She loved a lot of old-fashioned things, which showed around her house. Lace doilies, floral pillows, and ornate picture frames. They contrasted against her modern couch and coffee table, but showcased Kathy's personality.

As Dave stared at the couch, remembering that it had been the last place that they had been intimate a month ago, Kathy came back out from the washroom. She placed the stick onto the coffee table, and together, they both stared at it.

"Three minutes," she said.

Dave stared at the white stick. In a manner of minutes, things were drastically about to change, he thought as the clock continued to tick loudly behind him. It was when Kathy was in the bathroom that he realized something profound; he didn't want any more children. He might not have a choice in the matter, depending on what the stick told him in a few minutes, but that realization was suddenly clear as day in his mind. The desire to have a family was behind him. He *had* made a family, with someone whom he loved with all his heart, and that had blown up in his face. Half of that family was missing, possibly dead, and he'd never see them again. The part that remained was the most important thing in his life. And now, that could change.

Dave couldn't even fathom how he would tell Abby that she might be a big sister again. It would mean revealing that he lied to her about breaking up with Kathy. They would need to get married, or at the very least live together. Their families would suddenly become blended and entwined together, and Dave realized that was something that he did *not* want. He cared for Kathy, that he was sure of, but this white stick staring up at him from her coffee table made him see that deep down, he didn't want this to go the distance. This relationship was just skin deep and nothing more.

The sight of the stick made him feel sick. He held his breath as Kathy picked it up, the three minutes coming to their end. She held her breath too and brought the stick up at eye level.

Suddenly, she let out a loud exhale, a sigh of relief. "It's negative."

Dave too, let out a loud breath of relief. He fell back into the chair behind him and looked up at the ceiling. *Thank God*, he thought. When he looked back at Kathy across on the couch and their eyes met, he knew she felt the same. The relationship between them was over. Neither of them wanted this anymore, and definitely didn't want to go through scares like this again.

They said their goodbyes at the door, their last goodbyes this time, for sure, and Kathy said that she would confirm with him that it really was nothing once she conferred with her doctor. She was sure it was a false positive or a chemical pregnancy, for her bleeding was heavier when she went to take the test. Dave thanked her in advance for letting him know, wished her luck in the future, and they shared one last, long embrace.

As Dave got back into his car, he made a note on his phone to make an appointment with his own doctor for a vasectomy referral. He never wanted to go through this again. The thought of an accidental baby was not one that had ever crossed his mind over the years, and as he thought back to the few hookups he had, he couldn't believe how careless he acted, despite how safe the sex had been, and that his life could have changed forever in an instant. If it wasn't with Ronnie, he didn't want any more children. Plain and simple.

Abby
November 13, 2021

"Oooo, this one is cute," Joanna said. She tapped a button on her phone, and a pair of dog ears and a sparkly collar filtered over hers and Abby's faces on the screen. They made silly faces and Joanna snapped the picture. They cycled through a few other filters, one that made them angels, another that turned them into monsters. Each time they snapped the picture and Joanna saved it to her phone, Abby felt a twinge of jealousy.

For a few months now, she begged her dad to let her have a cellphone.

"Almost everyone in my class has one," she whined. Dad raised his eyebrows at her, and replied with the standard, "If everybody jumped off a cliff, would you?" retort every time.

"I promise I'll be safe," Abby said. "That's what it's for, safety."

Except it wasn't just for safety. Abby felt left out of the online chat groups through the various social media platforms. She wanted to take pictures with fun filters and save them to her *own* phone, not have to wait until Joanna e-mailed them to her later. Everyone else laughed about memes she hadn't seen, or viral videos she wasn't familiar with, and online challenges she had never heard of. She felt like she was on a different planet or stuck back in olden times. It wasn't fair that everyone was a part of this online world, and Abby wasn't because her father was too afraid of what lurked there.

A few weeks after that conversation, her dad gave her a phone. Sort of. Abby looked down at it now. It was shiny and pink, and incredibly old fashioned; it was a flip phone. There was no fancy touch screen, not even any apps. Although she could text on it, the phone was otherwise strictly for making calls.

"For your safety," Dad said. "Now you can call me if you're in trouble, and I can get a hold of you while you're out."

Abby felt like he didn't trust her. They talked about online safety in school all the time. She knew not to accept requests from anyone she didn't know, not to take inappropriate pictures, click on unfamiliar links, and to always go to her dad if she ended up in any trouble. She told him this, again and again, but he kept saying she was too young for social media. It was ridiculous. And so, the only way she was privy to that online world was when she went over to Joanna's house, and the two of them hung out in her room.

Joanna's room was like a teenagers. She had fun geometric prints on her bedspread, small lights that flashed through different colours, a plain round mirror that exuded adultness, and even a small vanity for putting on makeup. Abby knew that part of the reason Joanna seemed so much more grown up than her stemmed from her having an older sister. She had someone to look up to, to set the new fashion trends, tell her what was cool and what wasn't, and someone to blaze the path for her. Scarlet had an older sister too. Abby just had herself and her dad. And it was already clear that her dad was not up on the current times if he thought she was too young for a smartphone.

"Check this one out." Joanna interrupted Abby's thoughts. Just as she clicked on a new filter, one with pretty floral crowns, a message blipped up in front of them. Joanna giggled to herself suddenly and pulled the phone away from Abby.

"What is it?" Abby asked as Joanna clicked away. When she glanced up at the phone, Abby noticed Joanna's cheeks were pink. "Just this guy I've been chatting with," she said nonchalantly after a few moments. The air between them suddenly felt tense, and a small knot formed in Abby's stomach.

"What guy?" she asked. An uneasy feeling crept up inside her.

"His name is Josh," Joanna gushed. "He messaged me when I posted a picture in my soccer uniform the other day. We've been chatting a lot ever since. He's sort of my online boyfriend."

"So," Abby started. She glanced around Joanna's room and hesitated. Though they'd been friends for a few years now and would go to high school together next year, Abby still felt so square around her. She felt like she wasn't good enough to be her friend and Joanna didn't see it yet. Abby sometimes worried she'd bring it to Joanna's attention if she said something stupid or uncool. But the uneasy feeling inside her kept creeping up as she watched her friend type away on the phone. "So, have you met him? In person?"

It wasn't quite what she had wanted to ask, but it seemed to make Joanna relax, the air between them clearing.

"Not yet," she said after a moment. "But we were thinking maybe this weekend."

"Joanna..." Abby hesitated. "How—how do you know he's actually a kid?"

Joanna looked up from the phone and frowned. She huffed, annoyed at Abby. "Because," she said impatiently, "I just do. I know, I know, internet safety, blah blah blah, but I trust this guy, Abby. He goes to the high school across town, and said he was just out this way last weekend playing against ours. He's on their soccer team."

"OK, I was just asking," Abby said in defense.

"Well, maybe you should mind your own business," Joanna said in a harsh tone. Abby felt hurt. The phone between them blipped again a few times, almost urgently, and the little red light blinking screamed to Abby that this was a red flag.

"If he was some creep, he'd have shown it by now," Joanna said at last. "All we've done is send cute selfies back and forth, nothing more. He's Zoey's age."

That's still three years older than us, Abby thought to herself. Twelve was old enough for a cellphone, in her opinion, but not for a boyfriend.

"You can come with me to meet him," Joanna chirped as she clicked on the phone again. "You are my best friend, after all."

Hearing that, Abby smiled and relaxed. That comment made her feel good. "OK, that sounds good."

"Here, let's send a picture to him," Joanna suggested. They stuck their heads together and Joanna selected the flower crown filter. She sent the picture to Josh, and immediately, he replied.

> *U 2 r cute. Have u ever kissed each other?*

"Ew," Joanna laughed at the message. The knot in Abby's stomach suddenly twisted again and a sense of dread filled her. Before Joanna could reply, a second message came through.

> *Maybe u can both be my girlfriends. Does she have a profile 2?*

Joanna exchanged a look with Abby. She frowned at the phone and replied *no*.

"Joanna, I don't think we should talk to him anymore," Abby said. The thought of not being cool enough evaporated as her sixth sense took over. The messages made her feel uncomfortable. Joanna opened her mouth to argue, but another message came through first. This one included a picture.

> *That's 2 bad. The 2 of u are both rly pretty. Thinking about the 2 of u together makes me rly happy.*

"Oh my God, what is that?" Abby asked, horrified as she looked at the picture.

"Ew, it's a penis!" Joanna shouted. She closed the app and threw her phone across the room. The colour drained from her face and Joanna burst into tears.

Abby felt dirty. She stared at the phone on the floor, the red light blinking as more messages kept coming through and she shuddered at the thought of what else they might contain. What she had seen could not be erased from her memory. She felt violated, and knew what she had seen was wrong, but she didn't quite understand why. A small part of her felt proud knowing what Joanna had been doing was wrong. But as she looked over at her friend and wrapped her arm across her shoulders, she too cried. There was no pride in seeing her friend hurt.

"You need to tell your mom," Abby said once Joanna calmed down. Joanna sighed and pouted, and Abby wondered for a moment if Joanna would argue with her about it.

"I know," she whispered in a small voice, and Abby relaxed.

Mrs. Newcamp was horrified, as the girls expected. Joanna cried again as she spilled everything out. It upset her mother that she was talking to someone she didn't know and had planned to meet up with him that weekend. When they showed her the picture "Josh" had sent, Mrs. Newcamp confirmed Abby's suspicions that it couldn't have been a boy that was on the other end of those messages. She would report the incident to the police and hope they find the guy. Joanna told him a lot of personal information, against the online safety lectures her parents had given her, and she could be in danger now.

"No more phone for you," her mother said. Joanna argued a bit, but ultimately agreed.

When it was time for Abby to go home, she assured Mrs. Newcamp that she'd tell her father about what happened. But she didn't. She didn't want to give him the satisfaction that he had been right. The online world was more dangerous than she thought. All it took was one picture with a flower crown for this guy to expose himself to them. Suddenly, her old-fashioned flip phone didn't seem so bad, and she was no longer in a rush for a smartphone.

February 14, 2022
Dear Abby,

Sometimes I secretly wish the house would catch on fire and we'd all pass away peacefully in our sleep. It seems the easier option than waking up to another morning.

May 30, 2022
Dear Abby,

There are so many things I wish I could ask you. Did you ever feel this way? Did you too, suffer from this black void that comes out of nowhere and consumes your every fiber? Did you ever fear that when this black cloud was hanging overhead that it would just take one miniscule thing to send you over the edge and that would be it? Or was I the only one in the family born with this curse? I can only pray that I don't pass it onto my children.

The days are getting better again though. Summer is around the bend, and I have a small road trip planned with the kids. We're all looking forward to it. A change of scenery always does me good. Thankfully both kids are always sunny. At least, these two are. I don't think I have to worry about them. But Abby… I always worry about Abby. I have no way of knowing if she's OK. And that's my fault.

Dave
July 28, 2022

July 28th was always the worst day of the year for Dave. This was the day when he came home to find Ronnie was gone. The confusion, hurt, and heartache rocked him again every time on this day, whether he mentally prepared for it or not. Out of nowhere, he was reminded of what day it was, and the wind would get knocked out of him, and the rest of the day would be lost. Most times he'd keep it together until Abby was in bed, or a few times he sent her to Donna's house so that he could allow himself to wallow in pity and sadness in solitude.

This particular July 28th though, he prepped hard. At the beginning of the summer, he arranged with Jennifer Newcamp, Joanna's mother, to take Abby with them to their cabin in Kelowna for a week in late July. He was forward in his reason behind it. It was the first time he spoke more than a few simple pleasantries to the woman, and if he was honest with himself, he found her and her husband both a bit insufferable. They had money, and they didn't have a problem flaunting it. Jennifer was nice enough, not as pompous as her husband. Dave found her a bit aloof though, too busy in her own world to really *get* what was going on around her. But when he explained that this year was the ten-year anniversary of Ronnie's disappearance, she became quite serious and assured Dave no less than twelve times that Abby would be distracted and have nothing less than a good time. The assurances were overkill but appreciated. All Dave wanted was for his daughter to be having fun on the lake with one of her best friends and unaware of what day it was.

Part of him felt guilty about pushing Abby away. This was a time for them to come together. They would share stories of Ronnie, cry together, and heal together. And they *would*, Dave assured himself as he bunkered down into his man cave in the basement of his house. They would come together when Abby was home in a few days, and they'd talk about it. While he was happy that she would be distracted, Abby was a smart girl. Maybe she wouldn't quite piece together that he had sent her away on purpose because the lake trip idea and invite would come from Joanna and her mother, with Abby only needing to ask Dave if she could go, but she would bring up the anniversary herself at some point during the summer.

The main reason Dave wanted Abby away was because of the media. Last month he received calls from a Ms. Novak from the local news station. She was doing a feature on cold cases in the area, and as this was the ten-year anniversary of Ronnie's disappearance, it was to be her centre piece. Dave was speechless the first time the reporter called him, asking for his time for an interview. He stuttered a few words, if any at all, and hung up on her. Confusion was his initial reaction, quickly followed by abstract anger. Why on earth would anyone think it was appropriate to ask him to sit down for an interview about his missing wife? And son? Dave spoke little to the media ten years ago when it was fresh and current. Just because time had moved on, didn't mean Dave had.

When Ms. Novak called the second time, Dave hung up on her right away. The third time, she just asked for a quote or comment from him or Abby. He spoke to Ms. Novak that time.

"Stop calling. I have no comment. And don't you *dare* try to talk to my daughter about this," he snapped on the phone. Visibly upset, he left work early that day.

Ms. Novak had reached out to Donna and Gerald too. Donna gave a quick "it still hurts, but we hope they're happy and well, wherever they are," just to get the reporter off her back.

Despite his verbal warning to her, there were a few times in the past weeks that Dave noticed a slow-moving car in front of his house. He kept the blinds shut and curtains drawn. It didn't matter to him if his house looked the cliched dilapidated, shuttered house of a broken person if they got a shot of it on the news. Maybe it was a different reporter stalking his front door, but it didn't matter. Today, Dave was drowning them all out.

For most of the day, he stayed downstairs in his basement. If someone came to the door, he'd check the video from the doorbell camera. One was the newspaper boy leaving the paper on his porch again, despite the sign that asked to put it in a designated bin. Another was the pizza delivery guy at lunch time. Dave passed the time playing a video game online with random strangers, none of them the wiser that he was the focus of at least one news segment today.

When his hand cramped from being bent around the controller all day, and the day's sunlight became sparse through the basement, Dave stood and stretched. His spine cracked a few times, and spots appeared in front of his eyes for a few moments as they adjusted from the TV being turned off. His stomach rumbled, the pizza from lunch worn off, and he slowly resurfaced into the main entity of his house.

Today was a day for comfort food, and comfort food only. After rummaging through his cupboards, he landed on the idea of nachos for dinner. Three melted cheeses, olives, tomatoes, organic corn chips, and hot salsa in a bowl later, Dave sat content on the couch, his dinner in front of him. He took a deep breath and turned on the news. Curiosity got the better of him, as he knew it would, and he readied himself as much as he could.

The segment was a few seconds in already as he sat back and watched. A young female reporter, labeled as Cindy Ming in blue underneath, stood in front of his house with a microphone in her hand. Dave was going to complain to the station for sure. Nobody needed to know where they lived now.

"... ten years ago today, and still no trace as to what happened. Our own Lindsay Novak has the story," Cindy Ming said as Dave tuned in.

Lindsay's voice then took over the rest of the story as a picture of Ronnie appeared on the screen. Dave's breath caught in his throat, and he almost choked on a mouthful of nachos. It was the picture he provided the police with when Ronnie had disappeared.

"Ten years ago today, Veronica Sanders and her son, Eliot Sanders, disappeared from their home right here in the city without a trace. Car still in the garage, passports left behind, mother and son vanished in the middle of the night. Veronica left behind her three-year-old daughter, Abigail Sanders, alone in the house. David Sanders, Veronica's husband, would later come home to find his daughter alone, and his wife and son missing," Lindsay said. The picture of Ronnie changed to a picture of Eli. Dave's heart sank as he looked at the chubby cheeks, button nose, and bright eyes of his infant son. He remembered his bald head and his love of blowing raspberries.

Lindsay's voice continued on the screen. *"Police exhausted their search for weeks, and ultimately, came up empty handed. Just what happened to Veronica and her son? We reached out to David to get his thoughts, but he declined to comment. Many experts have weighed in on the mysterious case that took hold of our town ten years ago. Most agree that it was a sad case of post-partum depression, and that Veronica took the life of herself and her son, their bodies never found. Some believe that they might still be out there, somewhere, including Veronica's own mother, Donna Shaw. Donna says that no matter what the reason, wherever they are, she hopes they are happy and healthy. Well Donna, I think we'd all like to believe that."*

Dave nodded at the TV as he turned it off. It was what he liked to think too.

Abby
August 27, 2022

"OK, meet you back here in an hour? Hour and a half?" Dad suggested while checking the time on his phone. Abby nodded and waved him off. She walked down the mall's corridor, blending in with the people milling about, and then glanced back over her shoulder after a few minutes. Her dad had gone around the corner and was out of sight. Abby let out an exhale of relief and turned back the other way.

School was starting in about a week and a half. It wasn't just going to be another regular school year this time though. Abby was starting high school. Seventh grade was behind her now, and so was her time in elementary. Joanna would go to the same high school as her, which would be great for their friendship. Scarlet would be there too, as would Greyson, and all the kids from her elementary school. High school meant meeting tons of new kids. That meant that it was time for a whole new wardrobe, and thankfully her father agreed, after some convincing. But what her father didn't know when he had handed over a generous two-hundred-fifty dollars for spending, was that Abby was after a very specific piece of clothing for her new transition into high school.

Keeping an eye out for her dad as she walked down the corridor, Abby took a deep breath as she approached the store in question.

She wanted to get this out of the way and over with first because she didn't know what she was doing.

The lingerie store loomed in front of her. Shiny black marble floors welcomed her inside, and neon pink signs flashed before her eyes. The busty mannequins and their risqué outfits were intimidating, and Abby hesitated outside the store. She glanced around to see if anyone was watching, worried that someone she knew would suddenly pop up or that her dad would come back around the corner. With one last glance around and a deep breath, Abby quickly crossed over the threshold and walked into the store.

The inside of the store smelled heavily of some fruity perfume. Bottles lined the wall to her immediate left, and a display of underwear on a round table stood in the middle. Bikini cuts, thongs, boy shorts, lace, silk, cotton… there was one of everything. Abby didn't realize there were so many varieties of underwear. Nighties and other erotic looking outfits were to the right, and in the back of the store were the bras. They were Abby's intended target, and she bee-lined away from the rest of the garments towards the back.

High school was for the grownup kids. "Kid" wasn't even the right word anymore, Abby reminded herself. She was a teenager now, and teenagers didn't wear the little cotton bralettes from the discount store. They wore real bras, the ones with the clasps and cups. The last thing Abby wanted was to change for gym in front of the other girls and to be the only one still wearing a training bra. It didn't matter that she was still flat chested. Her training days were over, and it was time for the real thing.

The choice of bras was as complex as the underwear she had passed. There were sports bras with crisscross straps in the back and zippers up the front, push-up bras in bright colours, with tons of extra padding and scalloped edges, and strapless bras and corsets with boning in them. The wall towered before her and Abby looked from one kind to another, utterly confused as to what she was looking for. She knew nothing about bras and didn't have anyone to ask for help. Her dad would have been just as clueless as she was, and her grandma was out of town. Even if she *had* been in town, Abby wasn't sure if shopping for bras with her grandma would have been the best. It would embarrass her to bump into someone she knew while in there as it was, but it would have been a million times more embarrassing if they discovered her there with her *grandmother*.

"Can I help you?"

Abby jumped and turned around. A store assistant, a young woman in her 20s whose makeup was on fleek and had a perfect ballet bun on the top of her head, stood behind her with a quizzical look on her face. Though she asked Abby if she wanted help, her tone suggested that she really meant to say *are you lost?* The associate sized her up with a judging look, and Abby felt herself turn red and shrink. She quickly shook her head, and the clerk all but rolled her eyes at her as she returned to the front of the store.

The bras stared at Abby as she turned back to the wall. This was a mistake. She didn't know what she was doing, what she was looking for, or even how to shop for a bra. She'd just be bra-less for the rest of her life and cross her fingers that her boobs would never come in so she wouldn't have to worry about it. Another womanly thing lost on her because she didn't have someone to guide her through it. Abby felt her face turn even hotter as, to her embarrassment, tears sprang to her eyes. This was so embarrassing. She didn't belong here.

"You probably just want something like a basic cotton, t-shirt bra."

Abby turned back around. An older woman stood near her, looking at a silky red bra on the wall. She was the only other woman in the area. Abby wasn't sure if it was her who had spoken until the woman glanced over at Abby and nodded towards a section of bras over on the opposite wall.

"They're over there." The woman gave Abby a kind smile. The embarrassment died down a little, and Abby looked over to where the woman had gestured. The bras over there looked less intimidating.

"Thank you," Abby said.

"I find some of the sale clerks here can have a bit of an attitude," the woman continued. "Don't let her get you down. Let me know if you need any help. I remember how intimidating it was when I got my first bra without my mom."

Abby felt something twinge inside her. Part of it was sadness. The other part though, was a feeling of relief. Of recognition. This woman and her adult knowledge knew just what to say. She was helpful but also gave Abby her space. It was a moment that Abby would always remember, and she was forever grateful for that woman and her nonchalance.

When Abby met up with her father an hour and a half later, she felt happy.

"Find some nice things?" he asked as they sat across from each other in the food court, a big plate of poutine between them.

"Yup," Abby said with a smile on her face. She nodded as she took a big slurp of her vanilla shake. The food court buzzed around them, and the two of them sat in a comfortable silence as they ate their late lunch. Her bags were at her feet, filled with her new wardrobe for the next stage of her life. Two pairs of jeans, four new t-shirts she had scored on clearance, a new pair of sneakers, and, secretly tucked in amongst everything else, were her two new grown-up bras. She was ready for high school.

September 30, 2022
Dear Abby,

    I can't believe it! I had a meeting with the principal at the school today, along with a counselor. They think Eli should skip the fifth grade. I always knew that he was smart and mature, but this caught me off guard. I feel so proud. Eli and I talked about it, and he agreed. It won't be a tremendous change for him since he's in a five-six split class already. The school is quite small. So, the teacher and classmates will stay the same, but he'll be moving up to the sixth-grade curriculum. I'm so proud of him. I made his favourite dinner and dessert tonight to celebrate. I was worried that Lisa would be jealous, but she is just as proud. The two of them are still thick as thieves and support one another in everything. They're the best of friends, and it makes my life so much easier at times. I'm so glad they have each other.

Abby
November 23, 2022

    The rain drizzled outside of Abby's classroom window, pitter-pattering against the windowpane. The rain was nonstop since the start of the month, and she wondered when she'd ever see the sun again. Some days she felt like the rain mirrored her mood. Or maybe it was her mood that mirrored the weather. Regardless, the constant grey skies and wet grounds irritated her. She looked forward to getting a quick Hawaiian getaway with her dad between Christmas and New Year's, but it was still weeks away. Hopefully the sun would at least show its face again once more sometime between now and then.
    Science class with Mr. Everson was usually quite interesting, but today he just seemed to drone on and on and on. Abby lost track a good fifteen minutes ago on whatever it was he was lecturing about. From what she heard from Scarlet's older sister, Mr. Everson was one of the better science teachers at the high school, and Abby had agreed until now.
    High school was interesting. New friendships formed left and right, and yet, at the same time, students had fierce loyalties with those who had been together in elementary school. The girls all formed cliques quickly, and Abby was thankful that she already had two good friends heading into school at the same time, Scarlet and Joanna. She was even luckier that Scarlet and Joanna got

along, and the three of them had become a trio of besties. It would have been even better if they had more classes together, but Abby only had one class with Joanna this semester and none with Scarlet. Next semester looked better, but like her Hawaiian vacation, that was still weeks away.

When Mr. Everson took a break from his lecture and instructed the students to work independently, Abby stood from her seat and approached his desk.

"May I go use the restroom?" she asked.

"Sure," Mr. Everson said. He handed her a hall pass and off she went.

Abby took her time walking down the hall to the ladies' room. As she passed Ms. Vasallo's history class, she peeked in and saw Scarlet sitting near the front door. Scarlet caught her eye, and they made a silly face and winked at each other before Abby continued her way and Ms. Vasallo reprimanded Scarlet for disrupting the class. Abby giggled to herself as she pushed open the blue door into the bathroom, the adrenaline of almost being caught by the teacher rushing through her. The feeling soon died though as she walked into the washroom.

A loud series of sobs echoed within the white tiled walls. All the stalls were visibly open save for one at the end. As Abby walked in further, she saw a pair of hot pink sneakers poking out from underneath the stall door. She recognized the shoes and their purple laces immediately and felt a quick series of mixed emotions.

"Grace?" Abby finally asked after wrestling with her conscience. "Is that you?"

A loud snotty sniff came from within the stall as the sobbing momentarily stopped, followed by a mumbled, "Uh-huh."

Just as fast as students clicked with each other and instant friendships formed, it was easy to discern who to avoid. Grace was one of those girls for Abby. Right off the bat when they met in homeroom on the first day of school, Grace Sawyer rubbed Abby the wrong way. There was something flippant about her, the way she looked down her nose at nearly everyone, her expensive clothes, and immaculate hair styles. She even wore makeup. Grace had made some snide remark about Abby's sweater that day, which stung because it was Abby's favourite. Fortunately for Abby they only had to go to homeroom once a month, but unfortunately for her, Grace had shown up in her gym class as well. They were both athletic and an unspoken rivalry formed between them. She just didn't seem like an agreeable person and Abby didn't want to associate with her.

But hearing her cry now in the stall, Abby knew she couldn't ignore her. There was a guilt that built up inside her when she thought about doing just that, turning away and leaving the bathroom quietly without acknowledging what she heard, and Abby didn't like the taste of that guilt.

"Are you OK?" Abby asked.

More sobs came from within the stall. Abby looked down at her hall pass, wondering what to do. What would her dad do? *He'd ask her to talk it out,* Abby thought. That's how they always worked through their problems together.

Abby took a deep breath. A deep conversation with Grace was not appealing, but she had to be the bigger person here. "Do you… do you want to talk about it?"

The sobs paused again, and Grace blew her nose. The sound reverberated through the bathroom and made Abby think of an elephant playing a trumpet. A few more trumpets came from within the stall, and then at last Grace emerged. Her long black hair was a mangled mess, and black streaks streamed down her face from where her makeup had run. She looked like a sad raccoon, and Abby had to stifle a giggle at the thought, for she was clearly an upset raccoon.

"Oh, it's you," Grace said. She took a deep sigh, her breath hitching as another onslaught of tears threatened to pour.

"Do you want to talk about it?" Abby asked. She couldn't imagine what Grace would have to be upset about. The girl had nearly everything she wanted. Her dad picked her up from school in a fancy silver car, she boasted about the pool at their new house, and would tell anyone who listened about their upcoming ski trip in the Swiss Alps. The furthest place Abby had gone for skiing was Whistler, and she had quickly learned it was not her sport.

"N-Not really," Grace said. "Not to you at least."

A twinge of hurt ran through Abby, but more than anything, she felt annoyed. She rolled her eyes and headed for one of the open stalls, her need to pee suddenly coming back.

"Fine, whatever Grace." Abby rolled her eyes. "I was only trying to help. You don't need to be so rude."

Grace blinked in surprise. It surprised Abby herself, she was never that brash. Before she entered the stall, Grace reached out and softly grabbed Abby's arm.

"I'm sorry," she said after a hesitant moment. "You're right. I just… it's… I…"

Abby turned back around as Grace broke out again into incoherent sobs. With a stiff movement, Abby put her arm around Grace's shoulders, and let her cry it out for a few minutes. Once the wave of tears passed, Grace pulled away again and wiped the smeared makeup from under her eyes.

"So, what's going on?" Abby asked.

Grace sighed. Her lip trembled, but she spoke in a steady, quiet voice. "Today is my mom's birthday."

That didn't seem a reason to cry, Abby thought, but then Grace continued.

"She died at the end of July."

Any misgivings Abby had felt for Grace suddenly melted away and she saw the girl in a new light. The new clothes, gifts from her father to help mask the pain, the makeup to make to feel more grown up, the bragging about her big house and upcoming trips, all overcompensating for the pain she felt daily. Abby understood everything. Grace had built herself up as a hard exterior to hide the soft, broken person who was inside. And since it happened just before high school started, she could start fresh with this fancy, uptight popular persona and nobody would be the wiser about what was happening in her home and her heart. Everyone handled grief differently.

"Oh," Abby said. "I'm so sorry, Grace." And she meant it too.

Grace shrugged, not sure what else to say. Her most vulnerable secret was now out in the open, and if Abby had been a bad person, she'd have the power now to use it against her. But Abby wasn't a bad person. They were in the same boat. This sad exposed truth was something they had in common. And though she had never spoken the words aloud or admitted it to herself, for she wasn't even sure if it *was* true, Abby surprised herself again by saying, "My mom's dead too."

Her mouth felt dry and cottony as she spoke, and her stomach twisted like it did when she lied. But she wasn't lying, or at least, she didn't know if she was. But this idea, this notion that her mother was dead, was one that Abby had toyed with for a few years now. The idea first came up a few months after she made her father break up with his girlfriend, Kathy. A guilt had overcome her then, taking away her father's happiness and making him promise to hold out for something that may not even be possible. At the time, Abby hadn't come to the idea that it wouldn't be possible for her mother to not be able to come back. And when that rude awakening was realized a few months later, it was too late for her to go back and repair the happiness her father had found. And so, she buried her guilt away, and kept telling herself that it *was* possible, even though the idea seemed childish. Admitting it aloud now to Grace felt like a breakthrough, a breath of fresh air she didn't know she was missing.

"Oh, I'm sorry, I had no idea," Grace said. Her breath stopped hitching, and she was calmer now. She wiped her eyes again and turned around to face Abby. "How did it happen?"

Abby shrugged. "I don't know," she answered. Which was true. She did not know, and she likely never would. "I was only three."

Grace nodded. Abby worried for a minute that she would ask follow-up questions, like why she never asked her dad about what happened. But instead, she said, "Mine was a car accident…"

The tears started up again as she trailed off, and Abby wrapped her arms around her, fully this time. Grace sobbed into her shoulder. Abby held her for a long time, Mr. Everson's science class forgotten, her bladder still full, until the bell finally broke them apart and other girls entered the washroom. And though they never became close friends, Grace and Abby had an understanding from that day on, their athletic rivalry dissipated, and they cheered each other on instead.

January 8, 2023
Dear Abby,

 School is barely back in session from the winter break, and already there is trouble. It's rare for the kids to be in trouble, but today I was called in because of the both of them. Apparently, there is a boy in Lisa's class who is bullying her. I'm not sure why I wasn't told about this before, and I'm furious about it, but that's another issue.
 Anyway, today at lunch the boy was picking on her, and Eli caught wind of it. He swooped in, big-brother-mode activated, and hit the boy once it became clear that he would not leave Lisa alone. I'm just so shocked because Eli is not a violent person. Then Lisa played a prank on the boy once class had resumed. She claims the idea came from her friend, McKayla, but I don't know. She can be sneaky and conniving at times, so I wouldn't put it past her.
 They're both in trouble right now, as is the other boy. And of course, I got into a heated argument with this boy's mother. He's been tormenting Lisa for quite some time. I don't know why she didn't tell me about it, but she admitted to me tonight that she cries herself to sleep most nights. I'm so heartbroken. It reminds me of when Eli was first picked on when he started kindergarten. Of course, he and Tommy are still best friends now, even with Eli now a grade ahead. I don't see this working out the same though. And

there is only one fourth grade class, so it's not like Lisa or the boy could be moved to another classroom. Small town woes, I guess.

Abby
March 14, 2023

Scarlet's bubble-gum snapped at the desk next to Abby. Her blank stare reminded Abby of the zombies they saw in a movie last weekend. It had been a C-grade movie, something to do with people turning into zombies by playing a video game that enslaved them. They spent most of the night talking instead, and the details of the movie escaped her. But the look of the zombies matched Scarlet exactly.

Madame Le Croix lectured on and on at the front of the class. She wrote something on the whiteboard in front of her, pointed to it, and the class repeated it like drones. French was incredibly boring, and more than one of her classmates shared Scarlet's zombie-like state. But not Abby, not today at least. Today, something else distracted her, something that she didn't realize was sitting right in front of her face this entire time, and now she couldn't stop thinking about it; her crush on Greyson.

Abby had known Greyson for as long as she could remember. He lived down the street, and they had often played together in the summer months on the sidewalk. Hopscotch, bike rides, tag, chalk. Of course, they went to the same elementary school together too, but often were not in the same class, for Greyson was a year older. They had one year together when they were in a split class. That had been one of Abby's favourite years in school. Greyson was one of her oldest friends, and he was like a brother to her for a long time. A brother to replace the one she had lost.

But then Scarlet pointed out something at their sleepover last weekend. Abby had a crush on him. Abby brushed it off at first, but she slept little that night. Scarlet was right. Abby had a crush on Greyson. Whenever they played M.A.S.H. and they had to write the boys' names, she always secretly hoped that she'd end up with Greyson. Dancing with him in sixth grade was one of her fondest memories. It made her sigh dreamily when she thought about it, even though they had been children then.

Greyson was her first real crush, the kind where her stomach flipped, she felt sick when she looked at him, and an overwhelming surge of happiness would fill her whenever she spotted him. Sure, she had crushes before, in elementary school, but they weren't real. They were just the ones she said she had when her friends asked, but she didn't really know what a crush was. Everyone seemed to like Timothy Gillies, and so that's who Abby always said she liked too. This was different though.

And now, as she stared at him outside the window, butterflies flitted in her stomach. His gym class was at the same time as her French, and they often did drills outside on the field. She could see his curly brown hair and recognized his green gym shorts. Today they played rugby, and Greyson passed the ball to one of his friends. At one point he looked over towards the school, and Abby felt her cheeks flush. She knew he couldn't see her; the field was too far and the classroom window too small. But she blushed nonetheless, and her mind wandered. Maybe he would ask her out soon. Her dad probably wouldn't let her date yet, but they could do it in secret. Maybe he'd even ask her to the upcoming Winter Ball, and they'd share their first kiss…

"Abigail?"

Abby snapped back to reality. Madame Le Croix looked at her expectantly, with a twinge of annoyance. The rest of the class stared at her as well. Courteney Myers, whom Abby hated, whispered something to her stupid friend Michelle, and the two of them giggled. Scarlet rolled her eyes at them, and shook her head, bubble-gum snapping again. Abby felt her cheeks flush, and her palms sweat. She looked at the board but hadn't heard what her teacher had asked her.

"Je ne sais pas," she mumbled in response. Madame Le Croix sighed loudly and shook her head. She then repeated the question again and called upon the stoner in the back of the class. He miraculously answered the question, and Abby felt even more embarrassed. But soon the feeling passed, and she glanced out the window again. The gym class had moved on further down the field, and Abby could no longer see Greyson. She sighed and blew a blonde strand of hair out of her face. Oh well. Soon it would be lunch time, and Abby could try to spot him then. For now, as Madame Le Croix droned on and on, Abby doodled little hearts on the side of her notebook and daydreamed about how that kiss would go between her and Greyson.

July 29, 2023
Dear Abby,

The kids and I have started something new. We've taken up running together. Eli expressed interest in the track team but was too shy to try out this year. He's worried he's not good enough, and despite all my praise, he would not try out. But he's still very interested and determined, so we've taken up jogging together as a family throughout the summer to boost his confidence a bit and he'll try out next year. It's going quite well. I feel so good after a run, both kids are enjoying it, and we all find that we miss it if we skip a day. We go after dinner when the sun isn't as hot. I notice that my mood has been better since we started. It's true what they say about working out and endorphins. But you already knew that. You used to jog all the time. I wish I had gone with you. Maybe if I had and the habit developed younger, my depression wouldn't be as bad as it is now.

Abby
September 5, 2023

 Abby stared hard at herself in the mirror. Her pale skin reflected back as she studied it with her blue eyes. While some of her friends had broken out into pimples over that summer, Abby was fortunate to have inherited her father's flawless skin. That, his lips, and his dimples, which were once her most endearing feature but now she found them embarrassing and childish, were all that she got from him. The rest of what she saw was her mother.
 People constantly told her that she looked like her mother. The comments were inappropriate, or so Abby thought, considering that her mother abandoned her. Abby remembered little about her personality, but she would still see her face a lot in her dreams. Abby would go through the family albums that included pictures of her and study her face in secret. She could see the resemblance.
 In front of her on the bathroom counter were a couple of magazines flipped open and her dad's old tablet propped up against the mirror. Next to that was brand new makeup. Finally, her father gave in and told her she could start wearing makeup. Half of her friends started in the New Year, and her father was relentless on not letting her wear any until she was in the next grade. Well, today was the first day of school and Abby was ready to glam up. No more looking like a child.

Abby ripped open the packaging of her new eye liner with glee. She twisted open the top and looked at the black fine point pen. Scarlet informed her that liquid gel liner was the best. It looked intimidating to Abby, but she would try her best. Next, she opened up her mascara. The wand was cold and smooth in her hand, and the brush looked fluffy and soft when she twisted it out.

Once everything was open and spread out in front of her, Abby took a deep breath. She pressed play on her TikTok tutorial. The video sprang to life and the bubbly woman babbled on about products and techniques. Abby tried to follow along, but the woman went so fast. After pausing and starting more times than she could count, Abby groaned in frustration. She turned off the tablet and looked in the mirror. Her foundation was patchy and the eyeliner on her lids was uneven. Her right eye was thick and smoky, whereas her left was slim and classy. She looked nothing like the end result of the video or like the magazines she had opened for inspiration.

The face in the mirror no longer looked like a child. She looked like a clown. She couldn't go to school looking like this, and Abby started to cry. Tears of frustration spilled out of her eyes and the eyeliner ran. The open packages on the counter mocked her. This was nothing like how she planned her day. She would show up at school perfectly contoured, with a cool fishtail braid, and start the ninth grade off right. If her *mother* had been here, this never would have happened. She would have shown her what to do, which brushes were for which products, and Abby wouldn't have had to ask the cosmetic attendant at the store about which things to buy.

The more Abby thought of her mother and how she abandoned her as a toddler, the angrier she got. It wasn't fair. How could she just *do* something like that? Abby ripped open the makeup removal wipes and furiously wiped away the mess she had on her face. What was her dad thinking, marrying someone who would just leave her daughter behind? What an idiot.

Except, her dad wasn't an idiot. Abby stopped and stared at her fresh face in the mirror. Her dad was the nicest and smartest person she knew. He was always there for her, patient, and kind. He was her best friend, well, grown-up friend. Abby took a deep breath.

She couldn't ask her dad for makeup advice; he wouldn't know what to do. But she could take his usual piece of advice that he gave her when she got frustrated at new tasks. *Take a deep breath, be calm, and try again.* Practice makes perfect, or so they say.

And so, with renewed hope, Abby tried again. She didn't look at the magazines or watch any more videos. Her hands were steady, and she just did what she thought looked good and what made her feel good. Some simple eyeliner and mascara. And her favourite lip gloss, of course.

"There," she said with a final nod. Perfect. For her first time, anyway.

Dave
December 18, 2023

"Dave."

"Hi, Mom," Dave said with a deep sigh. She wrapped her arms around him as he stepped into her home, but he didn't quite extend the sentiment back.

The house smelled just the same as it always did. Citrus mixed with a tinge of cedar and smoke. It wasn't an overpowering smell, quite faint to be frank, but it made Dave think back on his childhood. It made him feel comfortable, despite how uncomfortable his relationship with his mother was still.

For years, his mom reached out to him to make amends. Sometimes she would get far, with Dave making plans to visit with Abby, before she would say something stupid or insensitive again, piss him off, and he would call everything off. Any snide remarks about Ronnie, missing Eli, *anything* really, would cause him to cancel. His mother was nothing but a headache in his life, and he had enough of those without her. But now was different.

"Where is Bruce?" Dave asked. "How is he?"

After a series of ignored calls and voicemails, and a few failed text message attempts from his mother, Dave called her back to learn that Bruce was sick. Sick enough that Dave kept his promise to come up and visit, purely to say goodbye to the stepfather he respected and admired. While he had nothing but a cold shoulder towards his mother for a decade now, Dave kept up with Bruce somewhat regularly. He was the olive branch that tied them together. It was through Bruce that Dave learned that the almighty Courteney turned out to be cheating behind his brother's back. The two of them divorced nearly three years ago. Courteney got full custody of the kids, the house, and the car, and drove Jeremy into the poor house. And yet, somehow, she still remained quite close to Pamela, and the two still got together often. Another testament of just how deranged Dave's mother was.

"Let me see my granddaughter first," his mother answered, waving her hands behind him. She ushered Abby in and pulled her into a tight hug. Dave turned to see Abby flash him a look of alarm and confusion. Dave's mother was not much more than a birthday and Christmas card in the mail each year. Abby barely knew her paternal grandparents. She knew of Bruce, since Dave spoke to him once every few months, but her grandmother was just a signature on the bottom of a piece of folded card stock. *Grandma Pam.* Dave barely let them speak on the phone in fear of his mother's insensibility.

"Um, hi," Abby said at last when Dave's mother pulled away.

"*So* tall," Pamela said. "And so beautiful. Just like your mother was. It's a pity you don't look more like your father, though."

"Mom," Dave warned. Less than two minutes in and it began. "Let me remind you. The main reason we're here is to see Bruce."

Pamela's smile faltered for a moment, and she sighed. She waved the two of them into the house and shuffled up the stairs and off to the left.

"Just leave your bag here," he muttered to Abby. "I haven't decided if we're actually staying *here* or if I'll get us a room in a hotel somewhere." He then went and followed his mother.

Bruce was propped up in their bed at the room at the end of the hall on the left. A machine was hooked up to him to help with oxygen, and another one beeped periodically. Otherwise, he looked the same as usual, except he was ten years older now than the last time Dave saw him. His hair was mostly gone, wrinkles lined his face, but Bruce's smile was the same when he looked up from his newspaper and saw Dave standing there in the hall.

"Dave!"

"Hey, Bruce," Dave said with a smile. "Still kickin', eh?"

"For now," Bruce said. Dave's smile faltered though Bruce had said it in good spirits. Pamela said that he only had a few months, if not weeks, left. That was the ticket that made Dave decide that he and Abby would spend Christmas with them. It would be Bruce's last.

The two of them chatted as though no time between them had passed. Abby came and sat with them for a bit, uncomfortable in the unfamiliar settings, but she laughed at Bruce's jokes in genuine, and chatted with him politely. Dave was proud of her. When Bruce commented on how much she looked like her mother, Dave didn't stop him because he knew Bruce would leave it at that, at the compliment that it was.

Hours passed as Dave spent his time with Bruce. Abby came and went a few times, and finally Pamela came in with dinner on trays for everyone. It was a delicious home cooked meal. That was one thing he missed about his mother. Her food was always the best.

"Come and help me with the dishes, Abby," his mother said once they finished their meal. Abby obliged, though she hated doing dishes. It was the one chore above all others that she argued about doing at home. She was too polite to be rude to an elderly woman she barely knew.

Once they left the room, Bruce sighed, content with food, and beckoned Dave to come closer.

"We need to talk."

"Oh? And what have we been doing this whole time?" Dave joked. But there was a serious look on Bruce's face that made Dave lean in closer in earnest.

"You need to check in on your mother more, once I'm gone," Bruce urged. Before Dave could interject, he continued. "I know that you two don't get along, that you have your issues, and that what happened with Ronnie made things worse. Jeremy will move in with her, I've already arranged that, but she needs to hear from you too. Things are hard for her. We've talked about this before on the phone. She misses you, Dave, and her granddaughter. Despite her odd relationship with Courteney, she rarely sees those girls either. All of her family has abandoned her, and I can't mend things for her once I'm gone. You know what it's like to be abandoned."

Dave inhaled sharply. "That's low, Bruce."

"I know, I know," Bruce said putting his hands up in defense. "But it's true. I think she only puts up with Courteney for some company. Courteney destroyed her older son. Jeremy is a puddle most days now, keeping to himself, dark and alone. I told him he needs to snap out of it and move in once I'm gone, and he's agreed. I know he'll hold it to himself. And I hope with him being here that Pam will get to see the girls more often. But you need to keep up with her too. Call her once a month, at the bare minimum. Let her speak to Abby too. And if she gets on your nerves... just let her. She's your mother, Dave. She's your family too. Don't let go of family when you've already lost some."

The sound of Abby laughing from the kitchen floated down the hallway. Dave's mother's laugh followed, and he felt a part of him relax. Bruce was right. And as he looked over at his dying stepfather, Dave felt a part of him crumble. He had to hold on to as much time with his family, what was left of his family, for as long as he could. Even if it annoyed the hell out of him. Because Bruce was right. He knew what it felt like to lose family, and he realized now that he'd let too much time go already with the family he had left.

February 1, 2024
Dear Abby,

 Well, it's finally happened. Tomorrow is Eli's birthday, and the gift he's asked for is to talk to his father. He wants to know more about Dave. I've gotten away with avoiding and tiptoeing around the subject long enough, and now I don't know what to do. My anxiety is skyrocketing. All I've ever told the kids is that their father lives across the country, and that they live with me. I told them that was the arrangement we had made, and that Abby chose to stay with him. They don't know the truth, and the lie I've told has turned to stone, and sits in the pit of my stomach with the other stones I've created over the years. I'm like that wolf from the fairytale. He has stones in his stomach, and then goes for a drink of water, is pulled into the river, and drowns. Maybe it's only a matter of time before I drown too.

Dave
February 29, 2024

"Chicken, pasta, toilet paper, Windex," Dave muttered to himself as he prowled the grocery aisles at the corner store. He repeated the items over and over as he strolled down the disorganized shelves, the bright fluorescent lights not helping his pounding head. Normally he would have typed the list into his phone, but his phone died at work because of not charging properly overnight. So, he had to shop as they did in the olden days, like when he was growing up, and he would just have to *remember* what Abby said they were out of. The week's full grocery shop would be on Saturday morning. This was just a few necessities to get them there.

"Windex," Dave said aloud as he grabbed a bottle of it off the shelf. The downstairs bathroom mirror was looking grungy, and it had bothered him for days now. Washing the windows and mirrors was one of Abby's chores, and she was quite good at keeping on top of them. It was his own fault that the mirror now looked like something out of a foreclosure, for she told him a few grocery trips ago now that they were out of the cleaning agent, but he kept forgetting to grab it. He tossed the bottle into his basket, continued to repeat his list, and moved down the next aisle.

The corner store was owned by a local family. It was an old fashioned Ma n' Pa store, with just enough oddity that they usually had what you were looking for. When Abby was younger, they'd ride their bikes together in the summer and get ice cream sandwiches. They stocked an off-brand name that was absolutely delicious, and that they couldn't find anywhere else. Maybe he would pick up a few tonight as a surprise. Their bike rides to the corner store had ended a few summers ago, Dave realized. Where had the time gone?

"Chicken, pasta, toilet paper, ice cream sandwiches," he recited, amending the list. The small stock of pasta appeared in front of him, and he grabbed a few different boxes. Abby didn't specify just what kind of pasta she wanted. He knew they had some spaghetti sauce at home, so he grabbed one box of that, but she also asked for chicken which may have been a hint towards chicken Alfredo, which they also had the sauce for at home. A box of penne went into the basket as well, for good measure. And for good luck, some good old-fashioned macaroni. The pasta inside the boxes rattled as Dave swung the basket around and turned the next curve. He stopped dead in his tracks and his breath escaped him.

Under the glow of the horrendous lighting, Kathy laughed down the next aisle. Her head flew back, and her eyes closed. She brushed the shoulder of a man, whose back was to Dave, standing beside her. The last time Dave saw her was two-and-a-half years ago, in her living room when she took the pregnancy test. Despite they learned they weren't meant to be, Dave felt his heart sink at the sight of her with another man. In another life, that could have been him making her laugh.

Kathy turned, and Dave's heart raced in panic. He thought about darting back down the other aisle and slipping out of the store, groceries be damned, but before he could move, Kathy spotted him. The smile on her face faltered for a minute, and he saw her deer-in-the-headlights reaction, same as his, the wheels in her head turning on whether she could duck out and pretend she didn't see him. Instead, she took a small breath, and smiled again as she headed towards him.

"Hello, Dave," she said. The smell of roses wafted from her skin, a familiar scent that brought Dave at ease. Her blonde hair was shorter, cropped to just above her shoulders, and straight with bright highlights scattered throughout. It reminded him of how it would naturally lighten in the summer.

"Hi, Kathy," he replied, thankful that his voice didn't crack. He moved his basket from one hand to the other, just to keep them busy.

An awkward silence began to envelope around them, and Dave was thankful when Kathy broke it. "How have you been? How is Abby?"

"Good, thanks," he said. "Abby's great, she's fine. How are you?"

The man she was with turned around at that moment and met up with them at the end of the aisle. Dave couldn't help but immediately judge him. He was a bit taller than Dave, lanky with little defined muscle. The glow from the fluorescent lighting made his skin look shiny and pale, but as he got nearer, Dave could see a slight tan. As he looked closer between Kathy and the man, he realized Kathy looked tanned too. The highlights in her hair weren't artificial, they were from the sun. Somewhere warm and tropical where they had been together.

"I'm doing great," Kathy said. "This is Lee." As Kathy gestured towards him, something shiny on her hand sparkled in the light. It caught Dave's eye at once, and he stared at her hand as she waved it towards Lee. Not just the massive sapphire of the engagement ring, but it was the tiny diamonds on the ring sandwiched beneath it that caught his attention. A wedding ring, a set, really. They were married. Kathy caught Dave's eye and then quickly lowered her hand.

"Hi, nice to meet you…" Lee hesitated as he extended his hand towards Dave.

"Dave, sorry," Kathy flustered. She ran her wedded hand through her hair. "Lee, this is Dave."

Some sort of recognition passed across Lee's face as he shook Dave's hand, and as Dave looked at him, past his glasses and glanced at his eyes, it was clear that Lee knew who Dave was. He knew the history between him and Kathy. This was an awkward bumping of two ex-lovers, with one of them now married and out with their new spouse. A void of uncomfortable silence sucked the air between them. Dave took a deep breath and took the first step on the high road to help them all escape the void.

"Nice to meet you," he said with a firm handshake. "Congratulations." He nodded towards Lee's left hand where a simple, gold band sat. Kathy relaxed a little, and Dave saw the tension leave her features once Lee wrapped his arm around her shoulders.

"Thank you," Lee said in a clear voice. "We just got back from our honeymoon."

"Where did you go?" Dave asked. The question was automatic and escaped him before he could react. Their answer didn't matter to him because he didn't care. A feeling of bitterness crept up within him, and he swallowed it back down to deal with later.

"We went to New Zealand," Kathy said in a dreamy voice. Her eyes were glassy as she flashed back to the wonderful time they must have had. Dave wished he had a watch on his wrist to use the time as an excuse to leave the conversation. "Lee's family originates from there, but he hadn't been there in, what was it, twenty years?"

"Probably closer to twenty-five," Lee said.

"That's great, I've heard it's a beautiful country," Dave said. The lighting of the store was making his head feel worse. He needed to escape, but he had to know one more thing. He had to know how Kathy was married to someone else, just two-and-a-half years after they broke up. "So, how did you two meet?"

Kathy's smile faltered. Her cheeks turned red, and she suddenly avoided Dave's eye. "We met through Alicia. He was her first taekwondo teacher."

Dave understood then. He nodded, they exchanged a few more pleasantries, and then Kathy and Lee went on their way. Dave paid for his items and left as fast as he could. The drive home was a bit of a blur, and it wasn't until Abby came into the garage and flicked on the light that Dave realized he had been sitting there in his car, in the dark, for who knows how long.

"Are you coming in?" Abby asked.

"Yes. Just give me a minute," Dave said. Abby went back into the house, and Dave slowly climbed out of the car. Alicia, Kathy's older daughter, expressed interest in taekwondo while they were sneaking around. He knew that she was going to start her first class a few weeks after Dave and Kathy's pregnancy scare. Kathy had met her future spouse right after they broke up. There was no mourning period for the death of their relationship, even if it had just ended up being intimate. It made Dave question everything, and he wondered just what he had even been to Kathy. Did she ever really care for him? Or had Lee been a rebound that somehow worked out?

The questions kept spinning in his head as he walked into the kitchen and put the bag of groceries on the counter. He knew he was just being bitter. This was the bitterness clawing its way back up his throat, and he could not swallow it back down. What he and Kathy had was real. If Dave's prior circumstances had been different, if Ronnie had died or if they had divorced, if she had been truly out of the picture, then he and Kathy would have gone the distance. But thinking of it that way made Dave feel bad too. He didn't want to be bitter towards Ronnie for leaving him, or towards Abby for making him break it off with Kathy, or towards Kathy for finding new happiness. He was just bitter, and he didn't know what to do with it. As Abby had once exclaimed to him when she was younger, he suddenly had all these *feelings* and didn't know what to do with them.

"Ugh." Abby's moody grunt and teenage death stare broke Dave out of his bitter trance. The grocery bag was in front of her, and she shoved it further down the counter, clearly annoyed. "Dad, you forgot the chicken."

"Sorry," Dave said in a small voice. Abby didn't notice his misery. She was in that wonderful teenage phase where she didn't notice or care about anyone else's well-being except for her own. Except now was a time that he needed someone to care about him.

Abby
May 25, 2024

    The setting sun's reflection sparkled on the ocean's surface. It was like staring at a million glittering diamonds and the warm breeze previewed the summer season ahead. The day had been full of fun and laughter, and now, Abby sat on a bench, with the boy she adored and a cone of bubble-gum ice cream in hand.

    Abby, Joanna, and Scarlet had planned this beach day for a while now, after weeks and weeks of dreary and irregular May rain. When the forecast came that finally they were going to get a break of sun and that it was going to be warm, *hot* even, they immediately planned a day at the beach. What they hadn't planned was that halfway through the day they would meet up with Greyson and his group of friends, and that the day would turn into an absolute adventure.

    The seven of them ventured off the main part of the beach, far out to where the promenade ended, and there was nothing but nature. The tide was far out, giving them access to rock formations and secret caves that were usually inaccessible. When the tide came back in, they raced the water back to civilization, and cracked up laughing when Nash lost his shoe halfway and had to run back as the tide rushed in.

    Joanna and Scarlet kept giving Abby a knowing look and winks all throughout the day. They'd heard a rumor that Greyson had a crush on her, and this was the perfect opportunity for them to get together. Abby kept throwing them *shut-up* looks back, worried that Greyson would notice, but a part of her felt elated. She had a crush on him since last year, maybe even since they'd awkwardly danced together when they were pre-teens. If he asked her out, Abby was sure she'd explode and die of happiness.

So, while her two best friends kept wiggling their eyebrows at her whenever Greyson was near, like when he helped her climb down the rocks to the beach, or when he sat beside her when they stopped at the *Fishin' Chippin' Pond* for lunch, Abby played it cool. They were just a group of friends all hanging out together. Abby didn't wiggle her brows at Joanna despite that her crush, Levi, was with them, but she supposed it wasn't as big a deal between them. They'd already gone out a few times, but it didn't seem serious. Actually, Abby wasn't sure what was going on with those two, she'd have to ask Joanna later.

As the day wound down, Abby and Greyson broke off to get some ice cream. It wasn't intentional, just happened naturally, as the others were feasting on a bag of pretzels one of the guys bought, but both Abby and Greyson were craving something sweet.

The entire time the two of them walked down the promenade to the parlour, Abby had butterflies in her stomach. This was the first time it was just the two of them for longer than when they'd walk home together sometimes or stop for a quick chat in the school's halls. Her hands felt sweaty, and it felt like her stomach was inside out, but she made it to the ice cream parlour unscathed. It was hard to believe that a few years ago, Greyson was just the neighbourhood boy, the one she'd sometimes play with outside in the streets, just another friend on her roster. And now he was *Greyson*.

Abby felt calmer now that they were sitting on the bench, looking at the setting sun and the sparkling ocean, and that she had her ice cream in her hands. Her hands couldn't shake if they were holding ice cream, and her stomach untwisted itself if she concentrated on the sunset's reflection on the water.

"Any plans for the summer?" Greyson asked after they sat for a few moments in a peaceful silence. The waves crashed in a soothing pattern, and the smells of sea salt and her ice cream tickled Abby's nose.

"Mmmm," she said as she finished another lick of bubble-gum. "Just the usual. You know, camping with my dad at first, and then no real concrete plans. What about you?"

Greyson thought for a moment and then gestured with his vanilla ice cream cone. "Soccer camp midway through July, but otherwise pretty open. I think my cousin is getting married in August, but I can't remember the date."

Abby nodded along. Greyson went to soccer camp every summer for as long as she had known him. Last year she had stalked the streets waiting for him to return, only to find out that his family did an impromptu vacation right after his camp had ended.

"We should hang out in the summer," Greyson continued. Abby glanced over at him, her stomach fluttering again. He looked straight ahead at the ocean as he said it, his ice cream forgotten in his hand. A melted streak was running over his thumb, and when he looked up to see Abby facing him, he turned towards her. "I had a lot of fun hanging out with you today. I'm glad we bumped into you guys."

"Me too," Abby stuttered. Her heart hammered in her chest as her eyes met Greyson's and he leaned towards her. Blue drops of ice cream fell from her cone and onto her favourite pair of shorts, but Abby didn't care. She was about to have her first kiss.

It was short, just a firm peck on the lips, but Abby felt time stand still for a moment. Her entire body tingled, and her cheeks turned bright red. His lips were warm and tasted like his vanilla ice cream. It was actually sticky too, when she thought about it later, but at that moment, it was perfect.

As they pulled apart, each went back to their respective cones, and Abby laughed when a seagull swooped down and tried to swipe Greyson's. She was grateful that the setting sun hid the brightness of her red cheeks, and the rest of the group found them shortly after.

When the sun was finally under the horizon, they disbanded and went back their respective ways. As soon as the guys were out of earshot, Abby told her friends what happened, and they erupted in excited squeals. Abby couldn't stop smiling, her heart beating fast and feeling full. She never wanted to let this feeling end and closed her eyes for a moment just to savour everything that had happened, the most perfect day. She couldn't remember the last time she had felt this happy, and never wanted to let it go.

August 4, 2024
Dear Abby,

    I caught Lisa going through our wedding album this afternoon. I shouldn't say "caught" her like she did something wrong, but I do keep the wedding album hidden. I did the right thing and sat down beside her, and we went through the pictures together. She said she loved my dress and wanted to wear it someday. I told her I didn't have it anymore, which is true; it's at Mom and Dad's. Eli came and joined us, and we all sat together looking at pictures of me and Dave. Eli is still getting over the fact that Dave was unable to call him on his birthday. I feel so horrible for lying. I don't know what to do any more. The whole time we sat there together, all I could think about was how I lied to Eli, told him that Dave was too busy working to call him on his birthday, and even worse, when I'd look over at Lisa, I'd just think about how her father doesn't even know she exists. I'm a horrible, horrible person.

Abby
September 20, 2024

"Bye," Abby said as she leaned in for a kiss. When her lips met Greyson's, small butterflies flitted in her stomach and a giddy feeling ran through her. It didn't matter that they'd been together for a few months now. Every time they kissed, or he brushed her hair out of her eyes, or when they held hands or he wrapped his arms around her, Abby felt like she was on cloud nine. It was a magical feeling and she never wanted it to end.

"I'll call you later," Greyson said when they broke apart. As he hoisted the strap of his duffle bag up his shoulder and walked towards the school's field for practice, he turned back and blew her a kiss. Abby felt her cheeks flush as she swayed slightly from side to side before Scarlet nudged her hard in the ribs, laughing.

"Come on, love bird," she teased.

Abby rolled her eyes at her. She waved back at Greyson and then hurried to catch up with Joanna and Scarlet. The weather had finally turned from summer to fall, and Abby shivered a bit in the cool breeze. She was still in between summer and fall mode, not quite transitioned to warmer clothing. Her new sweater was soft and fuzzy, a beautiful cream colour that she promised her dad wouldn't get stained within the first week, for she was a bit of a klutz. The sweater was warm, but she still wore her favourite summer jean shorts and comfortable black flats. Scarlet and Joanna were also still between seasonal trends, both in tank tops with thin straps, with fuzzy fleece leggings and boots.

"Give her a break," Joanna said when Abby caught up. They linked their elbows together and Joanna winked at her. "They're still in that lovey-dovey phase at the beginning of a relationship."

"I wouldn't know," Scarlet muttered under her breath. Scarlet had yet to have a boyfriend out of the three of them, while Joanna had gone through a few already.

"It's nothing to be upset about," Joanna said to Scarlet. "It'll happen when it happens. Men aren't the most important thing in the world, or so my mother says at least."

Joanna's parents were in the middle of a divorce, and Mrs. Newcamp was quite vocal on her true feelings about her soon-to-be ex-husband. Abby felt bad for Joanna being caught up in the middle of it. Her older sister graduated early and was already out of the house. That left Joanna to hear all about how her father was a "cheating bastard" and the "biggest pile of shit this side of the earth." Abby couldn't imagine hearing these horrible things about someone she loved from someone else she loved. But then again, her father was the best person she knew. Despite that her mother had left them for no apparent reason and put a hole in their lives that they seemed unable to fill, he never spoke ill against her. Abby said a few snarky things here and there when she really felt down about it, but her father never did. He was resilient like that.

Abby and Scarlet never knew what to say about Joanna's situation. Scarlet's parents were quite happy together with four kids, and Abby's parents were already apart, albeit a completely unique situation. So, an awkward silence hung around the three of them as they walked down the street to Scarlet's house. Finally, Joanna broke the tension again as she nudged Abby playfully in the ribs.

"So, now that you're dating someone, has your dad had *the talk* with you?" she asked.

Abby cringed. Before she could answer, Scarlet groaned. "I can't even imagine having the talk with my dad."

"I know, right?" Joanna shuddered. Abby stayed quiet for a moment. When she approached her dad about dating Greyson, he was cautious with giving his permission. She was only fifteen, which he thought was quite young, but he had also known Greyson since they moved in down the street. They talked about personal boundaries and curfews, but they didn't really have *the* talk. Abby knew her dad trusted her, and she appreciated that. The last thing she wanted to do was talk sex with her dad. It was something she had learned about in health class and from Joanna, who only knew so much about it because of her older sister.

Scarlet and her mother were very close and kept no secrets between them. Though Scarlet had yet to have a relationship, her mother had told her everything. Abby didn't have that option in her own family, and it was yet another point in her life she felt robbed of, another milestone, coming-of-age experience between mother and daughter that she was denied. It wasn't one, she felt, that her father or grandmother could replace, like a few others had been.

"No," Abby answered finally. She opened her mouth to continue but didn't know what to say. Her friends didn't notice and kept on walking, talking about when they had the talks with their parents and how awkward or hilarious it was as they tried to censor the topic as much as possible. It was times like these that Abby felt annoyed at her friends and their lack of delicacy. They wouldn't stop and take a moment to think if what they were about to say would be insensitive to Abby and what had happened with her mother. It was like they'd forget that her mother abandoned her, and that it had stripped her of having these moments that they took for granted with their mothers. She knew it was hard for them to understand because their mothers were right there, but it wouldn't hurt for them to try.

October 15, 2024
Dear Abby,

It's hard to believe that you've been gone for twenty-five years now. Even harder to believe that Abby is the same age I was when you were taken away. I wish you could have met your nieces and nephew. I like to think that if you were still here, I wouldn't have gone off and created this new, pretend life. Every day I feel like I am living a lie, a lie to myself, a lie to my children, a lie to my community. We look like everything is OK, but it's not. Every day I am still waiting for someone to stop and look at us and point it out. "Look! There's that woman and her son who went missing twelve years ago!"

Of course, I don't blame your death for what I've done. That would be crazy. But I like to think, in a parallel universe somewhere, you're alive and happy, and I'm happy too, still with Dave, our family whole.

Abby
April 21, 2025

"OK," Dad said in a calm voice. "Slowly push your foot down on the pedal and drive forward."

Abby gripped the steering wheel, the leather slick under her sweaty hands. The setting sun reflected in the rear-view mirror behind her as she checked around the empty parking lot, and she exhaled loudly, a breath she didn't even know she was holding. She was suddenly very aware of her right foot and for a moment, didn't seem to be able to figure out how to move it from the brake to drive. Once she figured it out though, she gently tapped down on the driving pedal. Her dad's car lurched forward in a jerky motion, further than she meant it to go, and she yelled a little in panic.

"It's OK! You're doing great," her dad reassured, though he made a crazy hand-stopping gesture as he said it. "Try again. Just *ease* onto it."

Abby nodded. She looked straight ahead at the empty parking spaces in front of her and slowly lowered her foot down onto the pedal. The car eased forward in a smooth motion, and she felt a small thrill rush through her. Two days ago, she turned sixteen, and the first thing she did was go out to get her learner's permit. It was exhilarating. Both Joanna and Scarlet were born later in the year, Scarlet in the summer and Joanna just after school started, and so for once, Abby would be the first one at something. Joanna was first at dating, Scarlet was first at getting her period. Driving was Abby's. It terrified a part of her. She and her grandma had a close call once when another driver ran through a stop sign. That was nine years ago, but as Abby had been an impressionable and sensitive child, it stuck with her. Since then, cars made her feel nervous, but getting a driver's license was a rite of passage, one that she would not miss out on because her mother wasn't here. This was a milestone that was usually allotted to dads, anyway. She knew her father was looking forward to this day just as much as she was. Maybe in part that was because then he wouldn't have to drive her to her friends' houses all the time, and she could do it herself.

She also knew it was because it was another chance for them to bond. The older she got, the less time the two of them hung out together. Abby had her friends and Greyson, and her dad... well, she wasn't sure what he did. He had work, but other than that, Abby wasn't sure what he did in his spare time. It made her feel guilty when she realized they weren't spending that much time together anymore. Time was going by quickly, and before she knew it, she'd be graduating high school, and going to university. That was still two years away, but those years were coming quick.

"That's it," her dad said proudly. "Now try turning left. Hand over the other..."

Abby turned the wheel. It was harder than she thought it would be, but the car followed her motion. It wasn't that fluid, but her next turn was better. Soon she was weaving around the parking lot at a slow, but confident pace. Her dad smiled beside her as she pulled into one of the empty stalls to park.

"Do you want to drive home?" he asked. They had been circling around the empty parking lot for an hour now. Though Abby felt confident in there, she shook her head. She didn't feel ready for the road yet.

"Not today," she said. With the car in park, she took her hands off the wheel and wiped her sweaty palms onto her sweatpants. "But maybe tomorrow, after some more practice in here."

"Sounds great, kiddo."

Abby rolled her eyes, even though the nickname made her feel nostalgic. He slipped them in now and then, and it brought her back to a more innocent time. They had been through a lot, the two of them.

As she looked over at her dad, Abby noticed the lines on his face, the greys that streaked his hair. Little details that crept onto his features without her noticing throughout the years. They had come a long way. And as she thought about how they had two more years together before she was thrust into adulthood, she wondered just what he would do once she was gone. He would be all alone. Abby would still have her friends and Greyson, she was sure. But her father had dated no one since she asked him to breakup with Kathy. He stayed lonely because of her. And soon she'd be leaving him. The ten-year-old within her still felt so guilty for taking away his happiness—just like Mom had done.

The sun set, and her dad got out of the car to trade seats. Once in the passenger seat, Abby turned to him as she buckled up.

"Hey dad, before we go home; do you want to go see a movie or something?" she asked.

Her dad smiled. "Yeah, sure. I'm not sure if anything good is playing though."

"That's OK," Abby said. She smiled back. "Let's just hang out for a little longer."

September 28, 2025
Dear Abby,

 I still can't believe Eli is in high school now. It's his second year, but because he skipped a grade it makes it hard for me to wrap my head around. When I look at him, I still see that sweet little bald-headed baby tucked in my lap on the airplane, en route to Maui and into the unknown. All of my babies are growing up. It's Lisa's last year in elementary, and Abby is in grade 11... she'll be graduating soon. I've missed her entire life.
 Lately, I've been seriously thinking about reaching out to Dave. I miss them both so much. There's nothing I wouldn't give to go back in time and re-do everything, to have kept us whole. I'm nervous though... what would he say if I reached out? I can't imagine what their lives have been like, what kind of impact of what I did has left on them. Is it better if I stay dead? Some days I wonder if I should just make that a reality. It would be the easier step to take.

Dave
October 13, 2025

"Abby, can you come help me please?" Dave yelled from the kitchen. He felt overwhelmed. Donna and Gerry would be here in an hour, and everything was a disaster. Various half-finished dishes of food lined his counters. Cookware piled high in the sink as the dishwasher ran its first load of prep-plates.

When he decided to take on Thanksgiving this year, Dave thought of it as a break for his in-laws. Year after year, they made a delicious meal for the four of them. Sometimes they'd invite their neighbours over as well, and they never expected Dave to lift a finger. This year, however, he stepped up. Gerry had knee surgery last month, and Donna's hands ached from arthritis. It wouldn't be fair on them to continue to host, and so Dave volunteered. Abby saw her grandparents less and less now that she was a teen and had a *boyfriend*, which Dave still wasn't used to, even though it had been a year now, so any traditions he could keep with them, he would. Even if it meant realizing he did not know what he was doing.

The mashed potatoes in front of him were lumpy. They refused to be smooth and creamy, and he wondered if he could somehow turn it into a potato salad instead. But, as he glanced further down the counter, he already had a Caesar salad prepared. That was one thing he knew how to do properly. And the turkey smelled good too, at least. So that was maybe two things that wouldn't be a disaster. The rest however…

"Abby!" Dave yelled again. The cranberry sauce still had to be made, his brussel sprouts were on the stove, and the scissor rolls were still in the freezer.

Abby came trudging into the kitchen with her phone in her hand. She was in the middle of a conversation with someone, the phone on speaker.

"Uh-huh," Abby said to whichever friend was on the other end. "And what did she say?"

"She said yes!" It was Joanna. "Like, what a slut."

"Language," Dave said in a stern voice. Abby rolled her eyes to the ceiling and groaned.

"Oh, hey Mr. Sanders," Joanna said without apology.

"I'll talk to you later, I want to hear the rest," Abby muttered into the speaker. "Byeeee."

Once the phone was in her back pocket, Abby turned to him with a concerned look on her face. "What happened in here? I thought you were making dinner, not harvesting alien organs."

Dave laughed aloud to that. Abby smiled and rolled up her sleeves as she looked at the surrounding mess. Dave knew she was going to suggest that he do the dishes while she tried to cook. Abby hated dishes. But to his surprise, she pushed her sleeves up higher and tackled the pile in the sink.

"I know, I know," she said at his shocked face. "But at least if I do the dishes, I won't be blamed for whatever abomination you're concocting in here."

Dave laughed again. "Fair enough. So, who is the promiscuous friend you two were talking about?" He didn't care, but lately felt as though Abby was slipping away from him. He knew it came with the teenage territory, and they grew further apart the past few years as she made her way through high school.

"That's classified information." Abby was in good spirits lately. When the two of them were together, all they did was joke around and laugh. The trick was to get Abby talking though, because otherwise she was just like when she first entered the kitchen, absorbed in her own world, and Dave was left out. It was hard when the one constant in his life, the one constant that got him through the hardest moment of his life, was slipping away. "Hold on. Dad… is something burning?"

Dave stopped trying to smooth out the potatoes for a moment and sniffed the air. There was no visible smoke, but something smelled off.

"Shit! The gravy!" he remembered. He abandoned the potatoes on one counter and ran over to the stove. The gravy looked like a congealed mess of burned goop. He switched the burner down to low, unsure why it was on so high in the first place and turned with a hand outstretched to Abby. "Quick, I need to stir!"

Abby dug through the dishes in the sink. When that proved fruitless, she pulled open drawers but still came up empty handed. "Where the hell are all of the spoons?!" she exclaimed.

"Oh—they might all be in the dishwasher…" Dave said with a certain dread. The burning smell got stronger; except this time it came from within the oven. Dave turned on the inside light and bent down to look. He could see nothing but smoke.

"Shit, shit, shit, shit," he muttered to himself. "Stand back!"

Oven mitts thrust on, Dave opened the oven and a cloud of grey smoke escaped. It filled the kitchen and the smoke detector beeped loudly. Abby ran and started opening windows, the cool fall air rushing in as the smoke rushed out. Dave brought out the turkey. It looked completely fine. Even more confusing, the thermometer said it still wasn't ready.

"Look, the juices ran over the edge." Abby pointed at the bottom of the oven.

Between the two of them, they soaked up the excess juices and stopped the burning smell. The gravy was a lost cause, and the mashed potatoes stayed lumpy. Donna and Gerry didn't mind though. The turkey was not as juicy as when cooked by Donna, but it ended up tasting quite good. The dinner was a success.

Once dinner was done, Abby played cards against Gerry, and the two of them laughed at the embarrassing story Donna was telling, a mishap she'd had at her latest book club meeting. Dave sat back in his chair, stomach full of food, and a content warmth spread through him as he smiled at the family around him. These days were numbered, and he knew he had to hold on to them a little longer each year.

March 22, 2026
Dear Abby,

I've made a promise. I told Lisa and Eli that we would visit their father this year, that we'd been talking, and we'd go out to visit at Christmas time. What I'll do when that time actually comes, I'm not sure. But they're both pacified by the idea right now, so that's a break from that. One step at a time.

Dave
May 16, 2026

 Dave glanced down at his watch and tapped his foot as he looked down the empty SkyTrain tunnel. He hated to look the clichéd part of an impatient man waiting for a late train, but it happened before he could stop himself. His foot tapped along at a rapid, arrhythmic pace as he exhaled loudly. If there was one thing he hated, it was being late. If there was one thing he hated more than that, it was being late when he was the boss and should set the example.

 It was the yearly trade show downtown. Dave had made a point of telling everyone to be there no later than 9AM, and yet here he was, 8:55AM, still at least fifteen minutes away. Driving was always a disaster in the city, which was why he opted, as he did every year, to park at the bus loop, take the bus to the nearest SkyTrain station, and then take the train to the convention center. Every year it went smoothly, except now. There had been a delay with the bus because of a medical emergency. This initially favored Dave, for he'd had to run back to his car for his wallet, forgotten on his seat. Now it appeared that the train was running late too.

 "Come on, come on, come on," he muttered. There was one booth that he had to be one of the first ten vendors to get in on the deal that they were setting up for their product. The last two years they sold out within the first half hour of the convention, and Dave was determined to be one of the ten this year. He needed this product to be on his shelves, and he would not let a late train stop him.

Dave whipped out his phone as he waited for the train, his foot still tapping away at a rapid pace.

Get to the SmoothiEco Booth ASAP he texted to his most reliable colleague attending the conference.

At last, he could hear the train's wheels squealing in the tunnel as it came nearer. As it approached the platform, Dave's phone rang. It was an unknown number. Normally, he'd not answer it and let it go to voicemail, but since it was the trade show day, he answered it just in case it was a vendor trying to reach him.

"Hello, Dave Sanders," he answered in his most professional voice.

The train screeched to a halt on the platform, the sound deafening anything the speaker said. Dave winced at the sound and dashed onto the train. He thought he'd heard a woman's voice on the other end but was unsure.

"Apologies, I'm on the subway right now," he said to the speaker. "Could you please repeat what you said?"

Nothing came from the other end. Dave could hear someone breathing, and a hitch in the voice, as though they'd been crying, or they were opening their mouth to say something. A noisy group of youths entered the train after him, and Dave plugged his other ear to hear the speaker better. Maybe he imagined the breathing sound, and the line was dead.

"Hello? Is anyone there?" he asked. Nobody spoke, but that time he was sure he heard someone inhale as though to speak. And then they hung up with an audible click.

Dave frowned and looked down at the phone. The number was not only unrecognizable, but the area code didn't match any of the local ones. It looked like the type of number that would come from across the country. He paused for a moment, trying to think of who he knew that might call him from such a number. It could have been one of the vendors, but there were only a few that were coming from out of province, and Dave couldn't think of why they'd be calling him. They were all signed up with him.

As the train lurched forward and stopped at the next station, and then the next, Dave shrugged at the phone and put it back into his pocket. It wasn't until he arrived at his own stop that a thought occurred. Could it have been Ronnie? Who else would call him, breathe but not speak? He didn't have any stalkers, none that he knew about, anyway. He was as Joe Average as the next guy.

Dave whipped his phone out again as he got off the train. The group of youths pushed past him, one of them huffing as he unintentionally blocked their way. Dave stared down at the numbers. It had to be her. After all these years, he still had hope. His heart raced as he pressed the *call back* button, and the phone rang. The palm of his hand sweat against the phone as it rang again, the conference and the SmoothiEco booth forgotten. The phone rang and rang and rang, but nobody picked up. There was no answering machine either. Dave hung up and waited a minute before trying again. The second time though, the phone didn't even ring once.

The number you have dialed is not in service. Please check your number and try your call again, the automated voice said. Dave cursed and muttered under his breath as he looked down at the phone number again. The more he looked at it, the more he doubted himself and his pulse calmed down. Maybe it was just a scammer. If it had been Ronnie, there would have been an answering machine. If anything, he thought to himself as the conference came back into mind and he sprinted up the stairs to the street's surface, this only proved to him that when it came to Ronnie, there would always be hope inside him. No matter how much time had passed.

June 11, 2026
Dear Abby,

Sometimes it feels like all I am doing is trying to keep my head above water when all I really want to do is drown. Drowning would be so much easier, and yet I keep on trying to swim.

Abby
August 2, 2026

"So, I guess that's it then," Greyson said.

"I guess so," Abby said in a clear voice. Her palm sweat, and the phone trembled as she held it to her ear, but she kept it together. She would not let Greyson hear her break down and cry. She would not let him know just how much this hurt her. Both Scarlet and Joanna had warned her this would happen, that as soon as he graduated, he'd break up with her. And she had refused to believe it. They had been together for almost two years. They would be the ones to last, they'd be those high school sweethearts who were together for seventy years. And yet, here it was. It was happening. He was breaking up with her, *over the phone*.

"Listen, Abby," Greyson sighed. "Maybe… maybe we should—"

"No, no," Abby said, her voice angry now. Tears trailed down her cheeks, but she made sure they stayed out of her voice. "You've made your decision and you've already said everything you wanted to say. You've made it clear, Greyson. I get it. We're done. Have a nice life."

She hung up before he could argue back and threw her phone across the room. It hit the wall and left a small dent. Her dad wouldn't be happy about that, but there was nothing *happy* about this situation, anyway. At least the wall was repairable. Her relationship was not.

Thinking about that, the finality of their conversation settling in her mind, Abby let out a loud sob. Tears splattered on her bedspread, and she threw herself onto her pillows and wailed as loud as she could. How could he think they were better if they were apart? They were perfect for each other. Greyson was her first love, her first boyfriend, her first everything. He wasn't like the other dumb guys at school, he was smart, respectful, funny; she had known him for years and he knew her. How could he think there'd be someone better out there than her? Did he really think he'd be happy with someone else? Because she knew the line about him needing his own space was BS. Clearly, he must have met someone at his university orientation and suddenly dating someone still in high school wasn't good enough.

Abby didn't know how much time had passed by the time the tears stopped. She'd need to re-charge to generate more tears. A water and snot stain were visible on her pillow when she finally sat up and she flipped it over to avoid looking at it. She rubbed her face with both her hands and sighed. A slow rage developed somewhere within the sadness, and everything in her room suddenly made her mad.

She jumped off her bed and marched over to the mirror above her dresser. Pictures of her and Greyson framed the mirror, and she ripped them off one by one. An old-fashioned Polaroid one was taken just two weeks ago at the fair. A paper cut sliced her finger as she crumpled them into a messy pile and added the few that were in cute frames from around her room. The girl in the mirror's reflection had a red blotchy face and Abby scoffed at it, but paused when she noticed the sparkle of the silver locket he gave her last Christmas. It was one of her favourite things, from her favourite person. A wave of tears came rushing up, and she cried aloud again as she ripped the necklace off and threw it onto the growing pile.

Across the room she rummaged through her closet for an empty shoebox. As she did, she also grabbed her favourite sweater, the soft pink one Greyson gave her for her birthday, and one of his t-shirts that she had borrowed when they went swimming at the lake at the beginning of the summer last year. It was one of her other most-prized possessions. It was an old retro-shirt that had Scooby-Doo on it. Greyson's grandma bought it from a consignment store for him a few years back because the show had been his favourite growing up. They went to the lake last summer, and Abby's shirt became ripped up when she fell into a bush. Greyson's dog, Boundary, had knocked her over in his excitement, and after they went swimming, Abby needed something new to coverup with, and the Scooby shirt hadn't left her possession since.

With the box in hand, Abby stormed away from the closet and back to her dresser. She crammed everything inside, the sweater, pictures, t-shirt, and locket. The lid kept popping off when Abby put it on, and this just made her angrier.

Abby stomped down the stairs and into the kitchen in a cloud of anger and hurt. She ripped open the junk drawer and fished out the first roll of tape she could find, which was duct tape. Perfect. That would not only hold it down, but would keep it sealed forever, and be harder for her to re-open if she had moments of weakness.

As she wrestled with ripping off strands of tape and holding down the lid of the small box, she heard the garage door open. Her dad was home and there was no time for her to hide now. She knew she'd have to tell him eventually, but she wanted a few more hours to herself to cool down or at least be a bit more composed. Not that he had never seen her at her worst before.

As soon as he stepped into the kitchen, her dad knew that something was wrong. The bag in his hand fell on the counter with a loud thud as he looked over at her, down at the box and the mess of tape in her hand, and Abby glanced at him quickly to see concern in his eyes. That was a mistake, because looking at him just made her want to cry harder. He was her safety net, and she couldn't even pretend to hide her emotions from her dad. He just brought the truth out without even meaning to.

Abby cut to the chase before he could ask. "Greyson and I broke up," was all she said. Finally, she stopped trying to rip off individual pieces of the tape and decided to just wrap the entire thing in one long strand. Her father said nothing at first, he just watched as she wound the tape around the box five or six times.

When she finished, he opened another drawer and handed her the scissors to cut the end.

"I'm sorry to hear that," he said at last. When Abby glanced up at him again, she could see that it caught him off guard. This was a situation he hadn't wanted to deal with, because he didn't know *how* to deal with it. This was another mom territory thing that was served on his plate because her mom wasn't there. He looked a bit like a deer in headlights but tried to compose himself for Abby's sake.

Abby helped him out. "I don't want to talk about it, OK?" she said, a bit harsher than she'd meant to. Dad relaxed a little and nodded. He pulled her into a hug, which she sort of fought because she didn't want comfort right now. She just wanted to wallow in her grief, cry for days, punch a few walls, and eat nothing but chocolate cake.

"That's fine," he said. "You talk about it if and when you want to."

What she wanted to do was pull away and storm back up into her room, to cry on her bed and throw the wrapped box into the depths of her closet. But instead, beyond her control, she sunk into the hug with her father and sobbed into his shoulder. Her tears had fully regenerated and now it would be his work clothes that would be water and snot stained. And she knew he didn't mind.

September 5, 2026
Dear Abby,

   I'm trying to see the light at the end of the tunnel. There has to be a light, somewhere. But sometimes I wonder if maybe you don't get to see the light until after you're gone.

Abby
September 7, 2026

    The lights of a passing by car reflected onto Abby's ceiling as she lay on her bed staring up at it. The last day of summer break was behind her, its warm night breeze floating in through her open window as the weight of the first day of school tomorrow loomed over her. Her school schedule was tucked in her backpack, along with her new notebooks and tablet. In some ways, she was eager to start the school year. It was a new beginning, in a way. She and her friends would be the seniors, top of the food chain. It was like a clean slate for her last year of school, a new start as a single young woman. Yet, it was also the first of many lasts to come. First last day of high school. To an outsider, it looked like she was excited and ready to go, with her backpack ready, and lunch pre-made in the fridge downstairs.
    But if she was being honest with herself, Abby dreaded the first day of school. The first day meant facing a ton of her friends who weren't in the loop about her breakup with Greyson. They'd ask her how her summer was, unaware that something now tainted it with their breakup last month. All of July, which had been wonderful and fun, was garbage now because of that bleak day in August, and the gloomy days that followed. The rest of summer was a drag. Abby ignored her friends for days before they finally came over to drag her out of the house. She was moody with her

father and spent most of her nights in her room, watching movies on her laptop under the covers with a bag of chips. It took her a long time to snap out of her gloomy-state, and now all that remained was a bitterness that she couldn't seem to keep in check. Anytime her dad said something nice to her, or tried to cheer her up, her response was some bitter remark under her breath. Sometimes he would call her out on it, but most of the time he let it slide.

It was a good thing that Greyson was a year older than her. At least she didn't have to worry about bumping into him in the halls at school. He'd be off in the city going to university. By November he'd likely have a new girlfriend, whereas Abby would still be single. She knew all the guys in her grade and none of them held a candle to Greyson. The days she did get out after their breakup, she deliberately took the long way to get to her destinations, to avoid passing his house down the street. This was a prime example of why you never fell for the guy next door, or four doors down in her case.

As another car drove by outside her open window, Abby sighed. A feeling of frustration crept up in her, and she let out a small groan. She had all these *feelings* and didn't know how to deal with them. Her eyes closed for a moment as she took a few deep breaths to keep from crying. It was hard for her to keep Greyson out of her mind. She needed to let it all out without physically becoming a blubbering mess.

An idea popped into her head, and she sat upright. Abby turned on the nightstand lamp and crossed the room to her cluttered desk. It was white with chipped paint, knickknacks, books, pens, jewelry, and other miscellaneous things scattered across it. Sheets of loose paper with notes, doodles, and pencils rolled around the drawer as she pulled it open. Underneath it all, she pulled out a sparkly green journal. It shimmered in the light that shone from her nightstand, and she ran her hand over the cover. She closed her eyes as she thought back to when her dad took her to the mall, and she had taken her time picking out the perfect journal. It was from another time when she also felt she had too many feelings to deal with, and the journal was her father's idea. Her childhood therapist had suggested it too. She dug around in the drawer for the small key that opened the lock. That was a feature that she thought was *so cool* because she had seen nothing like that at the time.

But when she opened the diary, the pages were empty. There were many times over the years that Abby sat down and tried to write into the journal. No matter what she tried though, whenever she put pen to paper, the words just wouldn't come. The feelings were no easier to get out on paper than they were to say aloud. She *wanted* to want to write in the journal, just like her mother had, to feel connected to her in some way and to have an outlet for all her fears, frustrations, and stress. But it just wasn't for her.

Now, as she sat down and stared at the empty pages again, she didn't know how to express herself. Her heart was broken over Greyson. All she wanted to do was curl into a ball and cry and wake up when the pain would be over. Or better yet, for him to call her, say it was all a terrible, stupid mistake, and for them to get back together. But neither option was coming easily to her anymore, especially Greyson taking it all back. She cried throughout the month of August, and now she felt like an empty shell, still sad and broken, but with no way to be repaired.

Abby closed the journal and put it back into the drawer. The warm summer breeze greeted her from the window, and she looked out to see the night sky was still quite bright. It was almost nine-thirty, still too early for her to even start to fall asleep.

Abby stood from her desk and grabbed a light sweater. She walked down the stairs with soft footsteps. The light of the TV flickered from the living room, and her father looked up from the couch as she rounded the corner.

"Everything OK?" he asked.

"Yeah." Abby exhaled slowly. "I just need to go take a quick run. Feeling anxious about tomorrow, and I just need to let some energy out."

Her father frowned. "A bit late for a run, don't you think?"

"Yeah, but I'll just go around the block twice," Abby said. Her father knew the route she usually took when she went for a jog. She waved her phone in front of him. "I'll have my phone on me the whole time, no headphones in."

"OK. If you're not back by ten, I'm coming to find you."

Once out in the fresh air, Abby felt better. The smell of summer still clung to the air, and it filled her soul with peace. With each slap of her sneakers on the pavement, she felt those inexplainable feelings disappear one by one, until she focused on the positives of the upcoming school year. Maybe one day she and Greyson would reunite, maybe not. At least she still had her best friends, and together the three of them would have the best last year of high school. It would be a year of friendship and fun, she decided. She had gone through her one bad thing of the year, and from here on out it would be smooth sailing. Or at least, she hoped it would be. The last thing she needed was more bad news.

NOW
September 8, 2026

Dave

Dave lay awake that night staring up at the ceiling. Sleep eluded him as he tossed and turned, the time on his phone growing by the hour. The day was exhausting. He learned so much but had even more questions. All this time, Ronnie and Eli, and Lisa, were on the other side of the country, in Newfoundland. Many times, Dave would imagine Ronnie and Eli living their life somewhere in Europe, probably Germany, or somewhere else in Hawaii. Maybe they had been daring and went to Japan or Australia. If he had known that they were in the same country…

Of course, that wasn't the most shocking news he learned from his son. He had another daughter. Eli said she was thirteen, her birthday was in April. That meant that Ronnie must have been just pregnant when they ran away. Not far enough along to have known when she left. Or at least, that's what Dave told himself when he did the math. If she had known, she would have stayed…. Right? Lisa was the name that Dave had picked out if they were to have another girl. It was his favourite girl's name, and though it had taken Ronnie a while to come around to it, she agreed. Then they had Eli and had to come up with a boy's name, which was a more arduous task. It meant something that Ronnie still used the name.

Dave's world flipped upside down again. It took him a long time to accept that life would just be him and Abby. It would be the two of them against the world. His family broke apart because of a mental illness he tried and failed to understand. And now that same illness was forcing them back together at a rapid pace. Dave thought that if he ever had contact with Eli again, their relationship would build slowly. Maybe they would just exchange emails at first, add each other on Facebook, and then eventually, after months of exchanges over social medias, they would meet up for coffee, depending on where Eli lived. They would never get the real father-son time they had been deprived of, because he would be an adult. Maybe Eli would have a family of his own.

But instead of months or years away, it was happening now. They booked a flight for first thing tomorrow morning. Dave would get to see where Eli grew up and meet his other daughter. Did Lisa even know about him? Did she know about Abby?

That was another reason Dave couldn't sleep. He kept thinking about Abby. Aside from her one outburst when Eli told them about the funeral, she barely said two words all day, to either of them. She missed the first day of school but went over to Scarlet's house the first chance she could get. At dinner, Abby ate silently as Dave told them they'd be heading out the next morning and that he called the school to explain her upcoming absence. Then she excused herself to pack, and he didn't see her for the rest of the night.

He didn't get to spend much quality time with Eli, either. The teen was shy, despite his courage to come out here and find his unacquainted father. And because of the time change, Eli went to bed quite early.

When it was clear that he wouldn't be sleeping tonight, Dave sighed and rolled out of bed. Best to start the day early and hope for sleep on the plane.

Once dressed, he went downstairs to find the kitchen light on. Abby sat at the counter, a cup of tea in front of her next to a plate of cookies, and her laptop open. When she heard Dave come down the stairs, she quickly closed the computer and pushed it away. Dave didn't have to ask what she was doing. He knew. She was looking at pictures of her and Ronnie from when she was a baby. It wasn't something that she did often, only when she was going through a very rough time.

"Couldn't sleep either, huh?" Dave asked. He started up the coffee maker and opened the fridge to get started on breakfast. Abby shook her head and took a sip of tea. "Hopefully we'll get some sleep on the plane."

"Do I have to go?" Abby asked into her cup. She avoided Dave's eye but glanced at him quickly when she asked.

Dave closed the fridge and gripped the handle tightly. He leaned his forehead onto the cool stainless steel and took a deep breath as he turned to face her. "Yes, of course you have to. She was your mother."

"She abandoned me," Abby said.

"Abby," Dave sighed. "Now is not the time. Don't pretend that you aren't grieving."

"I grieved for years," she said. "She's already gone for me and has been for a long time." She snatched her laptop from the counter and stormed off up the stairs. Dave let her go. He knew she was angry. She had every right to be. But he also knew that she was lying. Ronnie was never far from her mind.

Dave

The hustle and bustle of the airport hummed as Dave drummed his fingers on his knee. Abby sat next to him on his right, glued to her phone, texting furiously to one of her friends. Her mood did not improve after breakfast, not that Dave really expected it too. She was still bitter from her breakup with Greyson on top of the bombshell of Eli's arrival yesterday.

Dave glanced to his left where Eli sat. Unlike Abby and everyone their age he spotted in the airport, Eli sat with his phone put away and his nose in a book. Something thick and science fiction. Dave's brain still couldn't believe what his eyes saw. He took in the dark chocolate curls, the light freckles on his nose, his eyes just like Ronnie's. This was his son, *his son* who had been on missing posters, social media feeds, newspapers, commercials, and news reports for so many years. Did Eli know about any of that? To what extent, if any, had Ronnie explained things to him? Him and Lisa?

That was another thing Dave's brain didn't yet comprehend. He had a third child. The third child that Ronnie always dreamed about, the second girl they'd always wanted. He had so many questions, to the point where he wondered if he should write them down. But he didn't want to bombard his children with questions. This whole situation was just as bizarre, awkward, and difficult for them as it was for him. He was sure that they must have questions too. *Why did you stop looking for us?* Dave imagined Eli thinking. *If you cared so much, you would have kept looking. You could have tried harder. By letting go, you abandoned us just as much as she did you.*

Dave shook his head and the thoughts from his mind. One step at a time, that was all he could do to untangle this mess. The clock above the check-in desk moved slowly, and he took in a long breath. It smelled like airport, a mixture of sweat, greasy food, and a certain staleness that he could never put his finger on. He reached into his bag and brought out a pack of peanut butter cups. It was a pre-flight snack tradition he and Abby started on their first flight together after Ronnie had left. Personally, Dave was sort of sick of them, but traditions, and up keeping them, were important when Abby was growing up. The more that things were constant, the more that her trauma from Ronnie leaving resolved.

Once Dave ripped open the pack, he handed one over to Abby who took it without looking up from her phone. It pinged and buzzed beside him, and she clicked away as she shoved the snack into her mouth without so much as a word. Dave sighed and then turned to Eli.

"Would you like one? It's a pre-flight snack tradition Abby and I have." Dave smiled. Here it was, the first tradition he was including his son in, the first of many small olive branches to build the relationship between them.

Eli looked up from his book. With a glance at the snack, he shifted a bit in his chair and looked awkwardly at Dave. He wasn't sure if it was the drab airport lightning or his imagination, but it looked like Eli's cheeks flushed.

"Uh, thanks, I appreciate the thought," he said. That was one thing Dave noticed right away; Eli was quite polite. "But I have a peanut allergy."

Dave felt his stomach plummet. He fumbled awkwardly with the chocolate and hastily threw it into Abby's lap. She glanced up, puzzled, but took the remaining two cups without question and went back to her phone. Dave felt his own cheeks turn red and he ran a hand through his hair.

"Oh, I, uh, I'm sorry," he stuttered in a quick jumble of words.

"It's OK," Eli said just as quick, also keen to clear the uncomfortable air. "You didn't know."

How could I have? Dave thought to himself. There was no reason he should feel as terrible as he did, for it was true, there was no way he could have known. But all at once, Dave felt like the world's worst father. He had just offered his son poison.

"EpiPen's in my bag," Eli added as an afterthought as he turned back to his book. "If we need it."

Soon after, their flight boarded, and Dave was thankful. They left behind the situation in the airport terminal.

They could not get three seats together, which was initially a dilemma for Dave. There was no way that he was going to put Abby and Eli together. Abby was still quite hostile towards him and gave him the cold shoulder as Eli made himself a cup of coffee at breakfast. Dave knew some teenagers drank coffee, but it was so odd to see in his own house, because Abby wouldn't even try it. Eli was only fourteen, but who was Dave to lecture him that he thought he was too young to have coffee.

The dilemma then was, did Dave sit with Abby, for the two of them to comfort each other in whatever world it was they were about to enter together? Or did he sit with his long-lost son, Eli, to try to get to know him better, and try to get a bit of prep on whatever it was they were walking into? All night, Dave tossed and turned on what to do, among the other million thoughts that ran through his head, and Eli decided for him when he said he'd prefer to sit by himself. The decision hurt a small part of Dave, though he understood why Eli might want to sit by himself. Dave was a stranger regardless that they were related by blood.

Once they were up in the air, Dave tried to relax. He could see Eli sitting a few rows up and across, and that put him at ease. Abby took the window seat, and her headphones were in the minute the seatbelt sign went on, and she shut Dave out. She stared, moody, out the window, and Dave would give it a few hours before he tried to talk to her. With any luck, she'd turn to him when she was ready, and they would talk.

When the food cart made its way down the aisle, Dave jumped up from his seat and walked over to Eli. He too had a pair of earphones in, and his book still open in his hand. Dave tapped on his shoulder, and Eli took one earphone out, while placing his finger on the page to mark his spot as he closed the book.

"Did you look at the snack menu? Do you want anything?" Dave asked as he glanced up at the cart coming their way. He reached into his pocket for his wallet, but Eli put his hands up and shook them.

"It's OK, I can pay for my own," Eli said. Dave felt rejected again, and it was like a small, sharp prick in his heart. His lip twitched as he tried to smile.

"Please? It would make me feel better about earlier," Dave pleaded. Eli looked warily at him but then shrugged in acceptance. Dave happily bought him a bag of chips and a sandwich. Back at his own seat, Abby declined anything and quickly fell asleep soon thereafter. Dave looked back over at Eli, who chatted cheerfully with the elderly lady beside him, even laughing at one point. Maybe he should have pushed harder to sit beside his son, for now it left him alone with his own thoughts as he stared at the map on the screen in front of him.

As the little plane on the map got closer and closer to their destination, Dave became more and more fidgety. Once the overhead announcement came on that they were beginning their descent, Dave took a deep breath and exhaled loudly.

"Dad?"

Abby was suddenly awake beside him. He didn't notice her open her eyes, and he suspected she had been faking her sleep to avoid talking to him. But she turned to him now, big blue eyes glossy with a mixture of sadness and anger, as she said in a small quiet voice, "I'm scared."

"Me too, kiddo," Dave murmured. He held her hand and squeezed it, as he glanced back over to Eli who was back to reading his book. "Me too."

Abby

"Turn here," Eli instructed from the front seat of the rental car. Dad flipped on his signal and turned onto a long narrow road, lined with tall trees.

They had been on the road for what felt like an hour. Whatever small town her mother abandoned her for was far from the airport and city civilization. Something about that thought annoyed Abby as she sat in the back seat of the rented sedan. It smelled like hot dog water, and there was a questionable stain on the seat next to her. Eli sat up front because he was their GPS. They could have used the real GPS on one of their phones, but there was something rude about using an electronic map when they were going somewhere that somebody knew how to get to. Or at least, that's what her dad said when Abby questioned it.

Abby glanced at her phone. No new messages or texts from Scarlet or Joanna. They were still in school right now, four and a half hours behind her current time. She felt both jealous of and neglected by her friends. Jealous because it did not interrupt their lives like hers. They woke up and started their senior year of high school like they were meant to. Abby wanted to be with them. She should be in biology class with Scarlet right now, both rolling their eyes because they had Mr. Peterson as a teacher, and though he knew his stuff, he was so dry in his lectures that he made the Sahara look wet. Her friends did not know what she would give for a bit of normalcy, because she felt she was robbed of that her whole life.

And she felt neglected because, *hello,* this was a huge deal. Her long-lost brother appeared out of the blue on her doorstep after fourteen years, like something out of a movie. On top of that, her mother had committed suicide, and she had a secret sister. Scarlet couldn't believe any of it when Abby told her about it in person yesterday, and the two of them brought Joanna up to speed on the phone. It was the shock of the century; or at least it was yesterday. Neither of them had so much as texted her all morning.

Abby sighed and looked out the window. The trees continued to whiz past as they drove in silence down the road. Abby put her headphones in and closed her eyes as she listened to the ballad playing. It was the right mix of melancholy and calm that she needed right now.

Her mother was dead. *She's dead.* It was something she had repeated to herself since Eli let the bomb drop yesterday morning. Sometimes she whispered it to herself aloud. Other times she screamed it as loud as she could inside her brain, loud enough so that the hopeful five-year-old in her heard it loud and clear and would let the fantasies go about seeing her mother again. There would be no reunion with her, ever. There would be no chance to let her know how angry she was with her. No chance to ask her *Why? Why did you leave me behind? Why not Eli? Why me?* She would never get to hear her mother's excuses, never get to see her stutter on the spot, try to come up with some validation, because there was no valid reason. There was never a good reason to leave your child behind.

Abby opened her eyes and glanced over at Eli in the passenger seat. He sat quietly and looked straight ahead, waiting to point out the next turning point to Dad. Of course, he looked nothing like the baby brother she remembered, the one she made giggle and coo in her dreams. He was just some kid now, with whom she shared some facial features. It was hard not to see the resemblance between them.

Sometimes, when Abby was younger, and she tried to understand why her mother left, she would land on the idea that her mother hadn't wanted a daughter. That she had only wanted a son, and that's why she brought Eli with her and had left Abby behind. Except now that point was moot, because apparently there was another. The thought of having a sister out there made Abby's stomach rot. If she had hated daughters, then her mother would have abandoned Lisa too, right? Except she didn't. She kept her and Eli together, and the three of them grew up here, wherever *here* was that they headed to, some small town far outside of the big city. Abby had noticed a picture of Eli and a girl smiling together as the background on his phone. She had seen little of it, only a flash for a second, but she didn't need to see more to know that it was Lisa. They were close, and that thought too, made Abby's stomach churn. This other daughter had replaced her.

As they turned out of the tree-lined road, and signs of houses and shops appeared, Abby took another deep sigh and looked away from the back of Eli's head. She closed her eyes again and a single tear ran down her cheek as she thought of the one thing that was the most upsetting about everything. *She's dead*, she repeated to herself. *You'll never get to hug her again.*

Dave

Dave's palms sweat while he gripped the steering wheel as Eli instructed him to pull onto his street. They were ten minutes out from Ronnie's house now and the anticipation inside of him built to a degree that he couldn't handle.

The town was quaint and quiet. It was something out of a romance novel. Characteristic shops lined one of the main roads. They were once colourful, now faded over time from the sun and wind, which made them all more charming. People waved to each other as they walked down the streets and eyed the rental car with intrigue as they drove by. A few spotted Eli in the front seat and waved to him, and he waved back. It had that small town community comfort that made Eli feel at home, but made Dave feel like a complete outsider.

When they turned onto their street, Dave could see the sea out of the window, and it stretched for miles. Eli had the window rolled down a bit, and the smell of salt and fresh air rushed in. It was intoxicating and relaxing. Dave could see why Ronnie would want to live here. It was like a vacation spot with a homey feel to it.

"This is it, coming up on the right," Eli said at once. Dave's palms became slicker, and he swallowed a knot in his throat as he turned right and up the drive. He didn't know what to expect. Never in his wildest dreams did he think he would see where

Ronnie had lived all this time. In all his fantasies, she had come to him, to his house, the house that was meant to be theirs.

They pulled up to a small, picturesque house. It had a summer cottage feel to it, and it just screamed *Ronnie*. A big wraparound porch with a screened front door, the roof looked slanted and worn down, and the house was overall quite small looking from the outside. There was no garage. Dave pulled in behind an older model CRV. On its rear window was a stick family, a mother, a son, and a daughter. Tears welled in Dave's eyes, and his breath hitched for a moment. He hadn't even stepped into the house yet, and it was all hitting him too fast.

"I'm sorry," he said after they sat in the still car for a few minutes. "Just give me a minute."

Eli glanced at the parked car in front of them and then back at Dave. Something moved in Dave's peripheral vision on his left, and Eli said, "Take your time." He then stepped out of the car.

Dave closed his eyes for a moment to recover from the stick-family on the back of the car, and when he opened them again, he glanced in the rear-view mirror at Abby. She stared, neutral faced, out of her window, her earbuds still in, the soft sound of the music she listened to trickling out into the car. Dave followed her gaze over to Eli and the house.

An older woman stood at the front door on the other side of the screen. Eli moved up the stairs onto the porch, and she opened the screened door and brought him into a hug. Dave watched as his son's shoulders slumped, and when the woman pulled back, Eli nodded at something she said.

There was nowhere to hide now, and no way to pause time. Dave took a deep breath and stepped out of the car. He took care not to look at the back of the CRV again and walked up to the house.

The steps up to the porch sunk in the centers, and each one creaked as he stepped up. The pale-yellow paint on the house chipped and peeled, but the front door looked fresh. It was a robin's egg blue, and a homemade sunflower wreath sat in its center. Dave knew it was homemade because Ronnie loved making seasonal wreaths.

The woman at the front door gave Dave a sad, but welcoming smile. She was a good foot and a half shorter than him, with wiry white hair, and lines all over her face. Her eyes were kind and the same colour as the door. "Hello. You must be Dave," she said with an extended hand.

"Dave—Dad, I mean… this is Mrs. Hannigan, our neighbour," Eli introduced.

"Please, call me Alice," she said as Dave took her hand. It was soft and warm, and made Dave think briefly of his beloved grandmother.

"Hello, Alice. It's nice to meet you."

"And you must be Abby," Alice said. Dave looked over his shoulder to see Abby standing behind him. He didn't hear her get out of the car, but there she was. She shook Alice's hand in silence. "Sad circumstances to be meeting you all. Please, come in." Alice held the screen door open for them. Eli walked in first, Dave and Abby followed.

The inside of the house was just as quaint as the outside. A staircase was to the immediate right upon entering and disappeared upstairs around the corner. A rounded arch to the left showcased a small sitting room, where a faded blue loveseat and two matching armchairs sat together, a glass coffee table separating them. A vibrant green plant sat in the corner by the window. Dave could see Ronnie entertaining her friends in here. He pictured her laughing in one armchair, a cup of tea in her hands, with her feet curled up beneath her.

As they followed Alice into the back of the house, Dave glanced at the passing photos on the walls. There were a few recent ones of Eli in what looked like a soccer uniform, and a few others of a girl with matching brown curls. *She must be Lisa,* Dave thought. Most of the pictures were older though. A young boy with missing teeth laughed, covered head-to-toe in mud; a baby in a bright pink bathing suit smiled on a beach towel. They filled Dave with a sad nostalgia.

Another rounded arch at the back of the short hallway led into an open-concept space. The small kitchen was off to the left, another archway connecting it to the sitting room he saw earlier. A small, rounded kitchen table and four chairs sat in front of a small patio door, and the rest of the space opened into a living room. Across from a worn leather couch was a brilliant brick fireplace in one corner, and a modest older TV in another. Next to the TV was another doorway that seemed to lead to another hall.

"Can I interest you in some coffee?" Alice asked as she bustled in the small kitchen.

"Um, yes, please, that would be nice," Dave said back.

"I'll get it." Eli took a cup out of Alice's hand. "You sit down, Mrs. H."

The older woman didn't argue, and she sat down at the table. She gestured for Dave and Abby to join her. Dave hesitated a minute before sitting down. Abby crossed her arms and looked uncomfortable in the room. Dave pulled the chair out beside him, and reluctantly, she sat next to him.

They sat in silence as Eli made them coffee. Once he came over with a pot and mugs, he set everything out on the table for them. And to Dave's surprise, he brought a glass of water over for Abby. *Perceptive*, Dave thought as he helped himself to a cup of coffee. *He must have noticed she didn't drink any at home.*

"Well," Alice said with a hot mug between her weathered hands, "there's a lot to be said, and a lot to go through."

"Shouldn't we wait for Lisa?" Eli asked. "Where is she?"

"She's out for a run," Alice replied, "but should be back soon. I don't think she needs to be here for this. She's having a hard time, as we all are."

Alice glanced at Dave with an odd look in her eye. Dave felt his stomach twist, and he looked down in his coffee. Somehow, he just knew. "Ronnie never told you about us, did she?" he asked.

Alice shook her head as she took a long sip from her coffee. "Not much, no. Just mentioned once that her husband and oldest lived elsewhere. I'm not one to meddle. Families look a lot different nowadays than when I grew up. She left a note explaining what had happened. It was all quite a shock—I mean, everything was."

Dave looked over at Eli. He stared hard into his own mug, tears in his eyes, but they didn't fall. Alice reached over and patted his hand, and Eli grabbed it in his and squeezed it. Dave didn't know this old woman, but she meant a lot to his kids, that was apparent. She was the grandmother figure in their lives. Their real one would be a stranger, just like their father.

"I had no idea," Eli spoke at last. "I never really questioned it, you know? Your mom tells you that you live here with her and your sister, and that your dad and other sister live elsewhere. And it's just a fact. You don't question facts. We started to question it more recently, and—and—"

His lip suddenly trembled, and he closed his eyes. Alice scooched her chair closer to Eli and wrapped her small arm around him, and Eli sobbed into her shoulder.

"The kids had been asking to meet you," Alice explained. "And she promised that they'd go see you this Christmas. And Eli is worried it put her over the edge and…" She shook her head and looked away from Dave. She pulled away from Eli and held his chin, their eyes level. "I'm telling you what I told you on Monday. This is not your fault. When someone takes their own life, it's their decision. If… if she was nervous about Christmas, she would have done it closer to Christmas. You listen to me, Eli. It's not your fault."

Eli nodded as tears streamed down his face.

"It's true," Dave said. His own voice cracked, but he pressed through. "It's not your fault, Eli. I know you won't believe me, hell, I haven't been in either of your lives for fourteen years. But your mother, she had depression her whole life. This… suicide was something she'd thought of before. On more than one occasion."

Alice clucked her tongue and shook her head. "Terrible, terrible darkness. Such a shame. She was a wonderful person."

"Wonderful people don't abandon their children," Abby suddenly said. Dave looked over at her. Angry tears spilled down her cheeks, and her face contorted. She pushed away from the table, her glass of water knocking over, and stormed down the hall and out the front door.

Dave felt his cheeks flush as Alice watched his daughter storm out of the house. Eli looked hurt and bewildered. "I'm sorry for her," Dave stammered, embarrassed he had to apologize for her behavior.

Alice, however, shook her head and waved him off. "Everyone grieves differently. I can't imagine how all of this is for you. For me, she was a beautiful person. A sweet, kind neighbour, single mother, with two wonderful children. I knew she had struggles sometimes, with her emotions. But… it's like I've lost a daughter. I never would have guessed. I remember hearing about you years ago, when Eli and Ronnie first went missing. I'm sure the news coverings were bigger out west, but we had a few blips here and there. If I had known…" She sighed as she trailed off.

A silence filled the room as the three of them drank their coffees. Eli sniffled and wiped his tears away. A clock ticked on a wall nearby, and it reminded Dave of the clock in his own house.

"You must have many questions," Alice said at last. "I'm not sure I'll be able to answer all of them, but I can try."

Dave exhaled loudly. He had questions, hundreds of questions, many of which would now remain unanswered. The best he could do now was learn about Ronnie's life, the happiness she made for herself and focus on that, instead of the tragedy at hand. That he could do over time. The key questions now were about the future and where they would go from here.

"Yes, I have many questions," Dave said. "I'm not sure where to start." A small throat cleared as someone shuffled into the kitchen. Dave looked over Alice's shoulder and his entire world stopped as he looked at his daughter for the first time. His Lisa.

Abby

I hate everything, Abby thought as she stormed out of the house. The smell of fresh air, tinged with sea salt and something sweet struck her as she sat down on the top of the porch steps. They were here for five minutes, and already her dad forgot about her. Left her alone in the car, and now he was defending her mother's abandonment. She brought her knees up under her chin and hugged them close as angry tears continued to spill down her face.

A few cars whizzed by quietly on the street in front of her. A bird chirped happily somewhere in the distance, and all she could think about was how *peaceful* it seemed out here. It did nothing but make her angrier. If her mother had wanted to live somewhere more peaceful, why didn't she take her with her? Why did she have to leave her and Dad behind?

Her heart ached as she closed her eyes and sobbed quietly. Like Eli worried and wondered if he were to blame for their mother's death, Abby always wondered if she was to blame for her leaving. Had she been so hard to handle as a toddler that her mother gave up? How could she blame Abby for something like that? She had only been a little kid. She knew, somewhere *deep* down that wasn't the case. But sometimes that realism was too deep to reach, and Abby blamed herself.

When she opened her eyes again, a pair of pink sneakers looked back at her. She followed the sneakers up, past a pair of knobby pale knees, a pair of mustard yellow shorts and a grey sweatshirt, to a quizzical face staring at her. Abby scrambled up and wiped her tears away as she stared down the porch steps at who she presumed was her younger sister, Lisa.

There was no presumption really; Abby knew it was her. She had dark hair, the same as Eli, swept up into a messy bun. That was where their similarities ended. It wasn't the hair though, that gave away who she was to Abby. Lisa looked just like their father. Same square jaw and brown eyes, rounded nose, and full lips. The resemblance was impossible to mistake, and Abby stared in shock for a minute.

"You must be Abby," Lisa said after a moment of silence. Her voice was small and sweet, not quite unlike Abby's. "Hi. I'm Lisa."

"I know who you are," Abby scoffed. This was the replacement daughter. Suddenly, all Abby could see was red and green. Red with rage at her mother for abandoning her and then replacing her with someone new. And green with envy; envy that while she looked like her traitorous mother, Lisa grew up looking like their father. She didn't even *know* their father. She did not know what kind of wonderful person he was, and yet she got to look just like him. And Abby knew her father would be so happy when he saw that.

Lisa looked taken aback. She stared at Abby a moment and then opened her mouth to speak again. Abby pushed past her before she could. She didn't want to hear what her little *sister* had to say. She didn't even want her to exist.

Dave

It was later that evening and Dave felt exhausted. They spent the rest of the evening focused on the mechanical things that needed to be done. They planned the funeral. Alice had already contacted the home, the only one in the town, and the next date they had available was next Friday, like Eli had told them already. Once Lisa showered from her run, she joined them at the table, and together the four of them picked out floral arrangements, headstone fonts and engravings, and urns.

The question of whether they would stay here, in this small town together, or move back with Dave and Abby across the country was unspoken. Dave was taking this all one step at a time and didn't want to make any rash decisions or rush his children to decide on things they may not have even thought of yet. And so, they picked out a tomb marking for the cemetery here, where they had grown up and had their childhoods, and Dave picked out an urn to bring home with him, wherever that home may be. It wasn't the Ronnie he hoped to get back, but he was adamant on holding onto whatever piece of her he could.

The epitaph was a hard decision. Alice suggested the generic, "Beloved mother and wife" but Dave hesitated to agree. While Ronnie had been a beloved mother, *and* his beloved wife at one point, and forever in his heart, she had been missing as his spouse for longer than they were together. As much as he loved her, there was something about putting *wife* on the memorials that made him feel awkward. In the end, they all agreed on a simple "In loving memory" for both the tombstone and the urn.

It would have been nice if Abby was there to help them with the arrangements, but she avoided them at all costs, only reappearing quickly to eat a few pieces of pizza once the takeout arrived, and then she disappeared outside again.

"You and Abby can sleep in here," Eli said once they finished for the night. There had been no bonding yet with his new children, but that would come later as well. Right now, the focus was on Ronnie and saying goodbye. They'd have a week together before doing that, and Dave wanted to give the kids their space. Let them grieve how they needed to, and then they'd figure out how to move forward from there.

Eli showed them to Lisa's room upstairs. It was cramped but had a bunk bed in it. Lisa would be in his room, and Eli said he would take the couch. His room was tiny on the main floor, too small to even be a bedroom really, but nobody was about to sleep in Ronnie's room. Dave tried to protest and said he would take the couch, but Eli was firm in his decision. He was already like the "man of the house" despite how antiquated that idea was these days.

Lisa's room was like any typical young teens. Pastel floral duvets were on both the top and bottom bunks. Twinkly lights hung around the bottom bunk, and she had a heart-shaped silver mirror on the wall. Dave didn't want to pry into his new daughter's life too much, but he glanced at a few pictures on the walls. Lisa smiled with a friend in one. Many of the others were of her and Eli, highlighting how close their relationship was. There was one that stood out though, a picture of her and Ronnie. It looked recent, possibly even from this past summer. It was too painful for him to look at closely, but he also couldn't take his eyes off his deceased wife. She looked just the same as she had before, save for a few lines etched around her eyes and mouth. She looked happy.

As Dave rifled through his suitcase, he exhaled in disbelief. He had another daughter. Hearing it was one thing, but meeting Lisa was another. She was shy and polite, and she looked just like him.

It took his breath away, and he relived the moment now. Seeing her brought tears to his eyes. She was another piece of Ronnie left behind, a gift that he had only just received. Like Eli learned in Ronnie's suicide note that he was kidnapped, Lisa learned her father didn't know she existed. Too many webs to untangle in the first evening.

Just as he finished getting changed, Abby burst through the door. Already in her pajamas, she swung her duffle bag onto the floor and climbed onto the top bunk without saying a word.

"Where have you been all night?" Dave asked. Abby didn't answer. The springs of her mattress creaked as she rolled over and faced away from him. "Abby, don't ignore me. We need to talk."

"No thanks," Abby snapped back.

"Abby, please," Dave said. "This is hard enough as it is, for everybody. Don't make it any more difficult."

"Then here, let me make it easy for you!" Abby snapped. She rolled back over and grabbed the pillow and blanket from the top bunk as she climbed down. Without looking at Dave, she stormed out of the room and downstairs.

Abby

That night Abby tossed and turned, unable to sleep. Once she was downstairs, she wasn't sure where she would sleep. Eli was supposed to be on the couch. But he was nowhere to be found, so Abby took it.

The couch creaked with every movement as she rolled from one side to the other, and the unfamiliar sounds and smells made Abby uneasy. It was almost too quiet here. She needed the sound of a passing car's engine, or an ambulance siren from far away to put her to sleep. The night here was still, and it left her alone with her thoughts. It was too quiet to drown them out and lull herself to sleep. The time change didn't help either.

During the night, in a daze of half-sleep, she imagined what it would have been like if she grew up here. What would her life have been like if her mother had taken her with her? Maybe she'd have gotten a bigger house. Regardless, Abby pictured that she and Lisa shared a room. They'd have had late night chats, fought over dolls, and giggled under blanket forts. Sibling things that Abby missed out on, but that her brother and sister got to experience.

It would have been harder to run away with you, a small voice in her head whispered. *You would have slowed her down. She'd have taken you in a heartbeat, but it would be easier to hide without you.* Abby tried to ignore the voice, but it woke her several times. It was right. Abby was three. Three-year-olds weren't quiet. They asked questions, like "Where's Daddy?" and "When will he come to our new house?" Three-year-olds wouldn't understand. Even now, at seventeen, she didn't understand, but she would have known to play along.

If Mom brought her, and they moved here, etcetera… would she still have committed suicide?

Abby sat up on the couch as that thought passed through her mind. The soft ticking of the clock on the kitchen wall told her it was just past three-thirty in the morning. Three-thirty here, but only ten or so last night back at home.

Abby padded across the tiled floor and into the kitchen to help herself to a glass of water. The tap water tasted different here, but it was still comforting, nonetheless. It was cool and refreshing, and Abby closed her eyes as it slid down her throat. Maybe if she had been a part of her mother's life, she'd still be alive.

Something creaked across the room and Abby opened her eyes. Eli tiptoed through the living room toward the kitchen and paused when he saw her standing there. He nodded towards the glass of water in her hand.

"Couldn't sleep either?" he asked.

Abby shook her head. She felt a twinge of annoyance. Company wasn't something she wanted right now, but she was the stranger here. Eli walked up beside her and grabbed his own glass off the shelf.

As he filled it with water, Abby realized this was something they had in common. A glass of water was something they both craved when sleep eluded them. However, unlike Abby, who took small sips and savored her water, Eli chugged it all in one breath. As she watched him, she tried to remember the sweet little baby he was when he disappeared. It was hard to equate that person with the one standing beside her. Once done, Eli took a deep, long breath and sighed as he placed the cup on the counter with a loud *clang*.

"It'll be a while before I sleep properly again," said Eli, with an added "if ever," under his breath.

"Why is that?" Abby muttered under her breath. The question came out before she could pause to think.

"Oh, I guess I didn't tell you. Maybe only Dave—Dad…" Eli took a deep breath and glanced away from her. "I was the one who found Mom. I see her whenever I close my eyes now."

Something cold ran through Abby and she stared at Eli in shock. She didn't know and couldn't imagine what that must have been like for him. Her mouth opened to ask questions, but nothing came out. After a moment of silence, Eli looked over at her, staring agape at him, and he hastily ran his hand through his hair.

"It wasn't gruesome, or anything," he blurted, as though it were no big deal. But it was a big deal. He was the one who discovered their mother's suicide. And as angry as Abby was about everything, as angry as she was at Eli for being the one that she ran away with, she admired him. Three years younger than her, and yet with everything she saw of him so far, Eli was so much more grown up than Abby. "It just—it looked like she was sleeping."

Abby wasn't sure if that brought her comfort. In one small way it did, but overall, it didn't. It didn't make any difference because she was still standing in the kitchen of her dead mother's home, with her long-lost brother, at three-thirty in the morning. There wasn't much comfort in any of that.

"That must have been really hard," Abby said at last, in a quiet voice. Eli nodded. Abby noticed that his hands shook, and he fidgeted with his thumbs. She looked down at her bare feet and curled her toes. "Were you close with her?"

"Yeah," Eli answered without skipping a beat. He seemed to relax a little, and he leaned back against the counter beside Abby. "She was like my best friend. Always there for me—and Lisa. It was like us against the world, you know?"

Abby knew. That's how she felt about her dad. The two of them faced everything together; and yet right now, they were facing it apart. Abby didn't know why she was being so difficult. But she had all these *feelings* and didn't know how to deal with them. And when she didn't know how to deal with something, she became frustrated and mean.

So instead of nodding along and telling Eli that she understood, she scoffed and said, "No, I don't know. She left me behind. She didn't care."

Eli pushed away from the counter. His hands were in fists now and his face twisted between heartache and rage. Abby gripped the glass of water in her hand as Eli ripped into her and defended their mother.

"You say it like it was easy for her," he whispered angrily. "I can't imagine what it must have been like to have grown up knowing your mother left you behind. I only just learned what happened. To think that they declared me as kidnapped... it makes it seem like Mom was a bad person."

Abby opened her mouth to argue but Eli cut her off before she could interject.

"She wasn't," he continued. "And yeah, maybe she left you behind. And we'll never know why. But you were never far from her mind. You might not know about me, or Lisa, but we know all about you."

Abby was taken aback. Heat rose to her cheeks, and she placed her cup on the counter next to Eli's. "What are you talking about?"

"Follow me."

Quiet as a ghost, Eli wove his way back through the living room. Abby hesitated to follow. She wanted to stay angry, angry at her mother, angry at Eli, angry at anyone really. Feeling angry was better than the grief that kept trying to creep into every fiber. But her curiosity got the better of her, and she followed her brother into the small hallway behind the living room.

Abby hadn't seen this part of the house yet. The hallway was short. Two doors lined the walls, with a third on the end. The first door led to a bathroom. It was bigger than the tiny one upstairs, but it was still smaller than Abby's smallest one at home.

Next to it was Eli's bedroom. It was tiny, Abby noted as she walked by, the entire floor taken up by his mattress. Lisa's sleeping form hid under a pile of blankets, a mop of long curls poking out underneath and into the moonlight that shone through the small window. This meant that the last room was their mother's. Abby stood outside of the opened door, too afraid to cross over the threshold.

As Eli rummaged around for something inside, Abby placed her attention to the photos that lined the wall. There were frames of various sizes and colours, each one a frozen moment in time. Most of them were of Eli and Lisa, some as young children, others more recent. Abby's breath would catch whenever she'd see one with her mother in it. She looked just like she did in Abby's dreams.

More surprising, however, was when she came across of a photo of herself. It did not surprise her about the one when she was two and a half, sitting at the top of a slide; that was one her dad had framed at home, one of his favourites. It was when she came across more recent photos that she felt shocked. A picture of when she won her first race in track and field, another one of her and her grandma at the beach. They must have been pictures her mother took from online, posted by her dad or grandma.

In the middle of the hall of pictures were three of the biggest frames. They were all the same size and style, clean crisp silver frames. And in each of them were Abby, Eli, and Lisa's latest school photos. They hung neatly beside each other in a perfect row, and Abby felt a knot form in her throat as she looked at them. It was like any display of school photos she had seen at Scarlet or Joanna's house, their pictures beside their siblings. Not one was bigger or more important than the other. They were all equal, as children should be in their parents' eyes.

All at once, Abby was overcome with guilt for feeling angry towards her mother. The anger was there, but with confusion now more than ever. Here she was on display, just as equal to her brother and sister even though she hadn't shared a life with them. Her mother had put her picture up beside them just the same.

"Here," Eli said as he emerged from their mother's room. He thrust a worn-out journal into Abby's hands. "Read this and tell me she didn't care about you."

Abby opened to a random page and saw *Dear Abby* at the top. The writing was neat and slanted, a mix of cursive and printing. She shut the journal and shook her head, recalling what her dad told her years ago. "That's not me. She'd write to her sister who died when they were teens."

Eli rolled his eyes. "Just read it. Maybe then you'll have a little compassion. Living with depression isn't easy."

He then slunk back into his room and closed the door softly behind him, leaving Abby in the dark with the wall of pictures, the ghost of their mother's words, and her own confusion and grief.

Dave

Listening to Alice talk about Ronnie was surreal. As she and Dave sat together in the kitchen the next afternoon, Dave relaxed back in his chair and listened in awe about the way Alice spoke of her.

"She'll be missed at the soup kitchen," Alice said in a sad voice. "Father Simmons will have trouble finding someone to take her place."

"Ronnie attended church?" Dave asked in disbelief.

Alice chuckled. "Oh no. I try to attend on Sundays, but Veronica wasn't religious. She came across their volunteer program a few years after Lisa was born and volunteered every second Thursday night ever since. I don't think she missed a shift."

It was the little stories like that that painted a picture in Dave's head about Ronnie's new life. He learned she had a job at the local library and worked there for the last fourteen years. It didn't surprise him, as she had loved to read. It was a love she wanted to pass on to her children. One that never took off with Abby, Dave now realized as he thought on it, but it was clear with Eli.

Dave had little time yet to interact with his new daughter. Whenever the two of them were in the same room, Lisa became shy and quiet. She avoided looking at him, and when he would turn to include her in the conversation, she was already whispered away somewhere else. He wasn't sure how to break the ice with her.

It wasn't until the day after that Dave was alone with all three kids for the first time. Alice had other things to attend to, and Dave was both thankful yet terrified to have some time alone with his family. It was his time to figure out how to navigate his new role as a father of three.

Abby kept to herself for the most part. Holed up on a chair in the front living room for most of the day, her nose deep in what looked like one of Ronnie's journals. Dave left her alone to grieve in her own way. He didn't ask how or where she found the journal. Maybe she had ventured into Ronnie's room on her own. That was something Dave wasn't ready to do yet.

Eli helped show Dave where things were around the house that morning. Together the two of them made breakfast for the girls, and though he hid it due to the sobriety of the situation, Dave smiled at how natural it felt to be in the kitchen with his son. The awkward and jilted movements that Eli exhibited when he first showed up on Dave's doorstep earlier that week melted away, and he felt confident that his son was starting to feel comfortable around him.

"I obviously don't remember you," Eli said as he showed Dave his cramped bedroom. "But I've always had this framed by my bedside for as long as I can remember." He handed him a framed photograph.

Dave smiled as he took the frame out of Eli's hands. He remembered the moment as though it were yesterday. The picture was from the Hawaiian vacation they had taken that year. Eli was only a few months old in the photo. He was smiling, toothless still, and had chubby rolls on his arms. Dave held Eli on his knee at the beach, the two of them in matching swimsuits. Ronnie loved making the family match, and Dave had put his baseball cap on Eli's head. It nearly swallowed his head whole, the cap covering down to his eyes, but his smile appeared under the rim. Dave smiled broadly in the photo, a laugh on his face as the cap slid down Eli's face just as Ronnie tried to take the picture.

"This is one of my favourites," Dave said. He ran his fingers over the small baby smile and looked up at the grown son before him. So much time had passed since this frozen moment in his hands. "It was one of your mother's favourites too. It doesn't surprise me she framed it for you."

Eli half-smiled in response and took the fame back from Dave. He glanced from the father in front of him to the one in the photo, as though to confirm it was the same person, also reflecting on the missed time that had passed between them. He placed the picture back on the small windowsill above his bed and then shoved his hands in his pockets.

"Hard to believe you're here." Eli looked down at his feet as he talked. "Lisa and I were looking forward to meeting you at Christmas, and now…"

Dave's heart sank as his son choked up. He reached out to hug him, but then corrected himself in case Eli wasn't ready for that yet. Instead, he put his hand on his shoulder. "It sort of changes the whole tune of things, doesn't it? Not as exciting, more of a necessity."

Eli nodded. He shifted closer to Dave. "When Lisa and I first saw the movie *Parent Trap* as kids, we'd stay up late scheming on how to get the two of you back together. We didn't know the reason you were apart. Mom was good at avoiding and changing the subject. Now we know why. So, when she said we'd all meet at Christmas, those schemes and plans came back into our heads, and we laughed about them."

Dave smiled. Before he knew it, his whole arm wrapped around Eli's shoulders. It was then that he noticed how tall his son was. He was only fourteen, but already he was almost as tall as Dave, and came up right to his chin.

"I wish Mom were here to talk to about all of this," Eli said suddenly. Tears welled in his eyes, and his voice hitched. "I don't need any explanations; I just want to talk to her. I used to go to her with all my problems, and now I feel lost. Broken."

Dave pulled his son into his arms. Eli tensed for a moment, but then relaxed into the hug and broke down crying. Though they were still strangers, a sense of trust formed between them. Eli's soft curls tickled Dave's cheek as he held on tight to his son.

"I know," Dave mumbled. "I miss her too. I always have."

Dave

Later that afternoon, the rumbling of Dave's stomach prompted him decide what to do for dinner that night. It had been nothing but takeout since they first arrived, and tonight would likely be the same. The idea of cooking in Ronnie's kitchen made him feel uncomfortable. He knew eventually he would have to. He wasn't made of money and feeding three teenagers was costly.

There would be a lot of uncomfortable moments coming and he knew they were all unavoidable. Dave still had to talk to Eli and Lisa, but he settled on the idea that they would move back with him and Abby. It meant packing up Ronnie's home, likely selling a lot of her furniture and the house. It meant really saying goodbye to her and the life she built. All of that would come in a few weeks' time, but it loomed on him. He couldn't be off work forever and Abby couldn't keep missing school. They had moved on from Ronnie. Like she had created her new life, they had created theirs. And while it turned theirs upside down with the news of her death, they weren't quite as "on hold" as Eli and Lisa. Dave and Abby built their new life after their old one crumbled before them. Eli and Lisa's lives were the ones now crumbled.

Everyone was grieving, but it was at different stages, over different aspects. It was much more complex than Dave thought initially, and the more he thought of what he had to do, the supports he had to provide, the more overwhelmed he became. So, he did what he always did and took it one step at a time.

Another rumble from his stomach broke him from his thoughts, and he exhaled loudly as he crossed through the living room towards the kitchen. Something caught his eye on the back deck, and he paused mid-step.

Lisa sat at the patio table, back to the house, her frame silhouetted in the setting sun. A big sketchpad sat in front of her, and her hand moved across the page in a flowing motion. Dave had seen little of her all day. Neither of them knew how to act around one another yet.

Dave turned and headed to the back door. Not wanting to interrupt her right away, he watched through the glass door as she focused intently on the page in front of her. He had noticed a few little doodles on the walls in her room but wouldn't have clued in that it was a serious hobby. Her arms were swallowed in the oversized knit sweater she wore, the chill out here brisker than it was back on the west coast, but it was a beautiful evening to be outside.

Lisa's hand stopped moving for a moment, the billowing sleeves coming to a still, and she sat back in the chair. She then held up the sketchbook in front of her to study it, and Dave inhaled sharply. He slid open the door, and Lisa turned around at the sound of the squealing track, and quickly put the sketchbook back down on the table.

"I'm sorry, I didn't mean to startle you, but..." Dave said, speechless as he stepped over to the table. Before she could protest, he picked up the sketchbook with one hand and his other went up to his mouth in awe, as he choked back tears.

It was a portrait of Ronnie. The thick black lines were rough, a style that Lisa must have adopted, but it was flawless. The portrait's expression was serious, with a twinkle in her eye. She was older than when Dave had seen her last, and the realism that Lisa captured was extraordinary.

"You have a gift," Dave said once he regained his composure. He placed the sketchbook back down on the table, and Lisa placed an arm over it protectively. She glanced uncertainly at him for a moment, but then relaxed as she looked back down at the portrait.

"I love drawing," she said in a small voice. "I have for as long as I can remember. It's something Mom encouraged me to do." Lisa then picked up the sketchbook and hugged it close to her chest. She closed her soft brown eyes and tears spilled down her cheeks.

Dave sat down in the chair next to her. He placed a hand on her shoulder, unsure of what else he could do. Though her existence was unknown to him for all of her life, the need he felt to comfort her was natural and overwhelming. She was his daughter, just as much as Abby. Their relationship would be hardest to build and take the most care and time. And that wasn't a problem for Dave. He'd give it all the time in the world, to savour this one last gift left behind by Ronnie.

Abby

All day, Abby engrossed herself in her mother's journal. Since the moment Eli handed it over to her, Abby was both intrigued and terrified to dive into the mind of her mother. Finally, she would learn some sort of truth to help her with the closure of her abandonment, a finality that she was desperately searching for her entire life.

At first when she opened the journal, Abby was apprehensive to what she might find. She barely knew her mother, and yet she could very well stumble onto her last thoughts. But as she flipped through the dated and worn pages, she saw that Eli gave her one of the older journals. He brought her back to the very beginning, to right around the time when Abby was born.

The first thing that struck her was how similar her mother's writing was to her own. Abby wondered, as she looked down at the slant and neat loops, if her mother had held her pen in an awkward clasp like Abby did. By the time a teacher showed her how to hold it "properly," Abby was too set in her ways to change. Anytime someone really watched her as she wrote, they would comment on the odd way she held her pen. Maybe this was something her mother had done as well.

It wasn't long before her mother's words and thoughts absorbed her. For so long, Veronica Saunders had been this ethereal woman that Abby placed on a pedestal, a mysterious goddess from whom all Abby wanted was praise and adoration, but for all she knew was a terrible person for abandoning her family. And now, as she read pages upon pages of her words and thoughts, her mother became more human and less goddess. As a matter of fact, there were a few times it caught Abby off-guard, for her mother wrote things down how Abby spoke to herself in her own head.

It was odd, at first, to read what her mother wrote about her. Their time together was so short, and yet it was clear early on that Abby's mother cared for her very much.

Today Abby laughed for the first time, one entry said. *It's the most magical thing I've ever heard. I've never felt more elated, and now all I ever try to do is get her to laugh. Dave is better at it, of course...*

Another thing Abby picked up on, even before she got to the part where she was left behind, was that her mother doubted herself. Often, she would mention how Dad was better at something, or she'd question her actions.

Abby drew her first smiley face today. I've already ordered a special frame for it and made sure to write the date on the back. I re-arranged my photo wall to make space for it. I want it front and centre where everyone can see it...

We went to the beach today. Abby and Dave built a sandcastle, while I tried to relax and not let the morning sickness get the better of me. I've been trying to keep calm and excited about the new baby, but I can't help but think back on the post-partum depression from last time and...

Depression was something that Abby never took too seriously. Whenever her father mentioned her mom's condition, Abby thought he was using it as a crutch, and as an excuse. And yet, as she delved deeper into the journals, there was no doubt her mother battled something deep within herself. Even after she left with Eli, it followed her, and ultimately, consumed her.

Today Eli asked me if I was sad all the time because I miss Abby. He knows he has a big sister and doesn't understand why she isn't with us, just knows that she isn't. I told him I miss her very much and that it does make me sad she's not with us, but that it also wasn't the sole reason I'm "sad all the time." I guess I'm not hiding my issues from the kids as well as I thought I was...

The other thing that consumed her was her guilt for leaving Abby. The knot of anger towards her mother that Abby always carried deep in the pit of her stomach unraveled. And yet, every time Abby read a passage about her mother's guilt, she screamed at her in her head. *All you had to do was come home!* And maybe if she had, her outcome would have been different.

Once Abby finished the first journal, she struck up the nerve to find the next. Her mother's room loomed, an intimidating space of deep sadness. Or at least, that's how Abby perceived it as she stared at the closed door in the hall. How Eli had the strength to just waltz right in there, Abby did not know. Maybe it was because he already faced the darkest thing he could possibly find in there. All that remained for the rest of them to find were the ghosts left behind.

The door creaked softly as Abby pushed it open. The noise made her hesitate. It was like an alarm screaming about an intruder, and she paused, her hand still on the door, as she waited to see if someone would come running to stop her. But Eli was in the shower, and the last Abby saw of her dad, he was outside talking to Lisa. She would be undisturbed, for now.

The room was welcoming and cozy. A neatly made bed was in the middle, the blanket appearing soft and warm. Abby shuddered when she looked at it, once again trying not to imagine the horrors that Eli discovered on that very bed. She tried to avoid looking at it again as she surveyed the room.

More pictures lined the walls. These must have been her favourites, Abby figured, as she looked from one to another. There was one from her parents' wedding, one that Abby knew had been her favourite because her dad mentioned it every time they looked at it in their album at home. Most of them were of Eli and Lisa, which was only natural, but now and then there would be one of Abby. Rare pictures that her father would share online, evidence again that her mother was still in touch with them, even if they hadn't known it.

Abby went over to the nightstand first to search for the next volume of journals. The drawer proved to be disappointing, with little in it, just some lavender hand cream, a few stray bobby pins and hair elastics, and the novel that she must have been reading. It had a classy picture of a Victorian era looking road. The edges of the pages were worn and bent, and a beaded bookmark lay a third of the way through. There was something surreal about seeing the novel unfinished, never *to* be finished again, sitting there on the nightstand that knocked the wind out of Abby. These were the pieces of a life interrupted, a life ended prematurely.

Abby sat down on the bed for a moment to catch her breath, not taking into consideration that this was the last resting place of her mother. Her finger slipped under the pillow as she rested back on her hands, and it grazed something papery.

From under the pillow, Abby pulled out a worn photograph. Her breath caught in her throat and tears filled her eyes. The picture felt crinkly and had a bad bend in one corner, and it blurred behind the tears in Abby's eyes. Underneath her mother's pillow was the same picture that Abby kept under hers. Her mother's smiling face shone through the tears, and Abby's baby chubby cheeks, the picture so familiar that for a moment, Abby thought she was back at home in her own bed. All this time, the two of them had been together under each other's pillows, never far from the other's heart.

Dave

As the days crept closer to the funeral, Dave found it harder and harder to sleep. Every creak in the house seemed to whisper Ronnie's name. Whenever he did happen to catch a few moments of sleep, it bombarded him with memories of Ronnie. They melded together into deep, lifelike dreams, and when he woke up, the grief would be insurmountable. One moment she was beside him, laughing with her hair blowing in the wind as they walked together on the beach, and the next he woke up cold, and alone. Her laugh echoed in his head for a few moments as he grappled with what was real and what was a dream, and when the sound of it died down and Abby's soft snoring replaced it, his heart ached, and he muffled the sound of his sobs.

Because of this little sleep, Dave was usually the first one up in the morning. It was a surprise on Monday morning to find Lisa awake, fully dressed, and rummaging through her backpack when Dave walked into the kitchen to start a pot of coffee. She jumped as he bumped into one of the side tables, and he winced as he stubbed his toe.

"Sorry, I didn't mean to scare you," he hissed through the throbbing pain permeating through his baby toe. "I wasn't expecting anyone else to be up yet." Abby could sleep in until noon if Dave let her, which he had been, circumstances being what they were.

"Oh, yeah," Lisa glanced away from Dave, as though she were guilty of something, and quickly finished thrusting a notebook into her bag and zipped it up.

As Dave walked past her and into the kitchen to start the coffee, he saw an empty plate next to her bag. It was covered in breadcrumbs and a smear of jam, evidence that she ate a piece or two of toast already for breakfast.

"I um—I wanted to—" Lisa started to say. The coffee maker spat and hissed as the hot water poured into the machine, and the coffee spilled out the other end into the pot below. Dave looked up at Lisa, and again she quickly glanced away as their eyes met. "I mean, if it's OK with you… I was kind of hoping to go to school today."

Dave blinked, unsure of what to say. She and Eli missed the first week of school, as had Abby, which was understandable. Missing school wasn't even something that had crossed his mind. Nobody would expect them to go back anytime soon, and Dave wasn't about to force them to. He knew that Abby was eager to get back home and back into her normal life, but this new movement of grief was different for her. They hadn't seen Ronnie in years. Lisa saw her every day of her life.

As Lisa stared at him, waiting for a reply, he realized she was asking for his permission to go. She didn't phrase it as a question, but it had been. He was her guardian now. He made the rules, and she barely knew him. But by the looks of her packed bag, her mind was made, yet she still needed, or wanted, his permission.

Dave knew nothing about her school. All he could put together was that it was Lisa's first year in high school. Was it too soon for her to go back? She just lost her mother last week. Didn't she need more time to grieve? Would the kids judge her for going back? Would the teachers judge him?

What would Ronnie do? The question stung him somewhere deep in his soul, but he closed his eyes a moment as he tried to navigate the situation in front of him. He didn't know Lisa well enough to deny her this request. Perhaps she wanted to be surrounded by her friends, with people who comforted her as opposed to an estranged father and bitter sister. Everyone grieved differently. And while Dave didn't think he was ready to go back to work, maybe Lisa liked the distraction. Maybe it was something she needed and being stuck in her house was doing more harm than good.

"Of course," he said at last. Lisa exhaled a breath that she had been holding. "If that's where you want to be right now, then by all means. But please, call me right away if you want to come back, and I'll come get you."

"It's only a ten-minute walk from here," she said in a quick voice as she hitched her backpack up her shoulder. Dave felt himself deflate a little at the rejection. He wondered how long it would be before the two of them felt like father and daughter. Maybe not to the same extent as him and Abby, that would take a lot of time, more than just the few days they had so far.

As she walked to the back door and opened it, Lisa paused and looked over her shoulder back at him. "But I'll call you when I'm on my way home." Dave nodded, and as she slipped out the back door, a small smile spread across his face. The olive branch was there.

Abby

The floorboards beneath her feet creaked as Abby crept down the hall and faced her mother's bedroom door. It took her some time to find the courage to face the room again in search of the next journal, her last attempt abandoned after having found the picture under the pillow. Her father turned in early for the night, because he had to get up early in the morning to pick up her grandparents. Both Eli and Lisa were over at their neighbour's house. Abby was invited too, but she declined. Mrs. Hannigan seemed like a nice lady, but Abby didn't see the point in befriending someone she would leave soon.

It was a difficult conversation, but her dad announced today that they would sell the house, and Eli and Lisa would move in with him and Abby. They were both upset at the news, but unsurprised. It wouldn't be instantaneous; it would take a few weeks to sell and close the house, sell off the furniture, and pack up whatever her siblings wanted to keep.

Once the funeral was over, Dad would stay behind to help with all of that. Abby would fly back home with her grandparents and resume her life. This house and the trinkets inside it meant nothing to her. She felt like an intruder every time she sat on the couch, or when she slept in Lisa's bunk bed. Sure, her pictures were on the wall, but this wasn't a home to her.

She didn't envy her brother and sister. Abby couldn't imagine what it would be like if her dad died, and she had to sell off the comforts of her home, the place she grew up in, and move across the country. They all shared the grief of losing their mother, albeit that grief was different for her, but once the dust settled a bit, it would comfort Abby in her home, a safe and familiar place. Eli and Lisa would leave that behind along with their mother's resting place.

As she reached out for the doorknob, Abby paused, unsure if she heard the back door open. When nobody appeared around the corner, she took a deep breath, and twisted the knob. The door swung open, and for a moment Abby was hit again with the heartache of finding the picture underneath her mother's pillow. When she asked Eli about it, he explained that once the police and coroner had done their job in her room, Lisa put everything back in its regular place. Her mother really had slept with the picture under her pillow each night, and Eli said that she would show it to them often. It was one of her most prized possessions.

This time Abby avoided the bed and the nightstands all together. Eli said the journals were in her top dresser drawer. He offered to get them for her, but Abby said it was something she had to do for herself. She made a beeline straight to the dresser and ripped open the top drawer. It was a tall, old dresser, the colour of dark chocolate. The drawer squealed as it opened. Inside to the left was an array of undergarments neatly folded and sorted, and on the right were the journals. There were more than Abby expected, six thick volumes stacked neatly in pairs of three. Her dad wasn't kidding when he said that writing was a release for her.

As she pulled the journals out, something else caught Abby's eye. Pushed to the back of the dresser was a thick stack of envelopes. The stack was bound with bright coloured elastics. She set the journals down on top of the dresser as she pulled the envelopes out. Her name and mailing address stared back at her from the top envelope. The ink was faded, as though written from a long time ago, and the stamp was peeling.

Abby sank to the floor as she unbound the stack, and the envelopes scattered on the floor around her. They were all addressed to her, some of them stamped, some of them not. There were twenty or so, some written with blue ink, some with black. Some of them were wavy, as though her mother cried while writing it out, cried like Abby did at that moment.

It was suddenly all too much. Reading about how guilty her mother felt and how much she missed her in the journals, her school pictures on the walls stolen from social media, the worn-out photo under the pillow... and now finding these letters, solid evidence that her mother had needed Abby in her life but didn't quite have the courage to get her back. It was too much for Abby to handle, all these *feelings* that she couldn't process at once.

She left the envelopes where she dropped them and ran out of the room. Abby crept into the shared room where her father snored loudly on the bottom bunk. She quickly changed into a pair of sweatpants and threw on a sweater as she grabbed her sneakers. Tears blurred her eyes as she ran back down the stairs and nearly collided into Lisa.

"Sorry," Abby said as she slipped on the floor to stop herself. She wiped away the tears furiously as Lisa un-pressed herself from the wall. They stood there for a moment in silence by the front door, and Abby noticed the shoes in Lisa's hands. They were running sneakers, similar in style and colour to hers. "What are you doing?"

"I was just about to go for a run," Lisa said.

Abby took a step back and sized up her sister. There was no denying that Lisa resembled Dad more than she did their mother. She had his brown hair, which on her fell in perfect curls around her shoulders, and she had his hazel eyes. Her frame was thin and lanky, much like Eli's, and she sort of shrunk away from Abby's towering gaze. It was no surprise though, Abby thought, given how cold she had been to her these past few days. All this time, Abby pegged Lisa as a replacement for her. This was the daughter that Mom *had* kept, and Abby was the one she had thrown away. But now she knew better. It hadn't been like that at all.

"You like to go running?" Abby asked. Lisa hesitated for a minute before nodding. Abby wiped one last stray tear away and gave a small smile. This was something they had in common. This was something she could share with her sister. Abby held up her sneakers. "Me too."

Lisa sort of smiled back, still unsure of how to read the moment. She then shrugged as she asked, "Did you want to go with me?"

Abby nodded. She needed to let out her energy, let her feelings settle before she could work through them. A run would help, but she didn't know the neighbourhood and wouldn't know where to go.

Once out in the cool night air, the two of them jogged in silence. Lisa led the way, her pace on par with Abby's. The streetlights cast their shadows far behind them, and the stars twinkled above. They ran to the end of the block to where the road ended, and the beach began. There was a sidewalk that lined the sand, and they ran until the sidewalk ended.

Both out of breath, Lisa sat down on a bench at the end of the path. She put her hands on her head, and Abby took a deep breath of the fresh air. A seagull squawked nearby, and the sound reminded Abby of the beach back at home.

"I guess you found the letters, huh?" Lisa asked from the bench. Abby looked at her, confused at first. "I just—I heard you go into Mom's room and then you were crying…"

Abby moved to the bench and sat down beside Lisa. Her breath was shaky as she pictured the envelopes scattered on the ground, her mother's neat writing spelling her name and address on their fronts.

"Yeah," Abby said at last. She let out a long exhale and then inhaled again deeply. Her eyes closed as she tried to work through her feelings. They were a big, bundled knot in the pit of her soul, and she didn't know what to believe any more. For so long she was mad at her mother, so angry and hurt at what she had done to their family, and now, all at once, she felt so incredibly sad for her and what had happened. The anger was in the past, nostalgic in a way, but it still made it hard to move into the present. It was a constant presence throughout her life, and letting it go was surprisingly hard because being angry was easier than being sad.

"For so long I thought she didn't care about me," Abby continued, "that I had done something wrong, or she had preferred

Eli over me; and now to find out that all—all this time—"

Abby couldn't finish. Her tears started up again, and she sobbed before she could stop it. And like that time when Abby had comforted Grace in the school's bathroom, Lisa slid closer to her on the bench and wrapped her arm around her. It was awkward at first, the two of them working through the tenseness between them. But then all at once it felt right, and Abby leaned into Lisa, and she too cried. And they sat there, two sisters bonded together over the grief of losing their mother.

Dave

The morning was calm when the day of the funeral arrived. Dave awoke to the sound of birds singing away outside the window, and the soft snores of Abby on the bunk above. There was a peaceful stillness in the house that he tried to absorb for a moment, taking deep breaths as he readied himself for what was about to come. Today was a day that every step he took would be one at a time, slowly, and carefully, so as not to overwhelm his system with grief and despair, nor his children's.

Alice made them all a big breakfast. Fluffy pancakes with maple syrup, an array of fresh fruits, crispy bacon, and spicy scrambled eggs lay upon the kitchen table like a buffet. Dave and Alice ate together in a peaceful silence, and let the kids get up at their own pace. Each greeted the day differently.

Eli woke up first with a sombre air about him, still in his pajamas with his brown curls tousled and dark circles under his eyes. He headed straight for the coffee pot, as he did every morning, and gave Dave a curt nod in greeting as he passed. Dave gave him a soft clap on the shoulder, unsure what else to do but wanting to make physical contact. Until the funeral proceeded, there would be a dark cloud hanging over them all, unable to dissipate until they said their formal goodbyes and could proceed with proper healing.

Once his coffee was in hand, Eli turned to Alice who promptly wrapped her withered arms around him. Dave watched as his son deflated into the comforting arms of his elderly neighbour, the surrogate grandmother he had grown up with. Donna and Gerry were eager to become reacquainted with their grandson and meet their new granddaughter, but when Dave picked them up from the airport, they just left it at a polite introduction. It was too much all at once for his in-laws, and they said they would build a relationship with their new grandchildren once they were all back home and settled, once they had the chance to say their goodbyes to their daughter, certain now that she was never coming back.

As Eli piled food high onto his plate, Lisa came in next. The sound of her sobs preceded her, and Alice ran to greet her halfway to the buffeted breakfast. Her eyes were red, face swollen with sadness, tears spilling nonstop. It broke Dave's heart. He wanted to be the one to comfort his daughter, but he knew he wasn't a comforting source for her yet. So, he stayed back and watched as Alice murmured softly and stroked her soft brown hair. It would be difficult to take his kids away from this one last source of comfort. Dave wondered if he could convince Alice to come out and live their way. It was more expensive though and would be a big thing to ask of her.

Lisa was fully dressed already, in a simple long-sleeved, flowy black dress. Unlike her brother, she barely took any of the food presented on the table. She ate maybe two bites of a pancake and then pushed her plate away and moved to the couch where she sat and sobbed softly throughout the rest of breakfast.

Abby, unsurprisingly, was the last to wake up. The food was cold by the time she emerged through the hallway, and they had only an hour to go before they had to be at the funeral home. But she surprised Dave by being fully dressed as well. Abby's dress was shorter than Lisa's, with a fancy lace overlay, and she wore nude nylons underneath. Her blonde hair was brushed out and pinned back neatly, and her makeup already applied. Like Eli, she had a sombre air around her, and drifted silently into the room towards the food. Dave intercepted her and gave her a hug, not because she needed one, but because he did. Abby squeezed him back almost robotically. She didn't deflate like Eli or collapse into tears like Lisa. She stayed stiff. Everyone grieved differently, Dave reminded himself.

The funeral home was a short drive away. It was one of the fancier buildings in the area, with shiny marble columns, and stone angels perched on the roof's eaves. The director, Mr. Field, was waiting for them when they arrived. Donna and Gerry were already there too, and Abby ran over to greet them once she stepped out of the car.

Inside the funeral home was cozy and comforting. The sweet smell of the floral arrangements was the first thing Dave noticed as he stepped inside. A small stack of programs were tucked in a white basket off to the left of the door, and a wall mantle on the right held an array of pictures and mementos of Ronnie. Alice set up everything earlier. There was a picture of Dave and Ronnie from their wedding, another from when they were dating; most of the pictures were a mix of Ronnie and Lisa or Eli, or both. Any pictures with Abby were from when she was a baby. In the center of the arrangement was the drawing by Lisa that she had done the other day. It would be the first of many portraits she drew of her from memory.

As time ticked closer to the beginning of the end, people arrived. Dave stood with Alice, Abby, and his in-laws, and greeted them as they came through the door. Everyone shook Dave's hand with a small murmur of condolences. They would then proceed on to Alice, with whom they would speak more with, and usually give a tight hug. It formed a small pit in Dave's stomach, to be a stranger at his own wife's funeral. He and Abby stood like ghosts in the line, greeting people who gave them their sympathies, but who knew nothing about them.

Dave felt moved, however, by how many people showed up. There were some of Ronnie's coworkers from the library where she worked, parents of friends of Eli's and Lisa's, followers from the church where she volunteered, despite not being religious, and even a grocery store clerk with whom she chatted to regularly. It blew Dave away with how much Ronnie had touched people's lives in the community. She really had created a life for herself here and was not just hiding from her past. It made him smile a bit, to think that she had found some piece of happiness. A new sense of home.

When the director gave the cue, Dave and the rest of the family left the main hall and went to the waiting area in the back. Eli wrapped an arm around Lisa, who had not stopped crying once. Donna whispered something into Abby's ear, and Gerry chatted politely with Alice. A feeling of apprehension built inside of Dave, like the rising of lava inside a volcano. He suddenly couldn't catch his breath as he looked at his family around him, and all at once, Dave collapsed to the floor. Uncontrollable sobs took over him, and somewhere above him, he was vaguely aware that the door opened, and it was time for them to proceed into the main hall.

"I can't," Dave said amongst his tears. He tried to wipe them away, but his hands shook too hard for him to steady. He shook his head like a child. "I can't say goodbye to her. I just can't. I'm not ready."

Abby knelt in front of him. She took his hands into hers and pulled him up to his feet. "Come on, Dad," she said in a soft, but steady voice. "We'll do it together. Just like we do everything."

They entered the hall together. A sea of faces blurred as Dave glanced over them and then sat down in the front pew. Abby sat right beside them, their sides touching, and she kept holding onto his hand. The entire time, she remained a rock. Dave slowly found a sense of calm as he listened to the director and his scripted words. He heard little what Alice said, as Dave focused on a picture of Ronnie that sat up at the front. It was a picture from last summer, Lisa told him when they picked it out. They went to the beach, and Ronnie was in a good mood. She shielded her eyes from the sun, a laugh on her face, as a seagull had just stolen her sunglasses. What Dave wouldn't give to see that smile one last time in person.

He closed his eyes and thought back on all the times he *had* seen that smile. He smiled to himself as the memories unfolded within him, and he squeezed Abby's hand lightly.

It wasn't until Eli walked up to the podium that words turned from background white noise to actual comprehension. Eli looked smart in his black suit, his curls still unruly, but more put together than they had been this morning. The dark circles from under his eyes, and the sombreness that had circled around him cleared. Now, instead, he smiled at the people before him, an air of composure and peace.

"I know we're all here for a sad reason," Eli started. "But it wasn't a secret that Mom was sad for most of her life. At least, it wasn't a secret to my family. Not sad in the same way that most of us experience; she wasn't upset or disappointed about something. As a matter of fact, Mom was never upset or disappointed about much in her life. She wasn't upset about the time that I threw three rolls of toilet paper into the toilet all at once. She didn't so much as yell the time that Lisa thought that baking flour grew real flowers and poured the entire bag over the back lawn—and then went and stole Mrs. Hannigan's bag of flour because she wanted to plant a field in the front. And instead of getting upset when we painted her car because we wanted to enter it into the town's parade, she sent pictures of it to City Hall asking if we could be in it. Boy, we were the worst float that year."

Dave smiled as a few of the patrons let out loud chuckles. Eli was a natural public speaker, and he grinned.

"But she had a dark demon within her," Eli continued with sobriety, "and sadly, she could not beat it."

With his grin gone, Eli paused a moment as his voice cracked. He glanced from the paper in front of him, his hands shaking, over to where Dave and the family sat. Dave gave him a small nod of encouragement, and Eli folded up the speech.

"I thought long and hard on what I wanted to say while I stood up here," Eli said. "And I think, while it's hard to do in such a sad time like this, that the best thing to do is to look at the positives. I know Mom tried to, for as long as she could. She taught us how to look at the positive in all situations, because for her, that was a struggle. And she didn't want us to struggle like she did.

"The one bright thing from this dark event is that her family is back together now. And while I know she would have loved to have seen us together with her own eyes, I don't think that was ever going to happen. But I know she's looking down on us all now, smiling, and at peace. She'll be with us; me, my dad, and my sisters, forever. Because her last wish was to bring us together, and that wish came true."

When everyone had their chance to speak and all the words were said, the procession dispersed from the hall and out onto the grounds. This time, when people came to give their condolences to the family, they said more than just the generics to Dave. They'd mention a happy memory with Ronnie, a piece of her life that he wasn't able to witness. He didn't know if many of them learned the true reason they hadn't been together. If they did, nobody mentioned it or said a harsh word against her. And Dave appreciated that.

When one particularly chatty couple finally left Dave alone, he looked over to see Abby sitting alone on a bench. Her back was to him as she faced a small garden of flowers, the very last of the season before the fall frost set in and winter eventually put them to sleep.

Dave walked over and sat beside her. Abby's eyes were closed, silent tears falling down her cheeks. Her palm was open beside her, and Dave took it into his. She squeezed his hand and he squeezed it back. He too, then closed his eyes and listened to the wind. The breeze wafted past him and tickled his cheek. He smiled at the tingling sensation, cold against his own tear-stained face. It was one last kiss from Ronnie.

LATER

Abby
December 24, 2026

As the fireplace in front of her crackled, Abby snuggled deeper into the couch and pulled the white plush blanket up over her legs. The lights on the Christmas tree twinkled in the dim living room, and a rare Christmas snowfall fell outside of the window. It was picturesque and Abby sighed happily for a moment as she closed her eyes in bliss.

The last few months were a blur. It was weird at first to fly home after the funeral without her dad. Her grandma stayed in the house with her, even though Abby was old enough and responsible enough to be on her own. But the two of them needed each other to lean on as their grief would overcome them in waves. Abby was usually the saddest at night, and her grandma first thing in the morning.

It took two weeks for the Newfoundland house to sell and be cleared out. Alice had a fantastic realtor friend who helped get it on the market and sold quickly. They ended up selling the house with most of the furniture included. Eli and Lisa packed up their lives, all of their mother's photographs and trinkets, and by the second week of October they moved into Abby's house.

It was weird at first to share the house. For her entire life, it was just her and her dad. The spare bedroom next to hers upstairs was an awkward, mostly empty office space that neither of them used much. Now it was Lisa's bedroom. She decorated it much like her room back across the country, a string of lights, drawings on the walls, bright coloured sheets, and now she had a dozen photographs on the wall.

Eli took the spare room down in the basement. It was only half finished when he first arrived, but their dad and grandpa fixed it up quick. He had a collection of favourite novels on a bookshelf that also contained most of Mom's knickknacks.

Both of her siblings came into their own at their own pace. Abby did her best to make them feel comfortable. She gave them a personal tour around the high school, introduced them to her friends and their younger siblings who were about the same age. Lisa fit in right away with the artsy kids, and Eli with the school's book club. The two of them regularly video chatted with their friends back at home and called Mrs. Hannigan daily.

Now the house felt full. Eli started the coffee in the morning, and Abby even tried a cup. It was disgusting, and something just her brother and dad enjoyed. It was nice to have other bodies in the house. They started weekly game nights to break the ice and bond together, and their grandparents joined them half of the time. Eli and Lisa had yet to meet their dad's mom, but they would visit her during Spring Break. Their father spoke to his mom more often, more than Abby remembered him doing through her childhood.

When Abby opened her eyes again, she smiled at the four stockings hung up on the fireplace. There was hers and her father's, the same two stockings they'd had since Abby could remember. Next to them were Lisa's and Eli's, the ones from their childhood. All four of them were worn and full of memories of Christmas's past.

Above them, the mantel was full of photographs. There were the usual ones that Abby and her father had displayed over the years, and now the added new ones from Lisa and Eli. They had their favourites proudly displayed, interspersed with the others. In the center amongst the photographs was a hand-drawn portrait. It was one of Lisa's latest creations, and Abby stopped and looked at it every chance she could.

It was a picture of all five of them. On the left stood Abby and her dad, with his arm wrapped around her shoulder. On the right stood Eli with his arm around Lisa. And in the middle was their mother. She held onto dad's hand on one side and Eli's on the other. All five of them looked happy and calm. It was the only picture of the five of them that there would ever be, and it was perfect. Her sister had a gift, Abby thought, and without it, their complete family picture could never exist. The way she captured the likeness and realism of each one of them was extraordinary, and Abby admired her sister's talent.

It was a picture of the Christmas that would never be, a picture of the meeting that their mother promised Eli and Lisa. *Well, they made it here, Mom,* Abby thought to herself. They had made it together, to the promised Christmas to meet their dad and sister, and now they would be together forever. She had kept her promise, despite that she wasn't there with them.

That small thought made Abby smile. From underneath the fluffy blanket, she pulled out her sparkly green journal. The blank pages inside were still crisp, the colour of cream. When she opened the diary, the stale stink of resentment and anger trapped, wordless inside, escaped and the journal seemed to sigh in relief as the spine cracked lightly as Abby pushed it flat.

When she brought her pen to paper, the words came out naturally for once. She smiled to herself as the ink flowed from the tip and she felt her mother's presence around her.

December 24, 2026
Dear Mom...

ABOUT THE AUTHOR

Mandy Hayes is a Canadian writer who lives in Metro-Vancouver with her husband and three children. She has wanted to be a writer since being introduced to creative writing at the age of six. It's rare in life to find your passion at such a young age, and rarer still to have that dream come true. Mandy is grateful to be one of the lucky ones. In the event it doesn't work out, she does have an M.Ed degree to fall back on.

Find her online:
www.mandyhayes.ca

Like what you read?
Please leave a review using the code below!

Manufactured by Amazon.ca
Bolton, ON